NORIAN'S GAMBLE

(THE WOLVES OF NORBURY)

ROGER HYTTINEN

RAMBLING WORDSMITH PRESS

Norian's Gamble
(The Wolves of Norbury)

By Roger Hyttinen

Copyright © 2022 by Roger Hyttinen. All rights reserved.
Published by Rambling Wordsmith Press 2021

ISBN: 978-1-943005-58-1

Roger wishes to thank you for reading his work. Please consider leaving a review wherever you purchased this book. Also consider telling your friends about it to help me spread the word about my book.

Click or visit:
rogerhyttinen.com

LICENSE NOTES

CHAPTER ONE

"Sly Devil, I almost had you," Prince Norian said. He laughed and spun around the stick he was holding.

"Perhaps if you removed your blindfold, Your Highness," said the courtesan. "It could be that a bit more practice is in order."

"More practice?" said Norian. He went completely still for a moment. His long fingers clasped his weapon, and then, in one swift move, he swung it around in a wide arc and, with a loud clack, knocked the courtesan's stick right out of his hand. Norian yelped with delight.

"I must say that I didn't see that coming, My Lord." The courtesan shook both his hands in the air as if trying to get their feeling back. His stick now lay on the ground.

"Perhaps that will teach me not to mock me, Panus! 'Tis no way to talk to the son of your king. More practice indeed."

Norian removed his blindfold. His sea-green eyes twinkled, and a mischievous smile crossed over his red lips. At that moment, he caught his reflection in the castle window and nodded at it. Having recently passed into his twenty-third year, he was shaping into quite the strapping young man, or so his tutor had told him. He stood 6'4, and because of all the strenuous games and training he enjoyed with the courtesans—whom he referred to as his playmates—his muscles were hard and well-formed. He had long wavy brown hair and thick lips and was what many people in the kingdom referred to as fair. The only jewelry he wore was a gold torc with a crow—an homage to his pet corvus, Belkas. Norian spent his days dueling with the courtesans, studying his lessons and developing his senses. If one was to be king someday, one needed a well-rounded education. Or so he was constantly told.

The sudden sound of hooves made both men turn toward the path leading to the castle. A procession of seven horses trotted toward them. A large, stately black stallion led the train.

The courtesan's face paled. He shouted to the guards outside the castle door. "Quick, someone warn the King that Vadok approaches the castle!"

Norian looked at the courtesan, startled. "What is it? Who is this Vadok?"

"Someone you do not wish to know, trust me, Your Highness. Where is your father?" The panic was still evident on the man's face.

Norian heaved a sigh. "He would be at court, I imagine. But, Panus, I ask you again. Who is this person who has you so visibly distressed?"

"Vadok is a magician from a nearby village—a dark sorcerer, most would say. He's a ruthless man and one that you never want to see on your doorstep."

Norian creased his brow. "I wonder what business he has here?"

Panus watched the men dismount and tie their horses

next to the castle entrance. "Whatever the purpose of his visit, I'm certain no good will come of it."

"I thought my father's mage was the only magician around?" Norian said. "I seem to remember my father saying that there weren't very many left."

"Your father is mostly correct. There is a reason that there are so few." He swallowed and wrung his hands. "Vadok has vanquished most of them. Though I must admit this is considered hearsay and has never been proven, but whenever a magician has been found dead, it was rumored that Vadok had been recently seen in the vicinity. More than a bit curious if you ask me. Lad, if anyone is a black magician, it is certainly he. No, your father is right in that Vadok is not a magician but rather a black sorcerer, a devil."

Norian's face paled. "Do you think he came here to harm Wayf?" Wayf was the court mage who wasn't that much older than Norian. The two of them more or less grew up together, and Norian considered the man a close friend.

"I do not know," Panus said.

"Well, I intend to find out," Norian said, a note of determination in his voice.

"Norian, no. I beg of you, stay far, far away from him. The less Vadok knows about you, the better."

Norian shook his head. "If this so-called magician is as dangerous as you say he is, I'm not going to allow him to see my father without my presence."

Panus shot him a sharp look. "You are no match for him and his magics. However, I have confidence that Wayf himself can handle Vadok. Wayf is a powerful and adept magician. Don't underestimate him because of his age."

"Even against black magic?" Norian asked. "And you yourself just told me that this Vadok may be responsible for the deaths of several other magicians. What of them? Shouldn't they have been able to protect themselves?"

Panus took a deep breath and said evenly, "The King has given me the responsibility of protecting you. Keeping you away from Vadok is my primary concern right now. I must not knowingly put you in danger."

Norian thrust his chin forward in defiance. "Apologies, old man, but this time, you are overruled. If this Vadok rascal is as dangerous as you say he is, then as prince of this land, it is my responsibility to ensure that he causes nobody any harm, especially our King."

Without waiting for another word from Panus, he turned on his heels and headed towards the castle. Panus ran up beside him.

"I'm coming with you."

"It is unnecessary," said Norian. "There's no need to put yourself in danger."

"Your father is surrounded by his guards. I'm sure that Vadok wouldn't dare try anything."

"Ah, so now you tell me there is nothing to worry about? What about all this black magic and murder of mages you spoke of a moment ago?"

"Yes, he is indeed a dangerous man, that cannot be denied. I just don't want him to see you. It's best that he not learn of your existence."

Norian stopped walking and looked at Panus. A confused look crossed his face. "Why? What is all this about, then?"

Panus's expression paled. "I am only concerned for your well-being."

Norian creased his brow and squinted his eyes. "No, there is something more. There's something you are keeping from me. What is it?"

"It is not for me to tell."

"Ah-ha! So there is something!" Norian exclaimed. "Out with it."

"As I said, Your Highness, it is not my place to tell. You must ask your father."

"So I shall."

The two men reached the castle door. Vadok's men stood next to the doorway, three on each side. As Norian neared the entrance, one of the men made to step in front of him.

"Don't even think about it," Norian growled, glaring at the man. He put his hand on his sword and narrowed his eyes into what he hoped was a threatening glare.

The man hesitated, about to say something, then thought better of it. He stepped back.

"Who might you be?" the man asked.

"Who I am is no concern of yours," Norian responded. His voice was cold and deep, almost a growl. "You are a stranger at my castle, so you shall answer my questions. Not I yours. Where is Vadok? What business have you here?"

The man visibly stiffened. The shift in his expression signified his wariness. "Lord Vadok is in conference with the King and does not wish to be disturbed."

"What your master wishes," Norian said, speaking through clenched teeth, "matters not to me. And you know what is good for you, you shall not attempt to inhibit my passage."

All at once, four of the king's guards gathered at the door behind Norian to see what the commotion was.

"Is there trouble, Your Highness?" asked one of the guards. Each of the guards had his hand on his sword.

"Yes, is there trouble?" Norian repeated, never moving his gaze from the stranger's eyes.

Vadok's men moved back. "No trouble at all," responded the guard. "We only await the return of our master."

Norian approached the door and, with a wave of his hand, indicated to the guards to follow him. As he neared the chamber door, he could hear the sound of raised voices. "Do not follow, but wait here," he said quietly to the guards. "If I need any assistance, I shall call."

"Are you sure, Your Highness? What if the King is in peril?" one of the men asked.

"My father's personal guards are with him. I will observe the situation and shout if there is any danger."

The man bowed. "As you wish, Your Highness."

Norian opened the chamber door and, with an air of authority, walked in. He met his father's eyes. His father immediately shook his head and gestured for him to leave, but it was too late. Vadok turned around.

"And who might you be?" His eyes gleamed like sun on ice.

Norian crossed his arms over his chest. "I am Norian, Prince of Tregaron."

Vadok approached him. A foul stench attacked Norian's nostrils, a smell like sulfur or rotten eggs. He leaned so close to Norian that their heads nearly touched. "Ah, the beloved prince. My, my my, haven't you grown into a fine young man. I am sure your mother would be proud."

"That is enough!" the King roared. "You shan't mention my wife again. And your business here is not with my son. You shall not address him."

Vadok peered at Norian with steely eyes. He held Norian's gaze for another chilly moment and then dismissed him with a wave of his hand. He turned to face the King.

Vadok inclined his head politely to the King. "My apologies, Your Majesty. As you said, my business is indeed with you."

The King narrowed his eyes. "Get to the point, Vadok. Why have you come here after you were told never to return? What could you possibly have to say that would be of any interest to me?"

Vadok flashed a self-assured smile. "I wish to only be of service to you."

King Jamros leaned slightly forward in his chair. "Be of service to me? Surely you jest."

"You are a most powerful ruler, King Jamros, known and respected all across this land. But even the most powerful of monarchs can use some assistance at times." He again bowed his head. "That is why I have come. To humbly offer you my services."

"Again, in what capacity?"

Vadok looked up and met the King's gaze. "As your court magician, of course."

The King's eyes did not flinch. Instead, he indicated towards the young man at his side. "I already have a court mage. I have no need for two."

"So I understand," Vadok replied. "But my Lord, this boy is a mere child. He has not the experience and reputation as I. But of course, I would be happy to train him—take him on as my apprentice, if you will."

Wayf, the court mage, opened his mouth to comment, but the King laid his fingers against his lips to stop him.

The King's voice grew icy. He crossed his arms and said, "Oh, I am more than aware of your reputation, Vadok, and it is for that reason that I would never consider you for a position in my court. Moreover, I assure you that my young court mage is more than capable. I venture to say that even you would be surprised at how powerful and how wise he is.

Vadok let go of an evil laugh that was almost a chortle. "Wise? This child?"

"Not only wise," the King said. He paused for a moment, then continued. "But also good."

Vadok's face grew red. "What are you implying, Jamros? That I am not," he paused, narrowed his eyes, and said, "*good*?"

"I imply nothing," the King answered. "I have voiced my decision. There is nothing further to discuss."

Vadok's expression hardened. "You dare reject my offer? Any king would consider themselves fortunate to have Lord Vadok in their court to advise him. Especially in light of the fact that neighboring monarchs grow restless and look to increase their landholdings. Your kingdom would no doubt make a pleasant addition to anyone's assets." He wrung his hands. "You have erred, Jamros. Seriously erred."

"I think not," Jamros said tersely. "You have taken from me once and shall never do so again. My decision is final. I believe this meeting is completed. Good day, Vadok."

Vadok opened his mouth to speak but was interrupted by Wayf, who stood next to the King. His eyes blazed red. "His Majesty, King Jamros, has spoken. Please take your leave."

Vadok raised his arm as if ready to launch something at the mage. Then, all at once, two bright red fireballs appeared in Wayf's palms. They glowed brightly and crackled loudly. "I said go."

Vadok looked at the King and then directed his gaze

back to the mage. He closed his eyes briefly, then reopened them. He gave a curt nod to the mage and said, "We shall meet again. Soon."

He then moved his eyes to Norian, and an odd half-smile spread across his face. "And you as well, young prince" With that, he turned on his heels and headed towards the door. The King's guards parted to let him through. The door slammed loudly behind him.

"That went well, don't you think?" the King said. There was a nervous tinge to his voice.

Wayf laughed. "Very well, sire."

"Thank you, Wayf," the King said. "Who knows what he might have done had you not been here."

"One of Vadok's biggest flaws is that he overestimates his ability," Wayf replied.

"And underestimates yours," the King added.

Wayf smiled and bowed to the King. "You are most kind, Your Majesty. But we must not relax now that Vadok has departed. He is a vicious and malevolent scoundrel, and we must take his threat most seriously. Therefore, I shall add an extra-strong protection barrier around the castle that will hopefully deflect even the strongest magic. We must be on our guard at all times. Vadok may consider himself the most powerful magician ever to walk the earth, but there's no denying he's both formidable and dangerous—a man who, once he wants something, will let nothing stand in his way."

The King sighed. "I know that only too well."

Wayf looked confused for a moment, and then his face fell. "I am sorry, Sire. I did not mean to bring up—"

The King waved his hand and interrupted him. "No worries, Wayf." The King sighed loudly. "It's just that this swine's visit has brought back a lot of unpleasant and painful memories."

"Understandably, Your Majesty."

"So," said Norian loudly. "Is anyone going to tell me what in Brigit's name is going on here?"

The King and the young mage looked surprised as if they'd forgotten Norian's presence in the room. "Ah, my Son," the King said. "'Tis a long story and one best left for another time. What concerns me now is your safety and the safety of those in our kingdom." He nodded to Wayf. "And you, as well, my dear friend. I am more than familiar with his reputation for eliminating other magic workers."

"I shall be especially wary," Wayf answered. "Be assured, Sire, that I can handle Vadok and protect our kingdom."

The King nodded and turned his regard back to Norian. "But you, Norian, must be extra cautious. This man is a sorcerer and leaves nothing but death and destruction in his wake. He sees himself as my court magician and may not stop until he has accomplished his goals."

"This I understood from your discussion," said Norian. "But why? He has never shown himself here before. Or has he?"

The King visibly stiffened. "He is after power and control, my boy. From my understanding, he already has several kingdoms under his command."

Norian's eyes grew wide. "You mean he has murdered their kings?"

"Often, it is unnecessary for him to do so," Wayf answered. "It is said that he has proven himself able to control not only a king but also his people. So, though the king remains on the throne, it is Vadok who truly rules. Perhaps it is through his dark magics, perhaps through fear.

All I know is that thus far, nobody has been able to defeat him once he has taken control."

"What about you, Wayf?" asked Norian. "Could you vanquish him? Everyone knows you are one of the most powerful mages that has ever been seen here. You've brought down scoundrels before. So why have you not defeated him?"

"He's never come here before today, and our paths have never crossed," Wayf said. He cast a quick glance at the King, then looked back at Norian. "At least, not since I arrived."

"But could you defeat him?" Norian asked.

Wayf wrung his hands and smiled palely. "This I do not know. I have defeated black magicians who've attacked me twice before, but there is something different about Vadok. He emanates an evil that I have not yet encountered, and his magic is entirely different from mine—it comes from a different place, a darker place. And from my sense of him, I deduce that his powers continue to grow stronger. Are they stronger than mine? That remains to be seen. Still, he is careless and considers himself invincible. That could be his downfall."

"Norian and Wayf," the King said, "let us hope that after he left here today, he has moved on elsewhere. But regardless, we must be diligent in safeguarding the castle. Norian, I want two guards with you at all times, and for the moment, you are not to leave the grounds. No exceptions."

"But Father—," Norian began.

The King held up his hand to shush him. "It is most important that you follow my orders. If Vadok wishes to gain control of this kingdom, he may begin through you. And you are no magician. You have no way of protecting yourself from his vile hexes. He may think twice about trying to approach you if you are not alone."

"Why do you think he'd come for me? He barely knows who I am."

The King cleared his throat, and his voice grew hoarse. "It is how he operates."

Norian nodded, suspecting that his father was hiding something. But he knew better than to question him. "Very well, Father. I shall do as you request."

"And Wayf," the King continued. "You need to prepare should Vadok decide to return. You mentioned a protection spell of some sort?"

Wayf nodded. "I shall also consult my black arts books. If it comes down to it, I need to be certain of my ability to vanquish him. I have never fought evil such as his before, and it may be necessary to use dark magic should the need arise."

"But why wait?" Norian asked, throwing his hands in the air. "Why not just hunt him down and destroy him before he has a chance to do the same to us?"

Wayf smiled warmly and rested a hand on Norian's shoulder. "That is not how a true magus operates. If I were to go around and slaughter those who I believe might possibly be a threat to me at some later time, I would be no better than the black magician I was killing. Magic is to be used in defense only. 'Tis the way of the white magician."

Norian nodded. "Perhaps all this worry is for naught. Maybe he will never return."

"Let us hope," Wayf said, his smile fading. He tossed a solemn glance at the King.

"It is settled," the King said matter-of-factly. "Wayf, discover what you can on how to defeat this creature. Norian, you will stay close to the castle and maintain a state of constant vigilance. Perhaps we have nothing to worry about." The King let go of a nervous laugh. "He is, after all, only one man."

"That remains to be seen," Wayf said under his breath. The King and his son regarded Wayf, and with a puff of smoke, Wayf disappeared.

CHAPTER TWO

Vadok and his guard wrinkled their noses as a vile stench, a cross between a rotting corpse and boiling cabbage, caused both men's eyes to water.

"What is that awful smell?" Vadok's guard said, gagging.

"It is no doubt the witch," Vadok said, holding his hand in front of his nose and mouth. "We must be getting close."

The two men marched down the barely visible path. Dense vines hung to the ground and seemed to be getting thicker. The men had lost the trail a couple of times but managed to find it again. As they grew closer, the grass grew taller, the offensive stink grew more robust, and the biting bugs more abundant.

"Are you sure this is the right way?" the guard asked, swatting the bugs away from his face. "There doesn't seem to be much of a path here at all."

"Oh, it's the right way, all right," Vadok said. "The witch just doesn't want to be found. Her protection magic grows stronger with every passing second—I can feel it. The wench is powerful, I'll give her that."

They rounded a corner and spotted a small stone shack ahead. Its windows were boarded up with splintering, rotted wood, and across the blackened door, someone had scrawled in dripping red paint: *KEEP OUT OR ELSE!*. Beside the cracked, overgrown walkway, the yard was bare of grass, littered instead with the scattered bones of dead animals.

"Are you sure this is a good idea?" the guard asked, his voice cracking as he spoke. "Have you ever met this witch?"

"Silence, coward!" Vadok said under his breath. His harsh tone caused the guard to step back.

Vadok approached the door, his guard behind him. He raised his staff against the door and pounded three times in rapid succession. The loud knocks echoed throughout the forest.

A sharp, shrill voice echoed from inside the shack. "Begone with you!"

"Woman, open the door. I have business with you."

"I have business with no one," the voice responded. "I suggest you leave while you still can."

"Lord Vadok wishes to speak with you, woman. We've much to offer one another. Much indeed. Open up."

"*Vadok?*" the woman said, in a voice resembling the rasp of a baby crow. The sound of sharp footsteps clicked towards the door. The door swung open, and a foul stench assaulted the men's senses. Vadok stepped back, and his guard retched behind him. The woman was like a nightmare from a whispered old tale. Crimson rings circled her witch-black eyes, and her sallow, orange-tinged skin was thick with warts and twisted like knotted wood. Coarse gray bristles jutted from her sharp chin, and a few stringy tufts of hair clung to her scalp like the last strands of a horse's tail. She leered at the two men, lips parting in a crooked grin to reveal jagged teeth, yellowed and blackened like old tombstones.

"Good day to you, Vadok," the woman said in a sing-songy voice. She crossed her hands chastely in front of her and drummed her thumbs against her chest. Her smile sent a chill down Vadok's back. "And what brings you to a defenseless old woman's hut in the woods?"

Vadok's laugh rang throughout the woods. "Bah! Defenseless you are not, old hag. I know very well who and what you are. Allow me and my companion in. I have a proposition for you."

"Do you truly believe you have *anything* that would interest me?"

"How about power?" Vadok said.

The crone laughed and gestured in the air. "Power, you say?" She placed both hands on her stomach and continued to laugh. "I already possess more than I could ever need. Why, I could reduce you both to ash with nothing more than a blink, should I feel inclined. Power? Blah!" She spit on the ground towards Vadok's boots. "You are wasting my time, sorcerer, something I do not take kindly to."

"What good are your magics here, secluded in a shack not fit for the lowliest of servants?" Vadok asked. "I offer you the power of a king. A power to rule a kingdom. Perhaps the power to rule an entire region. A power where people bow down to you in fear and reverence. A power where you hold the lives of thousands in your hands, to crush or not." He paused and stared coldly into her dark eyes. "What say, you wench? Interested?"

All at once, he could feel movement in his mind, as if his thoughts were being flipped over one by one. The accursed witch was trying to read his mind! With an air of quiet sureness, he at once stilled his thoughts. Four steel doors slammed shut in his mind. The hag gasped and drew back, her eyes bulging in her wretched head.

"It appears you possess considerable power yourself, Vadok," the woman hissed. She then regarded him with a blank stare. "You may come inside." She pointed a gnarled finger at the guard. "*You* will stay outside."

"The guard accompanies me," Vadok said.

She shook her head forcefully. "No. If you wish to speak with me, you will do it on my terms." She pointed at Vadok. "I will allow only you into my home."

Vadok scowled. "Very well then. Only I will accompany you." He turned to his guard. "If anyone or anything approaches, kill them."

The door slammed behind them. Vadok glanced around the cramped one-room hut, surprised by how orderly it was given the crone's disheveled appearance. But the smell—gods, the smell—was enough to make his stomach churn. He scanned the room, trying to locate the source of the stench, but came up empty. Across the room, a shelf sagged under the weight of vials and bottles—potion ingredients, no doubt. Maybe they were to blame. Then again, his eyes drifted to the closet door nearby. Could there be a heap of rotting bodies behind it? It wouldn't be the strangest thing he'd encountered. Along the remaining walls, thick tomes lined the shelves, their spines choked with dust. Vadok found himself wondering what forbidden knowledge lay within their pages.

"Speak, Vadok," said the witch. "My patience grows short. I grant you only a few moment's time."

"You are familiar with Lord Jamros?" Vadok asked.

"The King of Tregaron? Aye, of course." She intertwined her fingers in front of her chest. "Is he the only king in these lands you haven't yet managed to sink your dark claws into?" She let go of a deep throaty laugh which changed into a rattle. "And wasn't there an incident with his wife several—"

"I've wasted little thought on King Jamros until recently," Vadok said, abruptly cutting her off. "In his employ is a court magician, one known by the name of Wayf, who could be problematic for us."

Her eyes held him. "I am familiar with this Wayf. It is said that he is most powerful for one so young. One of the most powerful magicians these lands have seen in quite some time."

Vadok visibly winced, then continued. "I was at the Jamros castle today and encountered this so-called mage. I am certain that he could be brought to his knees with minimal effort. Once having done so, his kingdom is there for our taking. As I'm sure you are aware, Tregaron is the largest and most powerful kingdom in the land, one that has never fallen to another. I think it is high time that this changes."

"You do, do you?" the crone asked. She gave another unnatural laugh. "If you are so confident that he can be overtaken, what are you doing here? Why are you not at Jamros' castle right now, slaughtering his mage and sitting on his throne?"

"I did not say he was powerless, witch," Vadok said. "Strength he does possess, but he is not invincible. The two of us could overtake him, I am sure."

She creased her brow. She stood in silence for a moment, her hands clasped in front of her. "And why should I help you? What is in it for me?"

"If you assist me in successfully crushing Wayf, you are guaranteed a spot at the castle with me."

She broke out into a smile. "With you? So you endeavor

to be king? That is not like you, Vadok. Usually, you kill the mage, bewitch the king and move on your way. So what is different with this king? Why the uncharacteristic desire to rule his lands?"

Vadok hardened his features. "We have a history, this king and I, as he took something of mine a long time ago that is now forever lost. I have not forgotten and swore that I would be someday avenged."

"Ah, yes," said the witch. "I recall." . "So this under-taking is one of personal vengeance." She shook a gnarled finger at him. "Beware, Vadok. Such missions are often sabotaged by the hatred of those initiating them."

"You know very well that hatred behind our kind of magic makes that magic all the more powerful."

"True," she replied. "But if that hatred is not controlled, such as when a blood-thirsty desire for vengeance accompanies it, unexpected results can occur."

"I've rarely been defeated, woman. I am more than capable of controlling my magic." He smiled faintly. "But this is not just about revenge. It is also about power. It is about you and I ruling Tregaron together. I have grown weary of traveling these lands. It's time I claimed a kingdom of my own—and carved a legacy into history. Perhaps once Tregaron is under my control, I'll look to other kingdoms to increase my holdings."

She laughed. "So much hubris. It may be your downfall, Vadok."

"I think not," he replied. "More than once, both kings and their mages have bowed before me, and it shall happen again with this king. Until now, I have never desired a throne for myself. It is time I do so."

"With my help," she said, her face expressionless.

He nodded. "If you assist me, you shall be court sorceress."

"What makes you think this is something I would desire?"

"Someone with your power and your capabilities should not be hidden away in a run-down hovel. It's about time you take your place at the head of a kingdom where you belong, to rule over these lands. Our names will be on the lips of peasants millennia from now."

"You do think highly of yourself, Vadok, I give you that." She studied him for a moment and creased her brow. "Perhaps you are right. Maybe it is time that I come out of hiding. I admit, I grow bored." She narrowed her eyes. "So what do you propose, sorcerer?"

"I have heard that you once cursed a magician with the scourge of the wolf. If I understand it correctly, such a dark curse would effectively overpower any white magical abilities the magician possessed, effectively making him useless as a mage. Is this true?"

The woman nodded. "You've done your homework, Vadok. Yes, you are correct. The bite of the wolf has the power to destroy evil—and magic utterly."

"But where did you find such a creature? I am not aware of any wolfkind in these lands."

"There is a lot that you are not aware of, Vadok," she replied. A half-smile appeared on her lips.

"What of the wolf?" Vadok asked impatiently, ignoring her insult. "Are there such creatures here in Tregaron?"

She ignored his question. "The problem with the spell that I use is once the wolf has carried out its purpose, it dies."

"And the human host as well?"

"Of course, they are one and the same," she said. Her

voice was sharp with impatience. "The spell requires two parts. First, you must find a human who bears the curse of the wolf. Then you must hex the creature when it is in human form, within three days after the dark moon. The spell will activate during the next full moon."

"What does the spell do exactly?" Vadok asked.

"When the next transformation takes place, the wolf will seek out the person who was designated in the spell. The spell ensures the wolf will bite the victim but not kill him."

"But why not kill him? It would be perfect with Wayf completely out of the way."

"What a silly question," the witch said. "Tell me, Vadok, why is the sky blue? The wolf doesn't kill the victim because that's how the spell works. That's how it was written. You should also know as well as I do that there is no magic in existence that can force one sentient creature to kill another against its will."

"How will this solve my problem?" Vadok asked.

The witch's lips parted in a menacing smile. "You mean our problem, do you not?"

"Of course, of course. Our problem. So what of Wayf?"

"Legend has it that a single bite from a wolf can rob a magical being of its powers entirely. This is because no magic can withstand the primal power of the werewolf. The bite then passes the curse onto the being—in this case, our young mage—so from that point forward, he himself will transform on the full moon." She then pointed an index finger at Vadok. "And that includes us as well." She looked away for a moment, as if in deep thought. "The bite of the wolf is especially deadly to our kind Vadok."

"What do you mean?"

"The lore states that a magician with a black heart will

instantly and completely die once bitten. Only evil can kill true evil."

Despite himself, Vadok rolled his eyes and then sighed. "Then we must ensure that we don't get bit." His gaze then locked on the woman's eyes. "So, will you help me?"

"I will help you."

"Do you know of a wolf?"

She nodded. "Aye. The doll-maker in the village. His daughter bears the curse."

Vadok cocked his head curiously. "I thought that such a curse is passed down from the parents. Does this mean her parents are afflicted as well, or was she bitten by another?"

The crone shook her head. "Once the hunters learned the truth about the girl's parents, they tracked them down and killed them. The child somehow escaped and was taken in by the doll-maker and his wife."

"Who apparently have done a good job of hiding the girl's secret. I have never heard tell of a werewolf anywhere near here."

The woman nodded. "The child's nature has been well hidden. Her true parents lived many days' journey from here, so the local townspeople are unaware of the girl's origin." She tapped her chin and locked gazes with him. "Didn't you tangle with a group of wolfkind about a decade or so back?"

He ignored her question. "How old is the girl?"

"I believe her to be about fifteen or sixteen." She chuckled. "She's hardly much of a girl anymore."

"What do we need to do to make this happen?" Vadok asked. "How do we force the child to bite the King's mage?"

The woman turned and walked to the left wall and, after a moment of glancing at the shelves, reached up and pulled down a thick book. She laid it so forcibly on the table that a glass vase flew off the table, landed on the floor with a loud crash, and shattered. The witch ignored the sound.

"It is in here," she said. She hunched over the book and began thumbing through the pages. Finally, she stopped. "Ah-ha! I found it." She hunched over to read. "This is it—the passing of the curse of the wolf through a bite." She was silent for a moment as she read. "Ah yes, it's all coming back to me. This is a relatively simple spell. A few herbs gathered during the waxing moon, a basic potion, and a simple incantation. The trick, of course, is getting the subject to drink it. Oh, and the magician must accompany the wolf on the night in question. To maintain the spell, proximity to the beast is a necessity. You must be as close to the creature as possible. This ensures that you remain in control of the girl's wolf and her."

Vadok looked over the woman's shoulder and read along with her. "The intended victim has to drink this potion?"

The woman nodded, still reading the book. "If I remember correctly, I think I cast a thirst spell and then conveniently showed up with a pitcher of water." She laughed. "Such a fool he was. So gullible."

"It's true, then. You've performed the spell yourself."

As she remained focused on the book, Vadok slipped a small dagger from beneath his cloak. In one swift motion, he seized the old woman by the hair and yanked her head back. Then, without hesitation, he drew the blade across her throat, pressing with all the force he could summon.

A loud gurgling sound erupted from her. She turned, hands to her throat, eyes wide with surprise. Her previously black eyes were now completely red. She raised her left arm as if to launch a hex at Vadok. But before she could complete the maneuver, Vadok screamed an ancient word, lifted both of his hands at once, and pushed into the air.

The woman flew across the room and crashed into the far wall, her arms glued to the floor. The knife then jetted from his hand to where the woman was sprawled out and buried itself deep into her chest.

Vadok grabbed an empty vial from the shelf, emptied its contents on the floor, and then walked towards the woman. He lifted her head and held the vial under her throat. A moment later, it was full of her blood.

"Witch's blood—no doubt it shall come in handy some-day," he said, holding the vial up in the air to inspect it.

He glanced at the woman's face. Her eyes had already gone dim. He let go of her head, and her corpse dropped to the wooden floor with a loud thud. He moved to the side as the blood continued to pool on the floor. After placing the vial in his pocket, he strode to the table, snatched up the book, and thrust it under his arm.

"Thank you, Ageentha. You've proven most helpful."

He opened the door to the shack, the book under his arm. "Let's go," he told his guard. "I got what I came for."

CHAPTER THREE

WAYF WAS OUT OF BREATH AND NEARLY PANTING BY the time he reached the King's chamber room. His shaking hand pounded on the door with more force than he'd intended. The happenings of the evening flipped over and over in his head. How was he going to face the King? How was he going to tell him that his son may soon die?

"King Jamros?" His voice cracked as he spoke. "I need an urgent word with you."

He waited and listened. Silence. He knocked again. This time, Wayf heard a grunt coming from the room, and then the sound of footsteps padding across the floor. The door opened. The King stood in this evening robe, his eyes were mere slits.

"Good grief. What is it, Wayf? Has something happened?"

The mage took a step back. His heart fluttered in his chest. "Did I awaken you, Your Majesty? I did not realize the lateness of the hour."

The King shook his hand in the air. "No matter. Come on in." The King gestured for Wayf to take a seat in a plush dark red chair and then sat down across from him. "Now, what matter is so urgent that it cannot wait until the morrow?"

Wayf's mouth went dry. He pointed to the pitcher of water on the table. "May I?"

The King nodded. "Of course, Wayf."

Wayf poured a splash of water into the glass and took a deep swallow. The water seemed to calm him.

"'Twas my divination," Wayf began. "Vadok's visit weighed heavily on my mind, and I found myself unable to shake it. So I performed a divination." Wayf swallowed. "It was much worse than I'd imagined. I prayed that I had erred—hoped I had somehow mistaken the prophecy. Thus, I laid out another...and another, all with the same results."

"Which is?"

"It is Norian," Wayf said.

The King was glaring now. "My son? What has he to do with a divination?"

Wayf watched the King, afraid to speak. He wrung his hands in front of him. "I do not know how to relay this to you gently, so I shall say it as I have seen it."

"Go on," urged the King. "What did you see?

"Danger," the mage replied. "I saw this dark cloud surrounding the boy, enveloping him, suffocating him like a black gale. It was dark magic I was seeing, of that I am certain. The feeling of this vision chilled me to the bone. I am sure Vadok is involved."

The King's face paled, and he stared at the mage expressionlessly. Moments passed. The King continued to stare, but said nothing.

Wayf finally broke the silence. "Sire?"

The King seemed to snap back to the present moment.

His voice was a mere whisper. "What can we do to prevent this?"

Wayf took a deep breath. "I suggest that besides the guards already protecting Norian, that you allow me to keep him under my watchful eye. I vow that at no time shall I leave his side until I'm convinced the threat has passed. Given that there is magic involved, I suspect only I can defend him against an attack."

"But how do you know you can do it?" the King asked. "How do you know you can defend Norian—and yourself—against this monster? You're well aware of this worm's reputation—his penchant for killing magicians. How do you know that either of you will survive such an attack? Did you not say you have already seen Norian's demise?"

Wayf closed his eyes to gather his thoughts. He hesitated for a moment. Then, "A divination represents what may take place if no action is taken, not what *will* happen. That is why magicians perform divinations—to understand the present course of events. This insight empowers us to intervene and change the outcome. By seeing the current trajectory, we gain the chance to shift it. It is said that to be forewarned is to be forearmed." He swallowed and then continued. "Now that we know there is to be an impending attack, we can take steps to prevent it—or at the very least protect Norian from it."

The King nodded. "But again, can you do it, my friend? Can you defeat him?"

Wayf reached forward and took both of the King's hands. He locked his gaze onto the King's eyes. "One can never truly predict the outcome of a battle, Your Majesty. I will say this, however. My magic is potent and grows stronger each day. Vadok himself knows this. In fact, when I encountered him here, I could sense his fear and wariness of me." He paused for a moment. "Vadok is also arrogant and overconfident. Such hubris makes a magician careless and causes him to underestimate his opponent. While he is wary of me, he still believes he is my superior. This belief will be his downfall."

Wayf winced when he noticed that the King's eyes filled up with tears. The King sighed.

"Wayf," he said. He slumped into his chair. "I cannot lose my son. Especially to him. I could not bear it again."

"I understand."

"I want him killed." His breath hissed through his teeth as he spoke.

"Sire?"

Jamros stared at Wayf with defeated eyes. "If he comes anywhere near this castle or near my son—or anywhere within your range of vision—I want you to destroy him. I should have done this the first time. I should have had him killed after he murdered my wife."

"Sire, nobody knows for certain whether it was Vadok who kidnapped her," Wayf said in a hoarse whisper. "It could have been a jealous villager or a resentful aristocrat who took her. As you well know, her captor was never found, and given that she no longer had a voice after her abduction, she was incapable of identifying who it was that hurt her. It could have been anyone."

The King's face grew red. "It was him! He made no effort to hide his desire for Emily, and each time she rejected his advances, the more aggressive and insistent he became. So, no, I do not think it was a coincidence that she died. I know in my heart and soul that it was the devil Vadok who murdered my wife. He robbed her of her will to live." The King wiped his eyes with the sleeve of his robe.

Wayf nodded and was silent.

"Wayf," the King continued. "Promise me you will take care of this. Promise me that he will not live to harm my son."

"Your Majesty," said Waif. "Since I do not possess a black heart, I cannot hunt him down and assassinate him in cold blood. The light masters would not allow it of me." He took a deep breath. "But I vow to defend you, your son, and your kingdom. Knowing what I know and seeing what I have seen, I will take any appearance of Vadok near you or Norian as a direct threat. Should this occur, I shall use every ounce of my power to destroy him."

"I appreciate that, Wayf." The King paused. "And you will stay by Norian's side at all times?"

Wayf nodded. "I shall. Your boy will be under my constant supervision." He creased his brow. "Although I am sure he will get suspicious of me. I've not yet figured out how I will handle that situation."

"Will you not just tell him what you've foreseen?"

"I would rather not if I can avoid it. I don't wish to frighten him by telling him his life is in danger. But if he gets too suspicious, I may need to."

The King heaved himself to his feet. "You shall do the right thing, of that I have little doubt."

"SO NORIAN," Wayf asked as they walked. They had left Norian's guards at the castle so they could converse in private. "Is there anyone new in your life? Anyone who sparks a bit of interest?"

"What you really want to ask me is whether I have

found anyone suitable for a wife. That is it, isn't it?" Norian said.

Wayf's eyebrows raised. "Where do you get such an idea from? I'm only taking an interest in my charge, my friend."

Norian smiled and shook his head. "Oh no, you don't. I'm not letting you get away with it. My father put you up to this, didn't he? I can smell it."

Wayf laughed. "Smell it? Perhaps you're taking your sensory development exercises a bit too far, are you not?"

Norian stopped, put both hands on top of his walking stick, and looked at the mage. "So you deny it, then? My father has had nothing to do with this conversation?"

Wayf let go of a sigh of exasperation. "Upon reflection, I suppose he did offhandedly ask me to speak with you and find out your marital intentions."

Norian nodded. "Just as I suspected. But if Father is so interested in my future, why doesn't he ask me himself?"

Wayf reached out and touched Norian's shoulder. "You understand how he is. It's difficult for him to talk about matters of the heart."

"Ever since Mother died," Norian added.

Wayf nodded. "Aye." He took a deep breath. "I hesitate to speak of your father while he is absent, but since he lost your mother, he has erected an internal wall around his emotions. It may well be that he is trying to distance himself from his pain. I'm sure he will come around in time. He must work through his grief on his own."

"Wayf, it's been nearly a dozen years. If he hasn't come around by now—"

Wayf interrupted him. "It can take a long time to recover from the death of a beloved spouse, Norian. Your father loved your mother more than anything. I personally had never seen a love as deep and intense as theirs." Wayf looked up for a moment as if in deep thought, then continued. "Together, they were awe-inspiring." He shook himself and returned his gaze to Norian. "The shock of her death nearly killed him, you realize. One says you cannot die from a broken heart, but your father nearly did. He had us all worried for quite some time."

Norian nodded. "If I remember correctly, you pretty much ran things around here for months on end, even though you were a newcomer to my father's court."

"'Tis true." A warm smile displayed on his lips, and he nodded. "Don't be too quick to judge your father. He may not show it, but he is still hurting, still healing."

The men continued to walk, silence falling between them. Finally, Wayf broke the silence. "Now, in answer to my original question..."

Norian giggled. "Oh. That."

"Yes, that. You are entering into your twenty-third year. Naturally, thoughts of an heir weigh on your father's mind. He has never been one to force you to do anything, but he would rest much easier once you've taken a wife."

"I suppose it must happen eventually," Norian said softly, without conviction.

Wayf creased his brow. "You do not wish this, then? Do you have no desire to couple with another? To find a woman to support you, to love you, to share your life with?"

"I don't know what I wish," Norian replied. "I haven't thought about it that much."

"I understand," Waif said.

"I'm not sure if you do," Norian replied under his breath, not intending that Wayf hear him.

Wayf stopped again and brought his hands up to Norian's cheeks. Then, he said in a soft voice, "I comprehend a lot more than you believe I do. Perhaps even more than you do yourself at the moment."

A confused look drifted over Norian's face. He shrugged his shoulders and smiled. "So what will you tell Father?"

"I will tell him we spoke of the matter, and you are taking it under advisement." He paused. "It may be prudent to you and him to gather together in the near future and speak about this."

"Would you accompany us?" Norian asked.

"If you would like," Wayf replied.

"I would," Norian said. "I'm never quite sure how to approach him when we're alone."

Wayf laughed. "He is human, you know, and he loves you very much. Never doubt this, Norian. He would do anything for you."

The men continued to walk without speaking. Finally, Wayf broke the silence.

"The moon is incredible tonight."

Norian nodded. "It seems especially huge this evening."

"The first full moon of the summer, the Strawberry Moon, often appears extra large in the sky," Wayf said. "Tonight is the perfect night for gathering specific herbs. Would you like to help?"

"I'd love to! Although my knowledge of herbs is lacking."

"Then it's about time you learn," Wayf said.

A loud howl broke the silence of the evening.

Both men froze in their spot. "What on earth was that?" Norian asked. "It sounded like some sort of wolf."

"No wolf that I've ever heard before," Wayf repeated.

Worry oozed from his voice. "Perhaps we should leave the herb harvesting for another time and move with haste back to the castle."

"What do you suppose that was?" Norian asked.

"I'm not exactly sure. Let's not tarry here to find out."

CHAPTER FOUR

THE WOLF AT THE OTHER END OF THE CHAIN GREW more and more restless the nearer they got to the Jamros castle. It took all of Vadok's strength — both physical and magical — to contain the beast. From the way the animal was reacting, he suspected they must be getting close to Wayf.

The spell had gone much easier than he'd hoped. Getting the girl to drink the potion took a bit of doing but once completed, her will no longer belonged to her but to him. The girl followed him out of the store and into the woods, where they waited for the moon to rise. Although he'd seen many incredible events over the years, to watch a human transform into a wolf surpassed all imagination. He couldn't help but wince during the metamorphosis. The girl crashed to the ground and writhed in agony as her internal organs grew and the entire chemistry of her body changed. The sound of bones cracking filled the air as her limbs elongated and her body grew larger. Hair sprouted over every part of her, and her feet and hands turned into enormous paws. Vadok had stood back in silent awe during the change but gasped aloud when her face first melted in, changed form and then jetted outward to become the muzzle of a wolf. He held tightly to the silver dagger in his pocket, ready to launch it at the beast should it try to attack. According to the book, the beast should be entirely under his command until the deed is finished, but one never knows with these things. More than once, the results laid out in a dusty grimoire were not always in alignment with what actually occurred. But the beast did not attack. Instead, it stood there, on all fours, staring at him as if awaiting further instruction. It was a beautiful creature, yet savage and powerful. Vadok felt a primal force bursting from the animal and was indeed surprised that there existed any magic at all that would contain such a beast, even for a short while.

Vadok looked at the wolf and tensed despite himself. The wolf was growling now, and thick globs of saliva dripped from its muzzle. Instinctively, he reached back into his pocket and grasped the silver dagger.

"You do know what you need to do, right, wolfie?" Vadok asked.

The wolf's head raised to look at Vadok, a menacing understanding in its eyes.

"Kill Wayf," Vadok said. "Not injure, maim, wound or cripple. Kill. Wayf must not live to see another night." He hoped the wolf would know what to do when the time came. All the ingredients in the potion and the incantation should have taken care of that. But again, old grimoires...

The wolf growled and jerked the chain. Then, its body stiffened, and it pointed its muzzle to the west. Vadok stopped and looked in that direction. On account of the moonlight, he could see two figures walking quickly toward

Jamros's castle. His senses told him that one figure was Wayf.

"Damn it all to hell," he said and then gazed at the wolf. "He is not alone. No matter. Kill both of them if you must. Understand? But Wayf is your top priority. He must perish this night." Vadok had no idea whether the wolf would actually kill his targets, given that the old witch had told him it was impossible to compel any creature to do so. But it was worth a try. And if the wolf doesn't complete the task, he'll finish them off himself.

The wolf looked up at Vadok, its eyes pleading.

"Yes, my beloved beast. It is time. Time to fulfill your destiny."

Vadok bent over and slipped the chain over the wolf's head. The wolf zoomed down the hill and towards the two figures at an otherworldly speed. This was truly a magical creature, Vadok thought, as he watched the wolf's movement. He clasped his fingers in front of him and smiled. Any moment now.

ALL WAS silent except for the clanking of the two men's walking sticks on the ground. Then, all at once, Wayf froze. He whirled around and, in one swift motion, shoved Norian behind him.

"Stay behind me," Wayf said in a voice that was barely above a whisper.

"What is it?"

"Danger. I do not know what yet. There is something—"

Before he finished his sentence, an enormous gray wolf

walked out of the darkness, snarling, teeth bared. A lengthy strip of saliva dripped from its mouth.

"Sweet Brigit, what is that?" Norian said.

Wayf raised his staff and pointed it at the wolf. "A foul and unnatural creature, a hybrid of man and beast."

Norian's breath came in short gasps. "You mean a were-wolf? They're real?"

"I am afraid so," Wayf said, sputtering. "I just pray that the protection shield I have placed around us is enough."

The wolf drew closer. Wayf's voice cut into the silence as he began to recite an incantation. Both of his hands gripped his staff.

Lupum ferum sisto, vi sanguinis et lunae.

Cor tuum quiescat, furor tuus dormiat.

In nomine antiquis, redeas ad pacem!

All at once, the wolf lunged. It seemed to fly through the air and hit Wayf's chest with such force that both men sprawled to the ground. The wolf stood on top of Wayf's chest, its yellow eyes boring into his. In one swift move, the wolf lowered his head, then stopped as if smashing into an invisible field. The shield was working. All at once, Wayf sensed a force gathering around him from all directions. Magic! There was another magician here, and he was working on destroying Wayf's protection shield.

"Run!" Wayf screamed to Norian. Even though he could no longer see Norian, he hoped he was within hearing range. "Run back to the castle!"

Wayf lost his breath, and his limbs froze in place. He tried to move his arms but was unable to. Whoever the magician was out there in the darkness, they were preventing him from moving a single muscle. Snarls echoed louder and louder as the beast gnawed at his shield, its magic splintering under the strain. Any moment now, the wolf would get through.

Wayf tensed his body and focused his total concentration on what was left of the shield, though it took nearly all of his strength to keep the animal from getting through and biting him. Desperately, his mind fished through his memories, looking for a curse that would work on a werewolf. But even if he'd remembered one, he wouldn't have been able to use it because his mouth was as frozen as his limbs.

He had to break free, no matter what. There was no choice here. His life depended on it. He closed his eyes and, with all his might, gathered up his remaining reserves to repel the magic that was freezing his limbs. His ears popped, and his body writhed. He was free.

But it was too late. Just as he broke the binding, a slimy strand of the wolf's hot saliva dripped onto his face—and Wayf knew the shield that had kept the beast at bay was gone. The wolf sprang toward Wayf's throat.

All at once, there was a loud crack, and the wolf stopped and reeled to the ground. Norian stood above the creature, the now broken walking stick in his hand.

"Norian, no!" the mage shouted.

Norian took a step back. The wolf rose onto all fours and slammed into Norian's legs, knocking him to the ground. He hit the ground with a thud, and the wolf's teeth sunk into his thigh. Searing pain tore through his leg, and Norian screamed.

The wolf's teeth tore a wedge of flesh from Norian's leg. The boy screamed again and tried to kick the wolf with his other leg, but the pain robbed him of any remaining strength. Norian heard Wayf shouting words he didn't understand. Just as the beast was about to bite Norian again, the wolf's body pitched and convulsed. It let go of a terrifying howl, and then it burst into flames. A blood-curdling death rattle emanated from the burning creature. Norian rolled over to get away from the fire.

In a moment, Wayf was at his side. He ripped a piece of cloth from his cloak and wrapped it tightly around Norian's leg. "This should stop the bleeding," Wayf said.

"Look, Wayf! It was a girl!" Norian said, pointing.

Though terribly burnt, Wayf was able to make out the form of a naked teenage girl on the ground. Wayf rose, took off his cape, and spread it over her body. He sighed. "Such a tragedy," he said. The weariness was heavy in his voice. "The young woman could not help what she became. She was cursed."

"It...she came out of nowhere," Norian said, still breathing hard.

"She was not alone," Wayf said matter-of-factly. He walked back to Norian and fell to his knees beside him.

"You mean there are more?" Norian asked. He glanced around him. "There are other wolves near here?"

Wayf checked the cloth bandage and sighed in relief—the bleeding had stopped.

"More wolves, no," Wayf said. "Magicians, yes."

Norian's eyes grew wide. "Do you think it was Vadok?"

"I am sure of it," Wayf said.

"It makes sense. That wolf came directly toward you. For a moment there, I thought it had you too."

Wayf creased his brow, and then his face fell. "Oh no! How could this have happened? How could I have erred so in reading the vision? How could I have been so stupid! So negligent! In doing so, I put you directly in the path of danger."

"What do you mean?" Norian asked. "We were just out walking. How could you have known?"

"But I did know," Wayf replied. He sighed. "Not about this precisely, but I had a vision of you surrounded by danger. I told your father about it and promised him I would protect you, that I would not leave your side. But it was me that Vadok was after, not you. By forcing you to be with me, I have doomed you." He wrung his hands and looked down at Norian. Wayf's eyes filled with tears. "I am so, so sorry."

"You did not force me to be with you," Norian replied through gritted teeth, wincing from the pain. "I wasn't even aware of the arrangement you'd made with my father. And I am certainly not doomed. 'Tis a mere animal bite, though a painful one, I give you that. It will heal in time."

Wayf shook his head. "No, my dear Norian. You don't understand. It is much more than a mere bite." He swallowed. "You now bear the dreaded curse of the wolf."

CHAPTER FIVE

BY THE TIME THEY GOT TO THE CASTLE, THE WOLF venom had already begun attacking Norian's system. His breath came in short, rapid bursts and sweat poured down his face. The shakes crept over his body, gradually growing stronger.

"What's happening to me?" Norian said, gasping for breath. "I hurt all over. My legs feel as though they are on fire. Sweet Brigit, I am hot!"

"Hold on to me," Wayf said. He put his arm around Norian's waist and held the boy close to him. "The werewolf's poison now flows in your veins. It's working to change your body."

Norian's eyes widened, and he felt his heart race once Wayf's words sunk into his foggy brain. "Change? Am I going to turn into a wolf now?"

Wayf shook his head and forced a smile. "Not now, no. Or at least, I don't think so. The bite is only turning you...," he paused, as if trying to find the right words. "Into something different."

"A wolf-thing."

Wayf nodded. "I'm afraid so."

As they reached the door to the castle, Norian broke away from Wayf and emptied the contents of his stomach. His hands shook violently.

He wiped his mouth with his sleeve. "How much sicker am I going to get?" Norian's legs grew wobbly, and all at once, they lost the strength to hold him up. Wayf grabbed him before he fell.

"I don't know," Wayf responded. "I know little about this disease."

"Disease," Norian repeated. His voice cracked as he spoke. He stared into Wayf's eyes, his face tight. "Am I going to die?"

Wayf opened the door with one hand, his other propping up Norian. He pushed gently on Norian's back to propel him forward. Norian forced them to stop once inside. "Well?"

"Norian, please, with these questions. I told you I know nothing yet. I will find out as much as I can, as soon as I can. But for now, you need to rest."

Norian allowed himself to be led to his room. Everything seemed like a hazy dream. He was barely aware of Wayf's hands undressing him, wrapping a bandage around his wounded leg and helping him to bed. He felt his head hit the pillow and then nothing.

~

"A WEREWOLF?" the King said. His face was white. "You are sure? There is no doubt about this at all?"

Wayf's head was bowed. He raised his eyes to meet the King's. "I am positive, Sire. I saw and then killed the beast myself. As I said, it attacked me first."

The King's eyes moistened. "How can such things be? I have always thought that such creatures were only of myth and legend, stories to scare the little ones."

"Ah, but how I wish that were true," Wayf answered. "But it pains me to say that they are very much real."

"My son will survive?"

Wayf took a deep breath. "I cannot promise you he will survive. The venom took hold of him almost instantly. He now lies in bed, gravely ill. I shall do all I can to discover how to help him."

The King nodded and stood up. "I wish to see him."

"A moment, Sire. There is more."

The King's brow darkened, and he sat back down. "I am listening."

Wayf clasped his hands, closed his eyes for a moment, and then reopened them. He met the King's gaze. "The bite of a werewolf releases a poison into its victim. The poison changes the body chemistry of the one who was bit, effectively turning him into the same type of creature."

"What?" the King's voice was so loud that it caused Wayf to jump. "You're telling me that my son is now in his room, turning into some kind of wolf?"

Wayf waved his hand in front of him. "Not exactly, Your Majesty. The werewolf is a hybrid creature. Most of the time, the person is as they were before they were attacked—fully human. If my understanding is correct, they bear no visible signs of the curse, and it's impossible to tell if someone is a werewolf unless it's the full moon. Therefore, Norian shall function as he always has."

The King's face reddened. "Only a moment ago, you said that he will be as the creature who attacked him—a beast. Now you are telling me that he will be as he always was. You speak in riddles, Wayf. Which is it? Make me understand."

"You are correct on both counts, Sire. The Norian you have always known shall remain. However, each month during the full moon, he will change. Norian will physically transform into the same type of creature who attacked him tonight, no longer resembling his former human self. Thus, he will remain until the sun rises.

"This shall occur once each month during the full moon?"

Wayf nodded, then creased his brow. "It is my understanding, yes. At least, this is what I have learned from what little I've read on the subject. I shall, of course, do extensive research immediately."

"Will this transformation affect my son in any other way?"

Wayf raised his eyebrows. "Sire?"

"During the other days of the month, will he be the same? Will he still be my son? My Norian?"

"I cannot answer that in complete honesty, as I know little of this curse. Physically, he should change only once each month. I do not know how or if the curse will manifest itself in his personality."

The King looked off into the distance for a moment, then returned his regard to Wayf. He clenched his hands into fists. "In that case, let us consider ourselves blessed that Norian was not killed during this encounter. We shall take any necessary precautions to protect ourselves and our people when he changes, perhaps lock him in the dungeons during this time. Having a beast for a son one day a month is a small price to pay. It could have been much worse." He stood up. "Take me to my son. I wish to see him now."

Wayf bowed. "As you wish, Your Majesty."

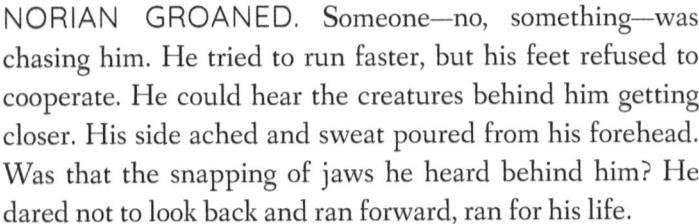

NORIAN GROANED. Someone—no, something—was chasing him. He tried to run faster, but his feet refused to cooperate. He could hear the creatures behind him getting closer. His side ached and sweat poured from his forehead. Was that the snapping of jaws he heard behind him? He dared not to look back and ran forward, ran for his life.

Just as he was sure that whatever was behind him had caught up and was about to bring him down, he fell to his knees, horrible pain in his gut. He awoke with a gasp, hugging himself tightly around his stomach.

He'd only been dreaming. He groaned as another squeezing spasm seized him. Why wouldn't the pain go away? He wanted to sleep some more until his body healed itself, but now the pain prevented him from it. He became aware of the sopping wet pillow behind his head. No doubt he has a fever, some sort of sickness. The agony subsided, and he let himself relax into the soft bed. He tried to ignore his aching muscles. He just wanted to sleep. Finally, the throbbing subsided, and he drifted off.

"Norian?"

The voice brought him back to consciousness. Someone was speaking to him.

"Norian. I need you to open your eyes."

Maybe if he just ignored the voice, it would go away.

This time, the voice sounded louder, closer. "Norian. Wake up. Now."

He forced his eyes open, but everything was a blur. It took a moment for his vision to focus on the two men standing at his bedside.

With an effort, he scooted himself up in his bed. "Father. Wayf. I do not know what it is. It appears as though I've some sort of dreadful fever." The weakness of his voice surprised him as he spoke.

Wayf sat down next to him on the bed and took his hand. He then gently laid two fingers on the underside of Norian's wrist. "His pulse is strong, Sire."

"He will survive?"

"I cannot say for certain, but he appears to be strong. He must survive the fever to be in the clear."

"My body hurts all over," Norian said. He flashed a weak smile at Wayf. "What's wrong with me? What illness is this?"

Wayf and the King exchanged glances. Wayf grasped Norian's hand tighter. "You do not remember the attack?" His voice was soft and soothing. "You don't recall what happened to you?"

Norian creased his brow. "I don't know. It hurts to think." He turned his head to meet his father's eyes, then shifted his gaze back to Wayf. "Wait. There was something. An animal." His eyes grew wide. "I remember. It attacked us!"

His father approached the bed. Wayf rose and stood aside, then gestured to the bed. The King sat down next to his son. "Everything will be fine, Son. You are fine. All we need for you now to do is to recover."

Norian nodded weakly. "It was a wolf that attacked us. It bit me in the leg. But why do I feel so horrible?"

The King turned his gaze to Wayf. "I would like to see the wound. I want to see exactly what we're dealing with here."

Wayf nodded and came forward. "Norian, I'm going to peel back the blanket and show your father where the animal bit you. Okay?"

Norian nodded. He closed his eyes, and Wayf pulled

back the blanket. They sighed in unison when they saw the blood-stained sheets.

"I'm going to unwrap your leg just for a moment," Wayf said. "It may hurt a bit. I shall try to be as gentle as I can."

Norian nodded. Wayf unfastened the pins that held together the bloody cloth that he had wrapped around Norian's leg. Wayf gently raised the leg so that he could unravel the wrapping. "Does this hurt?"

Norian shook his head. "It feels fine. Although my joints ache horribly."

Wayf smiled. "As long as I am not hurting your injured leg."

Wayf removed the last layer of cloth and let out a gasp.

"What madness is this?" the King said. "His leg is fine. There is no wound at all!"

"Apparently, Sire."

"What do you mean, no wound?" Norian asked. "I remember the thing bit me in the leg. The pain was agonizing." He pointed at the bloody wrappings. "See, I was bleeding."

"Calm yourself, Norian. Nobody doubts you," Wayf said. He turned to glance at the King. "I assure you, Sire, there was most indeed a deep gash on the boy's leg. As Norian pointed out, the evidence is here in the bloody bedding."

"But what of the wound?" the King asked. "By what sorcery is it no longer there?"

Norian bowed his head. "I cannot say for certain, as I have never tended to a werewolf's bite before today. What I do know is that these creatures are gifted with an uncanny power to heal. In fact, it is supposedly quite difficult to kill or even injure them when they are in their wolf state. It appears as though Norian's body is changing, and the first of these changes seems to be an astounding ability to recover quickly from injury."

"He isn't turning now, is he?" the King asked.

"Turning? What do you mean by turning?" Norian asked.

Wayf shook his head. "No, only on the full moon."

Norian sighed loudly. "Would you both stop talking as though I were not here? What do you mean by turning? And what does the moon have to do with it?"

"You do not recall our conversation, right after you were bit? When I explained to you about what it means to be bitten by a werewolf?"

Norian creased his brow. "No. I remember the creature grabbed my leg. I remember the pain, and then everything is murky after that."

Wayf folded his hands in front of him. "Norian, the creature that attacked you is called a werewolf. During the month, the werewolf is in human form, just as you or I. However, each month on the night of the full moon, the person carrying the curse undergoes a transformation in which they change into a wolf—the very creature we saw earlier. It's rare for someone to survive a werewolf attack, but those who do become as the creature who attacked them. They will transform into a wolf every month on the full moon."

Norian's heart thumped wildly in his chest. "What are you saying, Wayf? That I am now going to turn into one of those... things? That I am now some sort of monster?"

"If I correctly recall what I've read, yes. You now bear the curse of the wolf. But remember, Norian, you are going to be yourself most of the time. It's only one day a month on which you will change. The remaining time you will be as you always have been."

"And we can secure you in the dungeons on the full moon so you cannot to harm others," the King added. "Norian, know that we still love you. You're the same person you were before, except for this one day."

Norian's eyes welled up with tears. "But I don't want to be a wolf! Do you remember that creature? It was evil—bloodthirsty. Wayf, it tried to kill us!"

Wayf nodded. "I remember only too well, Norian. But please, look at it this way. We are both lucky to be alive. The creature might have killed us both. Is it not better to live and endure such a transformation once a month than to be dead for all eternity?"

Norian yawned as an overwhelming urge to sleep came over him. He nodded weakly. "I suppose." He paused. "Will it hurt?"

"I don't know. I will find out as much as I can."

Norian's head fell back on the pillow. He looked at the King. "You are not angry, Father, that such a fate has befallen me?"

"Of course not, my Son. It's not your fault. You were a victim."

"Need to sleep now. So tired." Norian's eyes closed, listening to the indistinct murmur of Wayf's and his father's voices. He could barely make out what they were saying.

"What now?" asked the King. "What is our next move?"

"To learn as much as we can about this curse and how it will affect Norian."

"How much time do we have?"

"Not much, Sire. We have until the next full moon."

CHAPTER SIX

NORIAN STOOD ON THE CASTLE BALCONY OVERLOOKING the courtyard. The morning sun sparkled on the water down below so brightly that he squinted. He sighed. Everything seemed so much simpler merely a few weeks ago. Now, nothing would ever be the same again. One fleeting event, one small bite, had changed his life forever. But what lie before him? He dared not even think of it. The events of that accursed night slowly unfolded in his mind, and he shuddered. He tried to stop thinking about it and dwelling upon it, but was unsuccessful. No matter how hard he tried to erase it from his thoughts, it remained, taunting him. How could he stop thinking about the beast that had turned him into a monster, turned him into a killer? If Wayf is correct, it's only once a month. That was one consolation, albeit a small one.

He sighed again, thinking about the rapidly approaching full moon. He would get through this. He had to. All he had to do was ensure his father locked him up on the night of the full moon so everyone, including himself, would be safe. He told himself to be grateful for what *didn't* happen that night. The events could have unfolded much differently. He might have died. Wayf might have died. Too bad that damnable wizard still walked free.

He caught sight of someone waving to him. He brought his hand up to his forehead to shield his eyes from the sun. When Norian recognized the young man below, he waved back. It was Leolan, the fabric shopkeeper's son. The boy looked exceptionally handsome today. Norian almost laughed to himself. It was silly of Norian to think of him as a boy, as he was only a couple of years younger than himself. He and Norian had practically grown up together, seeing each other almost every day during their childhood. When Norian had first developed a physical attraction to Leolan, he no longer remembered. What he did know was that it was an attraction he must never act on. He was a prince, and someday he would be king. Someone with such leanings could never run a kingdom. The people would never accept it. His father would never accept it. For that matter, he, himself, cannot accept it, and for this reason, he had never acted on his desires—except for once. He would have to marry someday, this was a given. There is no room here for any other possibilities.

He heard a step behind him and turned around.

"Oh, Wayf."

Wayf nodded. "Norian. I missed you at breakfast. I wanted to see how you were."

"I have no appetite at all this morning," Norian said. "Each time I thought about eating, I had to fight a bout of nausea. I imagine it is because of whatever now is running through my veins and that the full moon is tomorrow?"

Wayf creased his forehead. "Possibly. But Norian, you shall have to eat. Now is not the time to be of diminished strength. We know neither the effects of this new curse nor what the toll of it shall be upon your body when the change occurs. You must be as physically strong as possible. This may make it easier upon yourself."

"I shall try."

"I'm still amazed at how quickly you recovered from the attack. You were in bed for a mere two days and then back to your usual self. No wound, no remaining fever. These past couple of weeks, you seem to be the same Norian we've always known." Wayf ran his gaze over Norian's body. "However, it appears as though you've gained additional muscle since the attack. Your body is much fuller and tighter. May I daresay even bigger?"

Norian nodded. "I don't feel any different. It's almost like that night never happened."

"Apart from having no appetite, how are you otherwise feeling? Any odd sensations or pain?"

Norian shook his head. "Nothing notable. I do have a slight ringing in my ears, though I'm not sure if this has anything to do with the illness."

"But no remaining discomfort at all? How about the leg?"

"Nothing. No sign that anything happened at all. No marks, no scratches, and no pain. Maybe it all was nothing more than a bad dream?"

Wayf placed his hand on Norian's shoulder and sighed. "If only it were so, my friend. But unfortunately, it is only too real. But I need you to always remember—you are never alone. Your father and I stand beside you, and we both vow to do everything in our power to help you through this challenging time."

"But how?" Norian asked. "You said yourself that very little is known about my affliction. So what can you and Father do now that I'm this beast? A monster?"

"Norian..." Wayf began.

Norian's eyes dampened. "Nobody can help. I'm doomed."

"You are far from doomed. Again, it's only one night a month. We've already made preparations to ensure that you and the townspeople remain safe. And who knows? Maybe all of our worrying is for naught, and you won't turn at all. Very little is known about the curse of the wolf. All that I've read is myth, legend, hearsay, and conjecture. We simply don't know."

Norian thought about the handsome Leolan for just a moment, then banished it from his mind. Another boy's face popped into his mind: Thorne—the one and only boy he'd ever kissed. "What about relationships?"

Wayf creased his brow. "Relationships?"

"You've spoken to me on several occasions about taking a wife. This certainly cannot happen now, can it? How could I ever be with anyone and be certain that they would remain safe? What if they catch it from me? What if I passed this affliction down to my children?"

"Norian, I cannot answer all of your questions now. But I promise you, I will find the answers you seek. It is too soon for any of us to come to any conclusions. Give me some more time to see what I can find out. I just came across some old books about curses and supernatural creatures that may hold some essential information for us."

Norian swallowed, then nodded. "But what about tomorrow? We've run out of time. The moon will be full."

"I know, and preparations are already in progress. And I will be there the entire time."

Norian's eyes widened. "You cannot be there! I could hurt you or even kill you."

"I will not be in the same room with you, but right

outside. The cell has bars, so I'll be able to see you and talk to you as the change occurs." He brought both his hands to Norian's face. "You will not have to face this alone, Norian. I will be with you."

Norian gave him a sour glance. "I don't know if I want you to see me like that. I don't want anyone to see me like that." His voice cracked as he spoke.

"I can understand that. But you mean too much to me and the king to allow you to suffer alone. Additionally, being there to witness your transformation might provide me some insight on how I can help you."

Norian's face paled. "Father won't be there, will he? I don't want him to see any of this."

"Your father and I already discussed this. He will not be present during your change, only I."

Norian grasped Wayf's hands and looked him in the eyes. It was difficult for him to maintain his composure. "Wayf, you have magic. You are a powerful mage. Is there no way that you can stop me from turning?"

"I'm sorry, Norian, but this curse is beyond the scope of any spellworking that I'm aware of. Behind the curse is powerful dark magic that manifests as a physical change. As far as I am aware, there is no magic in existence that can counter the transformation. But that is only as far as I am aware. If there is a way, I shall find it. Know that I'll do everything I can to find a cure if there is one." He brought his hand up to his chin and wrinkled his forehead. "I may be able to do something, though. I could try to render you unconscious just before the moon rises. It could be danger-ous, but if it works, you may remain asleep throughout the entire episode. Oh, if I only knew what effect it would have."

"So you're saying that you could knock me out so that I'll never know or experience what happens?"

"That is the general idea. Of course, I don't know if you would remain unconscious throughout the change. Perhaps the change will awaken you. We also don't know if there's any danger in you changing while not being conscious. But if you are willing, we could try—know, however, that this is an untrodden path for all of us."

Norian's heart skipped a beat. "I don't care. I'm willing. I beg of you."

"Very good," Wayf said. Then in a voice that was close to a whisper, "But let's not tell your father about any of this, shall we?"

UNABLE TO SIT STILL, Norian paced back and forth continuously, feeling as though his body weighed him down. His skin itched, but yet it didn't. The itch existed somewhere deep inside of him, some inaccessible part of him. His stomach flipped, and his arms jerked on their own. Was this part of the curse? Was this his body signaling to him it was ready to change? So this is what he had to look forward to every month? Lucky him.

His stomach lurched again, but it wasn't from hunger. He had no appetite whatsoever. He recalled Wayf's earlier advice and he thought about forcing himself to eat something, but his nauseous gut informed him it would be in vain. Food would never stay down. It's possible the transformation required that his body be completely empty. He wished he knew more about how this worked. For that, he had to hope that Wayf would discover something more than what they already knew.

As the day wore on, he grew more and more restless. His muscles spasmed involuntarily, and he experienced the worse case of the jitters that he'd ever known. Moreover, he was hot. It was a cool day outside, chilly almost, yet here he stood, sweating like it was noontime in August. Several people had looked at him strangely as he wandered about the castle. That's not surprising, considering how he looked. Earlier, he'd glanced at his reflection in the mirror and the deep dark circles surrounding his bloodshot eyes stunned him. One cook even had asked him if he was feeling alright. How was he supposed to answer that? No, he was not alright, but how could he tell anyone that he was suffering from pre-werewolf transformation symptoms? He hoped he'd be able to sleep tonight, because no doubt there would be little sleep tomorrow night unless Wayf succeeded in knocking him out with his magic or one of his potions.

The day finally faded, and evening arrived. Norian's physical discomfort grew worse and worse as the night progressed. If he suffered like this the day before the transformation, what horrors awaited him tomorrow? He dreaded to think about what he might experience during the hours leading up to the change. Perhaps he could talk Wayf into putting him out *all day tomorrow*, not just at night.

Deciding that he desperately needed some air, he stumbled outside onto his balcony and sat in the back of the castle, watching the stars. He was more restless than ever, so he took in a few deep breaths, trying to calm himself as he stretched out on the floor. Judging by how utterly uncomfortable he was right now, he doubted that there would be any sleep tonight. His heart pounded in his chest, and a high-pitched ringing echoed in his ears. The ringing grew louder as he tried to relax. How would he bear this every month? It was nearly agonizing, what he was already experiencing—and the change was still a full day away.

His eyes latched onto the quickly rising moon, mesmerizing him. Transfixed by the glowing orb, he thought about the enormous power of it, the ability to change a man into a beast. All these years, and he'd never had even an inkling of this primal influence of the moon. Who could have ever guessed?

All at once, his stomach seized. He bounced into an upright position and grasped his abdomen. The pain was not subsiding and he wondered whether he should have forced himself to eat something. He glanced back up at the sky. The moon was rising, nearly at its peak. He wondered what he would be doing tomorrow night at this time. Would he be a wolf by then?

The ringing in his ears escalated. The pain in his stomach started spreading throughout his entire body—his arms, legs, hands, feet, and even head. It seemed as though his limbs were being stretched to their breaking point. He cried out, but his voice came out gurgled, as if there was something blocking his throat. *Dear God, please make it stop,* he thought. *I'll do anything.*

But it did not stop but rather increased in intensity. His body involuntarily flipped over onto his stomach. He screamed—or tried to—as an entirely new type of agony grabbed hold of him. The pain in his face felt as though someone were compressing his head in a vise, and he prayed his eyes would not literally pop from his face. An agonizing pulling sensation developed in his legs that stretched them to their limit. His stomach and his back hammered and thrashed as if there were a vicious animal inside of him trying to break its way out. It was then, in the midst of his pain, that he heard a distinct noise—a loud cracking, the unmistakable sound of bones breaking. He opened his mouth to scream but could not. In fact, he found himself incapable of making any noise at all. The cracking sound grew louder along with the suffering. His body lurched forward, and he was certain that his back had just broken in two. He expected he would pass out at any moment from the pain—prayed he would pass out. No one could endure this much torture for this long. The agony was beyond human comprehension. So this is what dying is like, he thought. Then, his mind grew cloudy, and the person he knew himself to be slipped away. He had no name, no identity. He simply "was." He became vaguely aware that at some point, his hands had become furry paws and that he now stood on all fours. Then, the pain suddenly stopped.

What power he now possessed! He had the impression that he could do anything, overcome anything. As he looked around, things jumped out at him. He could hear the smallest of creatures wandering around the grounds, and people talking in the distance. Then, a whiff of something caught his attention, and he lifted his nose to the air. It was a hare; he was sure of it. The luscious odor caused his stomach to rumble.

Must eat. Must hunt.

He found he was once again in a room with walls, and the light was so bright that it hurt his eyes. Norian padded back out onto the balcony and raised his head to look at the moon. It's raw, unleashed power filled him and fed him, and he understood then that the moon was the cause of everything—she was the mother of all. A rush of gratitude swept over him, and he opened his mouth to express his thanks. A loud, drawn-out howl came out of this throat.

He then licked his chops, jumped off the balcony, and bounded off toward the smell of food.

CHAPTER SEVEN

WAYF LIFTED THE COOL GLASS TO HIS LIPS AND TOOK A long drink. What a day. He had tried to keep an eye on Norian, but the boy made it clear that he didn't want to be disturbed. Moreover, he hadn't looked at all well earlier, and when Wayf asked him how he was feeling, Norian had snapped at him. It was uncharacteristic of Norian, who was usually soft-spoken and never had a harsh word for anyone. Wayf could undoubtedly understand it, though. He couldn't begin to fathom how his mood would be if he were in Norian's position. His mind drifted back to that horrible night, and he shuddered as he realized how close he'd come to being bitten by the wolf instead of the lad. He closed his eyes for a moment as a wave of guilt came over him, but then pushed the emotion away. This wasn't the time for self-reproach, for that would be of no help to Norian. But what would? He'd once again spent the day poring through his books, looking for something—anything—to help him put an end to the curse, or at the very least, stop the transformation. But could he prevent Norian from changing? There must be a way. If there was, he would find it.

An odd noise snapped him from his thoughts. What was that? It sounded almost like howling. His entire body tensed as he continued to listen. There it was again. And it sounded close. However, this wasn't any ordinary howling. This was not a wolf. His heart slammed in his chest as he realized what the sound was. *Werewolf.* He was sure of it. There was no mistaking that bone-chilling call. He abruptly got up from his chair and raced to the window, looking at the sky. But how could it be a werewolf? The moon was not full until tomorrow. Was he mistaken about how the curse worked? Could the transformation take place even before the moon was full? He'd never heard of such a thing, but then again, he hadn't done too much research on werewolves until recently. No, it couldn't be. He must be mistaken. Werewolves only appear on the night of the full moon, he was sure of it. Wasn't he? Wait, there was something he remembered reading...

All at once, a piercing scream rang out in the night. Someone was in trouble. Then, a deep panic seized him. Norian! He ran out of the room and slammed the door behind him.

He was out of breath by the time he reached Norian's room. He tried in vain to calm his shaking hands. His hand grasped the doorknob, and he took a deep breath, waiting for his heart to slow down. He turned the knob and pushed. His eyes grew wide, and his hands flew up to his throat, and he gasped. The room was in shambles. All of Norian's possessions were destroyed. His wardrobe and chairs lay in pieces, his clothes reduced to shreds. Deep scratch marks traced along the walls. Wayf grabbed hold of the nearest wall, trying to retain his consciousness. He gasped out loud when the village's warning bells rang out, signaling that there was danger afoot. Tears ran down his face, and he gasped for breath as the certainty of what had occurred took hold of him. The transformation had taken place a day early.

Norian had turned into a werewolf!

NORIAN OPENED his eyes and immediately shielded them from the bright sunlight. His entire body ached, and his mind was foggy, leading him to suspect that he'd drunk an enormous quantity of ale the night before. He tried to think about what he had done the previous night, but his head pounded too much. He closed his eyes again and sucked in a deep breath of cool air. Whatever had occurred, he must have had a marvelous time, given that he had no memory of it. He then noticed that something was not quite right. This was not his warm, comfortable bed he lay upon, but damp grass. A chill took hold, and his body shivered. He opened his eyes again and surveyed his surroundings. He found himself underneath a tree in the forest, and moreover, he was completely naked. His head spun as he slowly looked around, desperately trying to recall how he'd arrived in such a situation. Then it slowly came back to him—the excruciating pain, the sound of his bones breaking, his body changing.

He held both hands in front of him and breathed a sigh of relief as everything looked normal. But what had happened to him? Was it some sort of prequel to what would occur tonight? He shuddered as he remembered the agony of the night before. But how did he end up here? And naked nonetheless. Where were his clothes?

Norian tried to stand up, but his wobbly legs sent him back to the ground. He looked around him, hoping to catch a glance of his clothes, but saw nothing. He attempted to rise again, this time bracing himself against the tree. Intense dizziness hit him, but he managed to stay erect. He wiped the sweat from his brow and took a deep breath to calm himself. He was not only confused, but lost as well. Where on God's green earth was he? And why wasn't he at the castle in his own bed? He recalled the pain when his bones seemed to break, but after that, he remembered nothing.

He slowly placed one foot in front of the other and found he could walk without too much difficulty, as long as he took it slow. His head pounded, and his muscles still ached, but at least he was upright. He found a small brook and drank the icy water until the dryness of his mouth had passed. When he finished, he continued walking and was surprised to see a row of farmhouses up ahead. My goodness, how far away from the castle had he gone? He was in the village, at least an hour away from his castle. Luckily, he'd found an old blanket in one of the local barns and wrapped it around himself. At least now, if he encountered anyone, they wouldn't be shocked silly by a naked prince.

He continued to walk for what seemed like hours. Then, finally, the sound of someone calling his name rang through the woods. It was Wayf.

"Wayf! I'm here!"

All at once, Wayf came around the wooded bend. He appeared out of breath and a bit haggard-looking. He ran towards Norian, grabbed him, and then pulled him into a tight hug.

"Thank the gods you are alive!" Wayf said. He took a step back and looked at Norian. His brow darkened. "How fare you? Do you recall anything?"

"I'm a bit sore, but other than that, I appear to be fit."

He took hold of Wayf's shoulders. "But what happened to me? What did this damnable curse do to me?"

Wayf closed his eyes for a brief moment, as if in thought, and then reopened them.

"You don't recall?"

Norian shook his head. "The last thing I remember, I was at the castle. I awoke near the woods next to the village, with neither clothes nor memory of what had occurred."

With a wave of his hand, Wayf indicated a fallen tree on the edge of the path. "Let us sit for a moment." There was a serious edge to his voice.

"This can't be good," Norian said, gaping at Wayf.

Wayf gave him a weak smile. "Regretfully, it is not."

They both sat down on the log. Norian expectantly stared at Wayf, but Wayf's eyes looked off into the distance. He took a ragged breath, lowered his head to look at Norian, and then spoke.

"Do you remember anything else from last night?

"Very little. I was in my room, debating whether I should try to find something to eat, as I had fasted the entire day."

"But why?"

"No appetite. The mere thought of food nauseated me. I must have found something to eat eventually, though, as I am quite satiated now."

Wayf visibly grimaced and then indicated that he should continue.

"I was in my room when all of a sudden, a most horrid pain took over me. It came out of nowhere and immediately brought me to my knees. Its intensity grew, and for a moment, I swear I heard the wretched sound of my own bones breaking. I was certain that I would perish. Then nothing until I awoke this morning near the outer village."

"You recall nothing after you left the castle?"

"Wayf, I don't remember ever *leaving* the castle." Norian narrowed his eyes. "Tell me, what do you know?"

Wayf grabbed him, and once again, pulled him into a hug. Norian suspected immediately that something must be seriously wrong, as such an outward expression of affection was not typical for Wayf.

"There is not an easy way to phrase this, so I shall state it as it is. Last night, you transformed into a werewolf."

Unable to control himself, Norian's body began shaking, and he found it difficult to breathe. He finally gasped, "But...I thought...You are sure?"

Wayf nodded and gave him a weak smile. "Yes, Norian. 'I ran to your room last night and found utter chaos. I regret to say it is now all but uninhabitable."

"So that's what happened to me? I turned a day early?" He creased his brow. "Wait, was it, in fact, a day early? Did we somehow err? Was the full moon last night?"

"I am afraid not, Norian. The full moon is tonight. So we did not miscalculate."

Norian's eyes grew wide. "But how?"

Wayf sighed. "Yesterday, I discovered a little more about what it is you are facing." He placed his hands on Norian's shoulders. "I recalled reading that in certain rare circumstances, the curse does not cause transformation only on the full moon, but can do so the day before and the day after as well. Thus, you may transform three times a month as opposed to just once."

"Three times! But I thought it was only on the full moon."

"I thought the same. As I've told you, I have never encountered a werewolf during my lifetime, so this is as new to me as it is to you. I've been going by the rumors and wives' tales that I've come across over the years. Yesterday, I found a footnote in one of my old grimoires that mentions the three-night curse of the full moon. While it's supposedly extremely rare, it can occur. Unfortunately, I didn't pay any attention to it at the time and had almost forgotten about it." He paused, closed his eyes, and continued. "I'm know that this is not what you wanted or needed to hear right now, Norian. I'm so sorry."

Norian's heart pounded at the news, and his breath came out in quick gasps. His eyes teared up, and he broke Wayf's gaze. Three nights a month, he will turn into a beast! He shuddered as he recalled the unbearable pain of the night before. There was a bright side, though. At least he remembered nothing that had happened after he turned. He didn't remember being a wolf, and for that, he was grateful. He took a deep breath and tried to calm himself.

"Is there anything you can do to stop this? Can you somehow render me unconscious, as we've discussed?"

"As of yet, I have discovered nothing in my books that mentions the possibility of preventing the transformation. But we will try putting you under tonight. It just may work."

"I shall have to be locked up now for three nights lest I harm someone."

Wayf put his hands on Norian's cheeks and looked him in the eye. Norian saw him tense for a moment. "Norian," he said in a voice that was almost a whisper. A frown overtook his features. "There is more."

"What is it, Wayf?"

"There was an incident last night. A woman from the village."

It took Norian a moment before he understood what it was that Wayf was saying. Norian's heart clenched in his chest, and an intense dizziness fell upon him. Shaking, Norian stood up and covered his eyes with his hands. "It can't be! Please don't tell me I've harmed someone."

"I'm sorry, Norian. Unfortunately, she didn't survive the attack."

Norian looked up at the sky, his breath ragged. His body shook as sobs overtook him, and tears trickled down his face.

Wayf pulled him close. "Norian, it's not your fault. We didn't know."

"Of course it's my fault," Norian said through his tears. "Who else's fault could it have been? I am the one who killed her. I'm the one who is the monster."

"Now that we understand a little more about the curse, we can take proper precautions. We'll ensure that there's no possible way for you to escape."

Norian felt panic rise inside of him as a most horrible thought rose to the surface. "Wayf, did I," he paused, swallowed, and took a deep breath. "Did I eat her?"

"The specifics of the attack will not help you. What we need to do is—"

"Did I eat her, Wayf? Tell me!"

Wayf slowly nodded. "It appears so. There was not too much left of her when she was found."

Norian felt the bile of his stomach rise. He ran to the nearest tree and emptied his stomach, keeping his eyes closed the entire time. Over and over his stomach lurched until there was nothing left in it. When his retching finally ceased, he plopped to the ground and wrapped his arms around his knees. The sobs came of their own volition. He wanted to die.

He felt a hand on his shoulder and looked up. "I cannot

begin to imagine how difficult this is for you, my friend," Wayf said.

"I do not want to live."

"Norian, you must listen to me."

He shook his head. "This sort of life I do not want. I want to be done. I want it to be over."

All at once, Norian's ears popped, and he was jerked upright to a standing position without being touched. He jerked his head to meet Wayf's angry stare.

"There shall be no more such talk. Ever. Do you understand me?"

Norian stared, too stunned to speak. Wayf had never used magic against him before.

"I said, do you hear me, Norian?"

Norian nodded, trying to hide his rising anger. He thought of reminding Wayf that using magic against a prince typically results in the death penalty, but decided against it, given that Norian had just eaten a villager. "I understand."

Wayf poked him in the chest with his finger. "You are a prince. Someday, you shall be king. This kingdom needs a strong, brave man to lead it. And that man shall be you. There is to be no giving up here. You do not have that choice. Understood?"

Norian nodded.

"Good," Wayf continued. "Now sit back down, for I have more to tell you."

They both took their former places on the fallen tree. Norian rocked back and forth as he waited for Wayf to begin. Finally, he could wait no more. He had to learn the truth.

"The attack. Does everyone know it was me?"

"Nobody but the King and I are cognizant of the true

nature of the attack. Nobody else saw anything. Though village hunters went out to look for what they believed was a wild beast, they returned empty-handed, assuming the creature had moved on."

"Oh no, my father. How shall I ever face him? I'll never be able to look him in the eye again."

"You are his son, and he understands that this was out of your control. He is your father, and you are still his son. No matter what, he continues to love you. Vadok is to blame for this, not you."

Norian took a deep breath, fearful of angering the wizard again. "You mentioned me being king. Surely you know that this cannot come to pass now. What if the people should find out what I am? They certainly would not allow a murdering beast to rule them. Why, there would be an immediate uprising—and justifiably so."

"I know nothing of the sort, and we shall not spend our time speculating on what might be. What we need to do now is find a way to cure you."

"Cure me? But I thought you said that you aren't familiar with any way to stop the transformation."

"That much is true. I cannot do anything myself. But I did come across something of interest in an old journal last night, something that I'd completely forgotten about."

"A spell? Medicine that can cure me?"

Wayf shook his head. "Nothing like that. From what I read, most of the time, the curse is passed through blood. That is to say, people are born with it, receiving it from a werewolf mother or father. There are actually very few instances of people obtaining the curse through a bite."

"Probably because nobody ever survives an attack," Norian said.

Wayf squinted at Norian. "No doubt. Anyway, there is no known cure if the disease is transmitted through parents. But we don't know about your case. Perhaps since you weren't born with it, there might be something out there that is, as of yet, unknown to us—something that can, at a minimum, stop you from transforming, if not cure you completely."

Norian's eyes widened. "So, what are you saying? There is hope for a cure?"

"I dread to get your hopes up. But I think it would behoove us to explore all possibilities, no?"

Norian nodded. "Yes, of course. So what do you have in mind? What do I have to do?"

"How would you feel about a journey?"

Norian paused and wrinkled his brow. "You mean travel away from the castle?"

Wayf nodded. "While I was going through my old grimoires, I encountered an entry that talked about a hidden community of werefolk in a town called Norbury. It's about a nine or ten-day journey from here, possibly more. When I read it, I all at once recalled a story that was circulating several years back about that same village. Supposedly, people suffering from your affliction find a welcoming community there."

"What are you saying, Wayf? That I should leave my home for good and go live with a bunch of rogue werewolves?"

Wayf laughed. "Not at all. The passage mentioned that the queen of this community, Lady Auryon, is wise and willing to help those like yourself. Thus, she may know if there is any possibility of a cure or, at the very least, may have some idea on how to live a productive life despite the affliction."

"So I'm to seek out the Queen of the Werewolves? This is the hope of which you speak?"

"It's not much. I will give you that. We don't even know if this community actually exists. I know of nobody who has ever been there. But we need to explore every option, every possibility."

"Have you mentioned this to my father?"

"I mentioned it this morning, and he reluctantly agreed. But to be truthful, I'm not sure how well he was listening. He was in a bit of a panic because of your absence and the business with the woman in the village. We didn't have a search party set out for you, fearing that someone might associate you with the attack. So we're the only ones who knew you were missing. We shall need to discuss the possibility of this journey with your father when we get back."

"But how am I to locate this place—what was it again?"

"Norbury," Wayf said. "It is well outside the realm of our kingdom and not easy to find, from what I understand. But fear not—I shall have a detailed map drawn up at once, to at least guide you to the general area."

"But can't you accompany me? You're aware that I've done little traveling outside of these gates."

Wayf shook his head and rested his hand on Norian's shoulder. "I wish I could, Norian. But you must understand that I need to stay here and help your father protect the kingdom, especially now that Vadok is out for blood—my blood, apparently. And even if I could accompany you, you would have to go on alone at some point, for it is said that only those who are werefolk are welcome in Norbury."

"So this village consists entirely of..." he paused for a moment, swallowed, and then, "my kind?"

Wayf pursed his lips and absent-mindedly rubbed his chin. "It's not really a village per se, but more of a hidden community of outcasts. It's not like our villages, with their various shops and businesses. From what I gather, there is no real town to speak of— just scatterings of folk here and there. That is why I said it will not be an easy place to find. These people have made not being found their life's work."

Norian found the mere thought of traveling, especially alone, frightening. He had always been surrounded by people—Wayf, courtesans, tutors, and friends. But he had to admit that the idea of an adventure excited him.

"Is there no one who can come with me?"

"I'm sorry. But this is something that you shall have to take on by yourself. However, if your father agrees, I can travel with you, if you wish, up to the borders of our kingdom, but after that, you shall be on your own."

Norian thought for a moment. "No, if I'm going to do this, I may as well undertake the entire journey myself. I know the way to our perimeter. It's after crossing that perimeter that I'm dreading."

"That's understandable. I would suggest one of the servants accompany you, but there's a possibility they'd be killed once arriving in Norbury. Surrounding villages know to stay away—or face death."

Norian shuddered. "Death? And you want me to go to this place alone? Have you lost grip of your sanity?"

"That is why I am telling you ahead of time of the possible dangers, and it is your decision whether to go or stay. Let me say that you would not enter this journey without considerable peril. I do not hide this from you, as we have no idea what awaits you on the other side. There's a possibility that you could be killed instead of welcomed. But I am hoping that since you are one of their kind, they would be open to your presence in their village."

"But am I truly one of their kind?" Norian asked. "You

said yourself that most werewolves are born that way and not bitten. So I'm a freak even among the freaks."

"Norian, that is not true. I'm sure there are more out there like you. But I cannot make any guarantees as to whether you'll be welcomed, shunned, or driven out. Know that I do not suggest this undertaking without considerable reflection. When the thought first hit me, I planned to go to your room to discuss the possibility. That is, until I heard the howling."

Norian felt the red rise in his face. "Howling? I howled?"

Wayf nodded. "Aye, and a very distinctive, bone-chilling howl it was. But back to our journey. I considered the possibility before, but with this new knowledge that you will spend three nights out of each month in this new form, it might be wise to look even more urgently for anything that might help you. Inquiring among your own kind might be the smartest move at this point. It also may be your only option."

"That sounds so strange, my own kind. But perhaps you are right. If I am to be king someday, there is little doubt that I shall have to find a cure, if one exists, before I take the throne."

"Not necessarily. But that shall be a discussion for another day. The journey, then—you are willing to consider it as an option?"

"I'll do anything at this point. I just don't want to kill anyone ever again."

"Let us not dwell upon past actions, but instead look to the future. Agreed?"

Norian nodded. "Agreed. So when do I leave?" Norian asked.

"Not so fast. I want you to think seriously about this in

the coming days, weighing the pros and cons of such a decision. Because if you choose to go, you'll have to commit to it with your entire soul. It's not a choice to make lightly. But first, let us work on getting through the next two nights. Then, on the third morning, if you're certain you wish to embark upon the journey, you'll depart. You and I can walk together for the next couple of days, and I shall prepare you the best that I can for the journey." He paused for a moment and appeared as though he were in deep thought. "It's essential that you arrive there before the next full moon. I dread to think of you changing near a village."

"What about tonight? Where will I change?"

"We'll have to put you in one of the dungeons. I'll try to ease your discomfort with magic, if possible." He closed his eyes for a moment. "I'm just sorry that I was not there last night. But I had no way of knowing that the curse would run for three nights a month. So tonight, we shall be prepared."

"And Father?"

"We'll have a conference with him as soon as we arrive back at the castle." Wayf slapped him on the leg. "So let us start back. There is much to be done."

CHAPTER EIGHT

Wayf stood outside the locked cell, gazing at Norian's unconscious body. He took a deep breath and wondered what time it was—surely the moon would be rising soon. Earlier, he had concocted a potion that pushed Norian into a state of unconsciousness. It was a simple tincture composed of common herbs, infused with a powerful spell. He prayed it would work. So far, it seemed to do the trick. Norian's body lay prone on the cell floor, and Wayf could hear his heavy, rhythmic breathing. He smiled. If this worked, then a good portion of their problem would be solved. Perhaps Norian would not have to go searching for the Queen of Werewolves after all.

A loud groan escaped the unconscious man on the floor. Then, all at once, his body writhed and twisted. Wayf rushed to the door and grabbed the vertical bars contained within the small window. The moon must have risen. But the question is, would Norian turn? And if he did, would he awaken?

Wayf watched, his gut-wrenching in anticipation. Then

Norian's eyes flew open, and he gasped. His gaze met Wayf's through the window.

"Wayf! Help me."

Wayf closed his eyes and began chanting. A spell for deep relaxation. Sweat poured down his face as he recited the words he knew from memory. He chanted louder, trying to drown out Norian's screams. If the noise coming from the locked room was any indication, Wayf guessed his spell was having little effect. Seeing that the curse broke an unconsciousness spell, it came as no surprise to Wayf that a minor relaxation spell would be ineffective. Nevertheless, it was worth a try. It was all he had.

Wayf opened his eyes and peered inside the room. Upon seeing Norian, he gasped and instantly took a step back. Norian was on all fours, panting wildly like an exhausted dog. The skin on his back was pulsating up and down, looking as if something was ready to burst through. He could not see Norian's face, but it appeared as if the hair on his head was now twice as long as it was earlier. Then, a loud cracking noise erupted in the room, and Norian screamed—and screamed—and screamed. Wayf brought his hands to his ears, trying to block out the brain-splitting sounds of Norian's anguished cries. He tried to look away from the scene inside of the cell but found that he could not. His eyes welled up with tears at the sight before him, feeling truly helpless for the first time in his life.

Then the sound ceased. Wayf guessed that Norian's vocal cords had now transformed, making it impossible to create human sound. The cracking sound from the cell grew louder. Norian's back rippled and snapped, causing him to writhe wildly about the cell. His ripped clothes fell into a tattered heap on the floor. His arms and legs simultaneously extended, accompanied by sharp snapping sounds and thick black hair sprouted all over the boy's body. The worst to witness was Norian's face. Wayf watched in near terror as Norian's face compressed inward, appearing as though it was being smashed between two large boulders. Then it pushed forward and extended outwards, coming to a point.

A low growl came from the creature on the cell floor. It turned its head to the window, and bright yellow wolf eyes met Wayf's.

"Norian! It's me, Wayf. Can you understand me?" His voice shook and crackled as he spoke.

In one swift move, the creature bounded up to the window, its claws barely missing Wayf's face. It tried several times to reach him, a furry paw squeezing through the thin bars and swiping at him. It finally gave up. The animal now stood on all fours in the center of the cell, opened its snout, and let loose a loud, eerie, primal howl that sent shivers through Wayf's entire body. He was glad that they were deep within the castle basement, as this was a sound that would not sit well with the people of the village, especially considering what had happened the night before.

The creature began tearing around the cage, pouncing and throwing itself against each wall in an attempt to escape the locked room. It growled ferociously as it did so, and Wayf feared it would hurt itself.

"You might as well calm down, Norian. You are not going anywhere tonight."

His voice seemed to calm the creature. Their gazes met, and for a moment, Wayf could see and sense Norian through the wolf's eyes. It was almost as if the animal was trying to communicate with him.

"I'll be here all night," he reassured the creature. "You are not alone."

He then sat down on the stool next to the door, picked up one of his overly large books, and turned his focus to the words within.

~

A LOUD GROAN snapped Wayf awake. He jumped up off the stool, ran to the window, looked inside, and breathed a sigh of relief. Norian was once again in human form. He was naked, hunched in the room's corner. His body was shaking.

"Norian!" Wayf said. He drew a key from the pocket of his robe and unlocked the door.

He rushed to the boy and helped him to scoot his body up against the cell wall. Then he took off his outer robe and wrapped it gently around Norian's shoulders. Norian grabbed it from him and wrapped it around himself tightly.

"Wayf," Norian croaked. "Thank goodness you are here. Have you water perchance?"

Wayf smiled and nodded. He stepped outside the room and returned with one of the castle flasks.

"Here, drink up."

"So it happened again," Norian said.

"Aye, it did."

"Did the spell help at all? Did it at least slow down the transformation?"

Wayf shook his head. "You were unconscious until the moon rose, and then you awoke right as the change first began to occur."

"I remember waking up in the most horrible pain. The same wretched pain as before. I swear, if there had been a sword nearby, I would have cut my throat to make it stop."

"Norian, you mustn't talk like that. Remember our conversation from yesterday."

Norian nodded and said nothing. He took another long swig of the water. How could he possibly expect Wayf to understand? There were no mere words to describe the excruciating torture that this transformation brought with it. The agony of your bones snapping in two. How could he endure this month after month, year after year? And for three days in a row, nonetheless? But he would not give up yet. If there was a cure out there, a way of escaping this torment, he would find it.

"I can safely assume that you watched me change?"

Wayf swallowed. "Aye, I did."

"So? What was it like?"

"Certainly not one of my most favored scenes to witness. How much of it do you remember?"

"I remember extreme and absolute pain, torture, agony, misery,…need I go on?" He shuddered at the memory.

Wayf lowered his head. "I'm sorry, Norian. I don't wish to make you relive the experience."

"No, no. It's alright." He gave the wizard a weak smile. "I remember my bones breaking, just like last time. I wanted to cry out but found I was unable to. There were a lot of white flashes before my eyes, and my vision blurred completely. That's about all I can remember. Nothing until I woke up this morning."

"How do you feel now?"

"Like a stampede of horses has recently run over me. So Wayf," he said, pausing for a moment. "What did I look like? After the change, I mean."

"Norian, I really don't think that —"

"Tell me. I want to know. How hideous was I? Did I look like a monster? Were my eyes red?"

"On the contrary, Norian. You transformed into the most beautiful wolf I had ever seen. You were considerably larger than a standard forest wolf, completely black with yellow eyes. If it's any consolation at all, you were truly a majestic creature—though I admit, a tad frightening."

Norian smiled. "Hope I didn't frighten you too badly." He swallowed. "I really, truly turned into an actual wolf?"

"For the most part, yes," Wayf said. "Though you were perhaps nearly twice as large as a normal wolf, maybe even more. I think your eyes were different, too. They were such an intense yellow that they almost glowed."

"Incredible. Who could have ever guessed that such a thing was possible?"

"Seeing it in person is even more astounding," Wayf said. "Although watching you suffer as you did was very difficult for me. I felt so helpless during your transformation. I wish I could have done something to make you more comfortable, to ease your pain."

Norian smiled palely. "I know you would have done everything possible. Knowing you were here is comfort enough."

"Do you recall anything at all after your change?"

"What's funny is that the morning after the first time I transformed—yesterday morning—I recalled nothing. But as the day progressed, I got flashes of bits and pieces of the night before. Unfortunately, that poor villager was part of those flashes."

"That must be difficult. But Norian, this is important. Do you recall how things looked to you?"

"It was like looking out of my own eyes except that everything was a lot clearer, sharper. As the day went on, I recalled more and more. It was as though these foreign memories were supplanted on top of my old ones."

"This tells me that you both are sharing the same consciousness, at least at some level. What we need to do is to try to bring your own consciousness—that of Norian, the human—to the surface during the change."

"What would that do?" Norian asked.

"It might make you more aware of your actions. This could prevent you from harming others in such a situation; however, determining whether it's possible will require much more research. In the meantime, it's vitally important that you find the werewolf clan before the next full moon. Perhaps they know how to control their transformation. But regardless, you must not be alone or near a village when you change."

Norian nodded. "I understand. That doesn't leave me much time to find them, does it?"

"If you leave immediately the day after tomorrow and figuring in about ten or so days for travel, you should have nearly three weeks to find Lady Auryon. My map will narrow down the general location where to start looking. I would also venture to guess that the moment you enter their territory, all eyes will be upon you."

Norian's mouth grew dry as he pictured himself being ripped apart by angry wolves. His first journey out in the real world was to wander into hostile territory willingly, territory occupied by monsters. But it was his only hope, wasn't it? Perhaps if they did kill him, that wouldn't be such a bad thing. Facing a life of this curse was more than he wanted to bear. But he wasn't about to tell that to Wayf.

"I'll do whatever it takes, Wayf."

Wayf nodded. "I know you will. Now let's get you cleaned up and get some food into you. We have a long day of preparations for your trip ahead of us." He paused and sighed. "And you have one more change to get through before you leave."

CHAPTER NINE

NORIAN SPENT MOST OF THE DAY WITH WAYF, receiving instructions for his upcoming journey. Wayf had the court geographers draw up a map pointing the way to Norbury, which Norian now had in his possession. The prospect of the trip excited him, but he was fearful as well. It was his first journey away from the kingdom, and he didn't know if he would ever return. His stomach lurched at the thought of never seeing his father or Wayf again. But there was no way out of this one. His only option was to find this supposed Werewolf Queen and beg her for her help. Whether she could—or would—help him was the question.

Wayf let him loose for a couple of hours, during which he fenced with a courtesan. It had been a while since he'd used his sword, and seeing that he may be called to use it in a dire situation, he'd best be at the top of his game. It also didn't hurt that Thorne, one of the most handsome young men of the court, was the one with whom he practiced.. His groin stirred as he recalled the searing kiss shared between the two of them in the stables two summers past, and he'd never forgotten it. On that day, Thorne took Norian's horse

from him after a ride, and the two of them began conversing
—about what, Norian no longer remembered. What he did
remember was Thorne's hungry eyes as he'd run his gaze up
and down Norian's half-naked torso. Completely forgetting
himself, Norian had taken a step forward until he and the
boy were almost touching. Norian recalled the glistening
sweat on Thorne's chest and the musky scent of the boy.
Before Norian understood what was happening, Thorne
pushed him down onto a pile of hay and fell upon him. The
kiss that followed was explosive, and though it was Norian's
first and only kiss, it was one that stayed at the forefront of
his thoughts.

He'd secretly hoped for a repeat of that afternoon and
considered using his influence as the prince to sway the
young man, but unfortunately, it never happened again.
Which was for the best, really, given that he would have to
marry eventually and produce a royal heir. And what would
people say if they ever discovered that he had inclinations
towards the young men of the kingdom? What would his
father say?

He brushed the thoughts from his head, making final
preparations before following Wayf to the cell. He entered
the small room, and an odd, pungent odor immediately
struck him. A tinge of wildness hung in the air and
resonated with him on a primal level. An involuntary growl
rose in his throat as the pungent scent overtook his senses,
holding him, gripping him.

"Norian, what is it?" Wayf asked.

It took a moment for him to snap back to himself. "I'm
not sure. That strange odor—it did something to me. It was
like it was calling to me."

Wayf narrowed his eyes and then sniffed at the air. "I
smell nothing. Perhaps your senses grow stronger the closer

you get to your change. Maybe it's yourself you are smelling. Well, not yourself, really. Your other self."

"Possibly," Norian said. "It was the strangest thing. But it appears to have passed now."

"Are you going to give me the potion again?"

Wayf shook his head. "Given that it didn't prevent the transformation from occurring, there's no real sense in taking it for only a few moments of respite. I wish I possessed something to help, anything to make this easier for you, but alas, I'm aware of nothing."

"It's OK. I've managed these past two nights, I can manage again."

"Oh, one more thing before we close the door. Disrobe."

Norian creased his brow. "Disrobe? As in get naked?"

"Exactly. Why willingly destroy your fine clothing each time you change? At this rate, the cost of your wardrobe would bankrupt the royal purse in no time at all." He gave a nervous chuckle. "We should have thought of it last night."

"Good point." Norian undressed and handed his clothes to Wayf. He felt redness burn his cheeks as he found himself naked and vulnerable in front of the wizard.

Norian shivered. "I'm cold now."

"Here," Wayf said, handing Norian the old tattered green horse blanket he was holding. "This will help."

Norian took the blanket and wrapped it around himself. He nodded to Wayf, who then hugged Norian and stepped out of the cell. A metallic clang cut through the room as Wayf snapped the door shut behind him.

"I'll be right outside the door all night," he said in a low voice. "You are not alone."

No more than a few minutes later, the first sharp gut-wrenching cramp seized him and tore through his body. He screamed.

The change had begun.

~

"YOUR FATHER WISHES to speak with you," Wayf said at the breakfast table. "Alone in his study."

Norian nodded, his mouth full of food. He was ravenous. He'd had little appetite these past three days and literally had to force himself to eat. But, apparently, his appetite had returned in full force.

"Why didn't he come to breakfast?" Norian asked. "He missed seeing me make a glutton of himself."

"He was down several hours ago for breakfast, before dawn. He is having a challenging time with you leaving. This isn't easy for him, any of this."

"I know. I'm not anticipating saying goodbye to him—or to you. Especially since it's possible I'll never see either of you again."

"Norian, everything will be fine, I assure you. I can sense it."

"Is this your wizard sense talking here, or are you just trying to make me feel better?"

Wayf smiled. "Both, actually. But enough chatter. Your father awaits you in his room."

Norian sucked in a deep breath. "I am not looking forward to this."

"I'm sure he isn't either."

Norian's heart thunked in his chest as he knocked at the door. After his father's command to enter, he braced himself, opened the door, and walked into the room. His father sat at the table by the window, a pile of papers scattered on his desk. The man's appearance shocked Norian. His hair was disheveled, and the dark circles under his eyes indicated it had been some time since he'd slept. His father leapt up upon seeing Norian. He met him halfway across the floor and pulled him into a tight embrace.

He held Norian at arm's length, as if inspecting him. His eyes were puffy. "How are you faring, Son?"

"Well as can be expected, Father."

"I'm so sorry that I haven't seen you since your first...," he paused, then pursed his lips. "Change. In this, I have failed you."

Norian shook his head and made a dismissive gesture in the air. "Not at all. I understand. And truth be told, I didn't want you to see me like that. But Wayf was there—he helped me through it, so I was fine."

"How can you understand if I don't understand myself?" King Jamros asked. "I've been here these past three days trying to make sense out of everything that's happened." He looked at Norian with defeated eyes. "I suppose I haven't been very successful. I'm at a loss as to what to say to you. I want to help you but don't know how."

"Father, please do not punish yourself. It pains me to see you in such anguish."

The king put his hand on Norian's shoulder. "Here you are comforting me, and it is I who should be comforting you." He took a deep breath. "So you are well-prepared for your journey?"

"I believe so. The servants are packing my provision bags as we speak, and I've taken a few items of clothing with me."

"And weaponry?"

"I have the sword that you gifted me on my fifteenth birthday."

The king's eyes glistened. "Let us hope you shan't need it."

He then walked to the wardrobe next to the bed, opened it, and retrieved a small leather pouch, almost bursting at the seams. He handed it to Norian. "Here, take this son."

"What is this?" he asked.

"Gold," his father said. "If these people can help you, pay them as much gold as they want. Tell them there is more here in the kingdom. There is no price too high for your cure."

"Father, I —," Norian started.

"Don't," his father said, waving his hand in the air. "This is my decision. Just promise me you'll tell them you are willing to pay anything."

Norian nodded and held the pouch tightly to his chest. "I promise."

"Good. Now another thing. If we find it our unfortunate luck that the people of Norbury cannot help you, I want you to return to the castle immediately."

Norian swallowed. "I'm not sure I can do that."

The King's eyes grew wide. "What? Why would you not return to your home?"

Norian broke his gaze and looked down at the floor. "Because I am a monster."

The King grabbed hold of his shoulders. "Norian, look at me." Norian raised his eyes to meet his father's. "You are the prince. You are my son. Someday you shall be king. Those are the things that are most important and that you must not forget. This affliction you have, it's something we will get through together. It is only for three nights of the month that you suffer, and during that time, we will ensure that you and everyone else in the village are safe. This illness changes nothing. Your place is here."

"How can you say this, Father?" Norian asked. "How

can you think that the people of the kingdom would ever accept me—a foul, unholy beast—as their prince? As their king? Why would they accept a king who would prefer to eat them at the first chance?"

"Norian, stop."

"Think about it, Father. What would the people do if they learned their king was a monster and an abomination? They'd probably torch down the castle."

"Norian, you can't pretend to know the actions or reactions of others. Our people might surprise you." He paused for a moment and creased his brow. "Also, knowledge of your situation need not be shared with others. A serious illness is a man's private affair, whether he be prince, king, or peasant. Only those closest to you need to be informed about your affliction. We shall secure you during those three unfortunate nights, and life will be normal during the other times."

"How can a king just disappear for three days a month?" Norian asked. "Think about your own obligations. Many of them take you away from the kingdom for weeks at a time. There have been times of war where you've been gone for months. This would be impractical and impossible for me."

"There are many options," the king answered. "You can send others in your stead. You can plan your excursions around that accursed moon. Do not forget that there are many who love you and support you. You can and will fulfill your duties as a king."

"But what if I don't want to?" Norian said. His eye moistened. "The pain that this change causes is nearly too much to bear. Imagine, if you will, what it feels like to have every bone in your body break, to have your organs, your skin, the shape of your body snap into something else. Not once, mind you, but three nights in a row, every month for the rest of your life." Norian wiped his eyes with his sleeve, embarrassed at his tears. "I don't know how long I can bear it."

The King cupped Norian's face with his hands. His voice was almost a whisper. "Don't give up, son, I beg of you. I can't begin to understand what it must be like for you, but know that we will never stop looking for a cure. We will never stop searching until we find a way to ease your suffering. The answer is out there somewhere, it has to be."

Norian slowly nodded. "Thank you, Father."

"So do you promise me that no matter what, you shall return? Even if you are unsuccessful in finding a cure?"

"I do," Norian said. His voice sounded weak and strange to his ears. "I swear I will return, successful or not."

The king smiled. "Let us hope that this supposed queen can help you."

"Are you familiar with the village where I am going? About the people there?"

"Very little. King Zanian rules the land itself. You remember him?"

Norian nodded. "He's been at the castle to see you several times. He's the one with the long curly brown hair, right?" Norian remembered him because he'd found the king exceptionally handsome.

"Yes, that is him. Thankfully, we have good relations with his kingdom. Unfortunately, though the town you seek lies within his realm, it is a place over which no king truly holds sway. From my understanding, it is an area of rogues, cutthroats, and outcasts, a place where those who find themselves on the fringe of polite society live."

"Sounds like a lovely town," Norian said.

The King's brow darkened. "'Tis not a very desirable

place, I can assure you. I do not doubt that the people who inhabit this town are dangerous, with perhaps a low appreciation for life. This is my agony, Son. Every instinct I have as a father screams against sending you to such a terrible place. I would much prefer to keep you here, safe in our kingdom." The King bowed his head. "That is yet an option, son. You still can decide to stay."

Norian swallowed. "I know. But I have to do this, Father. If there's even the slightest chance these people or this queen can help me, I have to try. It may be the only chance I have of living a normal life."

The King nodded. "Understood. As difficult as this is for me, I want you whole as you were meant to be. But know that no matter what, you are my son, and I love you."

"Thank you, Father. I shan't forget your words."

"I neglected to tell you. Wayf shall accompany you part of the way."

"Wayf? But I thought I had to go alone?"

"Aye, that is the case. He shall accompany you only to the outer borders of our kingdom to help you get started on your journey. From there, you must go on alone. In the past, any time the rogues of Norbury have felt threatened, they have retaliated most viciously. Or at least, so goes the rumors. Strangers are unwelcome, even more so when they travel in mass. They protect their town with a vengeance. Believe me, Son, I wish I could send our entire army with you. But alas, that cannot be, for it would only drive us further away from the possibility of a cure for you. We must think of your safety as well as Wayf's."

Even though Norian had initially decided to journey the entire way alone, he now welcomed Wayf's presence, even if it was only for a short while. "Thank you, Father, for allowing him to come part of the way with me. It shall be an immense help."

They both stared at each other for several moments, an uncomfortable silence between them. Norian felt the tears welling up again, but he fought them back. Weeping in front of his father would do neither of them any good. Finally, the King reached out to Norian and hugged him tightly.

"It is now time for you to take your leave of me, my son."

Norian held onto his father even tighter, not wanting to let go. This time, the tears came—and he couldn't stop them.

He finally stepped back and nodded to his father. The tears blurred his vision.

"I know, Father." The glistening dampness in his father's eyes made it even more difficult for Norian to control his own. He took a deep breath. "I am ready to face whatever may come."

"You are my brave boy. Perhaps you are much braver than I would be, were I to find myself in your situation. I am so proud of you, and my heart goes with you as you travel."

Norian nodded again and turned to the door. He turned one last time at the doorway and looked at the King.

"Goodbye, Father."

A loud click rang from the door, and he pulled it shut. As he heard his father's muffled sobs echoing from the room, he turned and hurried down the hallway.

CHAPTER TEN

Norian's head pounded, and the sun hurt his eyes as their horses trotted through the green of the hills. Wayf seemed to prattle on endlessly about mundane life at the castle. As much as he loved his friend and teacher, Norian wished they could now simply ride in silence. He hated to think it, but he was almost looking forward to the time when they would part ways, and he could finally have some peace.

He then noticed that Wayf had stopped talking. He turned his head and met Wayf's expectant gaze.

"Well?" Wayf asked.

"Well, what?"

Wayf shook his head and laughed. "You weren't listening to me at all, were you?"

"Sorry. I'm a little anxious about what's to come."

"That is understandable. I asked how you were feeling?"

"Feeling?"

"Physically. It was only last night that you suffered through your last change. I can't help but wonder what kind of toll it has taken on your body."

"Apart from a colossal appetite, the same as before. Better, to be truthful. The only time I didn't feel right was during the day before each change. I had no appetite and my body ached all over. It all seems to have passed now. I am almost my usual self."

"Almost?" Wayf asked.

"There appear to be some side effects. No doubt it shall pass."

Wayf raised his eyebrows. "What sort of side effects?"

"Before the change, one reason I had no appetite was that the food smells were so overwhelming that they nauseated me to the point where I could keep nothing down in my stomach. What was strange was that I could smell every item the kitchen cook was preparing all the way from my room. That has never happened before."

"And this hasn't diminished?"

"Maybe a bit. Although I can smell that there's a rabbit hiding in those bushes over there."

"You can smell live animals?"

"It seems so," Norian said. "Although I didn't realize it until this moment. It's kind of an inner knowing, knowledge at the back of my mind that the animal is there. But my sense of smell for most everything is still intense."

"But it's no longer impacting your appetite?"

Norian shook his head. "On the contrary, this newfound sense of smell has increased it." He paused for a moment, not sure if we wanted to carry this conversation further. "I can see a lot better too."

"You're saying you've noticed a change in your vision? I wasn't aware that you've had difficulties in the past or that your vision wasn't clear."

"That's the thing. Neither did I. I always believed I had

perfect vision. But now, everything is so," he paused, looking for the right word. "Different. The world seems so much clearer and crisper, and even the slightest movement jumps out at me. It was a tad disconcerting at first, but I am getting used to it. Do you think it will fade in time? Maybe it's an aftereffect of the change that will diminish?"

Wayf rubbed his chin. "I wouldn't be so sure. This curse may have changed you biologically. Perhaps these newfound sensations are now a part of you, for you are not the same person you were before."

"What you really mean is that I'm not a person at all," Norian replied.

"That is not at all what I said," Wayf said, narrowing his eyes. "Do not change the meaning of my words to suit your mood." The sharp tone of his voice startled Norian. His voice softened. "You are indeed a person. Never, ever forget that. You are simply a different type of person, with new abilities that we do not yet understand. Hence the purpose of this trip."

"Wasn't the purpose of this trip to help me find a cure?"

"Aye. Naturally, that is our chief hope, to be sure. But we don't know what awaits you outside the boundaries of our kingdom. Perhaps there is indeed a cure. Perhaps there is not. Instead, you might find out how to best live with and understand this new part of you. Or learn how to make these transformations easier on yourself."

"But you're the court wizard. Can't you look at entrails or something to see if this trip is worthwhile?"

"I already have," Wayf said. "Not entrails, exactly. But I did perform a divination. Several, actually."

"And you neglected to tell me this? Why?"

"The response was unclear. However, what I learned is

that this trip will be indeed beneficial and that you will be rewarded for undertaking it."

"So, I will be cured!" Norian exclaimed.

"Not necessarily," Wayf said. "The divination showed that you would undergo a transformation, but more on an emotional level. There was no sign of anything physical. Now that does not mean you shan't find a cure, for perhaps you may. But apparently, the fates are not making this information available to me at the moment."

"Could it be that you perhaps did not understand the results of the divination or interpret them correctly? You yourself said that I would be rewarded for this journey. As it happens, the only reward for which I am searching is an end to this loathsome curse. So can it not be that this indeed shall be the reward I receive?"

"Alas, that is not what the divination indicated. The signs showed me that your reward shall have more to do with emotional growth, at least initially."

"Who in the hell wants emotional growth?" Norian asked. "If I am not to find a cure, then why am I risking my life in making this journey?"

"Norian, nobody truly knows what the fates hold for us. They are always careful never to reveal too much of their grand design. But what the signs tell me is that this journey is not only beneficial for you — it is essential." Perhaps you shall find a cure. I certainly hope so. But whatever the outcome, I am convinced that this is indeed a journey you must undertake."

Norian nodded and said nothing. They spent the next couple of hours riding primarily in silence, with Wayf making the occasional commentary on the landscape. Norian was wrapped up in his own thoughts—thoughts of his new life, thoughts about what lay ahead of him in this journey. Finally, Wayf's voice broke him out of his reverie.

"'Tis getting dark. We shall camp here. We've had a long and swift journey today. It is time for rest."

Norian was pleased to finally get off of the horse. He had lost all the feeling in his backside hours ago. In silence, the two men dismounted and busied themselves setting up camp. Norian smiled as Wayf began food preparation. His stomach growled at the anticipation of the upcoming meal. They had eaten nothing but a few morsels of dried meat as they rode, hoping to cover as much distance as possible. Based on what Wayf was retrieving from his overstuffed bag, it looked like their first meal away from the castle would be a good one. The amount of food that Wayf had packed into his smallish sack amazed him: an assortment of meats, breads, fruit, jellies, and vegetables soon appeared on the flat rock they'd decided to use as a makeshift table. Lastly, Wayf retrieved two shiny castle goblets, followed by a canteen of wine.

"Such a feast you've prepared, Wayf. This is extraordinary!"

"Seeing as it is to be our last night together, I wanted this meal to be something special."

"We are only together for one night?" Norian asked. "Tomorrow, you take your leave of me?"

"I am afraid so," Wayf said, snapping small twigs, which he then laid on the ground in a tee-pee formation for the fire. He stood up and brushed himself off. "We shall easily reach the boundary of the kingdom tomorrow. I shall then need to return to the castle."

"I didn't realize we would part so quickly."

"The western edge of Tregaron is only better than a day's journey from the castle. "

"I shall be alone for several days then?"

Wayf nodded. "Well over a week, I imagine. There are several villages along the way where you should be able to find an inn. Have you ample gold with you?"

"Father gave me plenty before I left."

"Ah, good. But be wary of rogues and bandits. There may be scoundrels lying in wait for unsuspecting travelers to happen by."

"I shall ride with one hand on my sword at all times," Norian answered.

Wayf flashed a warm smile. "Very good. I'm aware that I worry too much about you. I tend to forget that you are no longer the child you once were, but are now a fully grown man. Old nannying habits are sometimes challenging to cease, especially regarding those we care about."

"Nannying Wayf? Remember, you're not that much older than me."

"'Tis true. We aren't really that far apart in years. But as for maturity..."

"Watch it, Wayf. You're heading into some dangerous territory."

They both chuckled. Wayf gestured to the stick on the ground. "I brought the food, so it is up to you to light the fire."

A few minutes later, their campfire was blazing, and together, they both set about meal preparation. Soon, they both sat down to enjoy their bounty.

"I think this food tastes better than what we get at the castle. Wayf, have you ever considered changing careers and becoming a castle chef rather than the court magician?"

"My meal concocting is mostly limited to that which we are eating. Consider yourself fortunate that I am not in the kitchen, for if I were, it would ultimately lead to a castle uprising, if not a total revolution."

Norian laughed. "You don't give yourself ample credit. I find what you say difficult to believe based on what we're eating. Why, you are a marvelous chef."

"I bow my head to you in gratitude for such kind words," Wayf replied.

They finished their meals, washed up, and then rested against a massive boulder. Both men watched the twinkling stars in silence. Norian felt tired and sore, but satiated from the meal. He finally broke the silence.

"How long do you think it shall take me to reach Norbury?"

"I should not take you too much more than a week. Have you studied the map that I provided you?"

Norian lowered his eyes. "Not as much as I would have liked. I've been a bit occupied the past few days."

"Ah. Of course. Have you your map close by?"

"It's in the saddlebag." Norian rose and returned a moment later with a scroll. He spread it out over his legs and then pointed toward the center. "We're almost here, correct?"

"Yes, here's our kingdom boundary," said Wayf, pointing to a point on the map. "And there is your destination. It's unmarked, but somewhere around this area here should be Norbury. Based upon the villages between here and there, you should only have to sleep in the wild a few nights, hopefully not more than four or five. It'd be wise to consult the map regularly during your travels to ensure that you don't find yourself alone and out in the open past dusk. You'll want to plan your journey around the inns in the villages whenever possible. 'Tis better to cease traveling earlier in the evening rather than find yourself alone and vulnerable in dangerous territory."

Norian swallowed. He liked this less and less all the time. "I shall pay heed to your advice."

"Hopefully, we'll see your return in a month's time."

"After the next full moon, if all goes well," Norian added.

"I hope you realize how much you shall be missed by those at the castle. Everyone is quite fond of you." He paused. "Some especially."

Norian raised his eyebrows. "What do you mean?"

"The news of your imminent departure reduced one of the poor stable boys to tears. He seemed especially distressed when nobody would say when you would return." He locked his gaze with Norian's. "Thorne was his name, I believe. You know of whom I speak?"

Heat rose in Norian's cheeks, and he broke Wayf's gaze. An image of Thorne's beautiful face rose in his mind, and his groin stirred at the memory of the secret kisses they had once shared. At first, Norian was convinced that Thorne hated him, ashamed of what they had done. But then he slowly warmed toward Norian again, though neither of them ever spoke of what happened that day in the barn.

"Yes, Thorne has served me well," Norian answered, trying to keep his voice calm.

"He seems *very* fond of you."

"I am fond of him as well. He's a loyal and hard-working member of the staff." Norian couldn't help but notice Wayf extra stress on the word 'very.' He felt flushed and hoped his face wouldn't give him away.

"Ah. So you two are close, then?"

"Perhaps not the best of friends. We speak in the stables, and he prepares the horses when I need them."

"I remember not too long ago when you two were nearly inseparable. This appears no longer the case."

Norian wondered where Wayf was heading with this line of questioning. It was making him uncomfortable.

"We grew up, and I became much busier training, as my duties being a prince required."

"It had nothing to do with his father?"

"His father? What do you mean? I'm not sure if I even know his father."

"He certainly knows you. I overheard him once forbidding Thorne from ever associating with you outside of any court-required duties. He was especially adamant that Thorne never find himself alone with you."

Norian's cheeks burned hot, and his mouth dried. "I have no idea whatsoever why his father would say such things. I've had no direct dealings with the man, or at least none that I can recall."

"Apparently, it appears as though his father witnessed something between you and his son that he found—how shall I put it—somewhat untoward."

"No idea. Most curious, that." Norian started to rise, but Wayf brought his hand to Norian's shoulder and held him firm.

"Stay," Wayf said. "I have more I wish to say."

Norian remained silent and sat back down. He avoided Wayf's gaze.

"Norian, you can always talk to me about anything. I am your friend."

"I know," Norian answered. He really wished this conversation would go away. This was a topic he avoided thinking about. He certainly did not want to vocalize it, to discuss it with someone else, to admit that it was real.

"I have to get married," Norian said, surprised at the words as they left his mouth. "It's expected of me."

Wayf rubbed his chin. "Perhaps. Perhaps not. Times are changing. Attitudes are changing. There is a king in Penrith who rules alone, who has never taken a wife. What the people want is a king they can love and respect, a king who will protect them and take care of them. For many, what goes on in a king's bedchamber is of no concern to them."

"I've never bedded anyone," Norian said. He squirmed at the way his heart pounded in his chest.

"I suspected as much." He reached out and gently touched Norian's shoulder. "When the time comes, it should be with someone *you* choose—someone you *want* to give yourself to, completely and with all your heart. Don't concern yourself about what others may think. The most dangerous thing to a kingdom is to have a king who does not follow his own heart."

"I can't help but wonder what my father would think of this conversation? Would he so readily agree with you?"

Wayf smiled. "You might be surprised. He is much more progressive than you imagine. Being a good king requires one to be unprejudiced and nonjudgemental. This requirement extends to all aspects of a king's life. Even to his children."

"My father has a set idea of how a king should act and what's expected of one," Norian said. "He has questioned me many times about when I shall take a wife and stressed the importance of me doing so. I don't believe he's as forward-thinking as you believe him to be."

"Naturally, neither of us can assume what someone will say or do. But I've known your father for many years and he is a fair and just man. I also know the depths of his love for you. All I'm saying is that don't allow fear of what he might say keep you away from your home. He has sensed that you've distanced yourself from him, and it pains him."

"Only when he asks me if I've found my queen yet!"

Wayf laughed. "Then perhaps when you return, it might be time for you two to sit down and have a talk."

"And talk about what?" Norian asked. "I'm unsure about whether I want to even go in that direction. The unconventional direction, I mean."

"That's understandable. This journey will be an excellent opportunity for you to do some soul-searching. In my youth, I discovered that a journey, especially accompanied by a quest, can help a person understand who they truly are." He creased his brow. "Perhaps that is what the divination was trying to tell me."

"How long have you known?" Norian asked. "About that part of me, I mean."

"A while. Perhaps two summers."

"I'm not sure that I even know myself, for certain."

"It may take time. When the right person comes along, you will know, no matter what their sex."

"How are you so knowledgeable about this?" Norian asked. "I had never even heard of such inclinations and figured that there was something wrong with me, something unnatural. Something broken."

"My brother possesses similar inclinations," Wayf answered. "It was difficult for him to accept as well."

Norian widened his eyes. "Your brother? Aiden?"

Wayf nodded. "Aye. He struggled for years with his demons, finally coming to the point where he could reconcile himself to his true nature." Wayf flashed a sly smile. "It also helped that a handsome young man came into his life."

Norian felt his face redden. "I never would have guessed. Aiden gives no indication."

"And what sorts of indications do you suppose he might give?"

Norian chuckled and shrugged. "I have no idea."

"Exactly. He does not differ from any other male you might encounter. The only difference is that he has given his love to another man."

"Do you know if there are many more people like him?" He paused, then swallowed. "Like us?"

"Indeed, there are. They are just not readily obvious."

"I never realized. I thought that I...."

"Was the only one?" Wayf asked.

Norian nodded. All at once, a tremendous burden lifted from his soul. "I worried I was damaged, somehow."

"You're not. Only different."

"Apparently, in more ways than one."

Wayf creased his eyebrows. "Interesting observation. But yes. What you say is true. Sometimes it is our destiny to be different. Sometimes the path the gods choose for us is one not well-trodden by others."

Norian nodded and poked at the fire with a stick. He will have a lot of reflection to do in the coming days and a lot of decisions to make—and not just about the wolf."

"The young man Thorne," Wayf asked. "Have you strong feelings for him?"

Norian took a deep breath. Talking about such matters was difficult for him, as he was unaccustomed to doing so. Leave it to Wayf to put him in an uncomfortable position. But that was one reason he loved the magician. For as long as he could remember, Wayf would challenge him, stretch his boundaries by placing him in awkward situations. He was always the better for it afterward, though.

"Not really," Norian answered. "I did fancy him at first, but all we ever shared were a couple of clumsy kisses. At the time, I'd hoped that we would carry things a bit further. But then he pulled away from me and pretended that there was nothing between us. I was certain he hated me because I'd kissed him, though now I suspect that it was probably because of his father. But in answer to your questions, no, I have no romantic feelings for him." He smiled and blushed. "But I still find him incredibly attractive."

Wayf laughed out loud. "Norian, I cannot tell you how delightful it is that you are speaking so openly. But from what I recently witnessed at the castle, Thorne does not hate you. I'm guessing that the complete opposite is true, and perhaps he's experiencing regret now that you are leaving. But don't blame him. I think you're right in that I sense his father had a lot to do with Thorne pulling away from you."

"I harbor no bitter feelings toward him," Norian said. "So, do you think he's like me?"

"Possibly," Wayf said. "And like you, he may have a difficult time reconciling his feelings."

"I shall speak with him when I get back and tell him I hold no resentment toward him."

"That would be noble of you, for he may be going through the same doubts and uncertainties as you at the moment. It is not an easy road for most."

Norian nodded and then yawned. "I'm ready to retire for the night. I am exhausted."

"Yes, let us rest now. We have another long day ahead of us tomorrow."

CHAPTER ELEVEN

THEY AWOKE EARLY AND, AFTER A QUICK BREAKFAST, were back on their horses. Norian squirmed in his seat as they rode, his buttocks still sore from the day before. It would no doubt be a long several days.

A couple of hours in, the terrain turned rugged and untamed. At times, the path vanished entirely beneath the tangle of undergrowth, forcing them to push through thickets that grew thicker with every step. Finally, Wayf reigned in his horse.

"Why are we stopping here?" Norian asked, though he knew precisely why they were stopping.

"We are at the end of Tregaron. This is where I take leave of you."

"I figured as much," Norian said. "That doesn't mean that I'm pleased with it."

"Nor I. But you understand why you must carry on from here alone, even though every one of my instincts tells me to accompany you, to protect you." He sighed loudly. "But I suppose it's time for me to accept that you are now a man—a capable man, at that."

"I appreciate all that you've done for me, Wayf. Someday, I hope to reward you for all your kindness." Wayf jumped off of his horse and tied it to a tree. Norian did the same."

"Norian, I have already received my reward. Seeing the person you've become is payment enough for me—a strong, brave young man in every sense."

Norian felt himself blushing. "I'm not really sure how brave I am. I suppose the coming days will decide that."

"You've already shown yourself to be braver than most men in your situation. Deciding to take this journey into hostile territory demonstrates as much."

Norian sighed. "Thanks for the reminder, Wayf."

Wayf smiled and nodded. "You shall be fine. I can't proclaim what the outcome of our adventure shall be, but I do know that you shall eventually return to the castle to take your rightful place at your father's side. I have confidence in you, Norian." He reached out and took hold of Norian's hands. "Just remember how much you are loved."

"You're not making this parting easy, are you?"

Wayf laughed. "'Tis never easy to let a loved one go, but it is time. I've been away from the castle long enough already. I don't like being away too long from your father with Vadok as restless as he is. Who knows what that scoundrel's plans are? He has already made one offensive move." He paused and lightly touched Norian's cheek. "But no matter. Your father's army is powerful, and Vadok will be dealt with harshly should he attempt any aggression against the kingdom."

"Please be careful." Norian swallowed. "And be sure to protect my father."

Wayf waved his hand in the air. "Enough emotional

talk. You must be on your way, as must I. Be safe, my friend."

"You too," Norian answered. The tears stung his eyes.

Wayf pulled him into a tight hug. He bowed his head to Norian, untied his horse, and a moment later, he was gone. Norian watched his departure until horse and man disappeared from view.

THE REST of the afternoon passed without incident. How strange it was to be riding alone. He'd gotten used to Wayf's presence over the past couple of days, and upon reflection, he realized that there was rarely a time in his life when he was alone. He was always surrounded by people at the castle: Wayf, the courtesans, his tutors, or his father. So it was a rare occasion when he found himself alone with his thoughts. As prince, there was always some obligation to tend to, some matter which required his attention, some lesson to be learned. But here and now, he was not a prince. He was but a man—though one who carried a dreadful secret. He shook the thought from him.

An hour before dusk, he reached the first village. He'd consulted his map several times throughout the day to ensure that he was staying on the route that Wayf had outlined. Then, a red-haired boy at play by the roadside, just beyond the village bounds, drew his eye. The boy looked up at Norian.

"I don't know you," the boy said, giving him a wary look.

Norian smiled. "That's because I'm not from around here. I'm just traveling through."

"Where are you from?"

"Tregaron," Norian answered.

"Never heard of it. Is it far away?"

Norian nodded. "It is indeed far away. What village is this?"

"Why, it's Falshire. Everyone knows that. Is that where you're going?"

Falshire. That was the first village that Wayf had circled on his map. He was still moving in the right direction.

Norian shook his head. "No, I'm going to Norbury. Do you know it?" The boy's eyes grew wide. "Don't go there! That's a bad place. It would be best if you stayed here. It's better here. Plus, Miss Elora at the Tin Harp told me to send any strangers she finds her way."

"What's the Tin Harp?"

"The Inn." The boy pointed. "It's over there, right in the middle of town. It has a picture of a big 'ol harp and a mug of ale on the door. You can't miss it."

"You said that Norbury is a bad place. What did you mean by that?"

The boy shrugged his shoulders. "Everyone says so. Creatures are there."

Norian's heart raced in his chest. "What creatures?"

"I dunno, just creatures. Everyone says that you should never go there because of the monsters. They'll eat you if they find you."

"Is Norbury far from here?"

"You're not really going to go there, are you?" the boy asked, his eyes wide. "You mustn't."

"Regretfully, I must, as I have important business there. I need to find someone."

"Are you going to hunt the monsters? A hunter came through here a long time ago, but nobody saw him after that. Everyone said that the creatures must have eaten him."

Norian's mouth grew dry. Apparently, more people

know about werewolves than he had initially thought. So how come he'd never known they existed until he became one himself?

"Did he say what he was hunting?" Norian asked.

"He was a creature hunter. Everyone in Falshire told him not to go there, but he was stubborn. I didn't mind that he didn't come back. He was kind of mean."

Norian's heart quickened even more. "There are people who hunt creatures?"

The boy nodded. "All manner of 'em. You always can tell when someone's a hunter because they are the only ones who ever go to Norbury." The boy squinted his eyes at Norian. "How long have you been a hunter?"

"Oh, I'm not a hunter."

The boy wrinkled his forehead. "But then, why are you going to Norbury? Only hunters or creatures ever go there. And you don't look like a creature to me."

Norian let loose a nervous chuckle. "As I said, I have important business."

"What kind of business?"

"It's a secret." He leaned in close, his voice dropping to a whisper meant only for the boy's ear. "Official business for the King of Tregaron."

The boy shook his head. "I still wouldn't go there if I were you. Nobody who goes there ever comes back."

Norian nodded. "Thank you for the advice. Now, where is this inn you spoke of?"

"The Tin Harp? I can show you. Can I ride on your horse?"

Norian jumped up onto the horse. Then he reached down and pulled the boy up. The boy squealed with delight.

Norian tapped the horse on the side, and the animal

took off in a trot. The boy's words echoed in his brain. *Nobody who goes there ever comes back.* Suddenly, searching for the Queen of Werewolves didn't seem like such a good idea. In fact, it felt like a terrible one. He hoped Wayf was right when he'd said that no harm would come to him. Either way, he couldn't back out now. He had already invested too much into this journey and had to see it through to its conclusion. It was the only flicker of hope that he had. But it was best he didn't mention where he was going to anyone again. The last thing he wanted to do was draw attention to himself— especially if there were hunters about.

He found the Tin Harp with little difficulty. Luckily, nobody there asked any questions. He kept to himself until the following morning, when he was back on his horse heading out of town. He couldn't get the boy's words out of his head and was now facing his journey with a lot more trepidation than before. While he'd decided yesterday to continue forward, he couldn't help but wonder whether it was the right decision. Could suffering anguish three days a month be any worse than being dead? He had to admit to himself that over the past few days, he'd thought about the possibility of ending his life, especially when he recalled the excruciating torment of the transformation. But no, he'd made the right decision. He was ready for anything that might come.

Refusing to think any more about the matter, he turned his thoughts to Wayf and to their conversation two days earlier. Now, that was a conversation he never imagined would take place. It seemed as if Wayf had found a passageway into his innermost thoughts. The conversation did clear things up for him. At least he knew that the desires he felt were not just his own idiosyncrasies. The thought that there were others out there who shared the same inclinations warmed his heart. Why, Wayf's own brother was one of them. He smiled to himself as he recalled his stolen kisses with Thorne. The young man certainly was attractive. There was no disputing that. But did he have feelings for him?

No, not really. He had not, as of yet, known romantic love for anyone, male or female. While the thought of Thorne caused his heart to flutter, he decided that this was a road down which he would not travel, at least for the time being, if ever. He felt unnatural enough as it was, thanks to this whole wolf situation. He did not need to add a penchant for men to his problems. There was nothing he could do about the wolf inside of him— it will come out three days a month whether he wants it to or not. But he did have a choice regarding his romantic partners. He could choose whom he would love—or, in his case, who would one day rule beside him. Why would he willingly choose a path that would make him an outcast, that would cause people to despise him? This was something he could choose—it was one aspect of his life over which he had control.

Contrary to what Wayf believes, Norian couldn't imagine that the people of the kingdom would be too welcoming of a king with a male spouse. What shame that would bring to the memory of his father. He would accept the fate that was chosen for him—find a wife who would someday be his queen and fulfill his obligations to the crown. At least in that regard, he could be normal. He breathed a sigh of relief. One major decision was made. Now, all he had to worry about was facing this dreaded wolf queen.

On the sixth night of the journey, there were no inns along the route, so he camped out in the woods. This was the first time he'd ever slept in the forest, and being all by himself, he found the experience incredibly unsettling. He sat by the crackling fire with one hand on his sword. Who knows what creatures or cutthroats hid out in the woods at night? As he tried to calm his thoughts and instead focus on the sounds of the night, he noticed something strange. Except for the faint sound of crickets off in the distance, there were no sounds. All was quiet—almost disturbingly so. He slept that night with his hand tightly wrapped around his weapon.

The night proved uneventful, and the next morning he was back on his way. He was grateful that the next several evenings involved inns. One night alone in the woods in this territory was enough for him. He noticed that the number of villages became fewer and fewer and became less and less populated as he rode. People also seemed unfriendlier. Perhaps it was just that they deliberately seemed to avoid eye contact with anyone else. Even though he himself avoided speaking with others, the manner in which the people in these remote villages acted made him nervous. Everyone kept to themselves and seemed suspicious of everything and everyone. He was almost looking forward to finally reaching Norbury. Almost. Still, he was thankful that before each nightfall he was fortunate to come across a village with an inn, though some of the accommodations weren't even fit for farm animals. But it was better than sleeping out in the open at the mercy of god knows what.

Unfortunately, he saw no inn along the ninth (or what is the tenth?) night of his solo route. The map displayed only forest and nothing else, making it difficult to gauge how close he was to his destination. As he set up camp, a sensation of dread swept over him. He had been on the road alone for ten days now, only a little over two weeks remaining before the next full moon. He was in the middle of a forest, with no villages in sight and none listed on the map. How would he possibly find this Lady Auryon if she even existed? How would he find this village, where there seemed to be only trees for as far as the eye can see? His map was now useless, as it showed nothing more. He couldn't help but wonder whether this Norbury even existed and wasn't just part of some myth created to frighten children. He shuddered as he realized how little time remained for him to find it, if it even existed at all. If he didn't find the werewolf queen in the next few days, he'd have no choice but to return to the castle. The risk of transforming outside its walls was too great. He would risk killing no one else.

As he settled down to sleep, he noticed that once again, he heard no forest sounds. This time, even the buzzing of crickets had disappeared. He'd spent a fair amount of time outside around the castle at night and always noticed the nature sounds of owls, frogs, and birds. But now, there was not so much as a peep or a rustle from the forest's creatures. It wasn't the first time he'd noticed the unnerving silence. Earlier in the day, while riding, he had thought it strange that there was no birdsong to accompany him. He had stopped his horse for a moment to listen because the silence struck him as being so odd and unsettling. He wondered if the territory into which he was venturing had anything to do with it, for he was getting close to the domain of monsters. He hoped that this meant he was getting close to his destination. Close to either getting killed or cured. Again holding on to his sword, he drifted off to sleep.

He awoke to a sharp pain in his side, as if something had struck him. Norian opened his eyes, and the first thing that came into view was a dusty boot, which then kicked him.

Instinctively, he reached for his sword, but his hands returned empty. Where was it? It was then he noticed it a tree length away from him. Apparently, whoever stood over him had kicked it aside. All at once, something cold pressed against his throat.

"Wakey-wakey," a low, grumbly voice said. This time, the boot kicked him harder. He grunted and looked up. Three men holding swords stood above him, one sword resting on this throat. The boot now pressed down on his chest. "It's time to die."

CHAPTER TWELVE

THREE LARGE, DUSTY, MENACING MEN SURROUNDED Norian. All scowled at him simultaneously.

"Wait," said the youngest of the men. "I wanna understand what kind of fool would come to our territory all by himself. Only someone with a death wish would show up anywhere near here."

"Or a hunter," another man said.

The man removed his boot from Norian's chest, but the sword's blade remained firmly pressed against his throat. Norian's heart felt as though it were going to pound its way out of his chest. He couldn't die yet. Not when he was so close.

"What's your name, scum?" asked the man with the sword. "What makes you think you can wander anywhere you please without dying?"

"I'm looking for someone," Norian said. His voice cracked as he spoke.

"I'm looking for someone," the man mimicked in a singsongy voice. "Well, too bad that you're not going to find them, fool."

"Thomros, wait," said the youngest of the men.

"What, Deric? You're aware of the rules."

Deric sniffed and held his hand in front of him. "Smell him."

The man with the sword leaned forward and took a deep whiff. His eyes grew wide, and he stepped back, the blade still pointing at Norian's throat. "Well, fuck me! He's one of us."

"Yeah," said Deric. "And not only that, I think he's new. He smells different from us. Really different."

"Who are you?" the man named Thomros asked. "And what are you doing here?"

"Can you please remove the sword?" Norian asked.

"Not until you answer my question, wretch. Now, what devil are you?"

Norian tried to calm himself down but was unsuccessful. These men looked like the type that would kill him without giving it even a second thought. By the looks on their faces, Norian guessed they had no intention of letting him walk away.

"My name is Norian."

"Where do you come from?" Thomros asked.

"Tregaron," Norian said. "I mean nobody any harm. As I said, I'm looking for someone."

"All alone?" asked Deric.

Norian nodded. The third man stood off to the side with his arms crossed and glared at Norian. He said nothing, but the look on his face raised shivers on Norian's skin.

"Are you looking for the one who made you?" Thomros asked.

"I'm not sure what you mean," Norian said.

"The one who turned you into a wolf, stupid. 'Cause, we have one fundamental rule here: one wolfkind cannot kill another under penalty of death. So again, are you here looking for your maker?"

Ah, these men were werewolves, like himself. That's what they meant when they said that he was one of them. Norian felt hope rising within him. Maybe he'll make it out of here alive after all, and he just might find the queen in time.

"No. I'm looking for Lady Auryon. Do any of you know of her?"

Deric's eyes widened, and he stepped forward. "What do you know of Lady Auryon? And why do you seek her?"

"Someone told me she might be able to help me."

"Help you how?" Deric asked.

"A wolf attacked me and bit me," Norian said. "A wizard friend of mine told me that I might be able to find a cure—or at least learn more about my condition if I seek out the Queen of Werewolves, Lady Auryon."

Thomros snickered, and the others followed. "So you believe that this," he paused and let go another snicker, "Queen of Werewolves might cure you?"

Norian nodded. Were they mocking him? Was there, in fact, no such person as Lady Auryon? Or were they laughing because there was no cure?

"Are you acquainted with her?" Norian asked.

Thomros bent down and squinted his eyes. "Yes, she is known to us. But why should we take you to her? How do we know you don't mean her any harm?"

"But you must take me to her!" Norian exclaimed. "I've come such a long way. She's my only hope."

"For a cure," Thomros said. He smiled what looked to be a forced smile.

Norian nodded.

"Who told you of Lady Auryon? Who told you of this place?"

"As I mentioned, a wizard friend told me about it. He spoke of a place where I might find others like me—and said I should seek counsel from the queen who dwells there."

""How comes it to pass that a rogue such as yourself keeps company with wizards?" Thomros asked. "It's not as if wizards seek out our kind for frolic and friendship." He lowered his head and glared at Norian. "Wizards kill our kind. They do not help us."

Norian swallowed. "This wizard was my friend before I got bit. He's a good, loyal man. He would never harm anyone just because they were a werewolf."

"That remains to be seen," said the man called Thomros. "So, how are you acquainted with this wizard?"

Norian thought it best not to divulge that he was a prince and that Wayf was the court wizard to his father. "We grew up together," he said, which was not entirely a lie. "We ended up taking different paths, but still remained friends."

Thomros studied his face, almost as if he were trying to gauge the truthfulness of what Norian was saying.

"And your wizard friend couldn't help you?"

Deric punched Thomros in the arm. "Silly man. Magic can't cure us, so stop grilling the boy."

Norian smiled at the word 'boy,' for Deric appeared to be the same age as himself, if not younger.

"Something amusing?" Thomros asked.

"Nothing at all. So will you take me to the queen?"

The third man finally spoke. "Yes, we will take you."

"But he is a stranger," Thomros said. "Everything he said could be a lie. How can we trust him? He may very well be a hunter."

"Nah, he's a wolf like us," Deric said. "He's no hunter."

"It wouldn't be the first time that a vengeful wolf came through here looking for payback for what happened to him. Hell, it's not unheard of for a rogue wolf to turn hunter. It's happened. Remember when—"

"Enough," said the third man. He looked at the other two and indicated to Norian with a wave of his hand. "You certainly cannot be fearful of *this* scrawny pup?"

"Of course not," said Thomros. "I'm thinking of the pack. You know who would not be happy if we exposed our pack to an enemy."

Deric winked at Thomros. "The queen, you mean?" He made air quotes as he said 'The queen.'

"Of course. The Queen. You know how she gets."

"It is decided," said the third man. "We take the pup to Lady Auryon. Let it be up to her to decide his fate."

"So be it," said Thomros. "Just remember, it was your decision, not ours. Your neck on the line, not ours."

All at once, Norian wasn't so sure he wanted to meet this queen. If these three rough-looking men feared her as they appeared to, then she probably was not a benevolent and loving queen. But she was his only hope. Perhaps the queen would end up killing him. He couldn't help but wonder if he'd ever see his father or the castle again.

"On your feet, pup," said Thomros. "You want to meet Auryon, do you not?"

Norian jumped up to his feet. Thomros still pointed the sword toward Norian.

"Walk," said Thomros. "Your destiny awaits you."

Norian looked around. "Where's my horse?"

"Gone," said Thomros. "Now let's walk."

"Can you at least put down the sword?" Norian asked.

"I can't have you running off on me like a jackrabbit,

now can I?" Thomros said. "Nobody wants a rogue wolf running about the countryside."

"The pup will not run off," said the third man. "Remember, it's his idea to go to Auryon. Can't you see? He's desperate. I can smell it on him" He then raised his eyebrows then chuckled. "You don't think you can handle a young pup without your sword?"

"Fine," Thomros said. "Again, your neck."

Deric moved to Norian's left side, Thomros on this right. The third man followed behind. It made no difference that Thomros no longer pointed a sword at him. He was surrounded regardless. Just because there wasn't a sword at his throat didn't mean he wasn't a prisoner. He breathed a sigh of relief. His journey was nearing its end. He was finally going to see Lady Auryon.

THEY WALKED through the thick forest for what seemed like hours. Norian was anxious about what awaited him ahead. He feared that Lady Auryon would tell him she couldn't help him and that his entire trip had been in vain. There was also the possibility that she would have him killed. Who knew what the rules were for this society of werewolves into which he'd just entered? For all he knew, there were no rules at all. It could be utter anarchy and chaos. Although the three men who accompanied him had initially frightened him, there was something about them that made Norian think they were not the ruthless cutthroats he'd at first imagined. Upon reflection, he could understand their wariness and distrust of others—he was in much the same position: an outcast, someone most wouldn't think twice about killing.

To Norian's surprise, the forest all at once opened to a hidden town. He couldn't help but gasp when they passed through the thickness of the woods into a relatively large open village, complete with roads, buildings, and businesses. How could anyone hide a town of this size? There was no sign of its existence on any of the maps he'd seen, and Wayf had certainly made no mention of it. In fact, this was the opposite of what Wayf described. Several vendors stood before their stores, attempting to lure people inside. The many shops included Marcuson's Confectionary, the Mithroff Inn, Lea's General Store, Angus the Blacksmith, Troutt's Pharmacy, the Dusty Tomes Bookshop, and even a pastry shop. Though a couple of the buildings looked a bit run down, they all appeared to be thriving. In the center of town was the Norbury Community Center, which appeared as though they had recently remodeled it. The rhythmic clomp of horse hooves floated in from the street as there were a few people on horseback meandering down the primary thoroughfare, though most folks appeared to be walking rather than riding. It was perfect—a remote town in the middle of the woods. Surely there had to be guards along the outskirts of the town to prevent strangers from inadvertently stumbling upon it. Then he realized who his escorts were. He must have gotten too close to the town, and it was the job of the three men who accompanied him to ensure he didn't get any closer.

"Is this Norbury?" Norian asked.

"Aye, that it is," Deric answered. "Or as it is otherwise known, 'The City of Wolves.'"

"I didn't know that it was an actual town," Norian said. "It doesn't show up on any of the maps."

"That's the point," Deric said. "The fewer folks that know about us, the better. Oh sure, it's common knowledge that Norbury is a place where wolfkind can find sanctuary. But many people think that there are but a few clusters of wolves scattered here and there in the wild. Nobody knows how organized and self-sufficient we really are."

"Enough talk," Thomros growled. "He doesn't need to know our entire town history."

Deric grinned and leaned in toward Norian. "Don't be too concerned with him. His bark is much worse than his bite."

Thomros glared at Deric. "Any more barking comments, and it will be *your* head that I'll remove with my sword. And your tail too."

Both men laughed. Despite his earlier opinion of his companions, he was starting to like the men. At least Thomros and Deric. The third man, whose name he still didn't know, was too quiet, too mysterious for him to make any judgments. He frightened Norian more than the other two. Norian didn't like the way the man glared at him, as though he were planning his execution.

They stopped before a large, eerie building, the tallest structure in the village, from what he could tell. It looked old but wasn't run down. Two green cement gargoyles with giant wings and long pointed teeth guarded the entrance, making the building feel especially foreboding.

"Here we are," Thomros said. "The residence of the boss."

"The Queen lives here?" Norian asked.

"Huh?" Thomros asked. "Oh, yes, of course. The Queen. Yes, indeed she does." He indicated toward the door with his hand. "Why? What did you expect? Did you think she lived in a cave?"

Norian felt himself blush. "I actually considered the possibility."

"Sorry to disappoint you," Thomros replied "But as you can see, we're just like real people."

"Almost," said Deric. "Or at least some of us are."

"Enough chatter," Thomros said. He opened the door and made a grand sweeping gesture for Norian to enter. "Your Queen awaits."

CHAPTER THIRTEEN

A SERVANT LED NORIAN INTO A LAVISHLY FURNISHED room to wait. He assumed the men had gone to tell the Queen he was here. He prayed she would be willing to see him, to at least hear him out. Norian wrung his hands together to stop them from shaking and then, a moment later, crammed them between his buttocks and the chair. His heart pounded wildly, and he had little moisture remaining in his mouth.

Finally, the door to the room opened, and a young man entered. He had golden blond hair, a clear, smooth complexion, and the bluest eyes Norian had ever seen. It was a color that was so intense that it seemed to see right into Norian's soul. The man was a couple of inches taller than Norian and quite muscular, judging by the snug way his clothing fit him. Norian's first thought was that he had the face of an angel. He should be afraid of this man because, for all he knew, the Queen had sent him in here to kill him. But strangely, he had no fear at all. In fact, his earlier trepidation vanished and was now filled with a sense that bordered on calm. As he studied the young man, he had to restrain himself from gasping out loud at his beauty. This person had the strangest effect on him, and Norian found himself mesmerized by his presence.

The man studied him for an uncomfortable length of time, with a most curious look on his face. He looked as if he were equally perplexed by Norian, as if he had a burning question to ask him. Finally, the man stepped forward and held out his hand.

"I am called Kalen. I welcome you to Norbury."

When Norian grabbed his hand to shake it, a light jolt startled him. The man's eyes grew wide as they touched and seemed as surprised as Norian. Norian was positive that the stranger had experienced the shock as well. Who was this person? Was he some kind of magician? And why did Norian feel so strange around him?

Norian finally found his voice. "I am Norian, and I come to seek the Queen."

"Yes, my men informed me as such."

"They are your men?"

"In a sense. But more so, they are the village's men. They keep an eye out for any potential intruders."

Norian nodded. So he was right. The men who found him were protectors of Norbury. Norian tried to clear his thoughts, but the presence of Kalen made him nervous, made it difficult for him to think. He'd never experienced anyone like him and could sense a strange power emanating from the man.

"Why do you seek my mother?"

Norian's eyes grew wide. "The Queen is your mother? Oh, I'm sorry, Your Highness. I hope I wasn't disrespectful." Norian wanted to blurt out that he was a prince as well, but decided that it might be in his best interest to keep that fact secret for the time being.

Kalen smiled. "Yes, I am Lady Auryon's son—and I did not find you disrespectful in the least." He gestured to Norian to sit back down. Kalen took the chair next to him and turned it so they faced each other. He focused his deep blue eyes on Norian. "So, what brings you to see my mother?"

Norian couldn't help himself and blurted out the entire story, except for him being a prince. He told Kalen how he'd been bitten by a wolf under the command of a sorcerer, how Wayf had urged him to seek out the Queen of Werewolves in hopes she might help him—and finally, he recounted the journey that had led him to Norbury. He even confided to Kalen that he had killed a villager after his first change.

After he revealed the last of his story, Norian stopped and stared at Kalen, unsure of the man's reaction. The story had sounded strange to him as he recited it. He couldn't imagine what he must sound like to an outsider.

"You certainly have gone through a lot in a short time," Kalen answered. "I commend you for not losing your sanity through it all."

Norian smiled. "Sometimes, I'm not at all sure of how much of my sanity remains. A month ago, I never knew such things as werewolves existed. Now I am one of them."

"It is true that our lives can, at any time, take a drastic turn. Knowing this does not make it any easier." He squinted his eyes. "So what do you seek from my mother? Vengeance? Sanctuary?"

"A cure," Norian said.

Kalen's eyes grew wide. "How have you come to believe that my mother has a cure?"

"Wayf, the mage I mentioned, thought that since I was bitten and not born into it, she might be able to help me."

Kalen held Norian's gaze and was silent for several

moments. "We certainly can consult her and ask her if there is indeed such a possibility. So this last full moon was your first shift?"

"Yes, I was bitten, and a couple of weeks later, I shifted. Thus began my new life as a werewolf."

Kalen cringed. "Lycan," he said.

"I beg your pardon?"

"The correct term for our condition is lycan. We consider *werewolf* to be somewhat derogatory. Or you can refer to us as wolfkind. That works as well."

Norian's eyes widened. "So you are also a werewolf — I mean lycan?"

Kalen nodded. "I am. But this is not the case with everyone in Norbury. Many of the lycans in the village have human mates."

Norian instinctively flinched as if he had been struck. "Humans? I have not yet considered myself as something separate from humans."

Kalen reached out and touched Norian's hand for a brief moment. "Not something, someone. We are indeed separate from humans. Even though you were born human, you now differ from them. Yes, you are still human in many aspects. But in the species sense—the chemistry of your being—you are apart from them. You are special. You are lycan."

"It's a new way of thinking for me. Ever since the transformation, I've considered myself now separate from other humans, some sort of monster."

"No, no, no," said Kalen, with sudden emotion in his voice. "That is exactly the kind of prejudice we are working to avoid. This belief that because we change once a month, we are creatures to be feared and reviled is something against which we must constantly combat. We are not a monster, a demon, or a devil. We are only different, such as a crow differs from a hawk. That is all."

Norian found Kalen's voice to be lulling and calming. It almost mesmerized him, making him want to do or say anything to please Kalen. Norian shook the sensation away. Damn, the strange effect this man had on him! He had to be careful not to lose himself when they were in the same room together. The thought of it frightened him.

"With all due respect, Your Highness, I killed a woman when I turned. Is this not the action of a monster? A soulless demon?"

"You turned alone then," Kalen said. "Yes, that's right. You said that the mage killed the woman who bit you." He narrowed his eyes and took hold of Norian's hand. "I am so sorry this happened to you. It would have been easier had someone been with you. Someone like myself."

"What do you mean?"

"If you are a new lycan and you have no guidance during the first transformation, the inner wolf completely takes over, and you operate solely on instinct. But if there is an experienced lycan with you, they can guide you through the transformation by joining minds with you. We can teach you to still retain your consciousness and your personality through the change."

Norian sighed. "I wish I had someone with me the first time I changed. It was horrible. I did not know what was going on. The pain came out of nowhere, and at the time, I wanted to die. The next two changes were a bit easier as Wayf was right outside the bars where I transformed. Truth be told, the pain wasn't any less, but at least I knew what to expect."

Kalen raised his eyebrows. "I thought you said you were only bitten before this last full moon."

"I was. It has been only a few weeks since she attacked me."

"But you mentioned three transformations?"

Norian nodded. "The night before the full moon was the first time that I turned. That's why I was so surprised when it came. I believed that werewolves... er... lycans only changed on the full moon. The next night, I locked myself in one of the dungeons, and Wayf sat with me and helped me through the change. He thought that if he knocked me out with a potion, it would stop it from occurring. Unfortunately, that was not the case. I awoke just as the moon rose. And then I turned the third night again."

Kalen appeared visibly shaken. "When you initially recounted your story to me, you did not tell me you changed three times."

"I just assumed you knew." Norian's brow darkened. "Why? Doesn't every lycan change three times a month."

"Where did you get such an idea?"

"For one thing, it happened to me," Norian said matter-of-factly. "Plus, Wayf found it mentioned in one of his books. He said that there was an obscure entry in one of his grimoires that spoke of the werewolf changing not only on the full moon but the night before and the night after as well." He paused and took in a deep breath. "So tell me, do lycans not change three nights in a month?"

Kalen's face was white. "No, they most certainly do not. In fact, I know of no lycan who does, even those who'd been bitten."

Norian stood up and walked to the center of the room. His arms flew wildly about as he spoke. "How can this be? I did! What does that mean? Is something wrong with me? Am I abnormal even among the werewolves?"

Kalen rose from his chair and faced Norian. His voice

was soft and soothing. "On the contrary, Norian, you may be very, very special."

Norian could smell Kalen as he was so close, and the aroma of the man caused Norian's heart to pound wildly. His mouth dried and his hands trembled. He thrust them behind him so that Kalen wouldn't notice. Even though his heart rattled hard in his chest, the presence of Kalen next to him seemed to calm his raging emotions.

"Norian?" Kalen asked when he didn't respond. "Are you alright?"

Norian snapped back to the present and locked eyes with Kalen. He nodded. "I'm fine. So tell me, in what way am I special?"

"Before I say anything, let me consult with my mother. She knows more about it than I do. It has been a long time since anyone has encountered a wolf such as you. She would be the best at explaining what it means. But know this, Norian. You are neither an outcast nor abnormal. Rather, you are exceptional."

Kalen's words melted into him, and his knees quivered and grew weak. He wondered if he affected Kalen the same way that Kalen affected him? Probably not. Norian guessed it was his annoying penchant for men that made him feel so strange around the attractive stranger. Given that he'd decided not to follow that path, he had to be all that much stronger and resist any unnatural urges toward Kalen. Who knows how this strange community feels about men who lie with other men? He wasn't willing to risk it. Conscious now of his proximity to Kalen, Norian took a step back from him.

"I am so exceptional that I get to suffer three nights a month whereas other lycans only have to go through this once?" Norian asked.

"It is true that others transform only once during the

moon's cycle. But it need not be painful. We will teach you to manage it."

"But I don't want to manage it. I want to be cured. I want it to be removed."

"I'll know more about your options after I speak with my mother. I shall return shortly."

"Can I accompany you?" Norian asked. "I would like to explain my situation to the Queen in person."

"It's best if I approach her in person first. She tends to be overly mistrustful of strangers. I'll try to persuade her to meet with you this evening. But, for now, I shall send someone by to show you to your room. No doubt you'll want to rest after so long a journey."

Before Norian could respond, Kalen turned and was out of the room. Suddenly, a heavy ache filled his chest, an emptiness, as he looked at the now-closed door. He would no doubt have to be extremely careful around this Kalen.

CHAPTER FOURTEEN

"You're sure about this?" asked Lady Auryon. She gazed at her son. "You are positive he said that he shifted three nights in a row?"

Kalen nodded. "He was bitten only two moons ago and knew nothing of our kind before the attack. The first change came the night before the full moon. He transformed the following two nights as well."

Lady Auryon threw herself down on one of the chairs. She wrung her hands and then stood up again. "You understand what this means, don't you? You realize this changes everything?"

"I think so. I've heard the stories but never have I encountered one in real life."

"Besides your father," Lady Auryon said.

"Yes, besides Father."

"Do any of the others know?" his mother asked. "Does anyone else know that for the first time in over a decade, we may have a true Alpha in our midst?"

"If they did, they gave no indication of it. From what I

could gather, Thomros was a bit rough on him, so I'm guessing not. If he knew the boy was an Alpha, he would have never dared treat him as such."

"Agreed," said his mother. She breathed a sigh of relief. "So we need to decide what our options are."

"Our options? What do you mean?"

"Being Beta, you've been in charge ever since your father died. With this Alpha here, all of that is threatened. No doubt he'll want to come to power and take his rightful place as pack leader. But as he is not of our blood, he may find no use for either of us. It would not be the first time an Alpha has disposed of an existing pack leader."

"He's not like that," Kalen said. "He would never harm us."

Lady Auryon raised her eyebrows. "How can you declare such a thing? You've known the lad for all of fifteen minutes."

Kalen looked down, avoiding her eyes, and hid his sweaty palms behind him. "I don't know. I just sense that he means us no harm. There is an innocence about him—a gentleness—which leads me to believe that he would be fair and just."

"Perhaps. Though I am not so easily convinced."

"I am convinced."

"Strange way to speak about someone you just met." She paused, then in a harsher voice, "Look at me, Kalen."

Kalen raised his head and met his mother's eyes. "Yes, Mother?"

"There is something more. Something you are not telling me. Something about the boy."

Kalen's heart pounded against his ribcage. "I've told you all that he has told me."

"There's more Kalen. I can smell it on you. What is it?"

"From the moment I met him, I sensed an odd connection to him. The longer we were together, the stronger it became."

"What kind of connection? Maybe you sensed he was Alpha. They do have a singular effect on us."

Kalen shook his head. "No, it's much more than that. Deeper." He paused and swallowed. "Although I've never experienced it in person, from everything I've learned from others, there is only one conclusion I can come to." He paused and took a deep breath. "I believe this man is my mate."

Lady Auryon's eyes grew wide. "Your mate? You cannot be serious, Kalen. He is a male."

Kalen nodded. "I am aware of that fact. It's not like I willingly chose this. It isn't something over which I have any control."

She narrowed her eyes and stared at him for several moments. "Now that you mentione it, you have shown little interest in any of the local females, human or lycan. I suppose I've never really given it much thought before. Of course, you haven't mentioned it to me before either. How long have you felt like this? How long have you had this attraction to males?"

"For as long as I can remember."

"And you didn't tell me because?"

Kalen shrugged his shoulders. "I've never acted on it, so there was nothing to tell. My focus has always been on our pack, not on romantic inclinations or liaisons. Plus, you know what the men in Norbury are like. They would not take too kindly to their leader being a lover of men."

"Which is not up to them to decide. Leaders are created

by birth, and your birth created a Beta. They cannot fight their instinct in this matter. They must obey you and acknowledge you as their leader."

"That's fine in theory. But who knows how they might react? If something 'happened' to me, then someone from the village could easily take my place."

"Enough of such talk," snapped Lady Auryon. "We shall make no conjecture on the attitudes of others, for it serves no purpose. Instead, I wish to understand more of why you believe this Norian could be your one true mate."

"When we were in the room together, the feelings I had toward him were so unbearably strong that I could barely control them." Heat rose in his cheeks. "I had almost an uncontrollable urge to mate with him there on the spot. It was an urge I'd never encountered before. I've found other men to be attractive, that is true—but never to this extent. Nothing like this."

"It's possible the feelings you experienced were simply due to being in the presence of an Alpha. You haven't been near an Alpha since your father, and you were barely a man then. Often, just being near them causes odd feelings to stir in us."

"Perhaps. I don't know. All I can say is that I wanted him in a way in which I've wanted no one else."

"I must say, Kalen, these words are difficult for me to hear. Because you're a Beta, it is your duty to continue our bloodline. I've always hoped that you would father a new Alpha one day. I didn't even consider the possibility you'd end up mated to one."

"I'm sorry, Mother. I didn't want this. I'd always planned on ignoring my feelings and mating with a female for the good of the pack. I'd never even believed I'd find my true mate, as it's such a rare occurrence. But finding him changes things."

She sighed. "But the important question is: how does he feel? Does he recognize you as his mate?"

"I don't know. He appeared nervous, but given that he was in a new environment, a prisoner of sorts by the territory guards, it's difficult to guess what was going on in his mind."

She looked up as if in deep thought. "It certainly would not be the worse thing for you to be mated to an Alpha. I always feared that a new Alpha would appear and either run us out or kill us. It's happened in the past. But if this Alpha has the same feelings towards you as you have for him, it might be to our advantage. If he does not feel the same way, however, it could put us in a precarious position." She lowered her gaze to Kalen's eyes. "You are certain he gave no clear indication that he may consider you to be his mate as well?"

"Nothing for certain. There were a couple of moments when we were close together when I felt he wanted to kiss me as much as I did him. But this may have just been my own desire taking over as he is quite fetching. Wait, there was also the shock when we first touched."

"The what?"

"After we introduced ourselves, we shook hands, as is customary. When we did, I experienced an unexpected jolt, like static but taken to the extreme. The surprised and stunned look on his face revealed that he'd noticed it as well."

She considered this. "If he is your true mate, then he will feel the same. But it would be best if you were careful. Sexual advances made on an Alpha can be dangerous. In the old days, an Alpha would kill any pack member suspected of loving their own sex. By nature, Alphas are volatile and irrational. They'll defend with their life any perceived affront to their masculinity."

"But he doesn't realize he's an Alpha," Norian said. "Do we need even to tell him?"

Lady Auryon laughed. "You don't think others wouldn't notice it once he shifts before the full moon? This is something not easily concealed. No, even if we were to send him away, it would be found out. An Alpha is not easily hidden. Moreover, if we chased him off and if it ever came to light that we banished an Alpha, it would appear as though we did it for our own sakes—so we wouldn't lose our position in the pack. It would not look good for us."

"Then we must tell him," Kalen said.

She nodded. "It is an odd situation indeed to have to explain to an Alpha what it means to be an Alpha. I've not yet heard of an Alpha being created through a bite. We've always assumed the reason for this was so their village could groom them and train them to take over when the time came. Alphas are always created through birth, and if there are exceptions to this, I'm unaware of them. Of course, we need to keep in mind that it's rare for a wolf to bite a human. But no matter. This is something we shall deal with ourselves. I just hope he doesn't decide it would be better if he killed us."

"I don't think he would harm us. He's not that kind of person."

"So you keep telling me," she replied. "But he is an Alpha, and this always poses a potential danger for a current pack leader. For you. For me. Let us both hope that he is indeed your mate, for this may be the only thing that saves us. Is he aware that your mother lives here as well?"

"It is you whom he has come here to see," Kalen said. "He came here searching you out."

Her eyes grew wide. "Whatever for? What does he want with me?"

"He believes you to be the Queen of Werewolves. So he has come here hoping you might have a cure for his bite."

"Queen of Werewolves?" she said. "Good grief. Wherever did he get such a silly notion from?"

"A friend of his who is a wizard told him so."

"A wizard? This Norian has associates who are wizards?"

Kalen nodded. "So he says. This wizard told him that since his condition was not a condition of birth, perhaps there could be a cure. So he sent Norian here to seek out the Queen of Werewolves."

"I must say that I'm flattered to have such an honorary attributed to me." She sighed. "If only this were the case. But it is enough for me that my son is the Beta, the pack leader."

"Was the pack leader," Kalen corrected.

"You are still the pack leader," said his mother. "We do not even know if this Norian will stay once he finds out he is an Alpha. Perhaps he will prefer to create his own pack elsewhere."

"If the others find out, you realize there'd be no way they'd allow him to leave. They'd convince him to stay. Or leave with him."

"And that is why we must keep it a secret from them for the time being. At least until we find out what this Norian's intentions are."

"Shall I bring him to you?"

She nodded. "We had best tend to this as expeditiously as possible. Go retrieve him, and we will tell him together.

But do not tell him yet that you suspect he is your mate. If you're mistaken, it might prove deadly for us. Let us observe him first and see if there is any sign that he feels the same way toward you."

Kalen smiled at the thought of seeing Norian again. Trying to hide his excitement, he turned away from his mother and headed toward the door.

"Remember, be discreet," his mother warned. "You must hide your feelings until we know for sure that he is, indeed, your mate."

"I shall," he said, without turning around and shut the door behind him.

NORIAN SWALLOWED as he followed Kalen into the room. Since Kalen returned, the man had been much colder towards him than before. The warm, friendly demeanor that Kalen had exhibited when they first met was gone. Instead, he was aloof and curt. Norian also noticed that Kalen avoided eye contact and had not once looked at him since his return. He couldn't help but wonder what had happened since they last parted. He couldn't even begin to guess what had taken place with Kalen's meeting with the Queen. All he knew was that Kalen was completely different from before, and not in a good way. However, that did not slow down Norian's attraction to the man, and Kalen's peculiar effect on him remained. He had to be careful not to let it show in front of the Queen or anyone else. His very life may depend on it. If the Queen hasn't already decided to dispose of him, that is. That would explain Kalen's change of attitude toward him.

Lady Auryon was sitting on a plush chair when he

entered, and when she raised her head, he almost gasped in surprise. He never expected her to be so beautiful. She had long blond hair and a pale complexion. Her blue eyes matched those of Kalen, and she sent shivers right down to his soul as she looked at him. Her cheeks had a tint of rose to them, and the skin on her face was flawless. She rose, walked to Norian, and held out her hand.

"Greetings. I am Lady Auryon. Welcome to Norbury."

He didn't know whether to kiss the hand or shake it. Being that she was a queen of sorts, he inclined slightly and kissed it.

Should he call her Your Highness? Your Majesty? Apart from his mother, he'd never been in the presence of a queen before. "I'm Kalen. It is an honor to meet you, Your Majesty."

She indicated to two empty chairs with her hand. "Come. Let us sit and get to know one another a bit."

They walked over to the empty chairs. Norian glanced at Kalen, who quickly averted his eyes, causing Norian to feel a stab in his chest at the gesture. Norian took a seat next to the Queen. Kalen remained standing.

"I understand that you have traveled a long distance to see me," said the Queen.

Norian took a breath, trying to steady his shaking hands. He could feel beads of sweat form on his forehead. One wrong word to this woman could put his life in danger.

"Yes, Your Majesty," he said. "I've come to request your aid."

She waved her hand in the air. "Please call me Lady Auryon. There are no kings or queens here."

"You are not the Queen of Norbury then?"

Norian thought he heard a snicker come from behind him, but he did not turn to look.

"My family has indeed been the leader of the town for quite some time, but we are not of royal blood exactly. It is a complicated situation."

Norian nodded. "I apologize if I offended you. I believed you to be queen."

"No apology necessary." She smiled at him. "So I understand that you have gone through some changes lately."

He nodded. "Yes, a couple of weeks ago." He turned his head, and his eyes clashed with Kalen's. Once again, Kalen turned his head to avoid his gaze. Norian turned his regard back to Lady Auryon. "I know little about my condition. Practically nothing, to be truthful. I hoped that you might be able to help me."

"And what kind of help were you hoping to find?"

He gave her a shorter version of the story that he had recounted to Kalen earlier, again leaving out the fact that his father was King of Tregaron.

"That is quite an experience, young man," she said. She gave him a brief nod. "I am sorry that this happened to you. It must have been a horrible ordeal."

"It was, though I've come to accept it now." He clenched his fists. "But I swear that someday, I shall get my revenge. I will destroy Vadok one way or another."

Her eyes grew wide, and her face paled. She looked stricken. "Vadok? What do you know of Vadok? What has he to do with anything?"

"He was the one responsible for my transformation. He supposedly compelled a werewolf to kill me." He paused. "To be truthful, it was not me he was trying to kill, but my companion. Luckily, he was unsuccessful in either venture, although, as you know, I did not come out of it unscathed."

"Vadok is a very dangerous and evil creature." Her voice

cracked as she spoke. She dabbed at her eyes with her sleeve. "I would advise you to stay far away from him. Even though you are now lycan, you are no match for the likes of him. His magic is powerful and black."

"You've encountered Vadok yourself?" asked Norian.

Kalen looked at his mother wide-eyed. "Vadok is the one—"

"It is a story best left for another time," said Lady Auryon, interrupting him. She forced a weak smile. "We are gathered here to discuss the situation of our new friend."

"Of course," Kalen replied. He met Norian's gaze. The warmth in his eyes caused Norian's heart to speed up. A lump formed in Norian's throat. This was not the time to have randy thoughts about Lady Auryon's son. He inwardly chastised himself and forced his eyes away from Kalen.

"Norian," she said. Her voice was soft and soothing. "I am not clear as to what type of help you seek. Do you seek sanctuary here?"

"I seek a cure," Norian said. "I understand that if someone becomes a werewolf... er, lycan... through the bite of another lycan, then perhaps there is some way to reverse the process, some way to remove the curse from the blood."

She narrowed her eyes and reached out and took Norian's hand. Her voice was barely above a whisper as she spoke.

"I am so sorry, Norian. But if there is by some chance a cure, I am unaware of it. I have never heard of a lycan becoming human, regardless of whether they are created by bite or blood."

"There are no wizards or sorcerers in the village who might help?"

Lady Auryon shook her head. "None. Magic is forbidden in Norbury. I wish I could provide you some hope, but alas, it is best to accept the truth in matters such as this. You are lycan, like us. It is not something to be ashamed of, but rather a source of pride. You are stronger, more powerful than average humans with instincts and senses far surpassing those of the most cunning of animals."

Norian looked at her with his mouth open and said nothing. He fought back the tears that threatened to erupt at any moment. His disappointment engulfed him and dragged him down to depths he had not yet experienced. All was lost.

"Do not despair, young Norian, for you are not alone," Lady Auryon added. "Kalen and I will guide you and support you. We can teach you what it means to be a lycan and how to control your new abilities. You have come to the right place."

Kalen walked over and placed a hand on Norian's shoulder, but said nothing. He closed his eyes, inhaling Kalen's scent. Much to his horror, he felt his groin stir. He opened his eyes, debating whether he should push Kalen's hand off of him. He did not like the effect that this man's touch had on him. Norian's eyes met those of Lady Auryon and saw she had a strange, mystifying look on her face. Norian found it unsettling. He couldn't help but wonder if she somehow knew that he was having lustful thoughts about her son. In all of his years in the kingdom, he had always hidden his attraction to males. While there were undoubtedly many young men whom he'd found alluring, he had never acted on those attractions except for a couple of stolen kisses with Thorne. So why did this man affect him so strongly? Why was it that Kalen's very presence could blur his thoughts and make him question not just himself, but the path he had so carefully chosen?

"That is most kind of you," Norian said. "I indeed would like to learn as much as possible about my condition."

Lady Auryon creased her brow and then looked up. She held up her index finger in a wait-a-moment gesture. She glanced at the ceiling as though in deep thought.

"Magic, you say?" she asked after several long moments.

"Pardon me?" Norian asked.

She narrowed her eyes and met Norian's gaze. "You said that your bite resulted from magic? That this sorcerer compelled the lycan who attacked you?"

"That is my understanding," Norian said. "Vadok was there, and he seemed to be controlling the wolf."

"Hmm...he must has spelled the girl before she transformed because black magic doesn't work on us when we're in lycan form." She met Norian's gaze. "From what I understand, black magicians have typically feared lycans, for it is said that only evil can overtake evil. I personally don't consider lycans to be evil, but there might be something behind the legend. Black magicians are traditionally very difficult to destroy, but it may be possible that a lycan can kill a magician with a bite. That would certainly explain Vadok's fear of us."

"What are you getting at, Mother?" Kalen asked. "How can that help Norian?"

"It is common knowledge that if someone is hexed or cursed by a sorcerer, that the only way the curse can be lifted is by the death of the sorcerer. But there's a catch. The death of the sorcerer has to come at the hands of the one who is cursed. Since the bite of a lycan is said to be deadly to black magicians, Norian might be able to remove the curse himself were he to bite Vadok while in lycan form. The catch, is that Norian would have to kill the magician. Though Vadok didn't directly curse Norian, he is the source of the spell so it's logical then that exterminating the magician might reverse the spell."

"Kill the magician? Me? How would I do that? I've no magic. I'm just a normal man with no powers at all. I can't go up against a powerful sorcerer."

Kalen and his mother exchanged a curious look. Kalen looked as though he was about to say something, but Lady Auryon gestured to him with her hand, and he remained silent.

Finally, Lady Auryon spoke. "Do not underestimate yourself. You have more power than you realize. You only need someone to help you to tap into it, to discover it."

"You mean being a lycan?" Norian asked. "I have no control over that. I don't even remember what I do when I'm turned. It's a blank."

"That is easy to remedy," said Lady Auryon. "You simply haven't learned the proper way to turn. If another lycan is with you, they can teach you how to keep your consciousness and personality during the shift. Kalen will be present at your next transformation, so he can teach you how to do that. But that is not what I am speaking of now. You, young man, possess additional abilities that very few lycans have. It is a power that you can use to your advantage —power that can overtake and vanquish Vadok."

Kalen stepped in front of Lady Auryon and looked her in the eyes. "I thought you said we need to wait on this if you are speaking about what I think you are."

"It is best to tend to this matter as quickly as possible. I can sense the power just being in his presence, and no doubt others will be able to as well. So it is best to tell him and allow him to make his own decision."

Norian wondered if somehow they'd figured out that he was a prince. He tried to think of anything that could have given it away, but could not. "I don't understand what power you are both talking about. Am I different from other lycans? How?"

Lady Auryon brushed past Kalen and rested both of her hands on Norian's shoulders. He raised his eyes to meet hers, afraid of what she was going to say next.

"You are indeed different from other lycans, young wolf," she said. "You are an Alpha."

CHAPTER FIFTEEN

ALL THREE OF THEM WERE SILENT AS NORIAN glanced back and forth from Lady Auryon to Kalen.

"Am I supposed to know what that means?" Norian finally asked. "Is it something bad?"

Lady Auryon laughed, causing Kalen to snicker as well. "I forget you are unfamiliar with lycan ways. I assumed everyone would know." She took a deep breath and continued. "An Alpha is the dominant lycan in a pack. He is the leader and is one to be feared as well as loved. But his power does not extend only to his own pack. Any other lycan he comes across will immediately be overcome with the need to bow down to him, to do his bidding, to be subservient to him. Conflict arises when an Alpha lays claim to a pack already led by another. In such moments, the two Alphas must battle to the death, for only one may rule."

"How could I be an Alpha?" asked Norian. "I have done nothing special. I wasn't even a lycan until a few weeks ago. How can you say that I'm one of them? Maybe you're mistaken."

Lady Auryon shook her head. "There is no mistaking

this. A lycan knows when an Alpha is in his or her presence, so there is little doubt in my mind that you are indeed an Alpha."

"I don't want it," Norian said. "I cannot be leader here, for I have other obligations elsewhere. I wish to give it to someone else."

"It doesn't work like that," Lady Auryon said. "An Alpha is neither created nor crowned. It is not something that is bestowed. An Alpha is born. Like being a lycan, it is a part of who you are, a part that you cannot remove, no matter how much you might wish to. It is something to be proud of, young Norian, for every lycan parent prays their child will be born an Alpha."

Tears threatened to well up in Norian's eyes, but he held them back. Why did it seem as though his entire world were crashing down on him? So not only was he a werewolf, he was now expected to be some kind of leader. Would this nightmare never cease?

"I can't do this," Norian said in almost a whisper. "I do not want to be a lycan, much less king of the lycans. The only thing I want is for my life to go back to normal."

"What about killing the wizard?" Kalen said, his attention directed to his mother. "You said that a bitten lycan can be cured if he kills the wizard who caused his transformation. Would that not take care of both of his problems? He would no longer be Alpha for he would no longer be lycan."

"That is the myth," she said. "But whether there's any validity behind it remains to be seen. While it is certainly worth a try, I wouldn't put all of my hopes into this. Norian is better off learning how to be an Alpha."

"So my choice is between probably getting murdered by an evil wizard or staying here to be king of the werewolves," said Norian. "You say that I am this supposed Alpha but I don't feel all that powerful, certainly not powerful enough to single-handedly take on a ruthless dark sorcerer."

"Do not underestimate the power you already have, young Alpha," said Lady Auryon. "But there is additional power to be claimed, and it is not every Alpha who can obtain it or access it. You are one of the few who have that opportunity."

"What are you talking about, Mother?" Kalen said. "I'm unaware of any extra power."

She shook her head. "No, few are. That is why your earlier admission was so shocking to me after I realized the potential. After watching the both of you, I'm certain that you are right, Kalen—and if that is the case, the power you both would possess between you would be astounding. While an Alpha wields considerable power simply by being an Alpha, he is still somewhat incomplete. His true power lies with his mate. Once an Alpha completes the mating process with his true mate, then he can reach and tap into his genuine power." She narrowed her eyes and locked her gaze onto Kalen's. "And if his mate should by some miracle be a Beta, then the power between the two of them would be unparalleled."

Kalen's eyes widened, and he looked at Norian. Before he could fall into Norian's gaze, he turned his regard back to his mother. "So you believe me, then? It's not simply my imagination?"

"I can see and sense the same feelings on his part," Lady Auryon responded. "His heart races at your merest touch or glance."

"Again, you have lost me," Norian said, not really listening to them. "What is this talk of mating and Betas?"

"An Alpha is a powerful, albeit volatile creature. Simply by being the Alpha, he is already immensely strong and dominant. But if the Alpha should somehow be able to find his true mate, then his power is magnified, and he can command control simply with a glance. His senses are increased to such a point that others consider him almost otherworldly. Few Alphas ever find their true mate. To be truthful, few lycans ever find their true mate. Those who do are indeed considered fortunate."

"What is this, mate?" Norian asked. "Another lycan?"

"Usually, yes, although some lycans have human mates. A mate is your other half, you have no doubt heard the term 'soul mate'. It is the same idea. Lycans are never truly complete until they find their other half. They always feel that nobody is good enough for them, and any romantic partners they do encounter leave them somewhat unfulfilled and empty. It's an additional curse of being a lycan. For this reason, our kind are forever searching for their one true mate, but it is few who ever can find him or her. As you can imagine, this constant frustration does not make for happy lycans."

"This talk of mates doesn't concern me. I don't want this Alpha power, with or without a mate. All I want is to kill that accursed sorcerer and become a human being again. Can I do this or not?"

"It's complicated," Lady Auryon said. "And I shall need some time to dwell upon this. I shall think through our alternatives, consult with our pack scholars and give you my recommendations tomorrow. Until then, we all could use a good night's rest."

"I can't help but be curious," said Norian. "You suggested that I might have the opportunity to find my mate. Out of curiosity, would you happen to know who my mate is?"

"Ask Kalen," she said. "He will tell you everything." She

turned to look at Kalen. "And Kalen, whatever you do, take no action on this. It could jeopardize everything. Wait until I've reflected on the possible repercussions. There is more to this than meets the eye."

~

"LET US WALK," said Kalen. "We have the entire evening before us."

The two men left the building and walked towards the woods in the back. The only sound was the tweeting of birds and the occasional rustle of branches. They strode silently for several minutes along a dirt trail that wound around until they came to an edge of a lookout with a majestic view of the land. It seemed as though Norian could see for miles from where they stood, and a little swoop of vertigo hit him as he looked down. Norian breathed in the sweet scent of the nearby flowers. Then, another unexpected odor wafted to Norian's nostrils, causing him to shudder. His mind swam in confusion at the mere scent of Kalen next to him. He breathed in the sweet aroma of the man and resisted the urge to grab him in an embrace. Why did this person have such a strange effect on him? Once Norian resolved this issue with the sorcerer, he would need to make a conscious effort to stay as far away from Kalen as possible. This was the one person who could jeopardize his earlier resolve to marry and live a normal life.

Finally, Norian broke the silence. He brushed Kalen's shoulder, then quickly withdrew his hand.

"So, are you going to tell me about this mating and Alpha stuff?"

"Why don't we stop off at the creek right around the bend? We can have a rest and talk there."

They backtracked a bit, then took another winding dirt path which was more overgrown than the one they'd been on. Soon, a small stream came into view. Both men sat down, removed their shoes, and sunk their feet into the cool water. Kalen swallowed and finally spoke.

"I will tell you as much as I know. Much of this is new to me as well."

"Your mother seemed to think that you know enough to fill me in." He locked eyes with Kalen and immediately felt a tightness in his chest. "I believe she mentioned you might know who my mate was?"

"Let me start at the beginning. Or as close to the beginning as I can. You have already learned you are an Alpha, a rare thing for a lycan. It is indeed a fortunate pack that has an Alpha to oversee it. With an Alpha in charge, few would dare to harm anyone who is part of the pack, or even approach the pack, for that matter, not daring to incur the wrath of an Alpha. Before you came, there was another Alpha here. This was a long time ago."

"I take it he's no longer here, then?"

Kalen shook his head. "No, he was murdered."

Norian's eyes widened. "But I thought you said nobody would dare mess with an Alpha?"

"There was one who dared. I was too young to remember it, but according to what I've learned, this fiend thought he could be all the more powerful with a lycan pack at his disposal. When he first infiltrated the village, he wasn't aware that he'd stumbled upon a town full of lycans. But once he figured it out, he planned to kill the Alpha and take over the pack himself. Apparently, he knew nothing of our ways. Needless to say, it didn't quite work out the way he'd hoped. When the rest of the pack found out this stranger had killed our leader—our Alpha—they pursued the man. Regretfully, he escaped and has not been back since."

"Does anyone know who he is and why he wanted to control the lycans?"

Kalen nodded. "Yes, and you're familiar with him, too. His name was Vadok."

Norian gasped. "Vadok? The despicable scourge who had me turned into a werewolf?"

"The one and the same. Apparently, his aspirations have not calmed over the years."

"I'm sorry that the savage bastard killed your Alpha. That must have been very difficult for the pack."

"So, as you can see, you are not the only one who wishes vengeance. There is yet a bit more to the story." Kalen took a deep breath and then continued. "The Alpha who Vadok killed was my father."

"The Alpha was your father?"

Norian's head snapped up at the news, his hand flying to his mouth before he could stop it. "Oh, Kalen. I'm so sorry. That's terrible."

"It was, but it was a long time ago. So, now you can understand why my mother is so intent on you killing Vadok. Over the years, she has spoken many times of vengeance. Perhaps she sees you as the answer to her prayers."

"So your father was an Alpha, and I am an Alpha. Is there supposed to be some connection here? Am I supposed to be...what.... like your father now?"

Kalen laughed. "It doesn't work that way. It was only by chance that the Alpha was my father—and you, being an Alpha, have nothing to do with that." He paused, then scratched his chin. "At least I don't think it does. Yet I can't help but wonder how much of a coincidence it is that Vadok killed my father and then was responsible for you becoming a lycan. Kind of odd."

"Maybe it's no coincidence at all. Maybe it's my fate to kill Vadok."

Kalen raised his eyebrows and then smiled. "Perhaps. I've never been one to believe in fate until just recently."

"So, what can you tell me about being an Alpha? What was your father like?"

Kalen sighed. "I wish I could tell you more about my father. But, unfortunately, I only remember bits and pieces about him, and any knowledge I do have, I've learned from others. I remember he was incredibly handsome, though. Strikingly handsome... like you."

Heat rose up in Norian's cheeks, and he turned away to avoid Kalen's mesmerizing gaze. "So, was Lady Auryon your father's mate?"

"No," Kalen said, shaking his head. "They loved each other very much, but she was not his true mate. They'd known each other their entire lives, and once they became adults, they fell in love. Neither one of them had found their true mate before this and grew weary of waiting and searching, I suppose. My mother once told me her biggest fear was that my father's true mate would wander into town, and he would cast her aside. It is said that it's impossible to ignore the call of your mate and she was aware that if either of them ever encountered their mate, the marriage would be over. Luckily, neither of them ever did. My father died loving only my mother."

"So lycans don't always find their mate?" Norian asked. He tried to focus on the bubbling of the brook next to them rather than the honey scent of Kalen's breath.

"It is, in fact, rare for a lycan to find one's mate. Most search their entire lives for their mate, trying to find that missing piece of their heart. This is why it's not unusual for strange lycans to find their way into our pack. You see, some of us travel from one pack to another, always hoping our mate dwells within. My mother always said it's almost best to find another to love and forget finding your mate entirely, if only to obtain some peace of mind."

"But why not at least try?"

"Because if you do eventually find your mate and your mate dies, the other partner often dies shortly thereafter. From what I understand, the pain of losing your mate is so intense and gut-wrenching, it feels as though a part of yourself has died along with them. At that point, many feel the best and only option is to end their own life."

"So sad," Norian said. "I can't imagine what it must be like."

"I have known a few who have lost their mates, and it is indeed a sorrowful situation." He paused and looked at Norian. "I hope it never happens to me."

"Did your parents search for their mate before they met each other?"

"My father did. My mother told me that he spent a good portion of his early youth searching for his mate. Being an Alpha, finding his mate would have made him a mighty leader, one of the most powerful ever known in the lycan community. However, he finally abandoned the search when he realized he deeply loved my mother. I'm not sure whether he ever had any regrets about not finding his true mate, but from what others have told me, he and my mother were incredibly happy together."

"But what about my mate? Your mother said you could tell me something about it."

"I'm getting to that. So after my mother and father married, I came along. Although it is rare, an Alpha can father a Beta and that's what happened in my case. As I grew toward manhood, my Beta characteristics began displaying, much to the surprise of my mother and the rest of the pack. Regretfully, my father had already passed away by the time this happened. So once I reached adulthood, I took my place as pack leader."

"You're the pack leader? But I thought your mother was the Queen of Lycans."

Kalen chuckled. "I'm not sure where or how such a rumor started, but mother and I had a good laugh about it when you arrived here asking to see the Queen of Were-wolves. Though in a way, you are right. Being Beta, I have plenty of pack business to take care of, and much of it is delegated to my mother, who often deals with civil issues between pack members. So I guess it's not surprising some might consider her queen of the pack. She's a powerful lycan in her own right—one to be feared and respected. If I hadn't been born a Beta, she would have been the one to lead the pack, given that she was married to the Alpha. "

"So, what exactly is a Beta?" Norian asked.

"That's a complicated question. In the simplest of terms, the Beta is second-in-command to the Alpha. While just their stature commands respect, they lack the natural charisma of the Alpha. In the absence of an Alpha, a Beta naturally takes the role of pack leader and has the respect of the pack members. But mostly, the role of the Beta is to follow, support, and serve the Alpha and is more at ease doing so. I suppose this is why I've never been completely comfortable in a leadership position, but I do it because it's required of me. I'm lucky I had my mother to help me share the tasks and teach me. If my father had lived, my purpose would have been to help him with the pack, taking care of the lesser important issues, much like my mother is doing for me. But alas, I instead had to lead the pack the best I could."

"Do all packs have a Beta?"

Kalen shook his head. "While there are more Betas than Alphas, there is still not one born into every pack. In such a case, the widow or widower of the former Alpha takes charge of the pack. If there is none, then the strongest member of the pack, decided by vote, takes the role of leader. Even if a Beta should meander into town, this does not mean he would take over the pack. While a Beta has power of their own, it does not equal that of an Alpha. They don't have the physical presence and natural dominance of an Alpha, and the current pack leader would not be so willing to give over their power to a Beta. It has happened that an unsuspecting Beta has been killed because the current leader saw the intruder as a threat to their power."

Norian's head swam with all the information. His heart raced in his chest as he imagined ruling with Kalen by his side. "So, you're saying it's the natural order of things that you and I should rule together?"

Kalen stared at him for a moment, then tore his eyes away. "If you were to stay and accept your role as Alpha—and if you wanted me."

Norian stood up and crossed his arms over his chest. "It's not a question of whether I want you." He swallowed after the words left his lips, and his heart sped up. "You know my sole purpose in taking this journey is to find a cure, no matter what that may require. I have to at least try to kill Vadok in the hopes it'll cure me. It's nothing personal against you or lycans in general. I just want to be human again and return to my home. I hope you understand this."

Kalen nodded and then rose to his feet, kicking off the

excess water. "I do. But there is something else you need to be aware of before you decide."

"Kalen, I've already made my decision. This is something I must do."

Kalen locked eyes with Norian and then took a deep breath. "There is one additional consideration. You are my mate."

Norian gasped and took a step back. He tried to make sense of the words Kalen said. *You are my mate.* Could it truly be? This would explain the strange effect the man had on him.

"Why do you say this to me? How do you know?"

"I sensed it the moment I saw you," Kalen said. His voice was almost a whisper. "When a lycan meets their mate for the first time, there's an inner knowing that occurs, a stirring deep within the soul accompanied by an intense passion. That is how I felt when I first laid eyes on you. It was so strong it nearly moved me to tears. I didn't understand what was happening at first, and then when you told me you changed three nights in a row, I figured that simply being around an Alpha was causing these stirrings within me. But the feelings and yearnings became stronger until only one thought dominated my mind: mate."

Norian felt lightheaded. His heart pounded at the man's words, words he'd longed to hear ever since first meeting Kalen. But these were also words to which he must not succumb. His only objective here was to find a cure so he could return home to his people. He would not allow anything to come between him and his goal.

"You are mistaken," Norian said. His voice cracked as he spoke. "It is probably just as you said—being in the presence of an Alpha."

Kalen shook his head. "No. My mother noticed it too. She felt it."

"Then you are both mistaken," Norian said in a voice much harsher than he intended. "I am not your mate."

"Don't tell me you don't feel it too because I see it in your eyes." He took a step closer to Norian. "I can hear your heart race as I draw near to you. You cannot tell me you don't want me as much as I want you. You cannot hide it, Norian. I can *smell* your desire."

Norian took several steps back and, with the greatest of effort, tore his gaze from Kalen. The man was right. Norian felt it too—and in that moment, he wanted nothing more than to run to Kalen, wrap his arms around him, press their bodies close, and kiss him. He had never experienced such intense, almost all-encompassing feelings towards anyone before. But he had only one chance at a normal life, and he mustn't let anything deter him from that chance. His heart thunked as a deep, stabbing pain welled up in his chest, feeling as though his heart had been scooped out of him. Nevertheless, he could not give in to his desires and lose sight of his goal. Vanquishing Vadok was his only chance at a normal life.

"I don't know what it is you think you are feeling, but it is false," Norian said. "I apologize if I have given you the wrong impression."

Kalen's eyes filled with tears. He pushed Norian with both hands, causing Norian to stumble. "Liar! You feel it too! I know you feel it. You know I'm your mate. This isn't something you can ignore in the hopes it will disappear. *This will not go away, Norian.*"

The words blurted out before Norian realized what he was saying. "Even if we are mates, there can be nothing between us. If I am cured—and I shall do everything in my power to ensure it is so—I have responsibilities, obligations. I cannot rule a kingdom with another male at my side. My people would never allow it."

Kalen's eyes grew wide. "What do you mean, kingdom? Are you some sort of king?"

Norian flinched. He didn't want to let anyone know who he was. He'd learned this lesson from his father, who told him that when traveling, a king must never reveal his true identity, as disreputable people will use it against you. Kidnapping royalty is a way too common occurrence. Unfortunately, he had now let it slip who he was to Kalen.

"No, I am not a king," Norian said. He inclined his head politely. "I am Prince Norian to King Jamros, King of Tregaron."

"Why didn't you tell me? I'm sure my mother would love to learn she has a prince under her roof, a lycan prince at that."

"You mustn't tell her! It is too dangerous for me, my family, and my kingdom if it were to get out that the king's son had traveled to a lycan village in search of a cure." He fought the tears that threatened to well up in his eyes. "Now you understand why we cannot be mates, no matter what the connection is between us? A king cannot lie with a man, just as a king cannot be a wolf. This is why this trip here is so vital to me and why I must not fail in killing Vadok."

Kalen took a step toward Norian. "It doesn't matter who you are, king or peasant. The fact remains, you and I are destined to be together. This truth will not disappear, no matter how much you wish it. If you deny me, you shall always feel a part of you is missing." He brought his hand to his chest and rested it over his heart. "Even more so now that you know who your mate is. It is unheard of—no, impossible—to walk away from one's mate. It is akin to suicide."

"You underestimate my tenacity, Kalen," Norian said, the tears flooding his eyes. "The most important thing to me is my kingdom. I have trained my entire life with the expectation I will someday be king, and I will do everything in my power to prove myself worthy of the throne. You speak of destiny. While it may be true my emotions towards you are confusing, it is not my destiny to remain here and rule a werewolf kingdom with you. I wish I could, but I can't."

With that, Norian turned, snatched up his shoes and took off, running down the path without looking back.

"Norian!" Kalen shouted. But Norian continued to run until he was out of view. Kalen sighed, head bowed, and trudged back toward the house.

CHAPTER SIXTEEN

"You told him that dinner was being served now?" Lady Auryon asked.

Kalen nodded. He and his mother sat down at a large table with three place settings in a dimly lit dining room. "I knocked on his door and told him to come down to dinner."

"He still hasn't spoken to you since your walk this afternoon?"

Kalen shook his head. "I've tried several times. He remains secluded behind his locked door and has not come out of his room the entire afternoon, as far as I'm aware. I wish I knew what was going on in his mind."

"You must put yourself in his position," Lady Auryon said. "A mere couple of weeks ago, he was a young human man who believed that the rest of his life was completely mapped out for him. In only a short time, he has been attacked by and transformed into a lycan at the hands of a murderous sorcerer, traveled by himself to a dangerous known lycan village, been told that he's an Alpha, and has learned that another lycan—a male lycan, at that—is his one true mate. Be patient, Kalen, and give him time. This is a lot to process for anyone. That he's a prince further complicates the matter."

"But what if he leaves?" Kalen said. He slammed both hands down on the table. "What if I found my one true mate, and I can never be with him? What will become of me? How can I live after this?"

"You're overreacting. You cannot pretend to understand how the young man feels. Worrying about 'what-ifs' never does a body any good. Besides, there is more to this scenario than you realize. Norian shall soon face critical decisions—choices that will shape his fate."

"What decisions might those be?" said Norian, who was standing in the doorway.

Kalen's face flushed red. "Norian!"

Lady Auryon gestured to the empty chair next to Kalen. "Your Highness. Please join us. We've much to discuss."

Norian's head snapped to Kalen. "Damn you, Kalen. I told you that nobody is to know who I am. You just put me and my kingdom in danger."

"Posh," Lady Auryon said, waving her hand in the air. "Nobody is in any immediate danger. Your secret is safe with us. Kalen had to tell me because it complicates your situation even more." She gestured again to the empty chair. "Now come. Sit. We need to talk."

Norian sat down, deliberately trying to avoid looking at Kalen. His attraction towards the man was growing stronger, almost to the point of being unbearable. He would have to leave this village soon because the longer he stayed, the more difficult it would be to ignore his feelings for the handsome man.

"So I take it you know about the mate thing?" Norian asked.

"If you are referring to you and Kalen being mates, then

yes. I've been aware of this since the beginning. But it is up to you as to what will become of it. So you still intend to pursue Vadok?"

Norian nodded. "If that's the only chance I have, then I have no choice but to pursue this."

"Your father. Is he aware of what has occurred? Does he know you are lycan?"

"He was at the castle when I was attacked. Wayf brought me to him and told him everything."

"Wayf, this is the magician you spoke of?"

Norian nodded. "Aye, the court mage." He paused. "And also a very dear friend. He practically raised me though we're not too far apart age-wise."

"I take it this mage was unaware of any potential cure?" She asked.

"His knowledge of lycans is limited. That is why he sent me to you."

She nodded. "But he was unaware that you were an Alpha?"

"I think so," Norian said. "He was as surprised as I was when I transformed the night before the full moon."

"There are even many lycans who don't know a lot about Alphas," Kalen said. "Some have never encountered one. You are the first since my father."

Norian nodded, but avoided Kalen's gaze. "I would like to leave on this quest as soon as possible." He paused and swallowed. "After the full moon, that is."

"Before you make any decisions, there are things you need to understand first. It is important at this point that you do not close your mind to any possibilities. But it is essential to be informed of all the facts in order to decide your best course of action."

Norian crossed his arms. "My best course of action at

this point is to kill Vadok in the hopes that I'll revert to normal."

"How much do you know about Alphas?" Lady Auryon asked.

"Only what you've told me. That they are in charge of the pack and are somewhat charismatic."

Lady Auryon laughed. "That is part of it, yes. But there is so much more to being an Alpha, young Norian." She folded her hands and placed them on the table in front of her. "An Alpha is more than a mere pack leader. Because of their immense power, they are also the protector of the pack. It is only an Alpha who could protect a pack against someone like Vadok."

"But wasn't your husband, an Alpha, killed by Vadok?"

She sighed, and a wistful expression crossed her face. "It's true. Unfortunately, Vadok caught him unawares— caught all of us unawares. But my husband had not come into his full power because he'd never found his true mate."

"So you're saying that I am more powerful than he because I've a mate?" He glanced at Kalen and locked eyes with him for a moment. He returned his gaze to Lady Auryon when she spoke.

"Not quite. You actually must perform the mating ritual for you to come into your power. It is then that you will transform into the true Alpha lycan you are meant to be."

"And what is this mating ritual?"

A wicked grin crossed over her expression, and she made an obscene gesture in the air with her hands.

"Mother!" said Kalen.

She laughed. "Mating, of course! That's the ritual."

Norian raised his eyebrows and felt the heat rise in his face. "You mean sex?"

She grinned. "In a manner of speaking, yes. You need to

make love with your mate and, during the act, claim each other as your own with a bite. Of course, I've never witnessed such a mating in person." She pursed her lips, a playful look in her eyes. "I've only heard of the process. Once the deed is accomplished, you will come into your true power. You will indeed be a unique lycan, for there are few Alphas who ever achieve this."

"What kind of power? You mean the power to command people?"

"Leading a pack requires the power to command and be obeyed. But this power extends beyond the pack. Upon meeting you, people will instinctually become fearful of you and will experience an innate need to submit to you. Often, you can convince those to do your bidding with only a stare. And, from what I've heard, you'll be able to transform at will. That is to say, you would no longer need to wait for the moon to be full. You'd be able to shift anytime you want."

Norian shuddered as he recalled the unbearable pain of the transformation. "And why would I ever want to do that? Why would I ever want to suffer through that horrible, agonizing pain willingly? I would rather never, ever transform again. Right now, ending my life seems a preferable option to facing the next transformation."

She tensed up, and a confused expression crossed her face. "Pain? Whatever are you talking about?"

"Mother," Kalen said. "Remember, he didn't shift with his creator the first time. Instead, he shifted alone, unaware of what was happening. He had not learned."

Lady Auryon's eyes grew wide, and she brought her hand to her mouth. "Oh Norian, I am so sorry. I'd forgotten that you'd never learned how to transform properly. Nobody should ever have to shift alone the first time without the connection."

Norian squinted his eyes. "The connection?"

"When a lycan transforms for the first time, usually the entire pack is with him or her," Kalen said. "But it is a pack elder who guides the new lycan's transformation and serves as sort of a mentor, if you will. This mentor forms a mental connection with the new lycan to ease the transformation and step them through the process. During this connection, the lycan learns how to control the change, thus transforming with little pain. Without this connection, it is the body itself that controls the transformation rather than the mind." His gaze softened. "I can't imagine how painful that must've been for you."

"So you're saying that there is a way that I can transform without pain?"

"There is some mild discomfort, but shifting with an experienced lycan can help you to rise above it and not physically experience the most unpleasant part of the change," Kalen said. He met his mother's eyes, and she nodded. "I will be with you during your next change. I will guide you through it."

"But will that work?" Norian asked. "Remember, I turn the night before the full moon. Can you transform at will?"

"No, but we are both lycans," Kalen said. "That means that even though I'm not changing, I should, in theory, still be able to connect with you during the process and teach you how to complete it with as little pain as possible." He looked at his mother for a moment, then turned his regard back to Norian. "The connection is even stronger between us because we are mates."

"So do we need to...," Norian paused for a moment and swallowed. "Do we have to mate beforehand?"

Before Kalen could answer, his mother interrupted. "That is where things get a little complicated. Undoubtedly, transforming after the mating ritual would make it even easier upon yourself because you will have come into your full power. So, in effect, up to this point, you've only partially completed your transformation. A lycan bit you and, as a result of that bite, you've become an Alpha lycan. That alone is unheard of. But once you complete the mating ritual, your transformation will be complete, and you will enjoy the full benefit of your power. You would also physiologically change again. But this time, the change would instill itself in your physical human body as well." Her expression softened. "There is typically no going back from that. What that means is, once you come into your full Alpha power, it is unlikely that even killing Vadok would reverse it. It's possible, I suppose, but unlikely."

"Then, I will not complete the mating ritual."

Kalen crumpled into his chair and let out a soft cry. His mother reached out and gently touched his arm.

"Do not be too quick to make this decision, Norian. You perhaps do not yet realize what you would be giving up."

"Giving up? Having power over others is not motivation enough for me to give up my quest to kill Vadok. Why, once I become king, I shall possess all the power over others that I could desire. Instead, I think of what I would give up were I to stay. I am a prince! I have an obligation to my people to take over Tregaron from my father when the time comes. My ancestors ruled and protected this kingdom for centuries. I've no choice but to follow in their footsteps."

"Norian," said Lady Auryon. "There is always a choice."

"Not this time," said Norian. "I cannot walk away from my kingdom. I am the only son, the last of my father's line. I am the Crown Prince of Tregaron."

"But what if you fail?" Kalen asked. "What if he kills

you instead? Or what if you do succeed in destroying him, and the curse does not reverse itself? Then what? Will you go back and try to rule as a lycan?"

"I will decide that when or if the time comes where I need to make such a choice."

"Norian, please be reasonable," said Kalen. "You've an opportunity to rule your own kind. You said yourself that your people would never accept a lycan as their king. I know you feel it, the draw to stay here with your own people. To stay here with me."

The crushing in Norian's chest made it difficult for him to breathe. Was he making the wrong decision? It was true. There was an almost irresistible urge within him to take Kalen and make him his. But if he did so, then all hope was lost. "I'm sorry, but I cannot," Norian said. "I did not ask for this. This was imposed upon me. My only obligation right now is to find a cure so that I can resume my proper place in Tregaron."

"No need to decide now," said Lady Auryon. "The full moon is yet over a week away. Both of you must do some considerable reflection on your situation. Norian, as much as my desire for vengeance wishes for you to destroy Vadok, I must simply ask you this: can you truly walk away from your mate, from Kalen, and continue to live your life as though he had never entered it? Do not answer now. Think carefully upon it. As the full moon draws close, we shall talk again."

A loud knock on the door interrupted the conversation. The door opened, and a young servant boy entered.

"Yes, what is it?" Kalen said.

"Thomros, Deric, and Fruos wish conference."

"Tell them I'll be with them in a moment," said Kalen. "Have them wait in my chambers."

The servant bowed, then said, "It is not you whom they wish to see." He swallowed.

Kalen raised his eyebrows. "Then who?"

"They wish to see the new Alpha."

～

THE THREE OF them sat in stunned silence. Then, finally, Lady Auryon spoke. "Bring them here," she told the servant. Once the servant left the room, she glared at Kalen. "How did this happen? This information was not to get out. Kalen?"

Kalen shook his head. "It was not I, and as far as I know, nobody besides the three of us knows about Norian being an Alpha. It was Thomros and Deric who found Norian brought him here. No doubt they've figured out what he was. The effect that an Alpha has on you is not easily mistaken."

"Damn it!" Lady Auryon said. "Now, this is going to turn into something political."

"Political?" asked Norian. "What do you mean?"

Kalen turned towards Norian. "Being Beta, it has been up to me to lead the pack, and my mother and I have done so ever since my father died. However, a new Alpha in the village changes all of that. With you here, the pack will no longer recognize or accept our leadership, for it is in all of our deepest instincts to submit to an Alpha."

"But they don't even know me," Norian said. "They have no idea what sort of person I might be."

"It doesn't matter," Lady Auryon said, shaking her head. "You are Alpha, and it is in our blood to want to serve you, to recognize you as our protector and leader."

"I don't want to lead anyone! I only want to find a cure for this damned thing and go home, where I belong."

"It will not be that easy now that the pack knows about you," Lady Auryon said. "They will not be so willing to let you go. I'd hoped that this would not get out, but it was inevitable. It's difficult to hide an Alpha from other lycans." She sniffed the air. "Although, strangely enough, you are not that easy to detect. Perhaps it is because you are a new Alpha and were not born into it like most are. I have no idea. But it is not so weak that others wouldn't detect it. And apparently, that's what has happened."

Norian rested his head in his hands for a moment, trying to make sense of what they were telling him. Was he going to be a prisoner here now that the others have discovered him? "What if I tell the others that I don't want to rule and wish you both to remain as you are, as their leaders?"

"It doesn't matter what you say to them," Lady Auryon said. "The fact remains that you are the Alpha, and it is your duty to lead the pack. While our instincts towards an Alpha are strong, there is more to it than that. A pack without an Alpha is weak and vulnerable to attack—and there are many such packs, ours included. I've heard that outsiders believe I am Alpha, which has perhaps saved our pack from being attacked by other lycans. Perhaps that is how the rumor of me being the Queen of the Werewolves started." She gestured towards Kalen. "Although fortunate for us, we had a Beta in our midst. But regardless, for an Alpha to wander into our village is indeed a gift from the gods. The people will not let you go easily."

"But if I can command others as you say, can't I simply command them to allow me to leave and recognize Kalen as the valid leader."

Norian smiled as Kalen's hand moved over his hand and

then intertwined his fingers with Norian's. As much as Norian's mind told him to pull away, he couldn't. The sensation of Kalen's skin felt so right, and all at once, a hunger arose within him. A hunger for Kalen. Lady Auryon's voice pierced the fog he was falling into and snapped him back to the moment.

"It's possible. But in the meantime, you must go public. The pack will get suspicious if we try to hide you from them. Keeping you hidden away could be dangerous for us."

"In what way?" Norian asked. He squeezed Kalen's hand tighter, not wanting ever to let him go.

"To usurp the command of an Alpha is to ask for certain death. Even though Kalen is a Beta, they expect him to acknowledge and serve an Alpha should one ever make themselves known. If the people believe that the Beta—or anyone else for that matter—is trying to maintain power for himself over that of an Alpha, then the pack will kill them. They will always put the preservation and protection of the Alpha above anything else. I heard a story long ago about a pack that was led by a much-loved Alpha. Another Alpha wandered into the village, and before he even had a chance to introduce himself, the pack ripped the stranger to shreds. So you see, a pack will do anything—even kill another Alpha—to protect their own Alpha. It's fortunate for you that my husband is no longer alive, for you may have met the same fate upon your arrival."

"That's incredible. I didn't know about any of this."

"Of course you wouldn't," Lady Auryon said. "Only those who are part of the pack are familiar with our ways." She creased her brow. "Kalen, what is it? What is wrong with you?"

Kalen withdrew his sweaty hand from Norian's. The emptiness of the missing hand stabbed Norian in the heart.

He still dared not glance at Kalen, even though he could hear Kalen's breath come in rapid bursts.

"Nothing," Kalen said. His voice was more of a growl. "I am fine."

"You look shaken," his mother said. She then glanced back and forth from Kalen to Norian. "Ah, I think I understand. It is no doubt becoming more and more difficult for you to be so close to each other." She pointed to the empty chair next to her. "Kalen, come sit here. Thomros, Deric, and Fruos must not learn that Norian is your mate—at least not yet. If that knowledge becomes known, then there is no chance that they'd allow Norian to leave. In fact, it wouldn't surprise me a bit if the entire town forced you to mate on the spot."

Norian shuddered at the thought—the sheer wrongness of that sentence made his skin crawl. Kalen's hand brushed Norian's knee before he stood up. Damn you, Kalen. You are making this much more difficult.

Kalen rose, picked up his place settings, and walked around the table, taking the empty place next to his mother.

"You both must compose yourself," Lady Auryon said. She pointed at Norian. "If you still hope for a cure, then you shall need to keep away from Kalen. At least until you make a decision either way."

Before he could answer, a loud knock rattled the door.

"Enter," said Kalen.

The door opened, and the three men entered. They were the same men who escorted Norian to the village, the same men who Norian feared would kill him. So the third man's name was Fruos. He didn't recall anyone mentioning it before. The men removed their hats and approached the table. To Norian's surprise, it was Fruos who spoke first.

"So I was right!" he said. His eyes were wide as he

fixated on Norian. "You truly are an Alpha. I thought I sensed it when we found you, and the longer we were with you, the stronger the certainty became. Why didn't you tell us?"

Norian glanced at Kalen, unsure of what to do or say. Kalen gave him a brief nod.

"I did not want my presence to be known until I spoke with the Beta in charge. It was out of respect for the pack."

Fruos nodded and then creased his brow. "Understandable. But what was this talk of finding a cure? This wizard you spoke of when we found you?"

Norian waved his hand in the air. "Pretense. I was not ready for you to learn who I was, so I needed a tale to throw you off my scent until I figured out what I was walking into. Moreover, I feared that your village might house another Alpha who most certainly would wish me harm. I meant neither to mislead nor offend." It surprised him how easily the lies flowed from his lips.

Deric stepped forward, bowed his head, and met Norian's gaze. "But why have you not made yourself known to us? You have been here since yesterday, and yet you continue to hide out here. There has been no news since your arrival and were it not for the keen observation of Fruos, we wouldn't even have known that there was an Alpha right in our midst. This is indeed tremendous news for the village, no? A cause for celebration?"

Kalen stood and locked eyes with Deric. "It is important news for us all. But I ask that you not act too hastily. Norian is new to being an Alpha, new to being a lycan. He is staying with us to learn our ways and for us to help him with his first transformation."

Deric's eyes grew wide. "He has not yet transformed?"

"He has transformed only during one cycle," Kalen said.

"And that was without the aid of another lycan. Without any instruction or bonding."

The three men fixed their gaze on the floor. There was a silence for a long moment.

"I understand," Fruos said. He shuddered and looked at Norian. "That must have been horrible for you. But I am glad that you found us."

"It was indeed difficult," said Norian. "Thank you for your kindness."

"We are honored and overjoyed to have you here," said Thomros, speaking for the first time. "It has been a long time since we've had leadership."

"I beg your pardon?" said Kalen.

Thomros blushed and then nodded reverently. "I did not mean to imply that there was anything wrong with your leadership, Sir. On the contrary, we've been privileged to have you guide us these years and are thankful for your service to us. But as a pack, we naturally welcome the protection of an Alpha. So I apologize if my remark offended you."

Kalen waved in the air with his hand. "No apology necessary. I feel as you do."

"How long before we can announce your presence to the town?" asked Thomros, directing his gaze to Norian. "I am eager for the rest of the pack to learn that there is finally an Alpha among us."

"We ask that you wait until the full moon is past," said Lady Auryon. "This will allow Norian to learn the ways of the lycan and to come into his true power. The years I spent married to an Alpha have taught me well, so Kalen and I wish to pass this knowledge and wisdom along to Norian so that he may become the Alpha he is intended to be."

"Very well," Fruos said. "We've waited this long. I

suppose we can wait another couple of weeks." He turned his regard to Norian. "If there is anything we can do to ease your transition, Boss, don't hesitate to call on any of us."

"Thank you," Norian said. "I shall."

The three men started toward the door, then Fruos stopped and turned around to face Norian. His face glowed red.

"Oh," he said. "About the other day when we found you. The day we escorted you back to the village?"

Norian raised his eyebrows. "Yes?"

"Sorry I called you a scrawny pup."

CHAPTER SEVENTEEN

Norian stretched out on the bed in his room, allowing the events of the past several days to sink in. He'd spent them learning his way around the property and receiving teaching from Lady Auryon. He had told her that for the time being, he wanted to keep his distance from her son, at least until he had time to reflect—and time to make a decision. Though he knew it was for the best, it did nothing to ease the constant ache he felt for Kalen. How quickly his life had changed and how confusing things had become. His original quest to find a cure was now losing importance as Kalen moved more firmly into his heart. Try as he might, it was getting increasingly difficult to fight his feelings for the man. The mere presence of Kalen in the same room with him weakened Norian's resolve and muddled his thoughts. Kalen was the one person who could undermine everything he'd come here to achieve, namely, finding a cure and returning to his life at the castle.

His life at the castle now seemed like a distant memory to him, like someone else's memory. His heart tugged as he thought about his father and Wayf and everything he owed to both of them. It had been barely a week since he'd left the kingdom, but it felt like a lifetime. He supposed it made sense. After all, a fortnight ago, he was an entirely different person—he was a human being, a king's son. Now, he was not only a werewolf but the leader of werewolves—and was destined to rule with a male mate. Funny how destiny has decided that he would rule, one way or another.

All at once, a powerful scent attacked his nostrils, a familiar scent—one that immediately created a tent in his trousers.

Kalen.

He held his breath and waited. Finally, there was a light knock at his door.

"Norian," a voice whispered. "Are you awake?"

His heart quickened, and he prayed the evidence of his attraction to Kalen would dissipate. After debating a moment before opening the door, he took a breath and slid it open slowly. The appearance of Kalen did nothing to extract himself from his embarrassing physical condition. As the two met eyes, Norian's resolve weakened. He wanted nothing more than to grab this man and throw him onto the bed.

"Why are you here?" Norian asked, his voice cracking as he spoke. "You agreed you would give me time."

"Can I come in? I wish to talk with you."

"I don't think that's a good idea."

"Please, Norian. I haven't had a chance alone with you since you arrived. You have heard my mother blather on and on about your future, your decisions, your options, but you have not yet heard me out. I wish to explain to you where I fit in all of this."

Norian swallowed. "Very well. Explain then. You have my undivided attention."

"Not at your door. Let me in so we can talk as equals."

Norian stepped out into the hallway and shut the door behind him. "We can easily talk here in this hallway as equals."

Kalen raised his eyebrows. "What? You don't trust me in your bedchamber?"

"It's not you, I don't trust. I don't trust myself around you."

Kalen smiled. "That's a good sign."

Norian tried not to smile back, but the man's charm was too much for him, and a slight grin broke loose on his face.

"So again, I ask: why are you here, Kalen?"

All at once, Kalen's eyes filled with water. The sight of it tore at Norian's heart, knowing it was he who was causing this beautiful man pain.

"I am here because I cannot lose you. I am here because you are my mate, and this decision is not yours alone to make. My life and my sanity depend on what you decide."

Norian's heart pounded. He thrust his hands behind him so Kalen wouldn't notice their trembling. "Kalen, please don't make this any more difficult. I still need more time to reflect."

Kalen took a step forward. "What is there to reflect upon? You are an Alpha, and by some miracle, you stumbled into a pack who not only accepts you but welcomes you—a pack who enthusiastically awaits the day you step up to take charge. On top of all that, a member of that pack is your destined, true mate, something which few lycans ever find in their lifetime. How many more signals can the universe give you that this is the right decision? This is where you belong, Norian, with your pack. With me."

Norian took a step back and found himself pressed against the hallway wall. He wanted to push Kalen from him, to run far away, but found he could not. His legs were frozen, his heart rammed against his ribcage.

"Kalen," Norian said, his voice almost a whisper. "I can't."

"I know," Kalen said. "And I would never take that decision away from you. If your hope is lost because of me, you would never forgive me. Nor would I forgive myself. But that doesn't mean we can't do this."

Before Norian realized what was happening, Kalen pressed himself against him. Kalen's hardness pressed against his own and Norian groaned.

Kalen brushed a finger along Norian's lips, and then they locked eyes. "May I?" Kalen asked. "Please?"

"You may," Norian said in a voice he barely recognized.

Kalen gently placed his hands on the side of Norian's face and brought his lips to Norian's in a kiss that was almost like a whisper, a waft of air. Without thinking, Norian opened his mouth and allowed Kalen's warm tongue to enter. He tasted of mint, and Norian fell into the kiss, savoring the sensation of Kalen's mouth on his. He reached around and pulled Kalen to him tighter, Kalen's bulge pressing up against his own, causing him to press all the harder until his cock strained. Their tongues melded together as the kiss continued. All at once, Norian noticed another presence. His wolf. His wolf wanted out, and it wanted out now. It steadily rose to the surface, aching to burst through.

In a panic, he pushed Kalen away. His breath came in short, rapid gasps. "Stop!"

Kalen stared at him, eyes wide. "Norian! What is it? What is wrong?"

He shook his head, unable to speak at first. He was bent over, his hands grasping at his knees. Bile rose in his throat as panic seized him. "The wolf," he rasped. "I think I'm about to change. This is the same sense I had each time I shifted, right before the horrible pain came." He looked at Kalen with anguish in his eyes. "Help me. Make it stop."

He then heard Kalen speak, but not out loud. Instead, his voice was in Norian's head.

"Concentrate only on my voice. Now focus on your breathing. Breathe slowly, Norian. Slowly."

Norian's head snapped up. "How are you doing that?" he croaked. "You're in my head."

"Don't speak Norian. I'll explain later. Listen to me. Listen to the slowness of my voice. Concentrate on the slowness of your breathing. Fall into my voice and find calm. Listen to only me, connect with only me. Together, we find the calm, the peace. We are all that exists right now. You and me. Slowing down our breathing now. Slowing down our heart now. All fear disappears as we replace it with absolute serenity. Norian, I am with you. I am you. We're together, Norian, calm. Peaceful. It's time for the wolf to go back to sleep. It's not yet time to emerge. Sleep."

Before he knew it, calmness filled him, and the pain he was expecting never arrived. The wolf had retreated, pushed back deep inside of him. His breathing slowed, and his chest no longer pounded. He was safe.

"Now that wasn't so bad, was it? Didn't I tell you we were much better together?"

"I don't know what you did or how you did it, but thank you."

"I only connected with you on another level," Kalen said aloud. "Lycans can connect mentally and emotionally with each other. It usually takes a bit of practice to master. This is how we are guided through our first change. A more experienced lycan connects with the novice and is with them throughout the entire first transformation, teaching them how to master their wolf. It usually takes a while to build up the first connection." Kalen swallowed. "But with you, it was completely different. Before I realized what was happening, there was a pop, and the connection was instantly there between us. It is never this easy to link with another—it typically takes months of work beforehand and an abundance of patience to achieve. But with you, it was immediate. I imagine that it's because we are mates. It's only natural for us to connect on that level."

Norian nodded. "It appears as though I still have a lot to learn."

Kalen brought his hand up and lightly touched Norian's cheek. "Will you let me teach you? Let me show you that this life is not as bad as you imagine? Before you decide, allow me to show you our life from my perspective. You might be surprised."

Norian stared at him in silence for several moments. Then he nodded. "As long as you don't push me into physically partnering with you. I can't do that yet and risk throwing away my chances for a cure. I hope you understand."

Kalen nodded reverently. "I accept and will always abide by your wishes." He pointed to the end of the hallway. "Can we go into the drawing-room to talk? The hallways tend to have big ears."

Norian smiled and nodded. He followed Norian to the same room they had taken him to when he first arrived. When they entered it, a robust and gamey scent attacked Norian's nostrils, an odor he hadn't noticed the first time he was here. It was a familiar odor, maybe one that he'd probably encountered a long time ago, perhaps during his childhood but could not quite place. He took a deep breath and wrinkled his nose. His inability to identify it frustrated him. Then it hit him. It was lycans. He could smell that other lycans had recently been in this room.

Kalen gestured to an empty chair across from where he was standing. Norian sat down, facing Kalen.

"My first question is, what happened back there?" Norian asked. "Why was I starting to change? I thought I could only change during the three nights of the full moon."

"It also surprised me. Normally, lycans can only change during the full moon; the exception being the Alpha, who changes the day before and the day after as well. When my parents were first instructing me about our ways, I remember my father talking about a lycan's mate and how fulfilling it can be to find one's true mate. He also mentioned that if he had found his mate, he would have had even more power, with one of those powers being the ability to change at will. But being that he had found Mother instead, he figured The Fates did not intend for him to have such an ability—for my mother provided him with a different sort of power—one of love and devotion."

"So you think my wolf trying to come through had something to do with me kissing you?"

"It's likely. Though we haven't mated, I think the pull between us was strong enough to awaken the desire to shift."

"So you mean to tell me I might now change any time or any place, with no control over it?"

"That's not what I'm saying at all. I'm pretty sure that you can't actually shift during a non-full moon night, especially during the day and especially non-voluntarily. A mated Alpha, however, has *enormous* control over when they change, and as Mother said, you'd be able to change at will. You just haven't learned how to control your wolf yet."

"But we haven't mated! So why did I almost change back there? Was it just being close to you that made me feel like I was on the verge of transforming?"

"No. I think there is more to it than that. What appeared to set it off was when we began kissing. Tell me, what did you experience right before?"

Heat rose into Norian's cheeks. "While we were kissing, you mean?"

Kalen nodded. "Right before you became aware of the wolf."

"I was enjoying your touch and the softness of your lips when I began losing control. I had the sudden urge to bite you on the neck and throw you down onto the floor. Right as that thought crossed my mind, I felt it."

Kalen wiped his brow and then folded his hands in his lap. "I think I might have an idea what happened. I think your wolf wanted to mate with me."

Norian blushed. "I admit the thought had crossed my mind." He looked at the floor. "And it wouldn't be the first time I've thought about you in such a way."

"No, no, no. Not you, Norian, the wolf inside of you. It sensed you were kissing your mate so its instincts took over, urging you to take it to the next level. It wanted you to perform the mating ritual so it could come into his true power."

"You talk about the wolf as though it has its own mind."

"In a way, it does. While it is a part of you, it's also a separate being, with its own needs, desires, and instincts. So while the two of you do reside in the same body, there is a separateness as well."

"So you're telling me that every time I kiss you, the wolf is going to try to break through and make us mate?"

Kalen raised his eyebrows and smiled. "Every time you kiss me? I'm liking the sound of that."

Norian felt himself blush. "I'm not sure I would dare risk that again. The change is not something I look forward to."

"We will learn to control the change, just as we did earlier. You just need to make the wolf understand that you're in charge."

Norian wrinkled his brow. "And how do I do that? I barely kept him down last time and did so only with your help. If I were alone when the transformation started, I wouldn't have had a chance of stopping it."

"Norian, you underestimate your power. Don't forget—you are an Alpha. You have immense power at your disposal, both as a human and as a wolf."

"So you keep telling me. But what good is power if I don't know how to wield it?"

Kalen smiled. "That's where my teaching comes in. I can help you harness and master this power." He gestured to the middle of the room. "Stand up. It's time for your first lesson."

Norian paused for a moment before standing, unsure of what was going to happen. He still didn't trust himself around Kalen. The attraction between them was too strong —and if things went too far between them, there was a lot to lose on his part.

Kalen slowly approached him and stood a mere inch from Norian. He brought his face closer to Norian's, a little at a time. Norian stepped back, as difficult as that was.

"You can't," Norian said. "Not after what just happened. I don't want to go through it again."

"Trust me," whispered Kalen. "We can control this together." He locked eyes with Norian. "This is only a lesson. We've both learned that kissing me attempts to bring out the wolf, right? So it's the perfect opportunity to learn how to master your instincts and how to keep the wolf at bay."

Norian raised his eyebrows. "Are you sure you might not be taking advantage of the situation a bit?" He didn't tell Kalen that he wanted to kiss him back just as badly.

Kalen grinned. "Perhaps a tad. But it is an important lesson."

Norian sighed, and his heart thumped in his chest at the thought of awakening the wolf within him. He closed his eyes. "Right. Go ahead, then. I'm ready."

"No, Norian. Open your eyes. You need to look at me during this. I need you to be present."

Norian opened his eyes, and Kalen leaned in for the kiss. Before their lips even met, the intoxicating scent of Kalen sent Norian's senses into a state of high alert. He braced himself, and then Kalen's warm, soft lips pressed against his. He opened his mouth and slid his tongue between Kalen's lips. Their hardness once again pressed together. Kalen wrapped his powerful arms around him and pulled Norian even closer to him, allowing Norian to relish the firmness of Kalen's hard body. That's when it happened again. The wolf wanted to rise.

His body involuntarily tensed up, and he muttered unintelligible words during the kiss.

"*I can sense him too, Norian. Don't talk out loud. Think your thoughts.*"

"*The wolf...*"

"*He only wants us to mate. Tell him it's not time yet. But tell him calmly. Don't let his adrenaline overtake you. The way to counteract him is through the calm.*"

"How can I be calm? He's trying to get me to change. He wants to break my bones."

Kalen's body rocked back and forth and realized Kalen was nuzzling him, causing him to sway. *"Feel my calm, Norian. Listen to my heartbeat and connect with it. Calm. Remember, you are the master of the wolf. He is not the master of you. You have absolute control."*

Norian melded with Kalen as if the two of them were becoming one, and to his surprise, the wolf receded. His body relaxed as he noticed his own heart—both of their hearts—return to normal. It was then he realized he was still kissing Kalen. He pulled Kalen all the closer, savoring the gentle exploration of Kalen's tongue in his mouth. He sighed into the kiss, relieved the wolf had abated, but also delighting in the thrill that kissing Kalen was giving him. The urge to mate with Kalen, to take him entirely as his, was nearly overpowering. With an enormous effort, he pushed Kalen away. The hurt was clear on Kalen's face.

"We can't," Norian said. "Not yet."

Kalen nodded. "I understand. Not until you find out whether killing Vadok will change you back."

"But if that happens, then we'll no longer be mates, right? Will we still feel the same way about each other? Will you still want me the way you want me now?"

Kalen's eyes widened in surprise. "Norian, being mates has nothing to do with being lycan. What I mean is that a lycan can have a human mate, and some of them do. Sometimes the gods give us a lycan mate; other times, a human. We have no say at all in the matter. So even if you find a cure and end up reverting to being human, it's quite probable we would still be mates." He brushed his hand against Norian's cheek. "We'll always be mates."

Norian smiled and grabbed Kalen into a tight hug. So

he could be with Kalen and be human! He feared that if he found a cure, he'd lose Kalen forever, that they would no longer be mates. As hard as it was to admit it, he wanted Kalen with all his soul and found it more difficult to resist him all the time. The thought of the man no longer being in his life was too much to bear. It was not only his wolf who wanted to mate with Kalen. It was the man, too.

They pulled apart, and Kalen grinned. "What was that for?"

"I'm so happy with you. So happy I found you."

"You have a strange way of showing it, avoiding me as you have been. Why it's enough to hurt a man's feelings."

"I know. This has all been very confusing to me. There's been a lot to take in these past weeks. Who would have guessed my life could change so quickly, from being a bored prince to an Alpha werewolf with a male mate? Just trying to process it all has been challenging." He sighed. "And you have made my decision even more difficult. The draw I feel toward you is becoming difficult to resist. Yet, if I walked away from you, a part of me would surely die. I doubt that I'd ever be complete without you."

Kalen nodded. "Such is the way of mates. Mates complete each other—they are two halves of a whole, as my mother says. Once you find your mate, it's nearly impossible to walk away. This is why I am fighting so hard for you, Norian. My sentiments are the same as yours. Without you, life would lose its meaning."

"It's why I've been avoiding you," Norian admitted. "The more time I spend with you, the harder it will be for me to leave. I also feared that if I became human again, then this whole mate thing would be erased."

Kalen took a deep breath and closed his eyes for a moment. "Kalen, I think you misunderstood me. When I mentioned we would still be mates, I meant it only from my side. Our bond would still exist, but you would no longer experience it as you do now. While I said lycans could have human mates, it is the lycan who recognizes the human as his mate, not the other way around, though human mates do seem predisposed to love the lycan in return. So yes, a human can fall in love with a lycan, but they will never experience the mating bond in the same way as the lycan or the intense, all-encompassing emotions that go along with it. In these situations, the lycan is always at the mercy of the human."

Norian sucked in a startled breath. "Are you saying I wouldn't have the same feelings for you that I do now?"

"It's exactly what I'm saying." Kalen swallowed. "I would still feel the same way toward you as my mate, but the connection you feel with me now would be significantly lessened. Of course, you could still choose to be with me, to care for me—maybe even love me, if your heart allows it. But your emotions would never be as strong for me as they are right at this moment. Only I would feel the mate connection between us."

Norian's heart sunk, and his chest clenched, nearly to the point of pain. He would lose his feelings for Kalen. Even though they could still be together as lovers, the thought of breaking his mate connection with Kalen terrified him. Could he do it? Could he walk away from his true mate and throw away his chance at happiness to become human again?

Tears welled up in Norian's eyes. His pain was obvious in his voice. "I'm unsure of what to do."

Kalen pulled him into an embrace. "Whatever you decide, I am here for you. I will follow you no matter where you go. I will accompany you to Tregaron, if this is your wish. You will never be alone, no matter what happens. I will always be at your side."

Norian wiped his eyes with his sleeve and nodded. "I just don't know if I can willingly break our bond."

"If it's any consolation, you won't experience the pain and longing as you do now. Yes, the mating connection will be removed from your end, but hopefully, love will replace it. I can only hope that when it's done, you'll still want me in your life as your mate. But believe me, Norian—I will not easily let you go. I will fight for you."

Norian nodded. "I hope you understand I have to at least try. I cannot let my father down. Nor can I abandon my kingdom."

"Then, let us return to our lessons."

"What are we working on next?" Norian asked.

"I think we need to practice more on keeping your wolf at bay." Kalen winked. "And since kissing is the only thing that brings him up at the moment..."

"You're not going to make this easy on me, are you?"

Kalen smiled. "Not if I can help it. So pucker up, Your Highness."

Norian closed his eyes, a grin plastered on his face. "Bring it on, then. I'm ready for you."

CHAPTER EIGHTEEN

THOMROS, DERIC, AND KALEN CROUCHED DOWN IN front of Norian, sticks in their hands. A low growl came from each of their throats as they moved in closer to where Norian stood. In a defensive stance, Norian tensed his body, gripping the stick he held so tightly that his knuckles glowed white. He braced himself for the attack.

All at once, Fruos dashed around the corner, out of breath and stick in hand. "Sorry I'm late," he said. "There was an altercation in the village that I had to tend to." He joined the other three men, crouched down, and growled.

"Okay," said Norian, glancing between each of the men. "This is so unfair that it's ridiculous. What chance am I going to have against the four of you?"

"I was sure you would have learned to defend yourself at the castle, Your Highness," said Kalen. "No?"

"Your Highness?" said Thomros. "Do we have to call him Your Highness?"

"Pay no attention to him," said Norian, dismissing Kalen with a wave of his hand.

"Norian, you didn't tell our boys that you're a prince as

well?" Kalen said. "Gentlemen, I introduce you to His Majesty Norian, Crown Prince of Tregaron."

Deric's eyes grew wide. "You are the Prince of Tregaron? A lycan? Who could have ever guessed?"

Norian straightened. He glowered at Kalen. "Kalen, I told you that this is not information I wish to share. If word got out to the wrong people, we could all be in danger."

Kalen inclined his head. "You can trust these three with your life. They would do nothing to jeopardize the safety of their Alpha."

"So, are we required to call you Your Highness?" Thomros said, a smile on his face. "Or will boss do?"

Norian let loose with an exasperated sigh. "Norian will be fine. So back to the unfairness of this situation...."

"Remember, you are Alpha," said Kalen. "Taking on four of us should be nothing for you. My father could level an entire field of foes."

"Your father was an experienced lycan and warrior," Norian said. "Less than a month ago, I was human."

"No matter," said Kalen. "The wolf is a part of you now, as is being Alpha. Allow your instincts to take over. Move your mind out of the way and act."

Norian crouched down. A hot hit of adrenaline rushed through his body. "Very well. But I still think one-on-one, at least to start, would be more even-handed."

Kalen made a circle with his hands, and the four men charged Norian.

Norian braced for the attack. He tensed and then all at once, a growl rose in his throat. His limbs moved on their own, executing moves of which he didn't realize he was capable. He swung around and knocked Deric to the ground. How he sensed the man was directly behind him, he had no idea. His gut screamed to him to duck, so he dropped himself to the ground, just as the stick that Fruos held swung through the air where his head had been a moment before. Instinctively, he bounded back, reached up and, with one swift move, took the stick from Fruos, leaving the man open-mouthed and empty-handed. Now, with a stick in both hands, he shot up and extended his arms. With a crack, he connected with both Fruos and Thomros. A moment later, both men lay writhing on the ground. Like a whirlwind, he spun around and pointed his stick at Kalen's throat and inched him backward until he was pressed against the wall. He went to kick Kalen's feet from underneath him when his body froze. His mind bellowed in his head, *"Mate. Must not harm."*

He lowered his stick and took a step back. Kalen flashed him a toothy grin. "Whoa. I thought I was a goner there for a moment."

"You almost were," Norian said. He creased his brow. "But my mind wouldn't let me touch you. It knew who you were to me."

"The wolf knew," mouthed Kalen, apparently so that the others couldn't hear. "It understood that you were my mate."

Norian gestured behind him. "Do the others...."

Kalen shook his head. "Not yet. Let's keep it that way for the moment. Until your quest is complete."

Norian heard a groan from behind him, and both men turned around. The other three men were on their feet. Both Fruos and Thomros were rubbing their chests, groaning.

"Where did you learn to do that?" Thomros asked. "Your technique is amazing."

"You moved so quickly that I never even saw it coming,"

Deric added. "Next thing I knew, I was on my ass, and you were already gone."

"I must agree with them," Kalen said. "You were quite impressive."

"I've never fought like that before. Never have I taken on more than one person and remained standing. It was as if another force took over, granting my limbs a mind of their own."

Fruos dropped to one knee and bowed before him, and the others followed.

"You truly are Alpha," Fruos said, his head still bowed. "We are honored to have you lead the pack."

Norian took a step forward. As he reached Fruos, the man turned his head as if he were bearing this throat to him. Norian knew what that meant. The man was acknowledging Norian's role as Alpha.

He glanced behind him at Kalen and noticed that Kalen's eyes appeared misty. He smiled and nodded.

Norian touched Fruos' arm. "Please rise, all of you," Norian said. "It is unnecessary to bow to me, for I have done nothing to deserve it. I am only like you—a lycan trying to find his way in the world. All I ask from you is your friendship and guidance."

"No, boss," said Deric. He lifted his head to meet Norian's eyes. "You're much more than that. You are our pack leader and protector. You are Alpha and because of that, we honor you and follow you."

"Not to mention a prince," Thomros added. "A real one." The other three men snickered.

"It's true, you know," Kalen said quietly beside him. "You speak of your responsibilities to Tregaron and its people." He gestured toward Thomros, Deric, and Fruos. "But you now have a responsibility for the pack as well—a responsibility to all of us. Now, *we* are your people. We are your family."

The presence of Kalen so close to him, the feel and smell of his breath, attacked Norian's senses. A rush of lust soared inside of him, causing a tent to rise in his pants. He turned his head to Kalen, and they locked eyes. A look of lust was plainly visible on Kalen's face as well.

Norian brought his hands to his groin to hide his tented trousers from the others. He caught Fruos' eyes and observed the strange expression on the man's face. No doubt the man noticed his erection and perhaps even the way he and Kalen looked at each other. He cleared his throat.

"I appreciate your loyalty and your trust," Norian said. "But realize that I have much yet to learn. I am new to this life, as you all well know. I hope I can depend on you for your guidance."

Thomros, Deric, and Fruos all nodded. Norian noticed Fruos did not once break his gaze. He feared what his reaction might be should he discover that he and Kalen were attracted to each other—that they were mates. Norian would have to be extra careful around him.

"We look forward to you leading us on a hunt the day after tomorrow," Thomros said.

Norian raised his eyebrows. "Huh? What hunt?"

"The moon is full the day after tomorrow," Thomros said. "It will be our first hunt with our Alpha."

Norian felt himself blanch at the thought of the painful transformation that awaited him—that would take hold of him tomorrow.

"I am to lead you on a hunt?" he asked. "But I don't know how. I've never...."

"That's what we are here for," Kalen said. "We will

teach you. Although you will be surprised at how natural it will come."

"I don't understand," said Deric, a confused expression on his face. "I gathered that you'd already turned during the last moon. You did not hunt during it?"

A tightness gripped Norian's chest as he recalled the unfortunate villager that he had killed, that his wolf had killed. "I recall little of it. The change was unexpected."

"This time, it will be different," Kalen added. "We will run with our Alpha this full moon. But again, we depend on your discretion. We want to keep Norian's status as Alpha a secret for a bit longer. Only until he returns from his quest. He will run with us as a normal non-Alpha lycan."

"Ha! You don't really believe you can keep something like that from the others, do you?" Deric said. "Good luck with that. Why, I can tell you're Alpha just from being close to you."

Before Norian could answer, Fruos stepped forward. "What is this quest you speak of? Cannot we assist in this matter?"

Norian shook his head. "Regretfully, it is a private matter, one that I must handle on my own. But I shan't be gone long. I hope to return before the next full moon."

"I think that's enough practice for today," Kalen said. "We thank you for your assistance."

"We?" asked Fruos. He had a stern look on his face.

"Yes, we," Kalen said matter-of-factly. "As I was formerly pack leader in the absence of an Alpha, my mother and I have taken it upon ourselves to help ease Norian's transition. Remember, he has never even been in a pack before, much less led one. Given that my father once was Alpha and I am the pack Beta, we have the sacred duty to provide Norian with as much knowledge as we can."

"Shall we practice again tomorrow?" Thomros asked. "Although after the beating we took today, I'm a bit hesitant to volunteer again."

Norian laughed. "Let's wait until after the moon. We can then resume our sessions."

The three men nodded and walked through the door and into the building. No sooner was the door closed when Kalen rushed to Norian and held him.

"It was killing me not to be able to touch you, to feel you next to me." He brushed his lips against Norian's neck. "Your smell drives me wild."

Then their lips met, and Kalen's tongue entered Norian's his mouth. As their tongues dueled, Norian felt his wolf awaken and try to emerge. But now he understood how to suppress it, how to push the wolf back into its slumber. A moment later, the tenseness was gone. He relaxed and allowed himself to fall into the kiss. Once he became aware of both their hardness pressing against each other, he reluctantly pulled away. His breath came in quick gasps.

"Do you think this is wise," said Norian. "Somebody could come around the corner or through that door at any time."

"You're right," said Kalen, flashing him a devilish smile. "Let's go to my chambers."

"You are incorrigible!" Norian shook his head and smiled. "But as you know, there are other reasons why we cannot proceed further."

"But kissing is good," said Kalen.

"Not if kissing leads to other things."

Kalen feigned innocence. "Norian, I would never allow that to happen."

Norian shook his head again. "You do realize that I don't trust you at all, don't you?"

Kalen flashed an evil grin. "That's probably wise. For I am not one to be trusted."

Norian felt his face grow solemn as his thoughts returned to the upcoming moon. "I didn't realize that the full moon was almost upon us. That explains why I was so anxious and stressed all morning. My body is preparing itself for that awful change. Oh, how I am dreading it."

Kalen reached out and took both of his hands. "Norian, it shall be nothing like the last time. I promise you. I will be with you this time, and I swear to you, you'll barely notice the pain. I'll teach you the proper way to change, the painless way to change." He winked. "It could even give you an entirely different perspective on being a lycan. Who knows? It might even cause you to abandon your quest for a cure altogether."

Norian held Kalen's gaze for several moments. "Getting close to you has already caused my perspective to change." He took a deep breath. "Oh Kalen, if it were only a simple matter of you and me to worry about, then there would be no decision to make. There would be nothing that could stop me from staying here with you." He brushed Kalen's face with his hand. "But you know of my responsibilities, my destiny. I cannot let my father down. I cannot let my kingdom down."

"I understand," Kalen said in a low voice. "But that doesn't mean I have to like it."

"So, back to the change. Is there anything that I need to do to prepare?

"We've already been preparing for the past several days. You've learned our ways. You've learned how to listen to your instincts, listen to the wolf within. You've learned how to be a lycan. You are ready."

Norian sighed. "You make it sound so easy."

"Ah, but it ism Norian! Once you learn how to transform properly, you'll be amazed at how easy it is. Once this full moon is past and you possess that new knowledge, you no longer need to fear the wolf inside of you. On the contrary, you can call him up when you need him."

"I can't imagine ever needing to do something like that."

Kalen raised his eyebrows. "One never knows. Sometimes in battle, it can be more than helpful to have an unfair advantage."

Norian smiled. "I suppose so. Although I couldn't imagine exposing my secret like that."

"It may not be an ordinary foe that you'd be fighting. It could be someone like Vadok."

Norian rubbed his chin. "You have a point, given that a werewolf's bite is the only thing that can vanquish him."

"Or so it is said," said Kalen. "One must not be too quick to believe all that one hears. Though there is often a grain of truth to some of these sayings, myths, and wives' tales, most cannot be taken literally."

"In other words, try not to get my hopes up."

"I'm not trying to dash your optimism. Far from it. I just don't want you to be disappointed if things don't turn out the way you hope."

Norian nodded. "Tomorrow, during the change, will I be locked up somewhere safe?"

A surprised look crossed Kalen's face. "Locked up? What a curious question. Whatever for?"

"So I don't hurt anyone! Last month, I killed a woman while I was in wolf form. That must never, ever happen again."

"Norian, that only happened because you hadn't learned how to control your wolf. You let it take you over completely, and in the process, you lost yourself. It'll be different this time, I promise. I'll be with you all along the way. You'll have full awareness of what you do when you're in your other form. But moreover, you'll be capable of reasoning, of making proper decisions."

"Are you saying that I'll be aware as I am now with you? That I can make a conscious effort not to harm anyone?"

Kalen grabbed Norian's hands once again. "That's exactly what I'm saying. Last time, you operated on instinct alone. This time, you shall learn how to remain in control, to cause the wolf to bow to you."

"But what about you? You can only change on the full moon. So how will you be able to walk me through it."

"The same way that we connected after we kissed. We will link minds together, and I'll lead you. I don't have to be in lycan form to do it."

"But where will you be during this?"

Kalen creased his brow. "Right next to you, of course. It will be easier for you if I'm right there."

"No! I'll kill you!"

Kalen laughed and brought his hands up to Norian's face. "No, you won't. I promise you, you'll have complete control. You'll know precisely what you're doing at all times."

"Kalen, no. I can't take that chance. Last time, I lost control completely, and someone died as a result. I cannot allow that to happen again—especially with you." Norian swallowed. "I can't risk hurting you. I can't risk losing you."

"You will neither lose nor hurt me. You need to have faith in yourself and in me. Trust me, you will not lose control." He looked up and paused for a moment, as if in deep thought. "And even if, by some misfortune, you lost control of the wolf, I assure you I would have nothing to fear. Your wolf would never harm his mate."

"You're sure of this? There is no possible way?"

"None. The mating instinct overpowers all others. Once your wolf sees me, it will do everything in its power to protect me."

"I won't try to jump your bones or anything like that, will I?"

"Now, there may be a danger of that," Kalen said, flashing Norian a wicked grin. "So thus, it's vital that you keep your wolf under control." He laughed. "Being raped by a wolf while I'm in human form doesn't particularly appeal to me."

"No way, Kalen. I have to be locked up during this. You must do this for me."

"I'm teasing you, Norian. Your wolf would never try to rape me. Again, there's the whole 'not hurting your mate' thing."

"I hope you're right about all this. But it still would be safer to lock me up. Is there a cell or dungeon that you can put me in?"

"Unfortunately, our small village does not have all the modern conveniences that your castle has. We do someday hope to build a dungeon with the best stretching and torture devices gold can buy."

Norian narrowed his eyes. "You're making fun of me again."

Kalen's eyes twinkled. "Perhaps." He then took a deep breath. "If it makes you feel better, I could chain you to one of the gigantic oaks in the woods. There is little chance you'd escape."

Norian breathed a sigh of relief and nodded. "Yes, thank you. I would appreciate that." He took a deep breath. "I hope you understand. After the last time, I don't trust myself."

"I would probably react the same way. It hurts me knowing what you went through last time. This time will be different, I assure you." He creased his brow and then looked to the ground. "I just hope those chains will hold."

"What? The chains might not hold?"

"Don't worry. If they don't, I have a plan."

"What's that?"

"I'll just run you through the heart with a silver-tipped spear."

Norian felt his eyes grow wild, and all at once, a deep, vicious growl escaped from his throat.

Kalen smiled. "That's my boy."

CHAPTER NINETEEN

Norian threw his spear against the maple tree with such force that it buried itself several inches into the bark. It would undoubtedly be a challenge to remove it, something he would not do now. Today, he didn't have the patience for much of anything. His nerves were so much on edge that he wanted to scream. His body ached, he was restless and could barely sit still for more than a moment, just like last time.

He grunted and slammed himself on the ground next to the tree. He closed his eyes and tried to calm his rapid breathing. How he would remain in control during this change was beyond his comprehension. Hell, he could barely control himself now. He winced, remembering the look on Kalen's face when he'd snapped and told him to leave him the fuck alone. Acting like that was out of character for him, especially where Kalen was concerned. He never wanted to do or say anything that would hurt Kalen. It was this damnable upcoming change. Or pre-change. It made him crazy.

A strange sound all at once caught his attention. It was a

low squawk coming from the brush on his left. He stood still and squinted his eyes, trying to figure out what the strange noise was. It struck a familiar chord within him, making him think that he'd heard this sound before, that it was a sound he should know.

He slowly crept to the source of the noise. A sudden rustling of leaves caused him to step back for a moment, not knowing what sort of creature was hiding in the under-growth. Then, all at once, a large black raven crept out from under the bushes. It raised its head to look at him and let loose with a loud croak.

"Belkas?" He said out loud. He felt his heart thud in his chest as he stood frozen, staring at the bird. It was his pet raven that he'd left in Wayf's care. The bird was well-trained never to leave the castle grounds, and indeed it hadn't up until now. It had imprinted on humans when it was only a baby and since then, had followed him and Wayf around constantly. In all actuality, it was more Wayf's pet than his, as it was a rare moment when the raven was not at Wayf's side. While everyone referred to Belkas as his pet, the bird's heart truly belonged to Wayf.

So what was it doing this far away from the castle on its own? He jerked his head from left to right, half expecting Wayf to walk out of the forest. But all was quiet.

"Wayf?" he called out. He waited several moments, but there was no answer.

Another croak caused him to direct his attention back to the bird. Belkas appeared to be panting, and he teetered back and forth, seeming to have a difficult time remaining upright. His feathers were tattered and ruffled, as if he had just flown through a violent storm. Its eyes were opened wider than usual, and the bird locked his gaze on him as if he expected

Norian to do something. Norian held out his arm, and the bird flew up and landed on his wrist. The animal wobbled a bit, and Norian feared for a moment that it would fall. But it finally steadied itself and continued to stare at Norian.

"What are you doing here?" Norian asked, as if he expected the animal to answer. "How did you find me?"

As Norian eyed the bird, a strong, pungent odor drifted to his nostrils. Smoke. The bird had flown through a fire at some point. Norian felt his body seize up as the reality of the situation grasped him. Something must be wrong at the castle. Wayf would never have allowed Belkas out of his sight, but yet, here he was in Norbury. Wayf must have sent him. He must have somehow charmed the bird to fly to him —to let him know something was amiss at home. Norian's breathing became labored, and his intuition screamed at him. Fire. Someone had attacked the village! The village was on fire!

He locked eyes with the bird and noticed the knowing expression on the bird's face, almost as if the bird understood what he was thinking. The bird's head nodded up and down vigorously as if in agreement, and squawked loudly several times. The smell of smoke seemed even more potent now, and Norian's panic rose even further.

"Wayf sent you, didn't he? He sent you for help."

The bird stared at him and seemed to quiet down. Norian took a deep breath as he slid closer towards an inescapable decision. Vadok and his quest would have to wait. There remained only one thing to do now. He had to return home immediately to Tregaron, back to the castle. If indeed someone had dared attack his village, then Norian would see to it that it was a decision they would come to regret.

~

BELKAS CONTINUED to drink from the fountain in the backyard. Both Kalen and Lady Auryon stood silently with him as he explained his fears.

"It's impossible," Kalen said. "You cannot leave now."

"I realize that this is difficult for you, but it is something that I have to do. Can't you see? I sense deep in my gut that someone has attacked my kingdom. Someone sent the bird here as a plea for help, a request that I return to Tregaron. I must protect my kingdom."

"I understand that," Kalen replied. "And I can see the panic written all over your face. But you cannot travel now. Perhaps you have forgotten that the full moon is tomorrow? That means that you shall change tonight and the next two nights. I shall change tomorrow as well. We cannot risk being seen outside of the village. The hunters are a genuine threat to us and something not to be ignored."

Norian looked at Kalen, turned his glance to Lady Auryon, and then back to Kalen. He inhaled deeply, then nodded. "Yes, of course. I have to admit that I did momentarily forget the full moon and what that means for me. I was so concerned about my father and our kingdom that it'd momentarily slipped my mind." He rolled his eyes. "How I could have forgotten about it is beyond me, given that my entire body itches and makes me want to jump out of my skin." He creased his brow and brought his hand up to his chin. He smiled weakly. "I will take chains and a lock with me and chain myself to a tree before the change occurs. I'll make sure I'm well off of the road when it happens."

Lady Auryon shook her head. "It's much too dangerous to travel outside the boundaries of Norbury at the full moon. The moment you let loose with a howl, the hunters will come from miles around to find you. And find you they will—defenseless and chained to a tree."

"And moreover, you have not yet learned how to control yourself," Kalen added. He lowered his voice. "Remember what happened the first time you changed. We certainly don't want a reoccurrence. You could hurt someone, or someone could hurt you. The more times you change without controlling your wolf, the stronger your wolf becomes, and the more he takes over your being. This is exactly how rogue lycans are created. This is when you become truly dangerous—a constant threat to yourself and others."

"But I have to," Norian said. His voice cracked as he spoke. "You speak about your pack. But now it is my pack that is being threatened, for my people and my family are my pack. So it is my duty as the Prince to defend my kingdom."

"And it is your duty as Alpha to ensure that no harm comes to yourself," Lady Auryon said. She brushed her hand against Norian's cheek. "You are, as of yet, new and unrestrained. I understand your responsibility to your people, but don't forget—you have one to yourself and to us, too. You are the pack leader now, and we are your people. This is not something that will go away. It is also your obligation to learn how to retain control while in lycan form and how to fully use your lycan abilities. It would do no one any good for you to dash off in anger or panic before you learn how to control your wolf. As Kalen said, doing so may put others in peril, and eventually, you will be lost to yourself and to us. Wait the three days and learn with us. Learn what it is to be a lycan. Learn what it is to be an Alpha. Then you may go and take this knowledge with you. Do this, and you shall be stronger when the time comes to confront whatever awaits you in Tregaron."

Norian nodded, feeling defeated. "You're right, of course. Being out alone during this time of month scares me more than anything. I shall heed your advice and wait until after the third transformation. Then, I shall depart for my kingdom."

"You mean *we* will depart after the third transformation," Kalen said.

"We?"

"You certainly don't think I'm going to allow my mate to venture off on a dangerous quest by himself, do you? Not gonna happen, Love."

Norian shook his head. "I will not put your life in danger. I've no idea what the situation is like in Tregaron, and there is no way that I'm going to jeopardize your life. You need to understand this." He paused, then swallowed. "I just can't lose you."

Kalen put both of his hands on Norian's shoulders. Norian shuddered underneath his warm touch. Kalen met his eyes and then smiled. "Norian, I suspect that perhaps you don't understand how this works. Let me put it to you simply. A lycan does not leave their mate's side, no matter what the danger, no matter what the cost. Ever. It is not done, and I shall certainly not do it. I will be by your side to fight with you, to encounter whatever dangers may lie ahead. Norian, you will not undertake this alone."

Norian's face tightened. "As your Alpha, I command you to stay here."

Kalen smiled and then laughed. "Good try, but that doesn't work on me. You may be Alpha, but as my mate, we are equals. So you're stuck with me, like it or not."

Norian threw a glance over at Lady Auryon, hoping for

support. "You don't intend to let him do this? He could get killed."

"As could you," Kalen interjected. Norian ignored him and continued to stare at Kalen's mother.

Lady Auryon closed her eyes for a moment as the two men waited for her response. "No. I do not want my son to accompany you."

"See, I—" Norian began.

Lady Auryon held up her index finger between them to silence him. "But," she continued, "he must. No sane lycan would ever allow their mate to venture into a dangerous situation alone and unprotected. I know you've heard this before, but it is true and bears repeating. Once a lycan finds their mate, there is nothing that can tear them apart. If one of them perchance dies, then the other dies as well. And if the now partnerless mate doesn't die, then they may as well have because, from that point forward, life is meaningless to the surviving wolf. You see, Norian, Kalen is more than your mate. He is the missing part of you. He is you. Should one of you perish, it would be as though the other had lost all of their limbs."

"Tell him about Efrain," Kalen said.

Her face fell, and she nodded. "Efrain was a strong, powerful lycan, a true warrior. By accident, he found his mate, a lovely young lycan woman named Kara. She belonged to a small yet friendly pack in a neighboring village, and from the moment they encountered each other, they immediately were joined. We decided she would come to live with us and join our pack. Everyone in our village loved her and welcomed her, and she quickly became an essential member of our pack." She paused, wiped a tear from her right eye, and continued. "Fanatical hunters have attacked us several times over the years. One such hunter integrated himself into our village. Oh, he was sly, that one. He had us all fooled. We knew he wasn't a lycan, but he was so convincing that we mistakenly considered him an ally. He told us that his former wife, who unfortunately passed away from an accident, was a lycan. Her death left him to wander alone in the search for another pack that might accept him as one of their own, for he felt more at home with wolves than humans. All of our hearts went out to the supposedly lost fellow. But one evening, he found himself alone with Kara, and before she had a chance to defend herself, he slit her throat."

Norian gasped. She gave him a soft nod and continued. "I know not what his plans were. Did he think he could take all of us out, one by one, alone? Efrain immediately knew something was wrong with his mate. The connection between mates is a strong one. A lycan knows when their mate is in danger, hurting or," she brought her hand up to her throat for a moment, "or dead. It did not end well for our clever hunter friend. Efrain found him with Kara, both of them drenched in blood. He literally ripped the hunter apart with his bare human hands. After that, he was never the same. He would speak to nobody and always walked with his head bowed down, refusing to even look at anyone. Eventually, we barely saw him at all and it was rare that he left his house. Less than a month later, we found him dead in his bed. No one in the village could figure out what killed him, though I'd venture to guess he simply lost the will to live." She locked eyes with Norian. "Young Efrain died of a broken heart."

Nobody said anything for several moments. Finally, Kalen broke the silence, his eyes glued to the ground. "I do not want ever to go through what Efrain did." His gaze rose to Norian's. "I do not want to find out what life would be like without you. I couldn't bear it. Do you understand now? Do you know why I cannot let you do this alone? A mated lycan's utmost priority is the protection of his mate. It would be inconceivable for me to stay here without you now that we have found each other. I will not leave your side. Ever. It's not even open for discussion."

Norian took a deep breath. His hands were shaking. He had to tell Kalen the real reason that he didn't want him along.

"I get it. I feel it too. But you can't accompany me, Kalen. You just can't."

Kalen waved his hand in the air. "Have you heard nothing that we just said? Do you not grasp that you are no longer Norian but are now Norian and Kalen?"

"I can't stand being around you."

Lady Auryon's and Kalen's eyes grew wide. Both of them were speechless. Kalen looked crushed.

"I don't understand," Kalen said in a voice that was barely audible.

"Don't misunderstand me," Norian said. "I need you with every depth of my being. But the more I'm with you, the more I weaken. Your smell intoxicates me to the point of near insanity. Your voice makes me shiver, your touch causes me to lose my reason. My wolf tries to jump out of me every time you are near. I want you so badly that my resolve to find a cure is crumbling. I'm torn between my obligation to my kingdom and my desire for you, and I don't know what to do. Yes, I want you to go with me, with all my heart and soul. I never want you away from me, not even for a moment. But I don't know if I can survive a trip with you, without," he paused, "taking you completely. But if I do that, then my kingdom will be lost to me. My father will be lost to me. I could never return to my people."

"We are your people, too," Kalen said.

"I know. That's why this is so difficult."

Kalen took hold of Norian's hands. "I feel the same way being around you. But I promise you, I will always respect your wishes. I would never push you to consummate our relationship until the time comes that you are ready. I'll do everything I can to ensure that your resolve stays intact. I only want you when you are completely open and willing to have me."

"But that's the thing, Kalen. I desire you with every fiber of my being. I'm just afraid that I will give into that desire."

"I shall not allow it." He smiled at Norian. "I promise you, your virtue is safe."

"But what if I do defeat Vadok? What if I no longer am a lycan afterward?"

Kalen shrugged his shoulders. "I don't know. Nobody does. All we can do is do our best and follow our heart."

Hot tears welled up in Norian's eyes. "But I don't want you to die, like Efrain."

"I won't."

"How can you be sure? None of us knows anything."

"Exactly. So stop worrying. What you need to focus on is getting through the next three days and learning how to painlessly and safely transform. So let that be your primary concern right now."

"It's difficult when I have no knowledge of what's going on in my village. My father and Wayf could be in danger, or worse. This is not something that I can easily put out of my mind."

"You have to," said Kalen. "The transformation is going to happen whether you want it to or not. If the myth is wrong and it turns out that there is no cure for a lycan bite, then you need to learn how to live with this, to be our Alpha."

Norian nodded. "I understand." A painful cramp seized him, and he doubled over. He groaned.

Kalen rushed to his side. "It's only your wolf getting restless. Go to your room and try to rest. I'll come to get you shortly before moonrise."

"But first, come to the kitchen with me," said Lady Auryon. "I will show you how to make a tea that will ease your suffering. We all drink it several times throughout the day of our change. You will be amazed at how your symptoms will mostly disappear."

Norian allowed himself to be led to the door by Lady Auryon. He was shaking now, almost uncontrollably. He locked eyes with Kalen one last time before disappearing into the house.

CHAPTER TWENTY

His bones ached, his muscles hurt, and his skin was so sensitive that he could stand nothing touching it. The tea that Lady Auryon had given him helped most of the day, but its effects had now worn off. The panic welling up inside of him didn't help his situation, either. Even though he knew what was coming, he was in no better of a position than last time when the change happened. He recalled the initial pain of all three previous transformations, and he shuddered with dread.

Norian got up off the bed, giving up on trying to nap, and paced his room. He could sense the wolf within him scratching at his skin, demanding to be released. He closed his eyes and took a deep breath, trying to center himself and still his thoughts. A powerful, sweet scent then attacked his senses, bringing him to full alert. A tent rose in his pants as the erotic aroma drifted over him. A light knock sounded at the door, followed by the sound of Kalen's voice.

"Norian?"

Norian opened the door and tried to smile at his mate. Kalen stepped in.

"You look like a wild man," Kalen said. He reached out and touched Norian's shoulder. "Are you alright?"

Norian nodded. "This is something that I'll never get used to. The anticipation and dread of what's coming."

"After tonight, that will all change, I promise you. You will no longer fear the change but welcome it."

"Right now, I find that difficult to believe," Norian said. "I wish I had your confidence."

"It has nothing to do with confidence, only fact." Kalen gestured towards the door. "Come. It's time to go."

"Already? But the sun won't set for a good hour yet."

"I've prepared a place for us, a little ways away from the village houses. I wanted to make sure that we were alone and not disturbed. Not everyone knows yet that there's an Alpha in their midst. A lycan transforming before the full moon would no doubt raise more than a few eyebrows. So it's best that tonight, we be on our own."

Norian nodded. "Lead the way."

The two men crept through the woods for nearly half an hour before coming to a clearing in the middle of which was a vast burr oak tree. On the ground were strewn a couple of sacks.

"Did you bring the chains?"

Kalen raised his eyebrows. "Chains? Whatever for?"

"Kalen! Please don't tell me you didn't bring the restraints. We talked about this—you promised!"

Kalen shook his head. "I told you, there's nothing to worry about."

"Have you gone mad? When I turn, I kill. I've done it before. I cannot put your life in jeopardy."

Kalen placed his hand over Norian's. The warmth of his skin and the sweet scent of his mate caused Norian's heart to pump wildly in his chest. His wolf whined inside of him.

"You won't hurt me, Norian. It's impossible. As I told you, a wolf would never harm its mate. It simply cannot be done. When in lycan form, a wolf will put its own life in danger to protect its mate. It doesn't matter whether the mate is in lycan form or human form. The mate's safety comes above all else."

A new panic rose up in Norian. "What if I don't know that you're my mate? Last time, I remembered nothing at all."

Kalen laughed. "Again, not possible. Sit quiet and ask your wolf. Does your wolf know who I am?"

Norian closed his eyes and tried to still his mind. The wolf was there, scratching at his skin. He silently asked the wolf if it would harm Kalen. His wolf bristled at the thought, and a snarl rose from his throat. Then, one word clearly popped into his mind. *Mate*. With that word came an overwhelming sense of love and protection, emotions he had never experienced before on such a level. He then understood on a deep level that his wolf would never harm Kalen. He breathed an audible sigh of relief.

"Do you comprehend now?" Kalen asked.

Norian wiped the wet from his eyes. Speechless, he nodded.

"So you see that there is nothing to worry about. I will be here the entire time, and you will not hurt me. So push that thought out of your mind."

Norian opened his mouth to speak when a cramp seized his stomach, and he doubled over. Kalen grabbed him and wrapped his arms around him. The pain passed.

"It's time," Kalen said. He stood up and began removing his clothes. He gestured to Norian to do the same.

"What are you doing?"

"You don't want to damage your clothes, do you? That's

the first preparation you must make. It is also easier to transform when your body doesn't have to rip through restrictive clothing."

"But why are you stripping?"

Kalen pursed his lips and winked. "Why not?"

"Kalen...," Norian began.

Kalen laughed. "Don't worry. I'm not going to try to ravage you, especially with your change this close at hand. I only want to ensure that you and I are on equal ground—with nothing between us. Not even cloth." His face took on an air of seriousness. "Just like we did before, we are going to meld minds. But only more so this time. That is to say, we will go much deeper, all the way down, past your consciousness, to the level of your instincts. During your change, we will become one, and I will guide you through it all. What's important is that you do not let go, that you continue to listen to me, connect with me. Understand?"

Norian nodded. Kalen sat cross-legged before him, and Norian followed. He then took Norian's hands, and the two men locked eyes.

"My teeth ache," Norian said.

Kalen smiled. "Only for a moment. Now, steady your thoughts." Kalen then grasped fingers with Norian and pressed the fingers of Norian's right hand to his mouth. "Can you feel him, Norian? Can you feel the wolf inside?"

Norian's wolf snarled in response. "Oh yes, he's definitely there."

"Good. Now listen to me carefully. What I am about to say is essential. The moon is a powerful, sacred, and compelling object and is to be respected. But you must not allow the moon to overpower you, to absorb you. If you do, you will be lost. Though it is true your wolf is bound by the moon—and is a slave to the moon—*you* are not. Be certain to make that distinction. The moon has the power to overtake your wolf completely, leaving him to operate only on the level of its instincts. During the transformation, if you allow it, those instincts rise to the surface and take over. That's what happened to you the last time. Your instincts—or should I say, your wolf's instincts—took over and absorbed your consciousness. The moon's power is strong and primal, and operates at a level you haven't dealt with before. That is why it overtook you in the way it did. What is essential is that you focus on your sense of self during the change and do not allow the primal force of the moon to take over. Recognize the wolf as only a part of you, not your complete essence, and in so doing, you shall retain your consciousness. Don't fight the transformation, but you still will need to be firm with the wolf. Allow him to come through, but not take over completely." Kalen smiled at Norian. "Are you with me so far?"

Norian nodded. "I think so. But how do I do it? How do I keep my consciousness? Last time, I don't even remember it overtaking me."

"This time, I shall be right here, with you. I will be part of your thoughts, and you will learn how not to give your wolf complete control. And don't worry about losing control. Remember, I'll be a part of you—and I won't let the primal forces take over. Instead, I will ensure that your consciousness remains in the driver's seat."

"So, what do I have to do?"

"Just don't let go of my hands and keep concentrating on my voice in your head. I'll guide you."

Norian's nerves thrummed, and his skin felt too tight for his body. A deep, pulling ache stirred in his bones. "I think I might be getting close."

"Close your eyes. Breathe in and out. In and out. *In and out. In and out.*"

"You're in my head," Norian said in his thoughts. *"I can hear you."*

At the presence of his mate, the wolf stirred and made its intentions known.

"Kalen, my wolf wants to fuck you."

"Not gonna happen. Tell it to behave."

"So now what?"

"Quiet your mind. Be still. Can you hear my heartbeat?"

"Yes, it's in perfect timing with mine. Wow, we really are part of each other."

"Yes, we are."

"Ah - it's coming! It's hurting now."

"Stop thinking about it and focus on me. Focus on us. I'm part of you, Norian, part of your body and your soul. Can you sense me?"

"Yes, you're there. There's something else there as well."

"It's my wolf Norian. It is looking forward to meeting its true mate. We are joined as one."

"True mates."

"Norian, listen to me. Breathe with me. Hear and experience my heartbeat—allow us to meld. The moon is pulling at you, trying to unleash your wolf and let it take over. Do not let it! You are in control. The wolf is only a part of you, it is not completely you. You are in charge. Recognize your wolf. Honor your wolf. Respect your wolf. But control your wolf."

"Honor, respect, control. Got it."

"How are you doing?"

That was a tough question for Norian to answer. He was barely hanging on to his mind. His instincts wanted to take over, to rule him completely. But now, there seemed to be an invisible barrier between him and his wolf. It clawed desperately, trying to scratch his way through.

"*My wolf is not happy.*"

"*That's because he was the boss last time. No longer. Together, we will keep your consciousness on the throne. Let your wolf know he has a choice: to come out and play with you in control or to stay where he is. Those are the new rules.*"

"*He's not gonna like that.*"

"*He'll deal. Now for the important part. Visualize a glass floor. You are on top, standing proudly on the floor. The wolf is beneath you. He is always beneath you. He cannot break through the glass and get to you. This is the barrier between your consciousness and complete instinct. This barrier allows you to keep standing, maintain control, and keep your instincts where they belong. The moon will cause your body to change, but can no longer take your mind along with it. Can you see it, Norian? Can you see the floor beneath you and the wolf?*"

"*I see it... and sense it. It's growing thicker.*"

"*Good. That's what we want. We're letting your wolf know that he can come out but must stay on his level. Stay on the level of instinct.*"

"*He's calming down. Hey, my pain seems to have stopped.*"

"*I notice it too, Norian. Your pain is now my pain. That's the thing, love. Once you've managed to fight your instincts and not allow them to take over completely, your body no longer fights the change. The pain will be minimal. What you experienced last time was your mind and body fighting the moon with everything they had, but they lost control. The wolf is a moon-bound creature. You are not. As long as you keep this thought at the forefront of your mind, you will maintain control.*

"My insides are hot, like fire. Like lava. I'm burning."

"It's the last step of the change. Are you still with me? Are you ready?"

"I think so. Still with you."

"Barrier?"

"Still there. Damn, I'm hot!"

"Let it go, Norian. You have your consciousness. You are in control. It's safe to let him out. You are not alone. I'm with you."

"You're sure I won't hurt you?"

"Positive. It's safe."

And then it happened. A bright light flashed before Norian's eyes, and then a loud pop echoed in the night. His body shifted, transformed—and Kalen was right there with him—still guiding him. Norian held his breath for a moment, waiting for the pain, but this time, there was only a brief spasm. It was done. Norian could see his furry paws on the grass. He felt strong, powerful, free. He drew air deeply into his lungs, and all at once, a familiar scent drifted into his nostrils. Kalen.

He looked up to find Kalen, but he wasn't there. Instead, there was a beautiful white wolf with deep green eyes watching him.

"Kalen?"

"Norian, thank goodness. I was afraid I'd lost you."

"I can still hear you, even as a wolf."

"You succeeded. You've maintained your consciousness. All your instincts are still there—they drive you and teach you, but you are not ruled by them.

"But you! You're a wolf, too."

"How about it? It's the darnedest thing, that."

"*But I thought you could only change on the full moon.*"

"*So did I. I have never heard of a lycan who wasn't an Alpha changing before the moon.*"

"*Is it maybe because you were in my mind during the change?*"

The white wolf shook its head. "*No, though it could be because you're my mate and an Alpha. Perhaps you have the ability to transform those around you. Or it could be our bond, our connection.*"

"*Good thing you got naked with me, hey?*"

"*Good thing. Now Norian, look around you. What do you see?*"

Norian looked around him for the first time. Everything was different. Even in the dark, all the surrounding objects jumped out. He could see the individual blades of grass and the grooves in the bark of the trees. He saw a mole running through the grass and bristled. A desired to pounce, to hunt filled him.

"*Not yet, love. There will be plenty of time tonight to hunt. For now, inhale the scents of the forest.*"

Norian raised his nose and inhaled. A rush of smells attacked his nostrils, each of them sweet and delicious, and they reminded him of the night. He found them intoxicating, and he became dizzy with drunkenness. As he continued to sniff, a deep earthy odor attacked his senses, and his cock hardened. Then, without realizing what he was doing, he howled in delight.

"*Kalen, what is that scent?*"

"*I call it freedom.*"

Norian howled again, and Kalen joined him, creating an eerie melody in the quiet night.

"*This is a much different experience than last time,*"

Norian thought to Kalen. "Last time, the pain was nearly unbearable."

"Never again will you experience that. From this point on, you will see only the beauty and power of being lycan. You are part of our pack. You will never be alone."

"It's so different from anything I ever could have imagined. I almost see it no longer as a curse, but something else entirely."

"A gift, Norian. It is a gift."

Norian's stomach rumbled.

"It is time to hunt Norian. Your first hunt."

"Not exactly my first," Norian reminded him. *"Although that is something I prefer not to think about."*

"It is your first as a true lycan. Last month, you were only instinct, nothing more. This time, you are whole and complete. Come, it is time to run."

With that, Kalen dashed off. Norian threw his head back in a howl and then was in pursuit. Although the other wolf was no longer visible, Kalen's sweet scent was strong and seemed to pull Norian with it. Nose to the ground, he followed the sweet fragrance, charging through the woods, not really thinking at all. His senses screamed '*wolf*,' and he screeched to a stop. Before him was Kalen, frozen stiff, tail pointed outwards. Norian stopped, stunned by the most alluring odor. Saliva fell from his mouth.

"What is that new scent? It's familiar to me and I'm certain I've smelled it before, but I can't quite place it."

"Hare." He gestured with his snout. *"It is hiding from us in the bushes."*

Kalen lowered his head and focused his eyes. There it was, huddled down next to the ground, as still as a marble statue.

"It is yours."

Permission now given, Norian dashed forward, no longer aware of anything else except for the hare. The animal shot out from the bushes. Norian could smell its panic and fear, both of which drove him forward even more resolutely. Before he knew it, he had the hare's throat in his jaws. One quick shake, and it was done. Suddenly, Norian was next to him. He met the white wolf's eyes.

"Come Kalen. Together we can eat."

"No, this is your kill. There will be enough for me later."

"I want to share it with you. Kalen."

"The first is always for the Alpha."

"But I am not just an Alpha. I am your mate. I want us to be equals."

"Very well. I will share this first meal with you. But know that when we are with the others, the Alpha always eats first. If he chooses, he can leave some behind for the others."

In a moment, all that remained was a pile of bones. The rest of the night, the two wolves ran, hunted, and played. Norian had never felt so free, so unencumbered by worry. Having Kalen at his side, he was invincible and, for the first time, complete.

Norian was running at full speed when a nip on his back leg slowed him down. He stopped and swung his head around to meet the white wolf's eyes.

"It is time to return to the grove where we started. Dawn is not far off."

With that, Kalen turned and darted off. Norian followed. In no time at all, they reached their tree. Kalen snuggled at the base of it, and Norian curled up to him, his head resting on top of Kalen's. He inhaled Kalen's intoxicating scent.

Mate.

Within moments, he slipped into unconsciousness.

CHAPTER TWENTY-ONE

THE SOUNDS OF CHIRPING BIRDS AND CHATTERING squirrels pulled Norian from a deep, pleasurable slumber. As he slowly moved into consciousness, he became aware that he was not alone. He opened his eyes. A muscled hairy arm was tightly wrapped around his chest and a furry warm leg was tucked in between his own. But what really got his attention was an ever so slight tapping of something against his back, and it didn't take him long to figure out what it was. The thought of it caused his own cock to harden, and an ache grew in his groin. This was not exactly the best position to be in—lying naked in a field with the one man he wanted more than anyone. A man he must not touch. His mate.

He pushed the thought of sex from his mind and sunk in, enjoying the sensation of Kalen next to him. He gently stroked Kalen's beautiful arm as thoughts of last night's escapades replayed themselves in his mind. Norian remembered everything—the nearly painless transformation into a wolf, the freedom and power he'd experienced, his heightened senses, and the hunt. He recalled his last meal, and his stomach lurched in response. He'll have to get used to his new dining habits when in the other form. Though it nauseated him right now, he was in heaven at the time. The meat had satisfied a deep craving inside of him, a longing he hadn't even known was there. After he got his first taste, he remembered how he'd wanted more—and more he'd gotten. They both feasted on a couple of hares and several rodents. Kalen promised him that the next time they would try for a deer. He tried to push away the nauseating thought of eating raw animals from his mind and instead, he focused on Kalen. He reached over Kalen's arm, laid his hand gently over Kalen's, and slowly laced their fingers together. Kalen stirred behind him.

"You're awake?" Kalen whispered to him.

Norian had hoped this moment could have lasted a bit longer. This moment of quietly enjoying the touch of the man he was now sure he loved without having to worry about evil sorcerers or fighting off his natural desire to make love to this man. All at once, he began to question his goals. After last night, perhaps being a lycan wasn't so bad after all.

"I am," Norian finally answered. He held onto Kalen's arm tighter.

"Are you okay?" Kalen asked.

"I don't know how I could possibly be any better than I am in this moment."

Kalen laughed. "Much different from last time, no?"

"All because of you."

"All because of *us*," Kalen said. "We did this together. All you needed was a little guidance." He sighed. "I still can't believe I changed as well—and I didn't even realize it was happening until I was looking at you through my wolf's eyes. I have to ask my mother if she's ever heard of this before. The ability of a normal lycan to change before the full moon."

"I'd hardly say you're a normal lycan. On the contrary, you're pretty extraordinary."

"You're just biased because you're my mate."

Kalen disentangled their arms, leaving behind a coldness where his touch had once been. Norian shuddered.

"You're cold," Kalen said. Norian could hear rustling behind him. He hoped that the sound was Kalen putting on his clothes, for he no longer trusted himself around his naked, beautiful mate. Norian sat up and crossed his arms. He turned his head, and there was Kalen, still naked, gathering up their clothes, his hardness poking outwards. Norian swallowed, and then Kalen met his gaze. His face flushed for a moment, and he put the bundle of clothes he was holding in front of him.

"Sorry about that," Kalen said. "I should have put on my trousers straight away."

"No need to be sorry," Norian responded. "You're beautiful."

Kalen's gaze moved down Norian's body. "So are you."

With great difficulty, Norian broke the gaze and looked down at the ground. "But... we can't."

Kalen audibly released the breath he was holding. "I know. It doesn't mean that I don't want to more than anything." He paused, then tossed Norian's clothes to him. "I was hoping last night might have changed things. That you might decide being lycan is not so bad."

Norian laid the clothes over his groin to hide his own erection and gave Kalen a weak smile. "Last night was an experience I shall not soon forget. You made the change so easy for me and taught me so much, all in one night. And I remember it all! Last night's adventure with you was a gift

I shall treasure forever. But this doesn't change the fact my kingdom appears to be in peril, and I am next in line for the throne. I would love nothing better than to take you right now and make you mine. This longing for you is so fierce I can barely contain it. But I must. At least for the moment."

Kalen nodded. "As promised, I shall try to be patient. It's difficult not to be jealous of your kingdom, as it's the only thing that's keeping you from me. But wait, we shall, until we discover the situation in Tregaron."

"I realize how difficult this is for you. For the both of us."

The two men dressed in silence then sat against the tree, their arms and shoulders touching. Kalen turned his head toward Norian, considered him for a moment, and then stood up.

"Regardless of our situation, it is now time for you to prepare."

Norian creased his brow. "For what? To change again tonight?"

Kalen shook his head. "Tonight is the full moon and I believe it's time for the pack to officially meet you. Word has gotten around that there is an Alpha in our midst, so we couldn't hide you much longer, even if we wanted to. Though we'd initially said we'd wait until after the full moon to introduce you, it's apparent you're more than ready, and the best way for an Alpha to build solidarity with a new pack is to hunt with them. I'm sure everyone is more than eager to meet and run with their new Alpha."

Bile rose in Norian's throat. "But I can't!" He stood up, crossing his arms. "I'm not prepared. Why, I've barely learned how to transform properly. I am in no position to lead anyone, anywhere."

"Ready or not, you shall have to. It is your duty as Alpha of this pack."

"But I'm not Alpha of this pack. I'm not Alpha of any pack. I just want to get back to my kingdom and help."

Kalen looked stricken. Norian immediately regretted his words.

"But you *are* Alpha of this pack." Kalen's voice crackled with emotion as he spoke. "I am Beta of this pack, and as you are my mate and an Alpha. This automatically positions you as Alpha of the Norbury pack. So why do you keep fighting this? Why can't you accept who you are?"

Norian took a deep breath and took a step towards Kalen. "I do accept who I am." He then took Kalen's hands. "I'm scared, Kalen. I've barely adjusted to being a wolf, and now I'm tasked with being the leader of an entire pack. I've never led anything, much less a pack of wolves."

"How do you intend on leading a kingdom if you're afraid to be boss to a few lycans?"

Norian stepped back. "Now, you're not being entirely fair. Ruling a kingdom and playing head wolf are two different things."

"You aren't playing head wolf. You *are* the head wolf."

"So everyone keeps telling me. But I've had training my entire life on how to manage a kingdom. I know nothing of being head of a pack."

"All you need to do is listen to your instincts. The rest will come naturally." Kalen narrowed his eyes. "I've observed you these many days, and though you may not recognize it, your Alpha traits are strong. You need only to allow them to come out. And never forget that I am always here to provide guidance and to answer any questions you might have."

Norian sighed. "So, what is it that's expected of me?"

"First, you'll need to give a speech."

"Very funny."

"Not funny. True. You don't realize what a significant occasion this is for the pack. Do you have any idea how rare Alphas are? You being here, being part of this pack, is something few packs get to experience. An Alpha protects a pack, which in turn empowers it—strengthens it. It has often said that a pack without an Alpha is aimless and vulnerable."

"I'm sure you and your mother did a fine job of leading the pack."

"Not the same thing. While we did manage to maintain order, the pack didn't always respect our orders. Additionally, our pack was more susceptible to outside attacks without an Alpha."

"So I really need to give a speech?"

Kalen nodded. "All you have to do is introduce yourself, tell everyone where you come from and how happy you are to be part of their pack. They need something—someone— to restore faith in the pack and in themselves. Ever since my father was killed, the people here have almost lost hope. If even an Alpha can be killed, what chance do they have? They see an Alpha as someone who can protect them from outside influences like hunters and the likes of Vadok. An Alpha represents bravery and courage, but most importantly, hope."

"That's quite a charge you expect me to fill," said Norian. "I'm uncertain myself about my goals or even what my future will be. How can I convince them everything will be fine? Especially since I'll be leaving the day after tomorrow."

"Whatever you do, you must be careful not to tell them

that you are planning to leave. Such a declaration would most likely not end well for us."

Norian nodded. "I remember you said they would not be too willing to let me go." He raised his eyebrows. "But what about you? You were the leader here before I arrived. How can you leave them as well?"

"It's no longer up to me. You are my mate. I simply cannot allow you to go without me. And even if I stayed, I assuredly would be no good to the pack here because my mind and heart would be only on you. You see? Mates are forever. It's a deep soul-level bond from which one cannot simply walk away." He narrowed his eyes and studied Norian's face. "You know this."

Norian nodded. "I do. To be truthful, the thought of me leaving you behind terrifies me. But it also terrifies me to knowingly put your life in danger. I can't even begin to fathom what life would be without you."

Kalen reached and took hold of Norian's hand, intertwining their fingers. He gave Norian's hand a tight squeeze. "You won't have to. I'll be right by your side, no matter what occurs. No matter how many hateful sorcerers we have to battle. My mother will rule in my stead until we return."

"But about that speech," Norian said.

Kalen smiled. "You will be surprised how naturally it'll come to you. I've seen you in action. I've seen the Alpha part of you take over when needed. Have faith in yourself, and you'll do fine. Remember—just speak from your heart. Oh, and never lie to a lycan, for we can easily distinguish an untruth."

Not lie to a lycan? How was he going to pull that off? How would he convince the pack he was ready and willing to lead them when in truth, he was leaving town to look for a cure? Although this was no longer entirely true. His primary goal in going was to get to Tregaron and find out why Belkas, who looked and smelled like he had flown through an enormous fire, was sent to him without Wayf.

"Never lie to a lycan, you say? What will you have me tell them then? What if it comes out that I'm leaving?"

"If someone discovers your plan, you tell them the truth."

Norian raised his eyebrows. "And what truth might that be?"

"Tell them you must journey to Tregaron—your home—for the people there may need aid, that you are taking me with you as a reinforcement and will return as soon as you can. The truth."

"That's somewhat reassuring." He creased his brow. "You know what's funny about all this?"

"Something's funny about this?" A playful grin danced on his lips.

"More like peculiar. While I was growing up, I was forced to train constantly on how to rule as king. I focused my entire life on that far-off goal. And you know what? The mere thought of it terrified me. The last thing I ever wanted to do was to be king, to lead a kingdom. I secretly prayed my father would live to a ripe old age—that he would outlive me, so I would never have to take the throne. Leading others is something I've never wanted to do. And yet, here I am again. This time, I am reborn as an Alpha lycan, a completely inexperienced one at that, who is expected to take control and lead a pack. It seems I cannot escape this obligation—this duty of leading others."

Kalen smiled. "It's almost as if it's your destiny to be a leader, no matter what the circumstances."

"I wonder if you might be right? It's certainly looking

that way. The trouble is, I do not want it. I don't want to be a leader. I never did."

Kalen rested his hand on Norian's shoulder. "Unfortunately, it is not up to us to decide whether or not we like what the universe has in store for us. My mother says that the fates have a plan for each of us, and that plan doesn't necessarily coincide with our own."

"Yeah, I'm beginning to understand that," Norian said.

"So maybe it's time to stop fighting it. Maybe it's time to accept the fact that you are an Alpha and a prince, and do whatever it takes to fulfill those two destinies."

Norian locked eyes with Kalen, and both men were silent. Finally, Norian said, "You may be right. But how to choose? It is not an easy decision to make."

"What decision? Why decide at all? You're an Alpha and the Prince of Tregaron. Why can't you be both?"

Norian inhaled deeply. "It's impossible to do both."

"Is it?" Kalen asked. "Is it truly, Norian?"

Norian shook his head. "I should think so. That fact that I'm a lycan isn't something I can easily hide from my people. And if I did decide to try to rule, how could I leave this pack? They would see it as a betrayal, and I would constantly long for the life I experienced while here."

"You think, plan, and contemplate what-ifs way too much, Norian," Kalen said. "Sometimes you have to accept what is and work with what you have."

"But aren't struggles put before us for a purpose?"

"Why are you so stubborn?"

"Why are you so contrary?"

The men stared at each other for a moment, arms crossed, then both of them erupted into snickers.

"Kalen, you are utterly and completely maddening."

"I think you have it backwards, Your Highness. I see you as being the one who refuses to listen to reason."

Norian felt his face soften. A strange heaviness tugged at his chest. "I wish I could do both. I just don't see how it's possible."

"You might be surprised at what is possible and what people will accept. Don't underestimate others nor their love for their Prince—or their Alpha."

"I wish I knew what to do."

"One question you need to ask yourself now is: At this moment, how do you feel about being a lycan?"

Norian thought for a moment. There was no doubt in his mind that after last night's transformation, he saw things much differently. He no longer feared or dreaded the change and was no longer afraid that he'd hurt or even kill someone while in wolf form. And the power and strength! The freedom! Last night he was complete, perhaps for the first time in his entire life. And it was not only being a lycan. It was having Kalen with him, being one with Kalen. That's what it was—Kalen made him feel complete. Kalen was the missing element in his life, the one he'd spent his whole life searching for without even knowing it. His deepest instincts were telling him that he was fulfilling his destiny here with Kalen. Emotion welled up in his chest and in his eyes as he looked at Kalen.

Without speaking, he pulled Kalen to him and wrapped his arms around him with all of his strength. He shuddered in Kalen's arms and kissed him lightly on the neck. "You are what makes this all so difficult," Norian whispered. "And you are what makes all this seem okay."

"That's because it *is* okay," Kalen said, as he pulled away. A smile tugged at his lips. "As long as we're together, it will be okay. I'm not pressuring you into anything. Your future is your decision alone. Although I hope somehow, I'll be a part of it."

"How could you not?" Norian closed his eyes for a moment before opening them again. A sting of tears prickled at the corners. "Finding you has been the bright spot in my life and has made everything I've had to bear somehow worthwhile. Lycan or Human, I'm not about to give you up."

Kalen nodded. "Enough talk. You have a speech to prepare."

Norian's jaw tightened. "Ugh. Is there any way I can get out of this? I'm not prepared enough to give other lycans direction, being so new myself."

"No worries. I shall help you today. We'll work on it together."

Norian breathed a sigh of relief. "I would be most grateful."

"We better be getting back. The others will wonder where we've gone off to. And we've got work to do if we're going to get your speech done before sunset."

Norian nodded, and the two men walked away from the tree. Norian looked back behind him for a moment, trying to burn his surroundings in his memory. Last night was one of the most important events in his life, the night when he truly felt like a Lycan and an Alpha. He did not want to ever forget it.

CHAPTER TWENTY-TWO

Kalen and Lady Auryon sat across from each other on the fluffy white cushions in what Kalen called "The Pit." The pit was a sunken, circular structure at the heart of the room, lined with white seat cushions and matching off-white backrests tucked in behind them. Despite the fuzzy fabric covering them, Kalen found the cushions stiff and oddly unsupportive. They ringed the entire circle, leaving only a narrow gap—barely wide enough for a person to pass through. This lone opening served as the entrance and exit and was fitted with three dark brown steps that reminded Kalen of stadium seating.

In the center of the pit, a small fire crackled within a border of dark brick, radiating a gentle heat that lent the room an almost drowsy comfort. Suspended above by thick black chains was a large, dark gray cylinder hanging from the ceiling—its function a complete mystery. Kalen had given up trying to guess, chalking it up to strange decor.

"Have you heard of this before?" Kalen asked. "I never even noticed the change coming. I was guiding Norian through it, and then there I was, in wolf form."

Lady Auryon stared at him wordlessly and then drew a startled breath. "You're positive about this? Is it possible that you were so involved in Norian's transformation, so connected, that you simply imagined yourself changing?"

Kalen shook his head. "None. We spent the night together, running and hunting. Even if there were a chance that I was hallucinating, I certainly wouldn't have been able to keep up with him in human form. No?"

She gave a curt nod. "True." She creased her brow and rubbed her forehead. "I truly cannot recall ever hearing of a lycan, other than an Alpha, with the ability to transform before the moon. I suppose it might have happened, but certainly never not in this pack."

Kalen straightened. "What about you?"

"Me? What are you asking? Whether I've ever changed on a non-moon night?"

He nodded. "Father was an Alpha. Certainly, you must have joined minds with him when he changed." He knew he was taking a chance, bringing up his father. Lady Auryon had made it clear to him he was never to bring up the subject of her husband. Even after all these years, his death still pained her and remained a topic she found difficult to speak about. He recalled the time right after his father had passed. She spent months in her room in grief, coming out only to eat and even then, only when aggressively coaxed by others. During this time, Kalen had truly learned how to take charge, to take control of the pack, for his mother was in no condition to do so herself.

She shivered for a moment and folded her hands in front of her. "I was almost always there with him when he changed, even those nights before and after the full moon. I never tired of watching him transform. Yes, we would meld minds so I was able to experience the change with him. But

I never changed myself nor have I ever even tried. The thought never crossed my mind that such a thing was even possible."

"I didn't try," Kalen said. "It happened on its own."

She nodded and wrung her hands. Her eyes showed pain now. She locked eyes with him. "Have you and Norian," she paused, pursing her lips. "Mated yet? Completely?"

Kalen's eyes grew wide for a moment, and he shook his head. "No, not even close. Not that I wouldn't want to." He felt himself flush, but continued. "Norian still hopes that killing Vadok will cure him."

Lady Auryon grimaced at the name. "That is the only thing I can think of. You know that an Alpha who has mated is much more powerful than one who has not. I've heard it said that a mated Alpha is able to shift anytime he wants, moon or no moon. So this could be another one of his powers—the ability to cause his mate to shift with him."

"Even though we're not mated?"

"A mate is a mate. It may not matter that you've not physically mated yet, although that still surprises me. Maybe Norian is simply an incredibly powerful Alpha. Truth be known, Kalen, I've felt for some time that Norian is exceptional. I'm not sure how, but there's something different about him—something that makes me think he's not a typical Alpha. I've met my share of Alphas over the years, and being married to one, I speak from experience. Your mate is unlike the others."

"It's not surprising. He *is* a prince, after all."

They looked at each other for a moment, and then both burst out laughing. Kalen was glad to hear his mother laugh, for it was not something she often did.

"Perhaps it was his power as an Alpha, combined with

your bond as his mate, that caused you to transform alongside him." She pursed her lips and gave him a shy smile. "And once you truly mate with Norian, you both may be capable of so much more. It's possible that you'll develop additional abilities of your own, far beyond those of a typical wolf or typical Beta. Of course, as you know, I've never known a mated Alpha, so all of this is speculation and hearsay. But if what you experienced last night was any indication, there'll be many more surprises in store for you."

He nodded. "If we mate."

"If you mate," she repeated. She regarded him for a moment, then creased her brow. "You understand that it would be in your best interest to convince Norian to mate with you, and I mean completely. So that your two bodies meld to become one because—"

Kalen's felt his face flush red. "Mother!"

She laughed and gestured with her hand in the air. "Oh please, Kalen. I am neither delicate nor a prude. I understand what people do behind closed doors—even my son."

"It's not a subject I am comfortable talking about with you."

"Be that as it may, I am your mother, and you are the leader of this pack. There are certain pack matters I must discuss with you, and this is one of them."

"*Was* the leader of the pack," Kalen corrected.

She nodded. "That is even more reason why we need to have this conversation. And what you told me about last night confirmed it. I suspect that what happened to you when you guided Norian is only the beginning of what he might be capable of." She narrowed her eyes. "To have such a powerful Alpha would be good for the pack. This pack needs security so everyone can feel safe again."

Kalen shook his head. "I refuse to force this upon him. He has to make his own decisions."

"Even when the good of the pack is involved?"

"Mother, do not put that on me. It's not my decision to make. It is Norian's. I can't pressure him to choose between being fully human and ruling his kingdom, or being a lycan. He has a lot to lose if he stays a lycan."

"And we have a lot to lose if he doesn't," she said. She reached out and touched his hand. "Especially you, my son."

Kalen nodded briefly, considering this. "I'm aware of that. I don't even want to think about what a life without Norian would be like, and I hope it never comes to that. But, if he finds a cure, I shall still stay with him. I'll go to Tregaron if need be. It doesn't matter to me whether he is lycan or human. My love for him will remain unchanged."

Lady Auryon sighed loudly and shot him a sharp look. "But his love for you might. The mating connection is a characteristic of lycans. You know this. It doesn't exist in the human world to the extent that it does for us. So it's possible that his feelings for you—his love for you—will only continue to exist if he's a lycan. This mating connection is in his chemistry—in his blood. Yes, he loves you now, but if he were to revert to being human, that will undoubtedly change."

Kalen's felt his eyes glisten with emotion. He did not want to cry in front of his mother and allow her to see how heavy with worry his heart really was. He turned away for a moment, fighting back the tears.

"I've considered that possibility, and we've even discussed it. However, I cannot bother myself to be concerned with future possibilities and speculation. If Norian becomes human and no longer wishes to be with me, then that is what is meant to be. There is nothing I can do to change that."

"Ah, but you see, there is, Son," Lady Auryon said. "If you can convince him to mate with you, this possibility all goes away. He will be bonded to you for life."

"But what about what he wants?" Kalen asked. He turned his head and wiped his eyes. "He has a right to choose his own destiny."

"There are many that would argue against that," she said. "Being an Alpha comes with certain obligations, one of them being to his pack. While I agree that one's personal happiness is important, the security of the pack comes first. I know this first-hand from being married to an Alpha. Your father loved you and me, but the pack always came first. He ended up risking his life for the pack and dying for the pack." Her voice was heavy with emotion. "I imagine that many in our community would not be happy if they knew of his intentions to leave."

"But he is not of our pack," Kalen said. "He wandered in, looking for a cure. It's not his fault that it turned out he was an Alpha."

"Ah, but don't you see Kalen? He *is* of our pack. He's an Alpha, and his mate is the Beta *of this pack*. How can you say, then, that he is not a part of our pack? The way I see it, it's pretty darn clear that his calling is to lead us. He is one of us. He is ours."

"Even if he doesn't want it?"

She considered this for a moment, then nodded. "Life sometimes thrusts things upon us regardless of whether we want them or not, whether we're prepared for them or not. Your father once confided in me that when he discovered he was Alpha, he was absolutely terrified. He planned on running away from the pack so he wouldn't have to take on the responsibility of being a leader, convinced that being a lone wolf would be preferable to leading. He never wanted it. Never even fathomed it, actually. It might surprise you to learn this, but your father was exceptionally timid in his youth and always hung back in the shadows, never wanting to be the center of attention. Dreaded it." She chuckled. "Nobody was more surprised than him when his Alpha traits began to display. He certainly never aspired to become Alpha. But fate had other plans for him. In the end, he accepted his destiny and became a powerful and respected pack leader."

Kalen swallowed and stared at his mother. She was right. It was almost as if fate brought Kalen to Norbury—as if they were meant to find each other. As if he were destined to take over the pack.

"Mother, nothing would make me happier than if Norian were to agree to stay here with us, to stay with me. Believe me, I want that more than anything. But I can't coerce him to choose between us and his kingdom. He's only been a lycan for a month, but he'd spent his entire lifetime being a prince. How can he choose us over them after only such a short time? How can he choose between his love for his father and kingdom, or us?"

"There is no easy answer for you, Norian. All I can speak of is what is best for you and the pack." She brushed her hand along his arm. "It is only natural that a mother should look out for the best interest of her son. I want what's best for you."

"And the pack," Kalen said. The words sounded harsher than he had intended.

Her eyes grew wide, and she drew back. "Of course, the pack. This pack is a part of me, as you are. Your father worked hard leading and building it up, and it is our duty to him to ensure that it continues. Certainly, you understand my loyalty to it. The pack that protected us, provided for us, raised you."

Kalen nodded. "I get it. But I hope you understand that I also have an obligation to my mate to do what is in his best interest. Whilst I do possess a strong loyalty to the pack, I've also a duty to ensure Norian's happiness. I won't act against his wishes."

"So be it," Lady Auryon said. "But I want you to consider this and carefully reflect on it. In addition to the well-being of our pack, you must consider your contentment as well. Losing a mate can be devastating, and oftentimes, tragic. I don't want that for you, Kalen. It's so rare that one finds their mate. I just can't bear to see this opportunity— this gift from the gods—escape through your fingers. I couldn't bear to see you suffer through a broken heart. Remember Efrain."

"I know," he said. "I don't even want to think about the possibility of losing Norian forever. Besides, who knows if he'll even find Vadok or be successful in killing him? If he manages to succeed, it may not cure him, after all. There are a lot of what-ifs here."

She nodded. "What you say is true. But if there's one thing I've noticed about this Alpha is that he is determined. If he is driven to kill Vadok, then I have little doubt that he will succeed."

"If that be the case, I secretly hope that he never finds him."

She shook her head. "You might still work on convincing him that his place is here, with you. You know, one small seduction—"

"I won't betray him like that," Kalen said. "It must be his decision."

A ruckus in the hallway caused them both to turn toward the noise. A moment later, there was a loud rap on the door.

It was Thomros. He inclined his head politely before entering the room. His face was tight, and he appeared tense.

"Yes?" asked Lady Auryon. "Is something the matter?"

"Craig just returned from a nearby town. There is news of Vadok." Every pack member knew of the attack Vadok once made on Norbury and what he was capable of. Many feared he would one day return to Norbury to finish what he began.

Kalen cursed under his breath.

"So what is this news?" Lady Auryon asked. The concern was evident in her expression. "Is he close to Norbury? Has he been sighted nearby?"

Craig shook his head. "One week ago, he attacked Tregaron and is now in control." He swallowed. "He has killed their king."

CHAPTER TWENTY-THREE

Norian blinked and sat up, his heart still pounding. The nightmare was so vivid, so real. It was then he noticed the soft knocking at the door.

"Come in," he said.

The door opened, and Kalen entered the room. He avoided Norian's eyes, and Norian knew right away that something was wrong.

"Kalen?"

Kalen met Norian's gaze. He sat down on the edge of the bed.

"Had a little rest before tonight?" Kalen asked.

"Surprisingly. I never thought I could sleep seeing how wound up I was earlier, with the change coming on and all. Your mother's tea helped. It's amazing."

Kalen nodded. "Norian, there's something I need to tell you. I don't know the right way to say this or even how to say it."

"What is it? What has happened?"

"We've just received word that Vadok has entered your kingdom. He has supposedly taken it over."

Norian gasped, clenched his jaw, and his hands shook. He tried to control his breath and brace himself for the news that was coming. "Is there news about my father?"

Kalen took hold of Norian's hands and locked gazes with him. "I'm sorry, Norian." His voice was barely a whisper. "I am so, so sorry."

Norian fought back the tears that threatened to erupt from his eyes. He had just seen his father in his dream. It was just as the dream had foretold. He recalled his father telling him that it was his turn to rule, his turn to be king.

"So my father. He didn't...."

Norian closed his eyes and shook his head. "From what I understand, it was Vadok himself who murdered him."

Norian nodded, trying to keep down the rage that threatened to overtake him. He took a deep, shaky breath and met Kalen's eyes. His voice cracked as he spoke. "I felt something was horribly wrong from the moment Belkas appeared. I even just now dreamt about it." He widened his eyes. "Is there news of Wayf?"

Kalen shook his head. "I have heard nothing of anyone else—only that Vadok has taken control of Tregaron."

"Damn this accursed full moon!" Norian said, the tears now flowing freely from his eyes. "Moon or not, I leave first thing in the morning." He paused and hugged himself. "At least I know now where to find him. I shall have my vengeance."

Kalen rested his hand on Norian's shoulder. "I figured you would wish to leave right away. I will come with you. At least you know how to control the change, and together, we should be able to move under the radar of any hunters. We shall have to be especially stealthy—and careful."

Norian was quiet for a moment. His voice quivered when he finally spoke. "This changes everything."

"How so?"

"I'd hoped that my time to rule would come far off in the future. But it is here now, and my father's death is at the hands of Vadok. I cannot let him have my kingdom. I can't fail."

"And I shall do everything I can to help you."

Norian shook his head. "No. Things have changed now that Vadok is in control. It's way too dangerous for you to accompany me. This is something that I need to do alone, on my own. This is my fight."

"We've already had this conversation. There's no way I will let you go alone."

"And there's no way I am going to risk getting you killed," Norian said.

"It's no different from before, except there's more at stake now. I wouldn't be able to live without you, so I may as well die with you if that is to be our fate."

Norian stared at him and said nothing. He tried to figure out what to do. He couldn't risk Kalen's life, but this was his quest and his alone. His chest ached just at the thought of losing him.

"Stop scheming," said Kalen. "I can tell from the conniving look on your face what's going on in your head." He crossed his arms over his chest. "I'm going with you, and that's that. Don't even think of trying to escape me, for if you do, I'll be right on your tail." He tapped his nose with his index finger. "I'd be able to find you anywhere."

"No. I forbid it. You will not—"

"This is not up for negotiation, Norian. I *am* going with you. I will help you avenge your father and retake your kingdom."

They locked eyes for several long moments. Defeated, Norian's shoulders slumped. "If that is your wish. You realize that neither of us may return, right? There is no guarantee of your safety."

"I accept that. Wherever you go, I shall be by your side." He creased his brow and took hold of Norian's hands. "This is also a chance for me to avenge my father's death, as this scoundrel killed him too. I've waited a long time for this. Together, we will not fail."

Norian's tears started again. "I forget your father perished by this monster's hand as well." He sniffled. "I'm sorry, Kalen. I just feel so raw right now."

Kalen nodded. "We both will have time to grieve after Vadok is dead."

"But now, I must decide what to do once we kill Vadok."

"What do you mean?"

"What if I'm still a lycan afterward? I can't imagine that my people would accept me," he swallowed, "like that."

"We shall just have to face it when the time comes. So let us not worry now about what might be."

"There is also the issue of you."

"Me?"

"You are my mate. I am expected to take a queen and create an heir. The people of Tregaron would never accept a king with a male lover."

Kalen sighed. "Norian, you need to calm down and only focus on taking back Tregaron. We'll deal with whatever comes after—when the time comes. But, for now, let's focus on the singular task of liberating Tregaron."

"What of you? What if your pack should find out that we are mates?"

"Either they will accept it, or they will not. That's not a worry that weighs on me at the moment. But, truth be told, I have little doubt that they would ever turn their back on their Alpha—especially a *mated Alpha*."

Norian raised his eyebrows but took a deep breath. "You appear to have more confidence in people than I do."

"I find people will often surprise you." He brushed his hand against Norian's cheek, wiping away the tears. "I hate to even bring this up, but it's almost time for the pack to gather. It's come to my attention that everyone knows you are an Alpha. I stated to the others earlier that you would want to address them and officially introduce yourself to the pack, but of course, given the circumstances, I no longer expect this of you. I should also tell you that most everyone now knows you are the Prince of Tregaron. Once the news broke about what happened there, some people couldn't keep their mouth shut and let your secret slip. They wanted to express their concern for you." He gave Norian a weak smile. "'Tis not easy to keep a secret from this pack. But no matter. I shall tell them what had occurred in Tregaron and that you are grieving."

Kalen started to rise, but Norian grabbed his wrist. "No. I will speak to them myself. It is my duty to the pack, and I shall fulfill it."

Kalen's eyes grew wide. "But what will you say? It would be best if you didn't tell them you're leaving in the morning. They would not allow it."

"Perhaps it is *you* who underestimates people. They've encountered Vadok in their own city. I'm sure they'll understand what I need to do."

"Don't be surprised if they do not. They'll not easily let their Alpha go. What'll you tell them? Will you promise your return?"

"You know I cannot make any such promises. It all

depends on whether I succeed in killing Vadok — and whether my people will accept you as my mate."

Kalen smiled. "You mean that?"

"Of course I mean it. There's no life without you in it."

"Not so fast. Remember—we are mated by the bonds of the wolf, meaning that if you become completely human again, it's possible our mate bond will no longer exist on your end. You may no longer have any feelings for me afterward."

Norian brought both his hands to Kalen's cheeks. "I do not doubt for a moment that my feelings for you will remain unchanged. They are too deep to simply disappear, whether I be lycan or human."

"You don't know this, Norian. Once you're cured, you may go back to wanting to find a queen."

Norian smiled. "Kalen, I have always had an attraction to males. So it was no surprise to me when my mate turned out to be male. Perhaps it's you I should be concerned about."

Kalen raised his eyebrows. "Me? What do you mean?"

"Remember how surprised you were when you learned your mate was male? Perhaps when our bond breaks, it will be you who reverts."

Kalen blushed. "You are not the first man for whom I've felt an attraction."

Norian raised his eyebrow. "Do tell."

"Nothing much to tell. There was one other. We experimented a bit, but then decided it was best if things progressed no further. Plus, I imagine he was fearful that my mother would find out."

Norian laughed. "That doesn't surprise me. She can be a bit scary."

Kalen smiled, and then his face grew solemn. "It is time to speak to your pack. Are you sure you're up for this?"

Norian nodded and wiped his eyes with his arm. "Positive."

∼

NORIAN'S HEART pounded as he listened to Kalen address the crowd. It surprised him to learn that this monthly gathering was not only an opportunity for pack members to run together after the change, but also served as a monthly village business meeting.

Norian glanced around. The pack was much larger than he'd imagined, although he wasn't sure if every person present was a lycan. He thrust his shaking hands into his pockets. He looked around, hoping to spy water nearby, but there was none. His mouth was so parched that he wondered whether he'd even be able to utter a single sylla-ble. He wasn't usually this nervous about speaking in front of others as he'd done plenty of that in his village. Public speaking was one of those skills his father had considered essential training, and he'd had plenty of practice. No, he was nervous about having to tell the crowd that he could not be their Alpha, that he had to leave Norbury and wage war against Vadok. He knew how much they hoped to have an Alpha lead them and protect them. They'd also experi-enced an attack by Vadok during which he had killed their Alpha, so they understood how vulnerable they were. Norian shook himself, returning his focus to Kalen's words.

"Now comes the time to introduce the newest member of our community. I'm sure most of you have heard the news that we are honored to have Norian, Crown Prince of Tregaron, in our village. You have also no doubt learned that he is an Alpha, the first Alpha we have had here since my father. While this may seem to be an exciting time for us, Prince Norian's situation is complicated, which he will explain to you in person. Therefore, it is my honor and privilege to present to you, Prince Norian of Tregaron!"

The hooting, hollering, and thunderous applause startled Norian. He swallowed, nodded, and joined Kalen in front of the pack. The moment he stood next to Kalen, the noise stopped. Norian's eyes roamed over those present. He forced a smile.

"Greetings, brothers and sisters," he began. "I am grateful to be here among you and grateful for the hospitality that has been shown to me since my arrival. I especially am thankful to Lady Auryon and Lord Kalen for taking me in during an especially difficult time for me." A loud burst of applause interrupted his speech. He held up his hand to stop the cheering. This was going to be a lot more difficult than he had initially thought.

"I appreciate your enthusiasm and your support. It means more to me than you know. I wish I had good news to tell you. But alas, I do not. Some of you may have heard that my kingdom, Tregaron, has been attacked by the same scoundrel who infiltrated this village several years back and murdered your beloved Alpha. It is with a heavy heart that I tell you that during the Tregaron attack, my father, King Jamros, was killed, and Vadok has taken the throne for himself. Being the next in line, it is my duty and obligation to the citizens of Tregaron to remove Vadok and take my rightful place as King. What I am saying is that I cannot stay here and be your Alpha. This is not my home. My home is in Tregaron, not here, and I have a sacred duty to protect my people at all costs. I am terribly sorry. I never meant to deceive nor mislead any of you, and if my presence here has created false hopes, I deeply apologize." The bile rose in Norian's throat as he braced himself for the reaction. Without even looking behind him, he could sense Kalen's eyes bore into his back.

Several members of the crowd gasped, and there was a low rumble of murmuring. Then a loud voice broke through the rumbling.

"But you are Alpha!" Thomros said. The rest of the crowd grew quiet. "It is your obligation to lead a pack. It is pretty much your raison d'être. Or are you already obligated to another pack? Have you a pack in Tregaron?"

Norian shook his head. "Of lycans, no. But I consider the people of Tregaron my pack. You state that my reason for being is to lead a pack. But I have always been destined to eventually lead my kingdom as King. For this, I have been groomed since I was a child. Tregaron is my home, my bond. It is the place of my family."

"So, what was your purpose in coming here if you had no intention of staying?" Thomros asked.

The man was clearly setting a trap for him. Given that Thomros was one of the men who found him and escorted him to the village, he knew from the beginning the purpose of Norian's visit to Norbury, even though Norian had later told them otherwise. He understood that Norian's reason for coming to Norbury was to find a cure.

Norian locked eyes with Thomros. "I believe you know the answer to that."

Thomros gestured to the rest of the crowd with his hand. "But alas, the others do not."

Norian took a deep breath. "Very well. My story may help you all to understand my actions." He spent the next several minutes recounting the recent events of the past few weeks to the pack: the werewolf attack, his real reason for coming to the village, and his surprise at discovering that he was an Alpha. He left out the fact that Kalen was his mate, however. It was up to Kalen to share that bit of news with his people if he so chose.

When Norian finished, a young man stepped forward. He bowed and said, "Your Highness. My name is Corin." He met Norian's eyes. "Will you please tell us more about this cure you speak of? Is it true? Is it even possible?"

Before Norian could respond, Lady Auryon stepped forward. "You must keep in mind that Norian is unlike the rest of us. He was not born lycan. He was bitten, through magic, in an act of spite. According to a myth I once heard, it is rumored that if someone becomes a lycan through a bite caused by sorcery, that killing the sorcerer who compelled the lycan might restore them to their prior human state. I cannot verify the truthfulness of this myth. But Norian has decided to test it by attempting to eliminate the one who caused his situation. He plans on destroying Vadok."

"Vadok is one of us, then?" someone asked. "He's a lycan?"

Norian shook his head. "Although not lycan himself, it was his magic that caused the young woman to bite me."

Lady Auryon interrupted him. "Exactly. Sorcery controlled the lycan in question, so the origins of Norian's transformation is Vadok."

"But why seek a cure?" asked Corin. "What do you have against us? Have we wronged you somehow? Why do you seek to deny your nature and become human?"

"Don't misunderstand me. It isn't that I don't wish to be lycan. Rather, it is my obligation to the Crown and the people of Tregaron to restore peace to the land. My destiny is to be King, and I must do everything in my power to ensure the continuation of the kingdom that my father and his ancestors built. By taking my rightful place, I will be in a position to maintain peace throughout the land. There is more to this situation than my personal desires. Whether or not I wish to remain lycan is not my decision."

"Your logic is flawed, boss," Thomros said. "Why must you be human to be king? I fail to see the connection between the two."

"It would not be possible to have a lycan as a King. Such a ruler would never be accepted by his people. They would fear him, be suspicious of him, perhaps some would even try to kill him."

Thomros crossed his arms. "Hogwash."

"Thomros, regardless of your position in this village, I remind you that you are addressing an Alpha," said Lady Auryon. "As such, I suggest you watch your tongue. Such disrespect will not be tolerated."

Norian placed a hand on Lady Auryon's shoulder. "It's fine," he said quietly.

He then turned his regard back to Thomros. "So you think human citizens would allow themselves to be ruled by a lycan? That they would have no problems having such a creature in a position of power?"

"It wouldn't be the first time," Thomros said.

"What are you saying?" Norian asked. "Are you implying that there has been a lycan King in the past?"

"It's true!" someone shouted. "Lord Larius of Glendale was lycan."

Thomros nodded. "He was not only respected by his people, but also loved. He was a true warrior, and his people felt safe under his rule. Who would you rather follow into battle, a feeble mortal king or a king with the instincts and cunning of a wolf? And an Alpha at that."

"His people knew about him?" Norian asked. "They knew what he was?"

Thomros nodded and crossed his arms in front of his chest. "And they felt more secure because of it."

"I know my people, and they would never allow themselves to be governed by a lycan. I'm guessing that most of them aren't even aware that lycans exist. Hell, I didn't know they... er, we... existed until a short while ago."

"Perhaps you don't give your people enough credit," Thomros said. "It might surprise you what people will accept."

"Take this village, for instance," Lady Auryon said. "Not everyone here is a lycan. The humans who are here have chosen to be here willingly. They've chosen to love a lycan. People certainly can learn to love a lycan king. When my husband was alive, both lycans and non-lycans respected him."

Norian's mouth went dry, and he found himself unable to respond. Could it be? Could his people truly accept him for what he was? Could they accept having a wolf for a king? For the first time, he doubted himself and his intentions. Perhaps all this time, it was he who couldn't accept who he was, that he was no longer human. Maybe he was wrong all along. Power surged through him the moment acceptance settled in. His eyes threaten to water, but he fought back the tears. He mustn't cry here, not in front of the pack. Not in front of *his* pack.

He turned to look at Kalen, who nodded when he met his gaze, and Norian's heart melted. What was he thinking? How could he ever hurt this man? By not accepting who he was, by searching for this elusive cure, he was rejecting the love of this man. He was rejecting the love of his mate.

He turned his head toward Thomros, who was staring

at him expectantly, waiting for Norian to respond. Norian opened his mouth to speak, but his voice was buried deep in his throat. He had to consciously force it to the surface.

"You may be right," he said finally. "Perhaps it was my own prejudices and self-doubt that have driven me to find a cure. While I admit and recognize this, there remains the issue of my father's murder and the current situation in Tregaron. I must avenge my father's death and take back my kingdom. Vadok must not succeed. Tomorrow morning, I will take leave of Norbury. While finding a cure may not be the most important thing, I still need to carry out my mission of removing Vadok from power."

"No," a voice said from the crowd. Everyone turned to look at Craig, who stood next to Thomros.

"No?" Norian repeated.

"Yes," said Craig. "I mean, no. We cannot allow you to leave alone."

"Craig, I understand you feel my place is here, with all of you. But I cannot ignore my obligation to Tregaron and my father's memory. This is something that I must do and will do." He didn't want to tell them he wasn't going alone. That Kalen was going with him. How could he tell them that not only were they losing an Alpha, but the pack was losing their Beta as well?

"I think you misunderstood Craig," Thomros said. "He said that we cannot allow you to leave alone. So we are going with you."

Many in the crowd voiced their agreement. Kalen shrugged his shoulders and smiled when Norian met his gaze. Kalen was right. This pack wasn't going to give up their Alpha so easily.

"I cannot allow this," Norian said. "This is my quest, not yours. As you all know, Vadok is a deadly foe, and I will put no one else's life in danger. That creature has killed too many people over the years."

"So what, you mean to conquer him by yourself?" Craig asked, eyebrows raised. He crossed his arms. "What is your plan? How do you mean to do this, all on your own? With no magic?"

"I haven't decided yet, but I'm sure to work something out. I do have an army back at the castle."

"An army that is now under Vadok's control," Thomros reminded him. "If he hasn't already killed them all, that is."

Norian swallowed. "This is not—"

"Norian of Tergaron," Craig said, interrupting him. "You shall not face Vadok alone. Whether or not you accept it, you are our Alpha, and a pack always supports its Alpha. No exceptions. Just as we hope you would support us if there were a need. We cannot and will not desert you, Lord Norian. 'Tis not in our nature to do so."

Norian shuddered at the words, Lord Norian. Before he could say anything, Thomros spoke.

"Together as a pack lead by a powerful Alpha, we have a better chance of defeating Vadok." Thomros glanced around the crowd. "All the lycans in this pack shall accompany you. The humans will remain in the village for the moment."

"Certainly, you don't mean to leave the humans unprotected?" a young man in the crowd asked. He pulled the young woman standing next to him tightly into a protective hug. "What if someone attacks them when we're vulnerable? What if hunters come to the village? It wouldn't be the first time that hunters have used humans to get to their lycan mates."

"I shall stay and watch over your mates," Lady Auryon

said. "A couple of the younger lycans can stay with me as well. So you shall all be safe."

From what Kalen had said, Norian knew that Lady Auryon was a powerful and fearful wolf and would be able to protect her village if something happened.

All at once, Norian noticed the crowd tense and become restless. It was then he noticed the wolf rise within him. It was nearly time. He then heard Kalen's voice in his head. *"Remember, you are in charge. Do not allow the wolf to rise completely."*

Norian looked at Kalen and nodded, forcing his consciousness to stay in charge. He looked at the crowd and made a decision that he hoped was the right one.

"Very well," Norian said. "Tomorrow morning, we leave as a pack to Tregaron."

"But tonight, you run with us," growled Thomros. He was already in the throes of the change.

"Tonight, I run with my pack," Norian said. He then allowed his wolf to break through.

CHAPTER TWENTY-FOUR

Norian woke with Kalen's arms wrapped around him. This was becoming a habit, though an enjoyable one. He slipped Kalen's arm off of him, stood up, and brushed himself off. He found his stashed clothes a few yards away and dressed quietly. It was then he noticed all the sleeping figures in the meadow, all the lycans with whom he had run last night. He couldn't help but smile as he watched them sleep, their naked figures strewn about in the field. His heart tugged, and a strange warmth that he had not experienced before filled him. The warmth of kinship, perhaps? Pride? Whatever it was, he liked it.

He tiptoed to a nearby tree and plopped himself down. Last night was one of the most incredible nights he had ever experienced. While running with Kalen the night before last was beyond magnificent, last night had been extraordinary in a different way. Running with and leading a pack of wolves was beyond anything he could have ever imagined. He'd kept control of his inner wolf the entire time, which at first was a struggle. But he'd managed it.

As he glanced over the sleeping forms of his fellow

lycans, his heart clenched. How could he ever have believed he'd be able to leave these people? There now existed a connection between himself and them that was not there before, an unbreakable bond between an Alpha and the pack. His pack. He shuddered at the words, but yes, they were now his pack. He couldn't help but wonder if Kalen was aware of how Norian would feel after leading the pack on the full moon. Did Kalen guess that doing so would create this new connection between him and his fellow lycans? No matter, what's done is done. And if he had to do it all over, he'd do it the same way.

"You're awake," Kalen said, his voice startling Norian.

"Been up for a little while already." He tried not to look at Kalen's beautiful, naked body. "The rest of them seem to be in a pretty deep sleep yet."

"The change takes a bit out of a body," Kalen said. "I'm surprised you're up before everyone else. I'd expect you to be the most taxed of all."

"Me? Why?"

"You managed to bring down a buck all on your own. Pretty impressive maneuver there, by the way."

"Damn, I'd forgotten all about that." He shivered at the memory of killing an animal, then tried to push the recollection from his mind. "At the time, I didn't think too much about it and operated pretty much on instinct alone. I didn't make a faux pas of any kind, did I?"

"Not at all," said Kalen. "Actually, you scored extra brownie points with the pack."

Norian raised his eyes. "I did? How?"

"How much do you remember about taking down that deer?"

"I remember most of it, I think," said Norian. "I

remember picking up its scent, and then instinct took over. I don't recall thinking about anything at that point."

"No, I mean after you took it down."

"After?" Norian thought for a moment, and then his stomach did a flip. "We ate."

"But you didn't eat first."

"Now that you mention it, I guess I didn't."

Kalen smiled. "No, you didn't. You brought down the deer, stared at all of us for a moment, and then stepped aside. You put your pack first, a quality that I promise you nobody will forget. It's a sign not only of a true Alpha but a kind one."

"To be truthful, I have no idea why I did it. But, it seemed like the proper thing to do."

"There is an unwritten rule that the Alpha always eats first. But you broke that custom for your pack. At first, I feared their reaction, but once they realized what was going on, the love and respect that flowed from them to you were unmistakable."

Norian and Kalen locked eyes for several moments. Kalen broke the silence. "I probably should get dressed. The others should be waking up soon."

"Good idea. You're much too distracting like that."

Kalen left in search of his clothes and returned a few minutes later. By now, Norian had stood up and was leaning against the tree.

"You weren't wearing that last night," Norian said.

Kalen laughed. "The day after the change, it's pretty much a free-for-all. It would take forever to go through that vast pile of clothes to find the ones you were wearing the night before. It's easier to grab whatever fits."

"Isn't it kind of weird wearing someone else's clothes?"

Kalen gave him a strange look. "I've never considered it

before. It's the way it's always been done. But no, I don't think it's weird. These are all my brothers and sisters."

Norian nodded but said nothing. Emotion welled up within him at the realization that these were all now his brothers and sisters as well. Kalen's voice interrupted his thoughts.

"That was an incredible speech you gave last night, especially under the circumstances. You earned the respect of everyone there." Kalen flashed him a wicked grin. "And see? You didn't even have to lie."

Norian considered this briefly. "True. But I certainly didn't count on them coming with me." He paused. "Us, I mean. I'm still not sure how I feel about it. The last thing I want to do is to put anyone else's life in danger. Hell, I don't know any of these people. Yet, they're volunteering to be part of a war that may not end well. You truly have an incredible group of people who are part of your pack."

"Our pack," Kalen corrected him. "I realize this is all new to you, but it's what pack members do. We stand up for each other. Especially for our Alpha. There's a kinship between us, an unwritten and unspoken rule, that your problems are our problems and our problems are yours. Yes, we are all individuals with our own needs and our own desires. But underneath that, there is the bond of the pack, a connection that reminds us that we are not and never will be facing life alone."

"I feel it," Norian said. "I didn't until this morning. Things seem different now, clearer. For the first time, I'm part of something bigger than myself and sense that I really, truly belong. You know, I've never quite felt that I belonged before. Even at the castle, I've always been somewhere out on the fringes, not quite fitting in. But, after last night, that all changed."

"You experienced pack thought for the first time," Kalen said.

"Pack thought? What's that?"

"It's where the mind of your wolf melds with those of the entire pack. The wolf inside you met our pack and then became part of it. That's where this emotion you're experiencing is coming from. For the first time, your wolf acknowledges its place in the pack. That connection doesn't disappear when you transform back into a human. Just as the wolf is always a part of you, so now is your pack."

Norian drew a breath, trying to keep his emotions in check. "Now what?" he asked.

"You tell me," Kalen said. "You're our leader now, so it is you who needs to come up with a plan on what happens next."

Norian nodded. "I understand. I wish I was aware of the situation in Tregaron—whether the army is still with Vadok or with me. I don't even know who remains alive."

"In my opinion, we should wait until the next full moon to attack."

Norian's eyes grew wide. "Impossible! Why, that's a month away. That's too long to wait."

"You said yourself that the journey takes nearly two weeks. That's only an additional fourteen days to wait. If we attack on the full moon, we'll have the full power of the pack behind us. I doubt his army could overtake an entire pack of transformed lycans. Plus, that will give all of us an extra week to prepare. We can gather weapons and make arrangements for our absence."

Norian considered this for a moment. A part of him wanted to leave immediately and charge in. But Kalen was right. If they attacked as wolves, not only would they have the element of surprise, they would also have the might of the pack. Could Vadok hold back an entire pack of lycans? He wasn't sure. But he had to admit that they'd have more of a chance of surviving if they waited.

"You're right," Norian said. "It makes the most sense to wait and to gather up our resources." He paused and rubbed his chin. A plan began formulating in his brain. "We shall leave after one week's time. Once we get close to the city, I'll sneak in alone to assess the situation. This way, I'll get an idea about the best manner in which to attack. The rest of you will wait for my cue."

"You mean us, don't you? I'm going in with you."

Norian shook his head. "On this one, I'm holding my ground. Nobody is going in first except for me. I grew up in the city and know my way around the castle better than anyone. I don't want to worry about anyone else. You will remain with the pack."

"We will continue to discuss this further in the coming weeks."

Before Norian could answer, he noticed a naked man standing in front of him. "Boss, what's up?" the man said, rubbing his eyes. "We still leaving today?"

"There's been a change of plans," Norian said. "We will depart after a dozen days have passed. This will give us all a chance to tie up any loose ends and make a firm plan. Can you inform the others?"

The man nodded. "Sure. I'll wake them up now."

Kalen stepped in. "Let them know we will be holding a pack meeting in the general assembly room in two hours."

The man turned his regard to Norian as if expecting an explanation.

"A meeting?" Norian asked.

"You need to tell them the plan yourself." Kalen paused

and smiled. "So you have two hours to come up with a good one."

"I can't come up with anything too specific until I know for sure what's going on in the city. For now, we focus on getting to Tregaron in one piece and defeating Vadok by any means necessary.

"Spoken like a true Alpha," Kalen said.

CHAPTER TWENTY-FIVE

THE FOLLOWING TWO DAYS FLEW BY QUICKLY. THE night after the full moon, Norian changed by himself and spent the evening alone, hunting, running and thinking. He could tell that Kalen was disappointed that Norian didn't want to change together, but he needed some alone time. Plus, he wanted to ensure that he could change alone in Kalen's absence, without his guidance and without his wolf taking over. Surprisingly, the change was getting easier each time he shifted. It was almost as if his inner wolf understood that Norian would no longer give it complete control. The wolf seemed to stop fighting him during the transformation, allowing Norian to maintain full control throughout the change.

It was fantastic to run by himself, to let his wolf free for a night. Norian was on the verge of making an irrevocable decision, and he needed this night alone, a night spent in freedom with only his wolf. As he woke up the following morning, he smiled. He knew what he had to do.

He'd paced back and forth all day long, fists clenched and jumping at the slightest sound, leading Kalen to eye him warily several times throughout the day. It's true that Norian had wrapped himself up inside of his thoughts all day, not knowing how the events he had planned would play out. He couldn't stop thinking about his father, and it took everything he had to hold back his grief—his overwhelming urge to lose himself in his tears and his rage.

He sat in his bed wide awake. Everyone else had settled in, and the house was quiet. It was time.

He gently closed his bedroom door and tiptoed to Kalen's room. He knocked on the door as quietly as he could. A moment later, he could hear footsteps across the wooden floor. The door opened. Kalen's face registered his surprise.

"Norian?" He rubbed his eyes. "What's going on."

"Can I come in? I need to talk to you." Norian noted how delicious Kalen looked in his nightshirt.

Kalen paused for a moment, looking as if he wasn't quite sure what Norian had asked him. "Oh. Of course, come in."

Norian entered Kalen's room and made a beeline for the bed. He sat on the edge of Kalen's bed, hands folded in his lap.

"I hope I didn't wake you," Norian said. His heart slipped into slow, thudding punches against his rib cage.

"I was just on the verge of sleep. What's up?"

Norian reached for Kalen's hand and kissed it. He then scooted himself up next to Kalen until their bodies were pressed together. He slowly brought his head to Kalen's, and their lips touched. Kalen's lips parted, allowing Norian's tongue easy entry. Norian fell into the kiss when Kalen abruptly pulled away.

"What are you doing?" asked Kalen.

Norian raised his eyebrows. "Kissing you."

"Is that a good idea? We're in my bed, after all."

Norian hesitated, suddenly shy in front of Kalen. "I do." He stopped and took a deep breath, heading faster now towards that inescapable decision. "I've been doing a lot of thinking the past few days."

Kalen raised his eyebrows. "About?"

"About us and our future together."

Kalen flinched and locked his gaze with Norian. "So, are you going to share what it is you so urgently needed to tell me in the middle of the night?"

"You said that I would be more powerful once we mated, right?"

"It wasn't me who said that, but my mother. She said that there's no creature as powerful as a mated Alpha. What that means, I'm not sure. She wasn't sure herself. It was only what others have told her over the years."

Norian grabbed hold of Kalen's hands. "I think we should mate."

"What?" The surprise was evident in his voice and his expression.

"If we are to take on Vadok, we're going to need every advantage. If I had the power of a mated Alpha on my side, I should easily be able to overtake Vadok. Who knows? Maybe I'll even be able to ward off some of his magic. I'll sneak in, find out what I can about the logistics of his regime, and then we'll attack on the full moon. I'm guessing I'd be at my strongest then."

Kalen straightened and studied Norian's face for several moments. "So, you wish to mate so you can more easily vanquish Vadok?"

"Yes. I mean, that's not the only reason. You know I've wanted to mate with you ever since I saw you on that first day. You must know how deeply I care about you."

Kalen's face held no expression, and he locked on to Norian's gaze. "What about your quest to find a cure? If you and I do the deed, as it were, you will forsake your one chance to be completely human again. That was your point in coming here, remember?"

Norian nodded. "I know. But things have changed. I've fallen more in love with you than I ever thought possible. And..." Norian paused, trying to find the right words.

"And what?" Kalen asked.

"And I have to do whatever it takes to get my kingdom back from Vadok. I cannot allow him to remain in power. As prince, I need to protect my people."

"I see," Kalen said. There was now a somber tone to his voice. "In other words, you want to use me to increase your own power."

Norian shot to his feet. His heart clenched and he felt almost too pained to speak. "No, you misunderstand. That is not the only reason. You know how I feel about you. We are mates, destined to be together."

"Forget about us being mates for one minute," Kalen said. "For weeks, you've pushed me away, stressing how important it was to you to find a cure, and you made it more than clear that you didn't want me that way. So why the change of heart?"

"Ever since the night of the full moon when the entire pack ran together, I felt as though I truly belonged somewhere. I've come to accept that I am now a lycan and your mate. This is where I belong."

Kalen eyed him suspiciously. "But you mentioned your intention to attack Vadok."

"Of course. He's invaded my kingdom, and I cannot let that go. He has to be stopped. Surely you understand that?"

Kalen nodded. "And if you succeed? What then?"

"I haven't thought that far ahead. The most important thing is defeating Vadok."

"The most important thing is defeating Vadok," Kalen repeated in a voice so low that Norian could hardly hear him.

"That's not what I meant," Norian said.

"I believe it is, Norian. Let's say we mate, and you kill Vadok. Every time you look at me, you'll remember what you gave up because we mated—your chance to reign as a human king. I realize you want to defeat Vadok. I want him dead, too. After all, he's the swine that killed my father and many of my people. But a mate is for life. Consummating one's connection with one's mate is the single most important event in a lycan's life. I'm sorry, Norian, but the answer is no. I will not mate with you now."

Norian drew a breath, about to protest, but Kalen cut him off.

Kalen's eyes glistened as he spoke. "When or if we mate, I want it to happen because you wish to be with me until the end of your days, above all else. Not because it will strengthen you. Not because it might help you win back a kingdom. I want you to carry no regrets—not about us, not about the loss of your humanity, and not about the throne you left behind. Yes, I understand these things are important to you, Norian, and heaven knows, I wish to mate with you more than anything else. But I have to know deep down in my soul that you are mating because of me and only for me." He paused, closed his eyes for a brief moment, and then continued. "Right now, I don't believe that this is the case."

Norian lingered, staring at Kalen, not sure how to respond. His heart tugged in his chest, and a lump formed in his throat.

"But I do want you," Norian's voice rasped. "I want to spend the rest of my life with you, Kalen. Nothing is more important to me than you."

"Except your kingdom," Kalen added.

"Surely you don't expect me to give up on wrestling Tregaron from the hands of Vadok, do you?"

"Of course not," Kalen said. "And I will be right by your side, fighting with you every step of the way. And once this is over, and if you still wish to be with me, then I shall be here for you."

Kalen gestured to the door. "I think you need to go now, Norian. We will not speak of this again until the time is right."

Norian opened his mouth to protest, but no words escaped his lips. He nodded, rested his palm against Kalen's cheek, and left the room. The door clicked behind him.

He cursed himself and his clumsy, thoughtless words. He had had such high hopes for this night. How could it all have gone so wrong?

THE NEXT FEW days flew by, with Norian seeing very little of Kalen. Norian suspected Kalen was avoiding him, no doubt worried Norian would continue to push the mating thing, but he had no intentions of doing so. After the disastrous night in Kalen's room, Norian revisited their conversation over and over in his head and concluded that perhaps Kalen was at least partly right. One huge reason he wished to mate with Kalen was in the hopes it would give him—them—an extra edge over Vadok, that it would provide him with extra power that could help them be successful. But this wasn't the only reason. His heart constantly ached for Kalen, and he wanted them to be together more than anything.

But Kalen was wrong about one thing. If and when they mated, he would have no regrets. Norian loved his pack, loved his place in the pack, and loved Kalen. Instead of agonizing about his fate, he'd not only come to accept he was a lycan, but was proud of it. Of this, he would somehow have to convince Kalen. And yes, while he needed to restore peace in his kingdom, he was no longer sure he wanted to remain in Tregaron and rule afterward. There were many good men in his father's court who would do a much better job at it than him, of that, he had little doubt. Additionally, given that he was a lycan, it would not be in the kingdom's best interest for him to be king. It would be wrong to lie and hide his true nature from his people—and telling them the truth was out of the question.

When he thought about the possibility of a cure, of becoming human, he surprisingly no longer wanted it. More and more, he knew he belonged here, among his fellow lycans. In fact, he now feared killing Vadok would indeed cause him to revert to being human, and he'd end up losing Kalen forever. He had to convince Kalen of his sincerity before that happened, and time was running out.

CHAPTER TWENTY-SIX

THE PACK DECIDED TO LEAVE ON SATURDAY, NINE DAYS after the full moon, giving them about two and a half weeks to make it to Tregaron. Norian believed this would be more than enough time to get there, as it had taken him only a dozen days to arrive in Norbury. As they prepared to leave that morning, Norian looked wide-eyed at all the people waiting in front of the house, all the people waiting for him. From the window, he watched as more and more folks arrived. He counted forty-two of them and then stopped. While it delighted him that so many people were willing to accompany him on his quest—someone that they barely knew—he was also hesitant. It was going to be difficult to keep their approach a surprise. People tend to notice fifty or more people strolling about together in the woods.

A warm hand pressed on his shoulder and he turned around. Kalen was smiling warmly.

"Almost ready to get rolling?" asked Kalen. "By the looks of it, all the others are already here."

"I didn't think there would be so many," Norian said, his attention drifting back to the window.

"They are loyal, devoted people," Kalen said. "They've supported me and helped me ever since my father's death. Now they'll do the same for you. I consider myself fortunate to belong to such a community."

Norian nodded, saying nothing. At that moment, Lady Auryon entered the room. She walked up, hugged her son, and then turned her attention to Norian.

"May good fortune go with you, and may success find you each step along your journey."

Norian gave her a weak smile. "Thank you, Lady Auryon. I certainly hope that our mission will be successful."

Lady Auryon dismissed him with a wave of her hand. "Of your success, I have no doubt. Even a sorcerer as strong as Vadok is no match for a powerful Alpha, and you, my son, are one of the most powerful ones I have ever encountered. On the next full moon, Vadok will encounter something that will flood his chilly veins with fear: more than forty lycans, led by an Alpha, at his doorstep." She locked eyes with Norian, and her expression grew serious. "But that does not mean you can leave your guard down, especially during your journey. Because the King of Tregaron was your father, Vadok is no doubt searching for you at this moment. As long as you are alive, you'll be a threat to him. For not only are you the legitimate heir to the throne, the son of the father he murdered, but you are a lycan, the one thing that can destroy him."

"I shall constantly be on alert and am proud to represent Norbury in this battle. But you are certain that the bite of a lycan can destroy a sorcerer?"

"Not certain, no," she said. "But as with all such tales and myths, there is often at least some element of truth to them. The tale that I have always heard is that evil can destroy evil. Being that people consider lycans evil—and whether we truly are is a topic for another discussion—we can conclude that we could indeed be able to destroy other evil. Vadok certainly was fearful when he discovered that he'd attacked a village of lycans. Apparently, he did not know beforehand what he was walking into. Once he did figure it out, he subsequently assumed he could easily take over and have a lycan pack at his disposal. What he didn't know is that a local witch and friend of our pack placed protection wards around our entire village, thus making us immune to dark magic. Once he learned he couldn't use magic against us, he ran like the coward he was. If only it had been a full moon, his story would have turned out much differently."

The sadness weighed heavily on her face. Norian pulled her into a hug. "Thank you for everything, Lady Auryon," he whispered.

"Just promise me you will see that no harm comes to my son," she whispered. "He's all I have."

"I shall guard his life with my own," Norian said. "Of that, you can be certain."

She nodded her head. "And regardless of what happens, you are welcome here always. You have a permanent home in Norbury, young Alpha."

Norian inclined his head politely. "I thank you for that and shall not soon forget your kindness."

A gentle tug on his arm diverted Norian's attention. "They are waiting," said Kalen. His voice held an air of quiet sureness.

He looked at Kalen and then pulled him into a hug as well, burying his face in Kalen's neck. Kalen stiffened in the embrace. "Let us be off then," whispered Norian.

The murmur of voices in front of the house had grown

louder. When Kalen and Norian stepped through the front door, everyone grew quiet. Norian surveyed everyone and an intense surge of pride and gratitude filled him. Here were people he'd known only a couple of weeks, willing to uproot themselves, journey to Tregaron, and risk their lives for him. As his eyes moved from person to person, the physical fitness of the men and women impressed him. They all seemed in top physical form, as if they had been training for this moment their entire lives. It must be because they're lycans. He'd noticed that his own body had firmed up after he had turned, and muscles that he'd never had before suddenly appeared.

Norian glanced again over the crowd. Every person carried a sword with them, with most also having several smaller daggers on their belt. Norian no sooner wished that he'd had his own sword with him when Thomros stepped forward. He was holding a beautiful shiny silver sword.

"Boss, this is for you. It belonged to Kalen's father when he was Alpha of this pack. It now moves on to you."

"I can't accept this," he said. "It belongs with Kalen's family." He turned to look at Kalen. Although his eyes glistened, he was smiling.

"It was Kalen himself who gave me the sword to present to you," Thomros said. "It belongs to the Alpha of this pack. So it is now yours." His voice then increased in volume. "On behalf of the people of Norbury, please accept this sword as the new Alpha of the Norbury pack." He dropped to one knee, his head bent down.

"Go ahead," whispered Kalen behind him. "It's yours."

Without thought, his legs propelled him forward. As he reached Thomros, emotion overwhelmed him, and he had to fight hard to remain in control. He rested his left hand on Thomros's shoulder and retrieved the sword with the right.

"As Alpha of the Norbury pack, I accept!"

Thomros looked up and smiled, and a loud cheer arose from the crowd. Norian raised his hand to quell the noise.

He brought his hand to his heart. "This gesture means more to me than you can know. This morning, I am filled with gratitude for each and every one of you here. Your loyalty and devotion are not only noticed but appreciated."

"But today we leave on a perilous mission, and in a few weeks' time, we will face a deadly foe, one that many of you have encountered in the past. We leave today as one strong, united force. But understand that some may not return. I thus offer you now the opportunity to change your mind, to stay here in the village. You certainly will not be thought any less of for staying. In fact, I encourage you to stay, for I cannot promise anyone's safety. Vadok is a cruel and merciless sorcerer, and truth be told, I can't guarantee that any of us will make it out alive. It saddens me to put any of your lives in such jeopardy. For me, this is a personal mission, as he has stolen my kingdom and murdered my father. However, I am more than willing to face Vadok alone. So anyone who wishes to stay may retreat now back to their homes. I not only permit it but encourage it."

Everyone was silent, but looked back and forth at each other. Not one person moved. After a few moments, a young man stepped forward.

"Your Majesty," he said, bowing his head.

"There is no need to call me that," said Norian. "I am one of you, your equal. So please call me Norian."

"Lord Norian," began the man again. "We are all with you, danger or no danger. As an Alpha never deserts his pack, so does a pack never abandon their Alpha. Thus, we enter into battle with you proudly and willingly." The man stepped back.

"So be it," Norian said. "If there are no other comments, we leave immediately."

The crowd was silent as all eyes watched Norian intently. He raised his sword above his head. "Let us move on then to victory!"

"To victory!" The crowd shouted. And they were off.

~

THE FIRST FEW days passed without incident, although the going was much more complicated than it had been when Norian had come through alone. Then, he'd had the luxury of passing through the villages and finding lodging and food. However, given that there were nearly fifty of them, that option didn't exist. Kalen had pointed out that these towns were rife with lycan hunters and many of them still offered a bounty for the head of a wolf. Allowing the townspeople to see fifty lycans together would invite nothing less than a massacre. So they strayed from the main roads and passed much of their time bushwhacking.

"Why do you think there would be a danger for us?" Norian asked. "How would people know we are lycans?"

"There aren't many villages around here, and most folks know at least some people in the neighboring parts," Kalen said. "We've always kept to ourselves, so anyone seeing a large group of unfamiliar people could easily assume that we're from Norbury. So, no, it's much more prudent to travel this way. The one thing we do not need is to enter into any impromptu skirmishes with local villages."

"So there are really people who hunt you?" Norian asked.

"You mean us, don't you?" Kalen replied.

Norian felt his face redden. "Us," he repeated.

"There aren't as many hunters as there used to be. Over the years, a few rogue lycans have given the rest of us a bad name. These rogues had killed some humans, so naturally, people's first instinct was to eradicate all wolves. At first, people's conscience's only allowed them to hunt us during the full moon when we were in wolf form. Others, though it was against the law, hunted us even when we hadn't changed. Thus was the reason for forming Norbury, our protected fortress. It's been a few years since a hunter has killed a lycan, or at least so that we've heard about it. The killing of lycans is outlawed in most villages, but I assure you—there are still hunters out there, moving in the shadows, quietly seeking revenge for what was done to their families. Others are motivated by their hatred of anything they don't understand."

"Have there been many attacks on your village by these hunters?"

"Not too often, but every now and then, a hunter tries to invade our village. You learned what happened the one time they did succeed."

"I remember," said Norian. "He ended up killing one of the pack members."

Kalen closed his eyes for several moments, as if resisting a painful memory. "From that point on, we've had continual guards posted around all borders of Norbury. Most people are smart enough to leave us alone. Now you understand why Thomros and Deric were so rough on you when you met, especially once you expressed an interest in entering our village?"

"What do these hunters receive for killing a lycan?"

Kalen raised his eyebrows. "Besides revenge?"

"Is there a committee or something that rewards them for killing us? What is their purpose for hunting?"

"Truth be told, Norian, I don't know. I'm not aware of any committee or society that rewards them for what they do, though some villages used to offer a cash bounty for killing lycans and probably still do." He creased his brow. "Perhaps they do it for their own satisfaction and ego. As long as there have been lycans, there have been hunters."

"Nobody has bothered to figure out why or how to put a stop to it?"

Kalen thought about this for a moment. "I suppose not. I've always assumed it was because a lycan goes rogue now and then and terrorizes a village. But I must say you've aroused my curiosity about what drives the hunters to stalk us still."

"You've mentioned rogue lycans a few times. What makes a lycan go rogue?"

"What causes a human man to kill his neighbor or become a serial killer? What causes a human to betray a friend or steal from others?"

"Point taken," Norian said. "So it all boils down to our psychological makeup, then?"

"Mostly," Kalen said. "On rare occasions, a lycan finds themselves in the similar situation that you were in when you first arrived in our village. It's rare that someone is bit and survives, but it happens. They may suddenly find themselves shifting on the full moon with their wolf taking complete control, just as it did the first time you transformed. This is probably one of the most dangerous situations a lycan can find themselves in because eventually, the wolf takes over completely."

"You mean the person stays a wolf permanently?"

"I've heard of it happening," said Kalen. "It's an all-or-nothing situation. Either you learn to control the wolf and transform only on the full moon—or in your case, the three nights of the moon—or stay a wolf permanently and lose your humanity forever."

Norian shivered at the realization of how close he'd come to losing his humanity permanently. He wondered how long it would have taken for the wolf to seize complete control of him.

"It's a good thing that I found your village when I did," Norian said.

"It is indeed," Kalen said. "Otherwise, you might've been lost to me forever."

Norian looked at Kalen, but Kalen stared straight ahead, obviously avoiding Norian's gaze. This conversation would have to wait for another time. They walked in silence for quite some time. It was Kalen who finally broke the silence.

"The days pass us by quickly. Have you given any further consideration to your plan?"

"Only what you already know," Norian said. "All will depend on how reinforced the city and the castle are and whether there is anyone left who we can trust."

"Don't give up faith in your people," Kalen replied. "Even though they may be under the temporary control of another, they'll remain loyal to you."

Norian nodded. "I believe that to be true as well. I pray Wayf is still alive. He can be a powerful ally."

"He is the magic-worker you spoke of?"

"And my friend. However, I fear he is dead. Vadok was aware of Wayf's power, and Wayf was convinced that he—not I—was the target of the lycan attack. Vadok was trying to wiggle his way into my father's kingdom as a court magician. But, of course, my father saw right through him, as Vadok's reputation is well known."

"Then, let us hope he still lives," Kalen said. "We shall no doubt need all the allies we can get."

Norian nodded. "I'm pleased that everyone who accompanies us remains in good spirits. Let us hope they remain so as the days draw on. I had a much easier time of it when I came through alone."

"Much easier?" Kalen asked. "How?"

"I could stop in villages along the way and spend the night occasionally at an inn. Those villages were also essential for procuring food. I didn't think to pack enough for the entire journey. I have to admit that I worry about our food supply."

"That we didn't bring enough?" Kalen asked.

Norian shook his head. "No, I believe we have plenty. My concern is sleeping out in the open in the woods. There's a good chance that wolves or other wild animals could creep in during the night and steal our food rations. They could even feast on us as we sleep."

Kalen smiled, the first warm grin since they left Norbury. "Norian, you worry too much. No animal would dare attack us. We are lycans."

"But we're human and vulnerable now."

"We are never completely human," Kalen said matter-of-factly. "Even in our current form, animals know us and recognize us for what we are. They fear us because we are Alpha animals."

"Is that like an Alpha lycan?" Norian asked.

Kalen shook his head. "Not quite. An Alpha animal is one that is, how shall I put it, on the top of the food chain. We possess the cunning of a wolf with the intelligence of humans. Other creatures recognize this and tend to stay away. It is one of the reasons that we are on foot and not on horses. Imagine a horse allowing a wolf to ride it."

"Mine did."

"Huh?"

"I rode a horse partway on my journey to Norbury. The horse didn't seem to mind me at all."

"Curious." Kalen wrinkled his brow in thought for a moment, and then a flash of remembrance crossed his expression, followed by the smug look of satisfaction. "Ah, yes. That's because you're an Alpha. I recall my father was the only lycan in the village able to ride a horse. I'm not sure the reason. Maybe a horse doesn't dare disrespect an Alpha? I tried once, and it didn't end well for me." He rubbed his backside. "I figured that if an Alpha could ride, so could a Beta. I was wrong."

Norian couldn't help but smile at the mental image of Kalen being bucked off a horse. "That's good to know. I have to admit that getting attacked was at the back of my mind since we left, especially since we're carrying so much food."

"Now you needn't worry about that any longer." Norian could hear the teasing tone in his voice. "The only thing with which you need to concern yourself is how to regain Tregaron."

Norian looked away. "I'm not worried about that."

"No?" Kalen asked.

"It shall be done no matter what or how. It has to."

CHAPTER TWENTY-SEVEN

THE LYCANS GREW RESTLESS AS THEY DREW CLOSER TO their destination. Sometimes tempers flared, and Norian wondered if it was the stress at what lie ahead or the fact that the full moon was coming up quickly. They finally arrived at their destination three days before the full moon. It took the group much longer than it had taken Norian. They had nearly run out of time.

"What now?" Thomros asked once Norian announced they neared the castle.

"We wait until the full moon," Norian said. "Then we make our move. Until that time, we'll camp on the outskirts. Let the others know."

"Will do, boss." He hesitated. "But I have to tell you, this feels strange. Wrong."

"What do you mean?" Norian asked.

"There are no guards. If what you say is true and Vadok expects you to attack, then why isn't there an army around the perimeter? When I snuck near the castle earlier, I saw nobody—only a couple of armed guards outside the castle doors. But nobody was guarding near the woods at all. The castle appears undefended."

Norian rubbed his chin. "You're right. That is most curious. I wonder if Vadok knows we're coming and has set a trap?"

Thomros considered this. "I think we need to be extra diligent. We may not have the element of surprise on our side after all."

Over the past several days, Norian had engaged in repeated discussions with pack members, who insisted that they accompany him into the city. He understood their concern and desire to protect their Alpha, but held firm to his decision. He had to go into the city alone. Anyone with him would only slow him down, given that only he knew how to sneak in and out of the castle quickly. Moreover, going in alone assured the element of surprise, and they needed all the favorable odds they could get.

The night before the full moon, shortly before moonrise, Norian announced it was time and gave everyone instructions that if he does not return by morning, command was to defer to Kalen, and they should attack the next night after moonrise. Before anyone objected, he snuck off to transform.

Power surged through him as he trotted toward Tregaron. As he drew closer to the gates of the city, the silence surprised him. By now, the pub should have been full of people laughing, drinking, and singing. But his extra-sensitive ears picked up no such sounds. The silence was eerie. It was clear to him that things were not as they were. A sign outside the city gates confirmed his suspicion.

CURFEW: ALL CITIZENS MUST BE IN THEIR HOMES BY SUNSET OR RISK EXECUTION.

That was new, and told him that Vadok was indeed ruling by fear. He trotted through the gates and made his way toward the castle. Norian was surprised that running as hard as he did barely winded him. He discovered that though no guards stood near the border of the woods as Thomros had discovered, Vadok had posted guards everywhere outside of the castle, and the closer he got to it, the more plentiful they became. He was grateful that his black fur helped to hide him, as he could easily blend into the shadows.

He finally reached the castle and realized that there was no going in through the front. Armed men surrounded the castle.

"Hey!" a man shouted, and panic filled him. Norian froze and waited, preparing to pounce if necessary. "Get your lazy ass over here. You're late."

Another man jogged up to where the other two guards stood. Norian breathed a sigh of relief. So they hadn't seen him. But how was he to get into the castle? All at once, he thought of the main dining hall. In the basement, along the far wall, was a hidden room that gave way to a tunnel leading to the castle. It was truly a secret room, though the kitchen staff used it regularly to transport food back and forth to the castle dining hall. It was much quicker than dragging food down the road and through the front door. The food also was guaranteed to arrive warm.

Food smells attacked his nostrils, and his mouth filled with saliva. His wolf desperately wanted to hunt, to feed. *Not yet*, he told his wolf. *After our task is complete.* The wolf seemed to pull back, and Norian felt relief. The dining hall was dark, and there appeared to be no humans in the vicinity. Norian trotted to the front door and stopped. How was he supposed to open the door while in wolf form? How was he to get in? He pulled back and studied the front. The door was padlocked, and the wood was much too thick for him to break down. Perhaps he could do it, but the noise would no doubt arouse someone. He scampered to the side of the hall. Ah yes, there was one other way in—the window. He was unable to open it, but he might break the glass and get through. He hoped that the noise wouldn't give him away.

He retreated about fifty yards, crouched down, and with a running start, jumped and crashed through the window. The sound of the breaking glass wasn't as loud as he'd feared, and for that, he was grateful. His paws rested on the shattered pieces of glass. Norian shook his body, and bits of glass tinkled to the floor. Fearful of an injury, he looked himself over and could see no apparent bleeding. Luckily, his hide was tough.

He jumped over the glass and found the stairs to the basement. The food smells grew stronger, and his stomach rumbled. It appeared that roast beef had been on tonight's menu. He wondered if there was any left, but quickly shook the thought from his head. No time for that now. He had to get to the castle.

The basement was much chillier and felt good, its coolness a welcome break from the muggy night. The only sound was the clicking of his toenails as he walked, his wolf eyes allowing him to see perfectly in the dark. He thought it strange that nobody was guarding this entrance. Why hadn't Vadok sealed it off? The only explanation was that he wasn't aware of it. Nobody had bothered to tell him. This gave Norian hope that perhaps not everyone was entirely under Vadok's control. He had a difficult time imagining that any of the castle workers would support Vadok willingly.

He raised his nose in the air and sniffed. The food

smells grew weaker the further away from the kitchen he moved, and new scents took their place. Saltier ones.

Humans.

It was difficult to determine whether it was anyone he knew as the odors all mingled together. He finally reached the end of a tunnel which was sealed off by a large wooden door. Damn it! He'd forgotten all about the door. Norian pushed against it, but it held fast so he stood up on two legs, something he hoped he wouldn't have to repeat any time soon, and attempted to turn the doorknob with his paws. Despite the tight grip he managed to apply, the knob didn't budge. The door was locked, as he expected it would be. He meant to curse, but it came out as a snarl. Norian stared at the door for a moment and made his decision. He would simply have to break it down. There was no other way to get in. He lifted his nose high into the air and sniffed again. He smelled several distinct human odors, but none of them was strong, meaning that nobody had been near the door in a while. There were no guards in the nearby vicinity. He prayed he was correct in his assumption and that it wasn't just that the thickness of the door decreased his ability to smell what was on the other side.

He walked quite a distance backward until he felt that the space between him and the door was enough for a powerful running jump and thrust. He tensed and flexed his muscles. With his eyes glued to the door, he ran toward it. Just as he picked up as much speed as he could muster, he heaved himself in the middle of the door, to the left of the doorknob. The door flew open and hit the wall with a loud bang. Norian rolled and found himself sprawled out in the middle of the hallway. Stunned for a moment, he shook himself, then scanned his body once again. No damage done. He paused and listened, trying to gage whether the crash had aroused the interest of the guards.

Nothing yet.

His stomach rumbled again. He needed food and thought for a moment about what would happen should he encounter a guard, but shook the thought from his head. He promised himself that he would never again eat a human. But what if that human is an enemy? What if they attacked him first? Would he make an exception?

Norian shook his body, trying to rid himself of the disturbing thoughts, and glanced around. He knew precisely where he was. He was in the basement, close to the castle prisons. Typically, there was very little human activity here, except for the one guard who was permanently stationed in the hallway outside of the prisons. Who knew how much this might have changed under Vadok's rule? He wondered if Vadok even kept prisoners. From what Wayf had said, Vadok typically always kills his foes—he doesn't keep them.

As Norian trotted down the hallway, a new yet distinct scent drifted into his nostrils. A more potent, more familiar one. His heart started pounding rapidly in his chest. Could it be? Was the scent he noticed actually that of his friend and mentor, Wayf? Was he alive?

He ran faster now as Wayf's scent grew stronger. He briefly wondered how he was so confident that it was Wayf he was smelling, but then he remembered. Wayf was with him the second night he turned. Although he wasn't in control of his wolf at that time, his wolf remembered. His wolf knew Wayf.

He finally reached the door to the prisons, which surprisingly was wide open. The small table outside of the door that the prison guard usually occupied stood empty.

Apparently, he was right—Vadok had no need for prison guards. But what about Wayf's scent? It was so strong. Norian was optimistic that Wayf was somewhere nearby and alive. He moved slowly toward the doorway, ears perked up at attention. He stopped to listen one last time before going in and then stilled. There was someone close by. He distinctly heard the sound of steady breathing.

He padded cautiously toward the door and looked in. Only one of the prison cells was occupied, and it contained Wayf.

"Wayf!" he instinctively tried to shout, but it came out as a loud, snarling growl.

The noise awoke Wayf, and he turned to look at Norian. Norian smelled Wayf's fear upon seeing the giant black wolf peering in at him from the door's window, and then recognition sparked in Wayf's eyes.

"Norian?"

Norian nodded his large wolf head and walked into the room.

Wayf got up from the earthen floor and walked to the bars. He smiled, but all at once, his expression shifted into one of terror.

"No, Norian. You can't be here. Hurry, leave this room now!"

The words were barely out of Wayf's mouth when the cement door clicked shut behind him. Norian's head snapped toward the click, and he growled. Damn it! Someone had trapped him in here with Wayf, with no way out. So was there someone out there, after all? How did he not hear them or smell them?

"Magic," said Wayf, as if reading his thoughts. "Vadok was certain that you'd come back to the castle once you heard what had happened. He enchanted the door so that anyone entering it would be trapped inside. Funny, he did it just this morning, although he didn't expect you until tomorrow night. I wasn't about to tell him any differently."

Norian stared at Wayf and looked back at the closed door. Hot anger filled his veins. Idiot! He should have known that this was too easy. Upon seeing that there was no guard, he should have figured that it was a trap. How could he have been so dense? Vadok had expected him to come and to be in wolf form when he arrived. Of course he did. Vadok was well aware Norian would be much more powerful as a wolf, so it made sense that Norian would attack when in his lycan form. He wondered if Vadok realized that a wolf could destroy him?

Norian approached the bar and sat next to the door. It frustrated him that he was unable to speak. He had so much to tell Wayf and so much that he needed to know.

"I'm so sorry you're trapped," said Wayf, stepping back, keeping a safe distance from the bars. Apparently, he was afraid that Norian would reach for him through the bars. "I couldn't tell you what had happened, so I sent Belkas, hoping against hope the bird would reach Norbury—and that you'd be able to come. I imagine that the only reason I'm alive was to draw you here. From what little I've overheard, it sounds as if Vadok considers you a serious threat." He closed his eyes and sighed. "Oh, Norian, you shouldn't have come. I'm sure he plans on killing you, a deed that will solidify his position as King of Tregaron. If only you could understand me."

Norian turned his head and met Wayf's eyes. Norian whimpered and nodded his head.

Wayf creased his brow, his back still pressed against the wall of his cell. All at once, a look of recognition crossed over Wayf's face. "Your eyes. You're different from last time.

There's something else there." He studied Norian's face for another moment. "An intelligence. Can you understand me?"

Norian nodded again. He sat next to the cage, whimpered, and blinked both of his eyes.

"How can this be? The last time there was nothing left of you at all. You were a dangerous and untamed beast. What happened?"

Norian opened his mouth to speak, but only whimpered. He growled in frustration.

"It looks as though I have a lot more to learn about werewolves," said Wayf.

Norian wanted to correct him, to tell him that the proper word was lycan, but that would have to wait until tomorrow. Norian moved closer to the bars and pressed his body against them, his head facing the now closed door. He heard Wayf slowly approach him. Norian would have smiled were it possible. Wayf's fear had almost completely disappeared, though some trepidation remained.

Wayf reached out his right hand towards Norian, and, rethinking the action, quickly withdrew. "Can I touch you?"

Norian nodded, and Wayf's hand slowly stroked his head. Wayf's touch felt wonderful, and it made him realize how much he had missed Tregaron and the people he loved. Norian thought of the pack. He had failed in his mission, which meant that it was now up to the pack. He'd hoped that it wouldn't come to that. Norian had wanted to find Vadok and kill him himself without the pack ever getting involved. The last thing he wanted to do was to risk the lives of all those beautiful people who recognized him as their Alpha. Perhaps he shouldn't have been so pig-headed and should have listened to the advice of Kalen and the others. Advice that said he should not do this alone. Damn his pride. Now, look where it got him? He just hoped that Vadok didn't know about the pack. He also hoped that by some miracle, Vadok wouldn't kill him before moonrise.

"Norian?" Wayf's voice said softly.

Norian had become so caught up in his own thoughts, he'd momentarily forgotten about the presence of his friend. He turned and met Wayf's eyes.

"You have heard about your father?"

Norian slowly nodded his head.

"I cannot begin to express how sorry I am about what happened to him." His voice was barely audible. "He was a good man and was not only my King but also my friend."

He let loose with a long whimper, turning into a low howl. If he were in human form, Norian would be crying right now. His heart tugged, but the tears refused to come. Apparently, wolves can't—or don't—cry. He looked at Wayf and then hung his head.

"If it's any consolation, it was quick. I realize that doesn't help much, but I wanted you to know he didn't suffer." He sighed. "It's been a long few weeks. As I'm sure you suspect, everything's changed. All that is, except people's attitudes. Vadok has had a difficult time making the people accept him as their ruler, which has caused him to bring in a lot of his own people to run the kingdom. Your father's army is gone, replaced by his. There were uprisings and rebellions initially, but too many people were getting executed, so they mostly ceased. However, it's been quiet as of late. Perhaps people are finally accepting their fate. But I feel deep down that given a chance, they would overthrow Vadok and take their kingdom back without a second thought." He sighed. "But there seems to be little chance of that. Especially now that you've been caught."

Norian wished he could tell him about the pack, but it

would have to wait until morning. He hoped that he would have a chance to talk to Wayf before they came for him, to find out as much as possible about Vadok's strategy. But until that time, all he could do was wait. And if Vadok killed him, then it would be up to the pack to succeed without him.

Norian stretched out, laid his head on his paws, and prayed for sleep to come.

CHAPTER TWENTY-EIGHT

"Norian. Norian, wake up," a voice that was barely above a whisper called out to him.

Norian opened his eyes, all at once aware of the cold floor beneath him. It took him a moment to shake loose the cobwebs from his brain, typical for the morning after a change.

He lifted his head and glanced upward. Wayf was pressed against the bars and had a wild look in his eyes. Norian held Wayf's gaze, trying to figure out how he had ended up here. Then it all came back to him.

"Wayf!" said Norian, jumping up. He reached out and touched his friend. "It is so good to see you. I was so afraid that you'd met the same fate as my father."

Wayf gave him a weak smile. "'Tis good to see you too, my boy. But let me ask: Do you recall anything of our conversation from last night?"

Norian creased his brow and thought. "All of it," he said.

"But how can this be? The night you changed in my presence, you were naught but a wild beast. Even the next morning, you professed you could remember nothing of the previous evening's events."

"I have learned how to control the wolf," Norian said. "Or should I say, I've learned how not to allow the wolf inside to control me."

"I didn't realize this was possible. How did you learn such a feat? Did you find the Queen of Werewolves?"

Norian nodded. "Aye, but she's not exactly their queen. Perhaps she was once when she was married to their Alpha. But he found the same fate as my father at the hands of the same scoundrel."

"I may safely assume, then, that there was no cure to be found?"

Norian paused a little too long.

"What? There is a cure? If so, why haven't you taken it?"

"There is no known cure for lycanism," Norian said. "Although it is rumored that if one becomes a lycan through the act of sorcery, then killing the sorcerer might return the lycan to his or her human state. Whether this is actually true, nobody knows."

"So you're saying that if you slay Vadok, you could regain your humanity?"

"That is how the myth is recounted. But things have become," he paused, trying to determine how to explain his situation. "Somewhat complicated."

Wayf raised his eyebrows and studied Norian's face. "Then tell me everything. I am not going anywhere anytime soon, and it appears that neither are you."

"What about the guards?"

Wayf shook his head. "It is barely sunrise. The castle will not stir for some time yet."

Norian sat cross-legged next to Wayf's cell. He shivered. The cold was seeping into his bones.

"I forget you are naked," Wayf said. "We had better get you covered up." He moved to the back of his cell, retrieved a tattered green cloak and a faded orange tunic. He handed the items to Norian through the bars.

"Luckily, they provided me with a couple of changes of clothes. It would be difficult to explain how it came to be that you are locked in here with me, naked. It would no doubt arouse suspicion. Speaking of that, did you ever find out why it is that you can transform before the moon?"

"Yes," said Norian. "But let me start from the very beginning."

He then told Wayf, in whispers, everything that had happened to him since he left Tregaron: him being an Alpha, learning about lycanism from Lady Auryon and her son, running with the pack and the pack expecting him to lead them. The only thing he left out was the gender of his mate.

"My goodness," said Wayf, after Norian had completed his story. "You certainly have had yourself quite an adventure." He studied Norian's face for several moments. "So, you're an Alpha werewolf?"

"Truth be told, Wayf, the term is lycan. They don't like the term werewolf—probably because there's so much baggage attached to the word."

"Lycan it is, then," said Wayf. "I did come across this term while I was researching your condition. It's true what you've said. There are indeed very few cases of anyone turning into a lycan from a bite. I found this strange, judging by your condition the last time we talked. But now it makes sense. Once a lycan learns how to control the beast within, they are in full control. There are no more accidental attacks. Is it true?"

"That is my understanding. There have supposedly been unfortunate instances of the occasional lycan going rogue, but mostly lycans are no different from anyone else. Except for once a month."

"Did I not tell you something similar before you left?"

"Aye, you did," said Norian.

Wayf smiled warmly at Norian. "It is no surprise that you are an Alpha. One could say that it is your destiny, as you've prepared to rule as King since birth. You've simply ended up ruling a different type of kingdom."

"It must be in my blood," Norian said. "It appears as though I am indeed my father's son."

Wayf's expression faltered and grew dark, if only for a moment, but Norian caught it.

"What's wrong?" Norian said. "Did I say something?"

Wayf dismissed him with a wave of his hand. "Nothing. I only am concerned about what fate awaits us, now that they've captured you as well. You have come alone?"

As much as he trusted Wayf, Norian wanted to keep his plans a secret. It suddenly dawned on him that if Vadok had used magic to trap him, he could very well be using magic to eavesdrop on every word that he and Wayf exchanged, even their whispers. He mustn't take the chance.

"I've come alone. I must face Vadok on my own."

"You'll kill him then if given the opportunity?"

Norian hesitated. The answer to this question became more and more unclear with each day that passed. He straightened. "If given the opportunity, I will remove Vadok from the throne."

"Ah, my dear Norian. That was not my question."

"I know," Norian said. His voice sounded defeated.

"I'm sorry, my friend. I understand that this is one of the hardest decisions that you will need to face. From what I've gathered, you experience a strong bond with this new pack of yours, and they wish you to rule them. But ruling Tregaron is your birthright and your duty. You know this!"

Norian nodded. "Believe me, I have rehashed these thoughts repeatedly, and I am not any closer to a decision. There may not even be any such decision to be made. Given that I'm captured, my opportunities may now be limited."

"Perhaps. Perhaps not. There is still the full moon tonight in your favor, and from what you tell me, you also possess the powers of an Alpha. This may be an advantage, one of which Vadok is unaware."

"I suppose all will depend on the events of this day and whether Vadok will choose to slay me before moonrise."

Wayf closed his eyes and was silent for several moments. He wrung his hands. "Let us not think of the worst possible circumstances, but rather maintain our hope. It is all we have."

"But what of your powers?" Norian asked. "We still have those."

Wayf shook his head. "Alas, we do not. Vadok has somehow bound my magic. In my current state, I am no more powerful than a stable hand. I've tried everything I know to unbind them, but have met with no success. And even if I possessed my powers, my knowledge of dark magic is extremely limited. I suppose it might have behooved me to learn it if only to defend myself against it."

"Do you have any idea what his plan is?"

"Regretfully, no. He's only talked about dealing with you should you decide to show up. I wish I had thought sooner of some way to warn you of the trap."

"If I am killed today, then all is lost," Norian said.

"What happened to maintaining hope?"

"Sorry. I didn't count on getting caught."

"Nobody ever does," says Wayf.

They were both silent for several moments. Wayf finally spoke. "Tell me about this mate of yours. You said that if you mate with her, then killing Vadok would not remove the curse. This is true?"

Norian nodded. "I held off from mating for so long, fighting my feelings. My only goal was to cure myself of this affliction, to return to a normal life. But somewhere along the way, things changed. Or should I say, my feelings have changed. The more I became ingrained in the pack, the more I wanted to stay. It's like I finally found my place in this world." He met Wayf's eyes. "You know, I've always felt out of place."

Wayf nodded. "You have mentioned this a time or two."

"The past many weeks have been agonizing. I thought I was steadfast in my goal, but admittedly, I falter. I no longer know what is the right thing to do."

"Does your mate offer any advice?"

"He has supported me throughout all of this. However, when I finally agreed to mate, he refused me. He said that he didn't want to mate with me until I could convince him I was absolutely sure that I was willing to accept him as my mate and my place in the pack. Unfortunately, he didn't feel that I was ready to make that decision."

"Your mate is male, then."

Norian met Wayf's eyes and slowly nodded. "He is called Kalen. He is Lady Auryon's son."

Wayf took a deep breath. "Your mate is the son of an Alpha?"

"It appears so. From what I've heard, it is a rare occurrence for a lycan to find their true mate."

"Again, I am unsurprised that your mate is a male and one of royalty at that. We both knew of your inclination. Your destiny grows more interesting."

"That it does. It's come to the point where little surprises me now."

"This mate of yours," Wayf said. "Do you love him?"

Norian flinched back, surprised at the question. He then met Wayf's gaze. "With all my heart."

"When the fates place such machinations at our door, there is often a higher purpose involved. What that is, none of us knows until the time arrives. But what you need to realize is that our destiny is never freely revealed to those such as ourselves. Instead, the fates test us, sometimes over and over, to see if we are deserving of that which awaits us. I feel that the decision to mate with this Kalen was one of those tests."

Norian considered this. "So, did I pass?"

"Only you can tell that. But if what you say is true, that it is a rare thing for a lycan to find their mate, then who are you to reject such a gift?"

Norian nodded. "You are correct. I now wish I had found the courage to solidify my bond with Kalen when he offered it to me, offered himself to me. But now, all is lost."

"Perhaps. Perhaps not. I've a feeling that the universe is not through with you yet."

"I hope for all of our sakes that you are correct," Kalen said. "But if I were to mate with Kalen, then my destiny of taking the throne could no longer be."

Wayf regarded him, a curious look on his face. "Why should coupling with Kalen change anything? You are still the rightful heir to the throne."

"I would remain lycan, and any chances of beating this curse would be gone. How could I possibly take the throne?

I have asked myself and others this same question repeatedly, and it appears that nobody sees the incompatibility of a king with the wolf curse."

Before Wayf could answer, the scraping of the door against the cement caught both of them off guard. Vadok stood in the doorway with four guards. Norian took a step back, an almost involuntary reflex, as Vadok studied him with undisguised satisfaction. The sorcerer held Norian's gaze for a chilly moment.

"I didn't expect you until tonight when you'd be in your dog form." He brought both of his hands underneath his chin and formed a tee-pee. "No matter. I think this shall serve my plan even better." He laughed hollowly. "You have unknowingly made things much easier for me. For tonight, the entire city shall see that their would-be-King is a monster." He gestured to the men next to him. "Lock him up down the hall. I want four guards posted outside his cell at all times. Just in case he has friends."

The guards then dragged him out of the room and pushed him into one of the other cells down the hallway. "See you tonight, Princess."

CHAPTER TWENTY-NINE

"WHAT DID YOU HOPE TO ACHIEVE COMING HERE?" Vadok said, with a sharp voice that Norian thought could strip wallpaper.

Norian remained quiet, studying the man's face. Damn, even if Norian wasn't already aware this man was evil, his face was a dead giveaway.

"You're giving me the silent treatment? How adolescent."

"Your time will come," Norian hissed between his teeth.

"So it does speak, after all. Although I'm not so sure about the coming of my time and all that nonsense." He made a waving gesture in the air. "From where I am standing, you appear to be at somewhat of a disadvantage."

Norian took a deep breath. A sense of hopelessness crept through him, but he shook it off. He must not give up yet. His pack will attack tonight, no doubt. All he has to do is manage to stay alive until that point. Of course, that means trying not to piss off Vadok too much.

"If given half the chance —" Norian began.

"You shall not be given any chance. I shall see to it

personally." He flashed a self-satisfied grin. "But what to do to you? That is the question. I have imagined so many different ways to slay you, but yet none of them seem adequate. No, I need something astounding, something with meaning. Something people will remember for all time."

He stepped forward, closer to Norian's cage. "As long as you live, the people retain hope that you shall somehow return. That, of course, I cannot have. So tonight, you shall be slain, young Prince. But you shall perish in front of your people. All of Tregaron will witness your execution."

"What are you saying, Vadok? That you intend to kill me in front of the city? The people would never allow it. They'd surely attack."

A small, tight smile tugged at Vadok's lips. "Not only will they allow it, they will encourage it. They will cheer me on the entire time."

An explosion of comprehension slammed Norian as he slowly understood Vadok's plan. He was going to kill Norian while he was in wolf form, in front of his people.

A hollow laugh filled the room. "Ah, I see you've figured out my strategy. Yes, my dear dog, your people are going to see their beloved Prince Norian for what he truly is: a filthy, dangerous, man-eating beast. They will come to realize that as long as you live, they are not safe. And they certainly would not allow themselves to be ruled by a carnivorous hound. No, my dear Prince, your presence here is a gift to me and a blessing. For the people will no longer have the hope of some distant prince riding in to save them and will instead look to me: their new savior and protector."

Anger bombarded his brain, but Norian fought against it. As much as he wanted to tell this fiend precisely what he thought of him, it would do no good and would not serve his goals. The one consolation was that Norian would remain alive until moonrise. There was still a chance that the others would arrive in time. There was still a chance that he might rescue his kingdom. He gritted his teeth and looked at Vadok. There was no doubt about it: if given the opportunity, Norian would kill him.

"Feeling hopeless?" he asked with a sneer. "Afraid all of your dreams and goals are lost?"

Norian turned his head and said nothing. He braced himself for more.

"I no longer find your company amusing. I'll see you this evening, dog. Get ready to face your people."

Vadok let loose with a high-pitched chuckle, and Norian heard the heavy cement door close.

He surveyed his surroundings. The bars of his cell were solid, with no windows or any other moveable pieces. He knew these prisons well—these inescapable and impenetrable prisons. Nobody had ever escaped them.

It was impossible.

He was trapped.

He wished he were in wolf form so he could somehow let Kalen know where he was. He wondered if they still had the connection in human form. Kalen had mentally connected with him while they both were human, and they were able to converse back and forth. It was worth a try. He closed his eyes, scrunched his forehead, and called out in his mind.

"Kalen? Can you hear me?"

He waited for a moment. Nothing.

"Kalen? I'm not sure if you can hear me. I'm hoping so. Vadok has kidnapped me. He means to kill me this evening in front of the entire city. I imagine it will take place in the arena at moonrise. But he won't kill me until I transform.

The only hope is if you and the others are already nearby and can attack before they slay me. I pray that you can hear me. If you can, know one thing: I love you with all of my heart and soul."

Norian waited for several moments. Nothing. Disheartened by the lack of response, he spread himself out on the floor to rest. As usual, the previous night's change had exhausted him and he desperately needed to sleep—to recharge. As much as he didn't want to spend what might be the last day of his life sleeping, he understood he would need all of his available strength for tonight if it came down to a battle. He hoped it would.

He wasn't sure how long he'd been asleep when all at once, his nose picked up a familiar scent, and he snapped to attention. Kalen! He could identify the distinctive and over-powering scent of his mate anywhere. He was here to rescue him.

Norian rose and rushed to the bars, standing erect, waiting. His lover's scent grew stronger, meaning Kalen was getting close. All the once, the door slowly opened, and Norian's heart sunk. Kalen was being pushed forward by two guards, spears at his back.

"Norian!" Kalen said, rushing to the bars. "Thank the gods you're alive."

"But he won't be for long," snickered one of the guards.

"And neither shall you," said the other.

"Now, gentlemen," said Vadok's voice. "Is that any way to treat our most esteemed guests?"

The guards stepped aside, allowing Vadok to enter. He glared at one of the guards and Kalen. "Fools! He is one of them. I told you, keep them covered at all times."

The guard closest to Kalen held up his spear and pointed it at Kalen's throat. Norian saw that the tip was made of silver—a metal he'd learned was deadly to lycans. Norian could smell Vadok's fear. So the sorcerer was aware that a lycan could destroy him. That, of course, made his quest more challenging. He guessed Vadok was going to ensure that he was nowhere near any transformed lycan.

Vadok gestured toward Norian. The guard raised his spear and pointed it at him. "Back to the wall," the guard said. Norian let go of the bars, held up his hands, and plastered himself against the back wall. The guard opened the cage door and pushed Kalen inside. He then quickly locked it.

"So, you do have some pals about," Vadok said. "Who are you?"

Kalen glared at Vadok and said nothing. "Oh, another one too shy to talk? Maybe we'll just have your tongue removed, seeing that you're not using it, anyway. Guard!"

"I'm Kalen."

Vadok swung around and met Kalen's eyes. "Where are you from? Why are you here? How many are there of you?"

"I come alone with Norian. We have traveled together these past few weeks and have become friends.

"From one dog to another," said Vadok. He eyed Kalen suspiciously. "Again, where do you come from?"

"My home is Noredge Basin, the next town over. One day, I discovered Norian rambling in the woods, and we became friends."

"You mean you sniffed out the dog in each other," Vadok said. He laughed, and the two guards joined in.

Kalen nodded. "We recognized we were both lycans, yes. So I accompanied him on his quest."

Vadok's jaw clenched, and the veins in his face protruded. "And what quest was that?"

"To find a cure."

Vadok's eyes widened and then blazed cold. "A wolf cure?" He dismissed Kalen with a wave of a hand and laughed. "There is no such thing."

"That is true, sir," Kalen said. "We found that such a cure did not exist. It was then we learned about what happened in Tregaron. I accompanied Norian back to his home."

"For what purpose? To help him overthrow me?"

Kalen hung his head. "Norian is the Crown Prince. He has a right to the throne."

"Wrong," said Vadok. He folded his hands in front of his chest. He turned and studied both of the young men's faces. "And how were you planning to do it? To overthrow me? Why wouldn't you wait until the full moon when you'd have the advantage?"

"As you may know," said Kalen, "when the moon curse is upon us, we are no longer in control. Norian feared we would inadvertently kill innocent bystanders if we attacked in wolf form."

"Too bad you didn't," said Vadok. He locked eyes with Kalen. "That would have been your only hope. Regretfully for you, you shall also perish with your friend this evening. Two werewolves to play with!" He clapped his hands excitedly. "What fun! Such a treat the town shall have this evening. A spectacle, to be sure."

With that, he turned and left the room, the guard following. When the door was finally closed, Norian wrapped his arms around Kalen. He inhaled deeply, drinking in Kalen's essence, his scent. Norian hoped Kalen wouldn't notice the throbbing underneath his cloak.

"Kalen," he whispered. "Why did you have to come? Why couldn't you wait until tonight? Now he will kill us both."

Kalen brushed his lips lightly on Norian's face. "You called, and I had to come. I couldn't leave you here not knowing if...." His voice trailed off. "If he had killed you. After I heard you, I responded, asking where you were. After waiting nearly half an hour for your response, my worry increased. I had to find you."

"You could hear me?" Norian asked. "I wasn't sure if it would work. I remembered how we'd mentally communicated with each other before, so I thought I'd try it. But I received no message from you in return."

"When we're separated, it's a one-way deal."

"Meaning?"

"Even in human form, an Alpha can send out messages to his pack through his thoughts. Usually, it takes a lot of practice. My father used to do it, send out a general S.O.S. if there was trouble of any kind. I'm sorry that I'd forgotten all about it. It's been so long since there's been an Alpha around that the ability slipped my mind completely."

"So I can communicate with the others? With the other pack members?"

"Given that you did it with me, you should be able to contact the rest of the pack as well. My father could."

"But it's different with you," Norian said. "You're my mate, and we've done it before. So I pictured your beautiful face and thought about what I wanted to say."

"What we had was a direct communication link. It should work the same way with them. First, picture the group of them and bring to mind any faces you remember. Next, focus on connecting with them and on the bond between your mind and theirs. The bond is always there. You and the pack created the bond on the night they accepted you as their Alpha, and it shall remain till death."

"Whose death?" Norian asked.

"Such silly questions you ask. Yours. Theirs. Everyone's. So are you going to try?"

"What should I say?" Norian asked.

"You're the Alpha. You tell me."

Norian nodded and closed his eyes. He tried to picture as many of the pack members as he could.

"Now bring to mind what you want to tell them."

Norian pictured in his mind white words on a giant black wall as he thought them.

Pack members, this is Norian, your Alpha. Kalen and I have been captured by Vadok and he holds us in the castle's jail. He intends to execute us tonight after we transform. The event is to take place in the arena, located in the center of the city. If you are all still willing, I ask that you attack then and not before. I will try to signal you somehow when it's time. Do not enter the city until that time. I cannot stress enough the importance of this. It is much too dangerous, and Vadok's guards are no doubt on high alert. I shall see you all tonight.

Norian waited, wondering if he should try to send it again, but decided against it. Either it worked, or it didn't. He opened his eyes and met Kalen's gaze.

"It's done," said Norian. "I'm not sure if I succeeded, but I tried. I envisioned as many of the faces as I could and sent out the message."

"Let's hope it works," said Kalen. "Your earlier message to me came through loud and clear, as did this one. Of course, I'm sitting right next to you."

"I wish there was some way of knowing for certain that it worked. I don't want anyone else coming here and getting caught."

"It's out of our hands now," said Kalen. "All we can do is hope that it reached them." Kalen reached down and took Norian's hand.

"Won't they come charging in if you don't return?"

"They shouldn't. I told them that if I don't come back, to attack tonight."

"I hope they listen better than you do," Norian said.

Kalen raised his eyebrows. "Whatever do you mean?"

Norian laughed. "You understand my meaning perfectly. You disregarded my instructions and came, regardless of what I asked of you. You disobeyed the direct orders of your Alpha. What shall be done about it?"

Kalen shrugged his shoulders. "Perhaps you should punish me." His voice was barely audible. He moved his hand up and down Norian's arm.

"Kalen," Norian said. "What are you doing? You realize how weak I am around you."

"I want you, Norian. So fucking bad that I can't stand it a minute longer."

"What? But you said—"

"You were right," Kalen interrupted him. "The best chance to fight off Vadok is if we consummate our relationship. I was wrong in rejecting you. Hell, I was downright stupid. Ever since we've met, I've wanted you with every fiber of my being, and the one chance I had with you, I blew it. I suppose that leading a pack of lycans tends to inflate one's ego." He smiled. "This morning, it terrified me that I'd never see you again, that my mate would be gone forever. Then I was angry. Angry at myself for taking some exaggerated high road. I swore that if I got the chance to see you again, the first thing I would do was make love to you. That is, if you are still willing to have me."

Norian swallowed. "You were right in turning me away. At the time, I considered only myself and my kingdom. But things have changed. No, I have changed. Ruling Tregaron is no longer my primary goal. You are. You and this pack."

He took both of Kalen's hands. "If you will have me, I am yours."

Kalen inhaled a deep breath, held it, and let it go. "I need to make sure that you're absolutely certain. Part of me tells me to wait, and another part tells me to let go and to hell with the consequences. If things work out, you may kill Vadok tonight. You're so close, Norian, so close to this elusive cure for which you've been searching. So close to ruling Tregaron as a complete human. Are you sure you're willing to throw that all away now?"

Norian locked eyes with Kalen as if searching for the answer in his gaze. "I am," Norian said after a brief hesitation. "None of that holds any importance for me now. I've given this a lot of consideration over the past couple of weeks. A lot. And I always come to the same conclusion. You and the pack hold the highest place in my heart. I swear to you, Kalen, as Prince of Tregaron and as Alpha of the Norbury pack, that I have made my decision." He paused. "I choose you."

The sharp scent of male arousal filled the room. Norian's reason begin to slip as his animal side took over. He felt as though he were on the verge of shifting and closed his eyes tightly, trying to stop it.

"Norian," Kalen whispered. "It's okay."

Norian opened his eyes. "I came close to shifting. I was losing control."

"No. It's your wolf coming through. It knows that you are with your mate and what your intentions are. So let him come through, Norian. Don't worry, you won't transform, and you won't lose control. But let your wolf be part of this."

Norian nodded and looked at Kalen's face. His features looked different, wilder. No doubt Kalen had already allowed the wolf part of himself to come through.

Norian relaxed. His feral side arose, and Norian could feel the other presence inside of him, inside of his thoughts, inside of his soul. The wolf was there, just on the surface, and one thought arose in his mind: *Take Mate.*

If Norian had any hesitations, they were gone now. The smell of arousal from the two men grew even more potent, and Norian wondered if he could come just from that alone. He put his hands on Kalen's cheeks and pulled him into a starving kiss. Kalen's wet, warm mouth sent his senses reeling, and without thinking, he pushed Kalen to the floor, continuing to kiss him hungrily. Their tongues fought for control, with Norian eventually winning. The kiss bordered on brutal—hot and consuming.

Norian finally pulled his mouth away, and Kalen whimpered like a lost pup. Norian smiled, threw off the cloak. Kalen, in turn, ripped off his shirt and pants, tossing them overhead to the corner of the cell. Norian pushed his lover back down to the floor and then spread himself out on top of Kalen, for the first time feeling his mate completely naked underneath him. His muscular arms drew Kalen in tight, and he squeezed. Norian shivered and closed his eyes for a moment, reveling in the feel of Kalen's body beneath him— Kalen's erection pressing against his stomach. Then he let loose an instinctive growl and began to lick and kiss Kalen's neck. Kalen groaned and writhed underneath him. Next, Norian moved his mouth down Kalen's chest and stopped at his right nipple. Norian gave it a small nip, and Kalen thrust upwards.

"Norian! Ugh.."

Norian looked up, gave Kalen a brief smile, and continued his descent downwards. The more Kalen groaned and shuddered, the more intensely Norian kissed.

He moved his head right next to Kalen's impressive

erection. The sight of it was maddening, and he had to have it. The musky scent in the room grew even stronger. It filled Norian's nostrils and set his senses reeling. Norian dipped his head, stuck out his tongue, and licked along the underside of Kalen's cock. Kalen bucked and hissed through his teeth. Norian nuzzled his head into Kalen's balls and laved them with his tongue. His tongue darted underneath the sac for just a moment, the downward licks causing Kalen to gasp loudly.

"So you like that, huh?" said Norian.

"Please do not stop," Kalen said. "I need so much for you not to stop."

Norian snickered. "Don't you worry. There's plenty more where that came from."

He moved his mouth back to the leaking tip of Kalen's cock. He flicked his tongue a couple of times at the head and gently licked it on the underside.

"Please," said Kalen, the word sounding more like a hiss than a command.

Needing no further encouragement, Norian took Kalen's cock in his mouth. Kalen gasped, even louder this time. Kalen's precum was flowing freely, and Norian loved the tangy flavor. He loved having Kalen's cock in his mouth. It seemed so natural for him, so right. It was as if he'd waited his entire life for this one moment. His wolf was there, right there on the cusp of his consciousness, urging him on. He began by soft-sucking the penis and then increased his tempo. Kalen became more aggressive, grabbing onto Norian's head, trying to force more of himself into him. Norian relaxed his throat to accommodate Kalen's length and surprised himself by swallowing all of Kalen's cock.

Norian was sucking hard and faster now, driven solely by instinct. Then, without warning, Kalen exploded. A river of cum flowed into Norian's mouth. Just as Norian swallowed it down, his own cock twitched and spurted warm liquid over and over onto Kalen's leg. His body crumpled with relief.

Spent, Norian spread himself out on top of Kalen. He lifted his head and took Kalen's mouth in a starving kiss. Kalen broke the kiss.

"That was amazing," Kalen said. "I never imagined."

Norian's breathing slowly returned to normal. He tried to open his mouth but found no words. Another burst of aroma hit him—Kalen's aroma. His cock sprung to attention again, and Kalen wiggled underneath him. They locked gazes.

"You realize," Kalen said in a whisper. "As incredible as that was, you're not finished."

"No?" Kalen wanted more, Norian thought. He wasn't sure if he was up to it. His wolf first nudged him, then slammed him. *Must mate.*

Before Kalen answered, Norian pushed his shoulders against the floor and growled through his teeth. Norian ran his hands down the sides of Kalen's body and then inched backward until he sat upright at Kalen's hips. Norian looked down and smiled. Kalen was erect again. That didn't take long. Norian grabbed hold of Kalen's penis, bent his head, and licked around the head. He crouched and then spread himself out, his head level with Kalen's hips. Kalen's cock slipped into his mouth, and he sucked lightly, his tongue dragging up and down Kalen's shaft as he moved.

The cock flopped out of his mouth, and Norian nuzzled his head under Kalen's fuzzy balls. This time, he knew exactly where he was going. He laved at Kalen's entrance with steady, wet licks. Nonsense words came out of Kalen's mouth as Norian continued licking, his finger moving lightly along the crack. He probed his tongue inside of Norian, pushing it as far as it would go.

"That's it," said Kalen in rapid breaths. "Whatever you are doing...." And then his voice turned into groans.

He continued stretching Kalen's hole with his tongue and laving around the entrance, providing as much saliva lubricant as he could. He stretched him further, using one finger, then two, until he was satisfied Kalen was stretched enough.

"I need you inside of me," said Kalen. "Now, Norian. Please."

Norian looked up and moved to a kneeling position. "I want to see you when I'm inside of you."

Kalen nodded and shuffled down a bit. Norian put his hands on Kalen's muscular legs and slowly brought them up to rest on his shoulders.

"I don't want to hurt you," said Norian. "I've never done this."

"Go slowly at first. I'll guide you." Of course, Kalen didn't know what he was doing either, but Norian didn't question him. Norian spit in his hand and applied it to his penis.

Kalen's hips surged forward, and Norian pressed his tip against Kalen's entrance. "Relax," he urged Kalen, and slowly pushed forward. The entrance stopped him for a moment, and then he pushed firmly past the tight ring of muscle inside of Kalen. Without thinking, he slid all the way in. The feelings that now ran through him caused him to shudder.

"Kalen? Are you okay?" he asked, unable to open his eyes.

"I have never been better," he said, his breath coming in

gasps. Precum dribbled from his penis. "Now, take me, Norian. Be my Alpha and take me."

Norian's hips surged forward and then backward, his movements slow and firm. Kalen held his gaze, wordlessly begging for more. Norian's tempo increased, and he tried to push even harder, needing to be wholly joined with his mate.

Kalen's cock slapped against his belly with each of Norian's thrusts, now wet with moisture.

"Norian," said Kalen. "I can't stop."

Kalen's words brought Norian right to the edge. They groaned in unison, the groans growing louder and then turning into mingled howls. They took flight together. Higher and higher they soared until the explosion of white light. Before he realized what he was doing, Norian bit down on Kalen's shoulder. He pulled up and noticed that he'd drawn blood. They met eyes for a moment, then Kalen brought his mouth down to Norian's neck. There was a sudden stinging pain in Norian's shoulder as Kalen bit into him. They both convulsed and landed gently in each other's arms, shaking. Norian's muscles turned to goo.

"It's done," said Kalen through his rapid breaths. "We are now mated for all of time."

"How did we bite each other like that?" asked Norian. "It's almost as if we turned for a moment."

"We did, kind of. After you bit me and I glanced up at you, you looked just like your normal human self, except your teeth were razor sharp. I guess our wolves helped us to mate by giving us fangs when we needed them."

"I feel different," said Norian. And he did. After his climax, the wolf that hung to the end of his consciousness receded, but Norian knew he was still there. But something was different. It was as if he and the wolf were no longer separate, but one entity united and complete. A new rush of power surged through him, although at the moment, he couldn't quite figure out what it was.

"We are different," said Kalen. "I notice it too. It's like this force is rushing through me, waiting to be released." He locked eyes with his mate. "I've never felt so alive, so complete. So this is what being mated feels like."

"For the first time, complete." Norian added. He stretched out, and Kalen lay back, resting his head on Norian's shoulder.

"We should try to get some rest," Norian whispered into Kalen's ear. "We will need our strength for tonight."

Kalen nodded. "Should we get dressed?"

"Why? Are you worried about offending our hosts?"

Kalen snickered. He reached for Norian's cloak and draped it over them. "I don't think we have to worry about not having enough strength for tonight," Norian said. "I have a feeling that we'll have all we need."

CHAPTER THIRTY

NORIAN AND KALEN WERE BOTH PRESSED AGAINST THE wall, hands entwined, when the cement door opened.

"Ah, isn't that sweet," said the guard that opened the door. "A pair of star-crossed lovers, complete with the tragic ending and all." He ran his index finger across his throat in a cutting gesture.

The guard behind him laughed. "It's just about time to say goodbye to all of this, princess. Now, I've seen my share of executions, mind you. Especially recently, so there's not too much that'll surprise me. But Vadok says that tonight we will be more than surprised. Everyone will." The guard held Norian's gaze. "We usually behead traitors, but this time, we have instructions to poke you fuckers to death with our silver-tipped spears when it's time. Not sure why the switch, but I must admit my curiosity is peaked."

The second guard pushed two bowls of a gruel-like substance through the small opening between the bars. "It ain't much, but Vadok don't want us wasting no good food on prisoners. Especially those who'll be dead in a few hours anyways."

Norian reached for the bowls, and the guard stepped back, almost as if he were afraid of Norian.

"You have less than a half an hour to eat up. Then it's showtime." Both guards threw them a sneer and then left, shutting the door securely behind them.

"Hungry?" Norian said, holding out the bowl of slop to Kalen.

"I can never eat during the day of a change. My stomach is too topsy-turvy."

"I'm glad it's not just me then," said Norian. "I'm the same way."

An uneasy silence settled between them as they eyed the food. Norian closed his eyes and found his center. He breathed deeply, his breath falling into a steady rhythm as he visualized his pack members in his mind's eye.

This is Norian once again. The guards have told us we've less than thirty minutes remaining in our cell, after which I imagine they will take us to the city center. Vadok has instructed the guards to kill us at some point with silver-tipped spears, so be wary. Any spear that is thrust towards you could be deadly. I hope to see you all shortly. If given the chance, I will try to contact you all again before the change.

When Norian opened his eyes, Kalen was studying his face. "You tried to contact the pack again?"

Norian nodded. "Not sure if it worked, but right now, anything's worth a try."

Kalen's features darkened. He wrapped his arm around Norian's waist and pulled him close. "Norian, you mustn't give up hope. Things might not look good right now, but do not lose faith. Our pack won't let us down. Trust in that."

"It's not lack of faith in them that's bothering me. On the contrary, I am afraid for them. I dragged them into this damnable mess, and I feel responsible for their well-being.

Funny, they're almost like family to me now. And that's the kicker. I'm putting this new family in grave danger, and I hate it. Some of the pack members are barely adults. How can I protect them?"

"I understand exactly where you're coming from. Believe me, Norian, I've been there myself. So I know how protective we can become of our pack. But it's what we do. It's what a pack is all about. We help each other when we are in need. We jump in when there's danger. This might be a new concept for you, people you hardly know risking their lives for you. But you'd do it for them without thinking."

Norian briefly considered this. "You're right. I would. I hadn't thought of it before, but upon reflection, I would defend any of those people out there with my life."

"I'm sure you would," said Kalen. "You're the most caring Alpha that I've ever come across, including my father."

"Your father wasn't caring?"

"I wouldn't go so far as to say he wasn't caring. He cared about my mother and me in his own way, and all the pack members respected him. But he was somewhat of a hard man. Perhaps preoccupied is a better word. He was fair, but was harsh when required. But there always seemed to be something missing. There was a lack of warmth, I guess. Mother said that all Alphas are like that. That's why they're Alphas."

"You might have a point there. The words you use to describe your father sound similar to how I would describe my own. He was distant, often cold, but I always figured that such is the way of a king. Regretfully, I had no mother to comfort me. I suppose Wayf took that role in my life. I consider him more family than a friend."

"The magician," said Kalen. "Have you seen him?"

Norian nodded. "Aye. I found his cell last night, and it was where I first became trapped. They moved me into this cell today. Vadok used Wayf as bait to entice me here. Fool that I am, I should have figured as much. This morning, they moved me to this cell. Now that Wayf has fulfilled his purpose, I fear what may become of him."

"But he has his magics, certainly? Has he not the power to fight against Vadok?"

"None. Vadok has bound his magic. Wayf is working on a way to unbind it but regretfully is unfamiliar with most of the ways of dark magic."

"Let us hope he finds a way."

Norian smiled a faint smile. "I hope so as well, but I think we are on our own."

"Not on our own. Remember, we have the power of the entire pack behind us. Regardless of whether you success-fully reached them through your mind, they'll be here as soon as they transform. They would never abandon us."

"Let's just hope that they don't show up too late."

"So you know of Vadok's plans?"

Norian nodded. "He enlightened me this morning. He plans to cage me and present me to my people, letting them watch me shift—observe me become the beast that I am. Vadok figures the people will shun me and look to him for protection. Luckily, they'll be ready with their silver-tipped spears. I imagine they'll kill me while I'm still caged. Vadok would never dare let one of our kind run loose. That would be too much of a danger to him."

"I'm sure he means to kill me in the same manner," Kalen said. "You heard him earlier. He hinted that we both would be killed before the town." Kalen tapped his chin with his index finger. "This may be to our advantage."

Norian raised his eyes. "How so? We'll be trapped in the cage together."

"True. But together, we are much more powerful than alone. Especially now." He flashed Norian a wicked grin. "All we need is one chance, one distraction."

"Vadok is no fool," Norian said. "I'm sure he is well-prepared for this evening's events."

"He may have suspected that you would show up, but I could tell from his expression and his tone of voice that he was completely unprepared for my arrival. He's also unaware that you're an Alpha and have the power of an entire pack of lycans behind you. My guess is that he knows little to nothing of our ways, of what we are capable of, especially now that we're mated. This is definitely to our advantage."

"You make an excellent point," said Norian, nodding to Kalen. "But what of the cage? Will we have the power to break free?"

"'Tis difficult to say. But once we transform and meld our minds together, I suspect we'll be much more powerful than we'd ever imagined. My mother even hinted at such, though even she isn't aware of our full potential."

A sudden heat rushed to Norian's face. "You talked to your mother about us having sex?"

"Yes. Well, no, we never actually mentioned the word sex."

"But she implied it?"

"She's my mother and helped me to lead the pack. So of course, we talked about a topic as important as her son mating with an Alpha. She's the one who told me that consummating our bond would increase your abilities, although she didn't know how. She also suspected that my abilities might increase as well. It's all conjecture on her part, born from rumors. I suppose we'll find out soon enough."

"Let's hope it will be enough."

"Don't underestimate the power of our pack. Driven together with a common goal, they're a formidable force. Combined with our power, we should be able to accomplish whatever we have our minds set on."

"Even the impossible?" asked Norian.

Kalen grinned. "Norian, nothing is impossible for a lycan."

"Is it possible for me to meld with the entire pack like you and I do?"

Kalen considered this for a moment. "I'm not sure. My father never talked too much about his Alpha abilities or even pack business, for that matter. I wish I had asked him more questions, especially seeing that I was a Beta. It might've helped me to understand my abilities more." He paused and looked tenderly at Norian. "All I can say is that it's worth a try. Anything is worth a try. Given that you seem to be an exceptional Alpha—and I'm not just saying that because you're my mate—I would venture to guess that there's a good possibility. While growing up, I remember hearing an old saying to that effect, something like 'running as one mind with the pack.' I'm unaware if there's anything to it, but it wouldn't surprise me if a powerful enough Alpha couldn't cause the minds of the entire pack to fuse as one for a time."

"If I could communicate back and forth with the pack before and during their attack, it could be helpful."

"Then try, Norian. We'll need every advantage at our disposal if we're to survive the night." He paused. "The guards that were here earlier. Did you know them?"

Norian creased his brow. "Only one of them was known

to me, only because he brought me here this morning after I became trapped in Wayf's cell."

Kalen shook his head. "I mean, were they here before Vadok took over? Were these people you knew before? Your people?"

Norian stood frozen for several moments before he responded. "No. So far, I've not seen anyone I recognize. Those devils that were here earlier had no association with the court or the castle. Today was the first time that I'd ever laid eyes on them. I shudder to think of what became of my father's castle guards."

"Perhaps your people haven't been so quick to abandon you," Kalen said. "Obviously, Vadok needed to bring in his own guards to maintain order."

"We shall see if my people's devotion remains once they see their prince turn into a beast before their eyes."

Kalen gave Norian a weak smile. "From what I understand of Vadok, a beast would be a much more preferable ruler than that scoundrel."

Norian nodded, and both men were silent for several moments. A familiar restlessness and jumpiness settled over him, a warning that his change was not far off.

"I don't know what lies ahead for us this evening," Norian said. "But in case we don't survive...."

Kalen raised his eyebrows. "Yes?"

Norian felt his face flush. "I want—no, I need—to make love with you again. Right now. I need to be inside of you. I need us to be one."

Kalen flashed him an impish smile. "Who am I to argue with an Alpha?"

"I DON'T THINK I could ever tire of that," Kalen said, breathless.

Norian smiled. "Me neither. And I swear I become stronger each time we do it. A couple more times, and I'll be ready to take over the world."

"Now, that is the kind of attitude we need."

Both men looked at each other in silence, both aware that this might be the last time they would ever be together. Emotion rose from Norian's chest to his eyes, but he held back. He was an Alpha. There would be no tears, no hesitation tonight. He would not allow any doubts to creep into his thoughts. He must not. Somehow, he must triumph this night. There was everything at stake.

Before either of them could speak, the door opened. No less than a dozen guards appeared at the door, all armed with silver-tipped spears. Swords hung loosely from their belts.

One guard entered the room while the others held back. He was a brute of a man, at least two or three heads taller than Norian. His wild, dark red hair, long, scraggly, rusty-colored beard, and the feral look of his eyes made Norian think he was more beast than human. He wore scratched and faded body armor that covered nearly his entire body below the neck. He held his long spear in one hand and a large faded brass key in the other. Norian's sensitive nose picked up a vile stench coming from the man. The odor of the other guards wasn't much better.

"Up!" the giant guard said. "And don't try to escape. Lord Vadok gave us instructions that if either of you so much as flinched, we were to run you through."

He took a step forward, stuck the key in the lock, and turned. The metal bars squeaked loudly as the door opened. The guard stepped to the side.

"Out. Now."

Kalen and Norian exited the cell. The guards at the doorway split into parallel lines. They were halfway through when the guards to their left and right stepped directly in front of them. The nudge of a spear pressed into Norian's back.

"Move," a gruff voice said. Norian's wolf grew restless inside of him, hating the fact that he was a prisoner. The wolf, probably sensing Norian's panic, was itching to attack. Judging by the cramps, Norian sensed moonrise was no more than half an hour away.

Soon, his thoughts told his wolf. *Soon, you shall be free.*

CHAPTER THIRTY-ONE

THE ARENA WAS ALREADY CRAMMED FULL OF PEOPLE when Kalen and Norian arrived. All the people he had grown up with. All the people who had loved and respected him. Now here all of them were, gathered together to witness his death. Or did they somehow hope he would escape and rescue them from Vadok?

As the cage rolled to the center of the arena, Norian studied the people's faces. They seemed to contain the same expression—an expression of pity and fear. Many turned to avoid his gaze. He understood. It would embarrass him to observe anyone in his predicament.

The cage made a scratching sound in the dust as Vadok's guards pushed it to the center of the stadium. Norian smelled Kalen's fear now, and it grew stronger by the second. He realized that it was the first time he had ever detected fear on Kalen, and it greatly disturbed him. He wanted nothing more than to whisk his lover away to a safe place to ensure that no harm would ever come to him. But that was impossible. Kalen shared the cage with him. Whatever happened to Norian would happen to Kalen as well.

His heart tugged at his chest. Adrenaline rose in his body. His skin prickled and his muscles ached. It wouldn't be long now. The cage came to a squeaking halt. Guards immediately surrounded it.

"Ladies and Gentlemen," Vadok's voice boomed from somewhere in the stands. It figures he wouldn't dare to get anywhere near them. "Tonight, I have a special treat for you. For your entertainment, I present to you a familiar face. A face that many of you grew up with. A face many of you trusted and respected. But your noble Prince has kept a horrific secret from you, a secret that puts your entire kingdom in terrible danger. Knowing this was true, he came into your city yesterday with another creature such as himself. You see, my good people of Tregaron, Prince Norian is a werewolf. A vicious, blood-thirsty man-beast who would slay you and your entire family while you slept. A beast with no soul, no regrets. A beast whose only purpose is to rip you apart and eat you. If I hadn't stepped in and rescued you, this dog would have been your King. Imagine it! You and your families would have been at the mercy of his hunger and, I would say, his pity, but alas, there would be no pity from him. For you need to understand, kind people, that Prince Norian is incapable of showing pity, just as a lion shows no pity to a gazelle before it rips it to shreds. Luckily, I am here to protect you." A loud murmur arose from the crowd, but Vadok ignored it. "But you don't have to believe me. You shall see for yourself in a few minutes. You shall witness what kind of beast your Prince truly is as these two rip each other apart before your eyes."

The guards moved away from the cage, leaving it in full view. So Vadok assumed they would attack each other once they changed? He was now convinced that Vadok knew little about lycanism. Norian whispered to Kalen, "It will be okay." Kalen nodded.

Norian felt the change start to take hold of him, but this time, it was different. Instead of the usual fear that seized him before the transformation, an enormous surge of power ran through him. He felt his body shifting, but this time, there was no pain whatsoever. It was as if he were an onlooker rather than a participant. His feet turned to enormous paws, and his head pushed in as his muzzle extended. He was in his wolf form, but again, he felt that something was different. He looked over and caught sight of Norian, now a beautiful, snowy-white wolf. Norian knew now what was different. He was considerably larger than he'd been before. He practically looked down upon Kalen, who was standing next to him. Kalen's eyes were wide in surprise.

"You are nearly twice the size you were before."

"It appears so."

It was then that Norian noticed the setting sun. The moon had not even risen yet! Norian searched Vadok's face in the stands and finally found him. The surprise on his face was evident. Norian smiled inwardly. Then, suddenly, a powerful urge to contact his pack seized him, accompanied by a need to bring them to him. He padded to the end of the cage, and the guards instinctively moved back. He opened his mouth and a sound that he would never have suspected any being could make, escaped from deep within him. The howl—although it was more like a roar—reverberated through the arena. People instinctively brought their hands to their ears, trying to block out the harsh sound. The howl went on and on and. Kalen was lying flat in the cage, his head down in submission, paws covering his ears. Finally, Norian stopped.

"Now that's an Alpha," said Kalen in Norian's mind. *"I've never heard anything like that."*

Before he could respond, Norian smelled the pack, and they were close. It worked. They'd heard him. He was about to raise his head and howl once again when Vadok's voice shrieked above the crowd.

"Kill him! Spear them both now!"

The guards raised their spears, and just as they did, Norian threw his massive body with all of his might against the door of the cage. It snapped at the hinges and flew to the ground. Norian lunged at the guards.

The guards tried to run, but didn't make it very far before he took two of them down. He swung his head and saw Kalen take down two more. Vadok screamed repeatedly in the background, but Norian couldn't make out the words. Adrenaline filled his body and pounded in his ears.

From the side of the stands, more guards poured in, each armed with a silver-tipped spear. It looked like there were hundreds of them. Norian's body stiffened instinctively. How would the two of them overpower hundreds? Then, almost in answer to his question, a thundering roar erupted, and before he knew it, wolves surrounded the arena. His pack.

We're here, boss. Just in the nick of time, I'd say.

Well done, Thomros. Unless they surrender, take down the guards. But be careful. Their arrows are silver-tipped.

The guards drew closer, arrows raised. Once the people saw that other wolves surrounded them, they screamed but remained seated. Many of them looked around the stadium for an exit, but at least one wolf guarded each possible escape route. A guard fired his spear at a small gray wolf but missed and it landed next to a man seated in the stands. The man picked up the spear, but before he did anything with it, the gray wolf met his eyes and growled. The man quickly dropped the spear.

It's time, thought Norian. A collective growl of agreement reached his ears. *Attack only the guards, Norian said to his pack. Do not harm the townspeople. They are innocent. Only attack Vadok and his men.*

The lycans attacked.

The guards began throwing their spears randomly, hitting nothing in the process. The screams of the citizens grew louder, as did the shouts of Vadok.

"Get the big one!" he screamed. "Kill the big black one!"

Several large guards turned on Norian at once. He crouched, waiting. The men stared at him, frozen, as if afraid to make a move. A low growl came from Norian's throat. The men lifted their arms higher, getting ready to launch their spears, and Norian braced himself. He growled even louder. With that, the men dropped their spears, looked at each other, and took off running.

Norian caught sight of several guards moving in on a small white wolf. He pounced, knocking all the guards over. One of them lifted his spear, and Norian lunged, tearing his arm clean off. Blood spurted everywhere. Several other guards came at Norian with spears raised. Before they knew what happened, Norian took off one guard's arm and another's head.

Norian all at once felt panic fill him. Where was Kalen? He hadn't seen him since they escaped.

Kalen?

I'm at the west corner of the arena. I'm fine.

Norian turned his head, and he saw his mate, munching on the leg of a guard, the guard still trying to reach his fallen spear.

A loud, pain-filled squeal rang through the air, and Norian snapped his head toward the sound. One of Vadok's men had a large black wolf at the end of his spear. The guard laughed as he continued to thrust. Norian flew through the air at him. He opened his mouth, and his jaws closed around the throat of the guard. His head dropped off of his body and rolled down the aisle way. The wolf lie still, his yellow eyes open but empty. Norian's heart tugged. They would have time to mourn later.

The coppery scent of fresh blood was everywhere and was attacking Norian's senses, bringing out a part of him he never knew existed and nearly sending him into a frenzy. He looked around and caught sight of several guards ambushing another pack member. A white wolf nearby met Norian's eyes and nodded. They both attacked simultaneously. In less than a minute, five more guards were dead.

Norian looked around, ready to spring. Spears were flying aimlessly but luckily, hitting nobody. A familiar young man was running for an exit when a brown wolf bit into his leg. To his horror, Norian recognized Thorne as the human who had just been bit.

No! Not the people! Only Vadok's men. Don't hurt the townspeople.

I'm so sorry, Lord Norian. It was a mistake. I thought he was a guard escaping. I'll tend to him.

As much as Norian wanted to run to Thorne to see if he was okay, Norian knew he had to direct his attention on destroying Vadok. As Norian looked around, it surprised him that his wolves now outnumbered the guards. A few guards still fought on, but most of them were either dead or had fled. People were glued to the seats, eyes wide with terror. One woman met Norian's eyes, and she opened her mouth to scream. He shook his head, and surprisingly, she stopped and just stared.

"Fools!" a voice boomed from above. "Anyone who flees will be executed!"

Norian's eyes scoured the stand until he found Vadok. Though seven or eight guards surrounded him, Norian could clearly see the evil bastard. Norian padded through the stands, people gasping as he walked by. It stunned him that nobody ran as he passed by them—they simply sat still and watched him pass. He could smell their fear, but it wasn't an oh-my-god-I'm-gonna-die kind of fear. It was as if they somehow trusted him. The stench of Vadok's fear increased as Norian drew closer, but the offensive odor wasn't just fear alone—it was fear tinged with something else. Something dark and bitter. Vadok was still spitting out orders when a guard noticed Norian's approach.

"Wolf!" he screamed.

The other guards immediately raised their spears. Norian and the guards stood frozen for several moments. Then Norian opened his mouth and roared.

The men instinctively brought their hands to their ears, dropping their spears in the process. Then Norian noticed that the entire stadium had gone quiet. He turned and saw that everyone, people and lycans alike, had their eyes glued on him.

Vadok reached over and picked up one of the dropped spears. He shook it at Norian.

Norian moved closed, snarling as he stepped. Vadok then spit out some strange sounding words and a hot force hit Norian's chest. A fleeting pain ran through him, then disappeared. Magic! It surprised Norian that Vadok hadn't used it before now. The unexpected appearance of his pack must have thrown him off guard. Norian surveyed his body and noticed that he was fine. He drew in closer.

"Mors lupo. Mors ultima. Iubeo!" Vadok screamed, and another blast hit square in the chest with the same result as before. The sorcerer's magic couldn't hurt him. He was immune to magic. He tried to laugh, but a growl came through. Kalen's voice busted into his thoughts.

Now's your chance, Norian. Avenge your father and my father. Avenge all those that have fallen at this madman's hands. Do it.

Norian lunged. Vadok held up the spear and thrust at Norian. Norian twisted his body to avoid it. He landed behind Vadok. Lady Auryon's words echoed in his brain.

The bite of a lycan can kill evil.

Before Vadok could turn around, Norian dove, mouth open. His jaws crashed down on Vadok's leg. As his teeth broke the flesh, a jolt of power ran through him, flinging him backward.

A stream of curses was flying from Vadok's mouth. He spun around and around, shouting strange words. The wound in his leg spread, growing blacker and blacker around the edges, and as it did, Vadok's physical appearance also changed. First, his skin yellowed and sagged, and then his eyes clouded over. He held onto the wound with both hands and glared at Norian through his murky eyes.

"You think you have bested me? It takes more than a dog bite to do me in, scum. But I have the comfort of knowing that you will eventually follow in my footsteps, and I shall be waiting for you when the time comes. I can already sense the rising darkness in you. After all, you are your father's son." He grinned. "*Son.*"

He gurgled once and began spinning around, faster and faster, until he was a blur. Norian crouched, ready to pounce on the spinning figure, but the effect was dizzying. There was a loud, sudden plop!

And then nothing.

Vadok was gone.

Damn it all to hell! He had escaped!

Norian roared. If he had been able, Norian would have cried. He was so close. So close to ending the evil that is Vadok.

He turned, and the entire arena stared at him in silence.

Come.

The rest of the wolves joined him. The people sat unmoving as the wolves silently passed by, one by one, in a long silent procession. Norian looked once at everyone and gave a loud howl. He then ran off, followed by the rest of his pack.

CHAPTER THIRTY-TWO

AFTER VADOK ESCAPED, THE WOLVES RETREATED AND stayed close to the city. The following morning, Norian and Kalen entered the town. Norian couldn't even fathom what the townspeople's reaction might be now that they knew his secret, knew what he really was. For a brief moment, he'd considered simply disappearing back to Norbury with the pack, but thought better of it. He would not do that to Wayf, and Norian had to see him one final time to ensure that he was fine. He owed Wayf that much. He also wanted to check in on Thorne, the young man who was accidentally bit the night before. Thorne would most likely transform on the next moon, and Norian had to ensure that the boy didn't undergo it alone, as he had.

Norian walked through the streets on the way to the castle with his head down. He didn't want to cause a distur-bance or be driven out of Tregaron before he'd had a chance to see Wayf. Still, a few people recognized him.

Surprisingly, several people greeted him enthusiasti-cally as he passed. "Good morning, Prince Norian!" He nodded in acknowledgment.

He entered the castle and started heading toward the cells when he heard a familiar voice in the kitchen.

"Norian!" Wayf shouted upon seeing him. He pulled Norian into a tight hug. "I was so worried about you after they told me what had happened. You did it! You drove that evil bastard away from here. You succeeded."

Norian shook his head. "Not just me. My pack."

Wayf smiled. "Ah yes, the pack." He turned to Kalen. "And I imagine that this would be...?"

"I am called Kalen. I have heard a lot about you from Norian. He speaks highly and fondly of you."

Wayf waved his hand in the air. "Posh. It is all of you who brought this kingdom back to order, and I speak for the entire city in saying that we are eternally grateful. The unspeakable horrors that man brought to this kingdom." He shook his head and moved his gaze from Norian to Kalen. "And we have you all to thank."

"But we didn't truly succeed," Norian said. "Vadok still lives, although he appears to be significantly weakened. I had hoped to slay him but didn't get the opportunity." Norian locked eyes with Wayf. "I thought the bite of a lycan would do him in. Both you and Lady Auryon told me he feared lycans because only evil can destroy evil."

"And that is the key, my friend. You are *not* evil. You are just..." Wayf paused as if searching for the right words, "Different. Now Vadok, on the other hand, is pure evil, and as far as I know, he always has been. His dark magics are so ingrained in his soul that it would no doubt take a powerful wizard to bring him down."

"Could you do it?" asked Kalen. "Norian says you are one of the most powerful magicians he knows."

Wayf scratched his chin. "Possibly with some research. But there is a ring of truth to that 'evil killing evil' myth. It's always easier for a black magician to kill another black magician. Or any creature of true evil, for that matter. The question is: Can I learn dark magic without sacrificing my soul in the process? Learning such magics has been the downfall of many a mage."

"I'll save you the trouble," said Norian. "I swear on the grave of my mother and father that the next time I see Vadok, I'm going to tear his head off. Evil or not, nobody can live without a head."

Wayf chuckled. "I imagine not. Of course, the trick is getting close enough to him to pull it off. Remember that powerful magics protect him. I'm surprised that you could even bite him like you did."

"His magic didn't appear to work on me," said Norian. "He hit me in the chest with a bolt of something. I felt it, but it didn't hurt me. Vadok looked just as surprised as I was."

"Being in lycan form protected you," said Kalen. "It's common knowledge that magic doesn't work very well on us when we're in lycan form."

"There's more to it than that, I think" Norian said.

Wayf raised his eyebrows. "Why? What do you know?"

"It was something Vadok said. He said that I have evil inside of me and will follow in his footsteps. Then he said that I was my father's son. Do you have any idea what he meant?"

Wayf stood frozen, simply staring at Norian, saying nothing.

"Wayf?" Norian said. "What is it?"

Wayf gestured for the two men to sit down. "I promised your father I would never tell you. Promised him that as far as anyone would ever know, you were his son. I didn't think you'd ever find out."

"What are you saying?" asked Norian. "Find out what?"

Wayf took a deep breath. "That you are Vadok's son."

Norian felt stricken. His thoughts crashed, one into another, as he tried to make sense out of what Wayf was telling him. "But father always said that my mother died of an illness when I was a child."

Wayf wrung his hands. "That's not entirely true. You see, Vadok—or at least we believed it to be him—captured your mother shortly after your father married her. Your father spent several months searching for her. His men finally found her and rescued her. As much as Vadok tried, he couldn't win her heart. I can't imagine what he was thinking, believing that the Queen of Tregaron would accept his affections. From what we could put together, after he realized he would never have her, he abandoned her. So yes, when your father's men found her, she was still alive, but she was in rough shape, suffering from numerous beatings and god knows what other kinds of torture. We discovered shortly thereafter that she was also pregnant."

"With me," Norian said.

Wayf nodded. "Aye. Vadok had taken liberties with her during the time she was captive. But no matter what, your father never stopped loving her, and he vowed to her he would raise her child as his own. We would keep it a secret from everyone, especially Vadok. Your father assumed Vadok was unaware of the pregnancy as your mother was yet in the early stages. Apparently, he was wrong."

"So, how did my mother die? I don't remember anything about her."

"She died when you were five years of age, though she was never the same after we found her. Throughout her pregnancy and up until the day she died, she never spoke a word nor did she ever leave her bed. For five long years she languished, unresponsive, until her body gave up."

"Why can't I remember hardly anything about her?"

Wayf took a deep breath. "I'm partly at fault for that. You were so distraught after your mother died that your father and I decided to ease your suffering. He asked me to cast a memory spell so that you wouldn't remember the worst of it. You were so young, and it was so difficult to explain everything to you. Your father felt that it was just easier this way."

Norian dismissed him with a wave of his hand. "I harbor no ill will against you, my friend." But he thought of Vadok, he could barely contain the rage that arose with him. Bile rose in his throat, and he clenched his fists. "So Vadok killed both my mother and father?"

Kalen grabbed Norian's hand. "I can't imagine how difficult this must be for you to hear." Norian looked at him and nodded.

"Vadok said that he sensed a rising darkness inside of me," Norian said. "Is this true, Wayf? Am I evil?"

"While it is true that you are Vadok's son, you are also your mother's," Wayf said. "She was a loving, good person, as are you. One thing I've learned over the years is that everyone has a dark side of their personality. We all possess the potential to be evil. But it is always a choice. You alone choose what kind of person you will be."

Norian took both of Kalen's hands and looked at him. "I hope you don't think less of me now that you know this horrible secret."

Kalen creased his brow. "How could you ever think that? You are my mate. You are part of me."

"But I am also the son of the demon who killed your father. His blood runs through my veins."

Kalen briefly considered this. "You are not Vadok. You are Norian, one of the most powerful Alphas these parts have ever known. I do not hold you guilty for the sins of your father. On the contrary, the good you've already done shows your true self."

"What good?"

"You have freed our people from a terrible tyrant," Wayf interrupted. "Imagine how many more lives would have been lost if he had continued his slaughter, his daily executions. No, Norian, you are a good man. Perhaps the magic in you has helped you become the powerful man that you are. I sensed it yesterday when you were trapped with me. I sensed a power in you, a power I had never noticed before."

"I should say so," said Kalen. "What you did to the pack yesterday was unheard of."

"What do you mean?"

"You and I shifted before the moon had even risen, which surprised me enough. But according to the pack, when you called them with your howl, you caused the entire pack to shift at once simultaneously, well ahead of the moonrise. I would never have fathomed that such a thing was even possible, but yet, you did it. The pack is still talking about it this morning."

"You said that a mated Alpha has additional abilities," Norian said. "Maybe that was part of it."

"Mated Alpha?" asked Wayf, blushing. "I guess I need to do more research on lycanthropy."

Norian stood up. "It is time for us to take our leave," said Norian. "Know that you are always welcome in Norbury."

"What madness is this?" said Wayf, wide-eyed. "You

can't leave. You are now King. Or soon will be after the ceremony."

"Impossible! The people know what I am. They saw me yesterday in wolf form. I can never be King."

"That's where you're wrong, my dear Norian. This morning, all of creation was abuzz with what you did yesterday and how you saved them from Vadok. There's already talk of the coronation ceremony, and preparations are currently being made. You being a lycan, changes nothing. You are the rightful King of this land."

"You mean they would allow a lycan to rule them?"

Wayf laughed. "Allow you? They welcome you! Yes, at first, they were terrified when you transformed into an enormous wolf, and then an entire pack of wolves showed up. But it soon became clear to everyone what was going on—that all of you were no threat to them but were battling Vadok and his men. Who better to lead and protect a kingdom than a lycan who is also an Alpha?"

"But I can't desert my pack," Norian said. "I've made the decision to stay with them and have promised them I would be their Alpha when this is all over and done with."

"Understood," said Wayf. "But you are also King of Tregaron. So why not move your pack here?"

Norian looked over at Kalen, and he was smiling. Norian had not even considered the possibility of moving all of Norbury to Tregaron. Could the two worlds coexist together?

"Norian," said Kalen. "Your people want you to rule them. We want you as our Alpha. So moving the pack here is the perfect solution. Our people would no longer need to live on the fringes, forever fearful of hunters. And you Norian, you'd have a ready-made army."

"Do you think the people would agree? Be willing to move here?"

Kalen met his gaze. "I can't say for sure, but I'd venture to guess that everyone would jump at the chance. Let us go speak to the pack and see what they say. If they agree, we will send a contingent back to Norbury to propose the move to those who remain."

Norian looked at Kalen. "Are you sure about this? It's a lot to expect of them."

"We'll all talk it over and decide from there."

Norian was silent for a few moments. He looked at Wayf. "If the people will have me, then I shall be honored to be their King." He turned his gaze to Kalen. "And be the pack's Alpha."

"Good," said Wayf. "Let us now go greet your people. They've long awaited your return. We are going to have a busy, busy next few days. We have a coronation to plan."

CHAPTER THIRTY-THREE

After Norian left the castle, he found Thomros and Deric waiting for them outside. They looked nervous, but both wore smiles.

"What are you doing here?" asked Norian. "Is something wrong?"

"We were concerned for you," said Deric. "After last night's events, we didn't know what the reaction of the townspeople would be, and we certainly weren't going to allow you to wander into hostile territory alone. There could be hunters here, for all we knew."

Norian chuckled. "This isn't hostile territory. Tregaron is my home."

A flash of hurt crossed Thomros and Deric's expressions. "I mean, was my home," said Norian. "But it could be once again, depending on how the pack feels about our proposal."

"Huh?" asked Deric. "You lost me, Boss."

Norian recounted the conversation they'd had with Wayf, including his suggestion that Norian and the pack settle in Tregaron. "What do you think?" he asked the two men. "Do you think the pack would ever go for it?"

"Wherever you go, the pack will follow," said Thomros. "If you wish to live here, then the pack will live here."

"I'm not sure how I feel about uprooting everyone from their home," said Norian. "It might be wrong and unfair of me to expect them to—"

"Can I say something, Boss?" Deric interrupted.

"Certainly, Deric. What's on your mind?"

"The only reason we created Norbury was that it was far away from the other villages and offered us the most protection from hunters. We've always been outcasts, living on the fringes, never belonging anywhere. This might be the pack's first chance to be part of an actual village—to have a purpose other than merely surviving and defending ourselves. I think most if not all the pack members will eagerly agree to the proposal. We'll always be the Norbury pack, no matter where we actually reside."

Norian held gazes with Deric for several moments and nodded. "So be it. We'll propose to move the pack after we leave here. But first, I have other business."

"What's that, Boss?" Thomros asked.

"One of the townspeople was accidentally bitten last night, and I want to check in on him." Norian swallowed. "He isn't merely a resident of Tregaron. He's also my friend."

"Sorry to hear that," said Deric. He swallowed. "You know he's probably going to be a lycan now, right?"

Norian nodded but didn't reply. Instead, he turned and began walking toward Thorne's home. He thought about his first time transforming and how terrifying and painful it was. He recalled how the wolf completely took hold of him and drove him on instinct alone. This would not happen to

Thorne. If he were indeed a lycan, Norian wanted his first transformation to be as painless as possible.

Thorne's father answered the door, and Norian feared that there would be a confrontation, but surprisingly, the man stepped aside and said nothing.

"How is he?" Norian asked.

"Not well," said his father. "A fever has overtaken him, and he slips in and out of consciousness. But there was a miracle as well. My daughter went to change his bandages a short while ago, but the bite was gone. It has completely healed as though nothing had happened."

Norian glanced at Thomros and Deric, and both nodded. There was no doubt about it. Thorne would be a lycan in one month's time.

"Can we see him?"

"Of course," said his father. "This way." He led the men down a dimly lit hallway and then into the first room on the right. Thorne's eyes were open, and he was sitting up in bed.

"Prince Norian?" Thorne asked. "Is that you?"

"Yes, it's me. How are you faring?"

"Hot." He smiled. "I was bitten by a real, honest-to-goodness wolf. How fantastic is that?"

"What do you mean?" Norian said. He glanced at Deric and Thomros. There was the oddest expression on Thomros's face that gave Norian pause. Thomros was staring wide-eyed and open-mouthed at Thorne, like Thorne was an unknown species he'd never seen before. Norian turned his regard back to Thorne.

"I've never seen such extraordinary creatures," said Thorne. "The way they took care of Vadok's men and flung them about as if they were scarecrows." His grin increased. "And one bit me."

"I'm so sorry about that," said Norian. "That was never meant to happen."

"It's fine," said Thorne. "Strangely enough, it's all better this morning. It's completely disappeared, like it never happened."

"Yes, Thorne, about that." Norian gently explained to him about lycans and how he would transform himself during the next full moon.

Thorne was quiet for several moments as he took it all in. "It's okay. No, more than okay. It's terrific!"

Norian widened his eyes in surprise. "Okay, not the reaction I expected."

Thorne wiped his brow with his arm. "Don't you see? The wolves saved the village. They were heroes. Our saviors. I'll be proud to be one of them." His eyes grew wide and he pointed at Norian. "Wait, you're one too! That's right! You and that man turned together in the cage before all the chaos and fighting."

"That's right. I'm one too. We'll talk more when I get back."

"You're not leaving Tregaron, are you?"

"Right now, I need to talk to the other people I came here with and make a proposal to them. If it goes well, I'll need to take a quick trip but will be back before the next moon. But in case I don't make it back before the next moon, I'll ask a pack member to stay behind and watch over you. They'll guide you through your first change, if I'm not here. But know that I'll do everything in my power to return before that happens. Either way, you won't be alone."

Norian jerked to attention when he heard a low growl from behind him. He turned his head and locked gazes with Thomros, who still had that unseemly, wide-eyed expression on his face.

"No," Thomros said. He turned his regard to Thorne.

"What do you mean, no?" asked Norian. "What is it you disagree with?"

"Man, what's wrong with you?" asked Deric.

"No pack member is staying with him except me."

"Don't be silly," said Deric. "We're the village protectors. We'll get one of the younger ones to stay."

Thomros growled again. "No. He is mine."

Norian and Deric stared at each other for a long moment. "What are you talking about?" asked Deric. "You don't even know this boy."

"Mate," said Thomros. "Must protect mate."

"Wait," said Norian, pointing at Thorne. "Are you saying that..."

But before he could finish, Thomros pushed Norian and Deric aside and sat on the bed next to Thorne. Thorne stared up at him, a confused look on his face.

"I think you lost me," said Thorne. He again wiped the beads of sweat from his forehead with his arm. "But I can't think right now. I need to get back to sleep. Suddenly, I don't feel very well. Why am I so hot?"

"We'll leave you, now," said Norian. He touched Deric's shoulder. "Let's let him get some rest. I remember how horrible the first couple of days were."

"I'll stay," said Thomros, his eyes never leaving Thorne. "I'll make sure he's comfortable."

"Well, if that just doesn't beat all," Deric said, his eyes locked on Thomros.

Norian chuckled. "It certainly appears as though things are going to become quite interesting around here." He glanced at Thomros and Thorne, shrugged his shoulders and grinned. "Quite interesting indeed."

~

Looking for your next paranormal adventure? Check out my latest offering "The Golem's Guardian." Brooklyn librarian David discovers he can create magical clay protectors—just as a dark sorcerer threatens the city. Ancient magic meets modern love in this LGBTQ+ story!

PLEASE LEAVE A REVIEW

If you enjoyed *Norian's Gamble*, I would love it if you'd let your friends know so they can experience Norian and Kalen's adventures as well. If you leave a review on the site from which you purchased the book, Goodreads or your own blow, I would love to read it! Email me the link at
writerdude@wisguy.com

If you'd like to be notified when I release new books and receive a short story in your inbox every week, please sign up for my newsletter at http://rogerhyttinen.com/newsletter/

Thank you so much for supporting my work!

Questions? Comments? I'd love to hear from you! Contact me at:
writerdude@wisguy.com

CONNECT WITH ME

Click or visit the link below for my newsletter, including exclusive stories, bonuses and advance notice about upcoming work.

Subscribe To My Newsletter

Connect with me:

Follow Me On BlueSky

Like Me On Facebook

Visit My Blog

CHECK OUT MY OTHER BOOKS:

Standalones

A Touch of Cedar

Christmas Cookies that Sparkle

Ghost Oracle Series:

Nick's Awakening (Ghost Oracle Book 1)

Anaconda! (Ghost Oracle Book 2)

The Magician's Secret (Ghost Oracle Book 3)

Ghost at the Prom (Ghost Oracle Book 4)

Camping with A Ghost (Ghost Oracle Book 5)

Nick's Destiny (Ghost Oracle Book 6)

Wolves of Norbury series:

Norian's Gamble